LLANDRY

THE DRAYKON SERIES: 4

CHARLOTTE E. ENGLISH

ISBN: 9789492824202

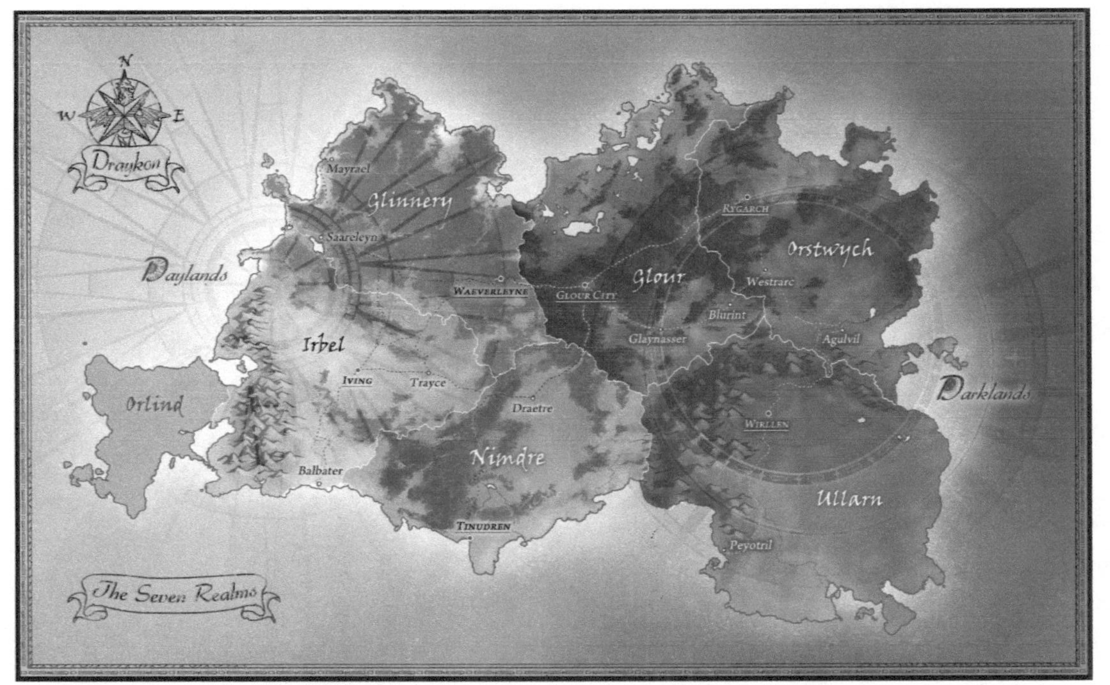
N
W
E
S
Draykon
Daylands
Mayrael
Glinnery
Saareleyn
Waeverleyne
Glour City
Glour
Rygarch
Orstwych
Westrarc
Blurint
Glaynasser
Agulvil
Darklands
Irbel
Iving
Trayce
Draetre
Wirllen
Orlind
Nimdre
Balbater
Ullarn
Tinudren
Peyotril
The Seven Realms

THE JOURNALS OF LLANDRY SANFAER, LADY DRAYKON

Entry One: An Introduction To These Records

Lady Draykon.

This is my title. It was bestowed upon me by the Elders of Glinnery themselves, and in front of a hall full of witnesses.

Two long moons later, I can still scarcely believe it.

I am Llandry Sanfaer. You may have heard my name. I am a citizen of Glinnery, one of the Seven Realms, even if I no longer live there. I am of the winged folk. I am a jeweller. I am shy, to my despair — probably more so than anybody you have ever met.

And I am a draykon. Shapeshifter, sorcerer, nightmare of the skies. Until recently, we of the Seven had forgotten the draykoni entirely, their absence from our world so extended that we no longer believed that they had ever existed.

It was me that brought them back. I did not know, then, what I was doing. I Changed… and the world changed with me. It is too late, now, to reverse those events, or to return the draykoni to their former dormancy. Some wish, fervently, that it were not so. We bring magic and wonder and life to the Seven — and we have also brought chaos, fear and war. There are those who will always condemn us.

I am not always certain that they are wrong.

Other pens have recorded the events of which I speak. Accounts have been written and re-written, by scholars almost as authoritative upon such points as I. I have given my side of those stories, over and over again. It is not the purpose of this journal to repeat that tale.

This endeavour is about the future. It was suggested to me by Lady Evastany Glostrum, a friend of mine since those confusing days. She is far better versed in the arts of politics and a public life than I; she has been submerged in both ever since she was born.

Llan. The coming years will be difficult for us all, but for you more than anyone. The return of the draykoni is, by and large, laid at your door, and not everyone is delighted with this development. Now the draykoni tribes and the people of the Seven must find a way to co-exist. It will not be easy. It falls to you, to Ori and to Avane to bring about peace, if you can.

There will be those who will question you, blame you, even curse you. When that day comes, it will be well for you to have a record to hand; an account, if you like, of everything you have done, and everything that you have attempted.

I have no doubt that she is right. Part of me wishes that she had not warned me, thereby stripping me of the bliss that ignorance can sometimes be. It is harder than ever to take up this duty, knowing that blame and accusation are likely to be part of my reward. But she is right.

Besides that, dear Llan, these are momentous times! Someday a little further in the future, scholars will look back on the events of our lives, and wonder. If they do not have first-hand, authoritative accounts upon which to draw, then history will remember us falsely. I undertake to commit my perspective to paper, and I urge you to do the same.

She has promised that I may read her account, when she chooses to declare it finished. I have promised that she may read mine.

Here, then, is my record of events following the draykon war upon the city of my birth, Waeverleyne. I swear that it is a true and faithful record, to the best of my knowledge and information.

This account begins in the year 1913, on the eighth day of the seventh moon. I cannot yet say where it will end.

Not even half a year has passed since I discovered my secret heritage. Perhaps I ought more rightly to say, since my heritage discovered me. My first Change came upon me without warning, and I was defenceless against it.

Prior to that change, the draykoni had receded so far from public memory that we had recast them as mere legend. Absent from our realms for hundreds of years, with all records of their history expunged from our libraries, they had dwindled into tales. We told each other stories of creatures bigger than houses, with wings like sails and scales of every imaginable hue. They could breathe fire, we said. They could swallow a human child whole, and frequently did.

I was the first person to suffer the Change. I say suffer because it was by far the most painful experience of my life. Try to imagine, if you will, that every inch of your skin tries to turn itself inside out; your organs expand too quickly for your beleaguered body to hold; your bones splinter and break themselves in their haste to reform, and then mend in the blink of an eye. Your heart pounds about a thousand beats a minute and you sweat away most of your body's water under the appalling pressure of it.

And then, when the searing pain is finished and all is quiet once more, you are... other. Everything around you has inexplicably shrunk, for it takes a little while to realise that it is you that has grown. Your face feels strange, because where there was once a mouth there is now a protuberance which can only be described as a snout. Wings you may be used to, if you are Glinnish like me, but not like these. These are indeed the size of sails, and they weigh differently upon your lengthened back. And I cannot even begin to describe how differently scales feel to skin.

When you look down and discover your arms to be more aptly described as forelegs, and that you are sporting wicked claws a few inches long upon what used to be your hands... I would like to think that panic would be a normal reaction.

I panicked. It wasn't pretty.

Things are very different now, for me and for the wider Realms. I have grown almost as comfortable with my draykon form as I am with my more familiar, two-legged shape. I have grown to love the mist-grey colour of my scales, and the powerful wings that carry me farther and faster than ever my Glinnish pinions could do.

And I am far from the only draykon in the Seven. The next to shift were Orillin Vance of Glinnery and Avane Desandry of Glour, both of whom are now my dear friends. We have been through much together, and I know that I can count on them both to be with me through every step of whatever is to come.

There is Pensould. He was the first of a different type of draykoni to return: the lost ancients. Sunk into a deathlike state and subsequently revived, he is pure of blood, for unlike the rest of us there is no human in him at all. There are others like him. It is difficult to keep track, but our best estimate at present is that there are now nearly forty living draykoni, of one type or another — ancients like Pense or hereditaries, as we have begun to call those like me. Most of them are ancients. There are few hereditaries, yet not so few as we initially believed. Lokant records identified only three of us: Ori, Avane and me. As it turns out, we three were only those with the very strongest draykon heritage — virtually bound to shift, sooner or later. There are others, their blood more liberally mixed. It is harder for them to Change, and they require more of our help, but they are finding their way.

Our numbers are steadily rising. We must make a place for ourselves somewhere in this world — away from the Seven, to my regret, for after the war there are many who will never trust us again. As the Lord and Ladies Draykon, it falls to Ori, Avane and me to attempt to maintain peace between these disparate peoples. It is a daunting task, and one that I do not feel prepared for. It has fallen to me by chance alone; a mere accident of ancestry has placed me here, and I am petrified of failure. The consequences would be severe — another war, perhaps, at worst.

But I must try, and I will. With Pensould and my friends at my side, perhaps I can survive this next year without another total disaster.

Hah. Who am I kidding.

The real beginning of this story was a few weeks ago. Pensould and I are settled in Iskyr now — the Upper Realm, as the humans still call it — and that is a major change in itself. I don't know if you have ever visited the Uppers, but I imagine not. It is dangerous up here, at least for most people. The place is unstable; it changes all the time, and without warning. One moment you might be strolling through a beautiful meadow full of flowers, three suns shining balmily upon you and the air full of fragrance. Two minutes later, the meadow is gone and you have fallen into a thicket of brambles with venomous thorns an inch long. Or fallen into the sea. Or a ravine. The changes cannot be predicted, and if you are a human with no magics, there are few ways to protect yourself from them.

And that is just the landscape. This world is also populated with all manner of animals. They are beautiful, wondrous and fascinating without exception, but some of them are brutal, aggressive and incredibly dangerous, too.

This is why humans have, for the most part, confined themselves to the Seven Realms and kept away from the Off-Worlds. But these dangers do not apply to the draykoni, or not in the same way. These are our worlds. We were born here, steeped in the mystic energies of these realms of perpetual light or endless darkness. A draykon may refashion the world around them, in whatever image they so choose.

This is not as easy as I make it sound. Manipulation of those energies — amasku, we call them — is difficult, and tiring. It is a wild force, hard to contain or direct. I cannot lightly tackle it alone, not to make grand, sweeping changes. Certainly not without exhausting myself.

But two draykoni together may achieve more, especially if their initial goal is merely to create a home for themselves. Pensould, my mate, is an ancient, and as such he is stronger than I. We travelled into Iskyr together, and chose a spot we considered pleasing. It Changes often, of course, but it returns most frequently to a peaceful configuration: a low valley covered in tall, blue-green grass, sloping down to the shores of a wide lake of rippling silver waters. We created a tree next to the lake, a glissenwol like those of my home in Glinnery. Beneath its vast mushroom cap we added a house: not a wooden-built construct, but a dwelling growing naturally from the trunk of the tree itself. I am winged even in my human shape, and when he chooses to take a human shape Pensould follows my lead. There is safety in the heights. Together, we exert just enough of our will over our little valley to keep our tree stable and safe, no matter how the land shifts beneath us.

It is a modest beginning, considering the volume of work before us. But it is a start.

One morning about two weeks ago, I was sitting atop a large rock not far from the lake enjoying Pensould's remarkable cooking for my breakfast. He is a marvel that way, and you wouldn't think it to meet him. Ancient beyond words, with little recognisable humanity even in a human shape, he is one of the most powerful draykoni I have ever met, and frequently impatient with what he calls absurd human customs. And yet, given a stove and a seemingly haphazard jumble of ingredients, he produces marvels.

Anyway, I had been given a delightful concoction of fruits and grains to eat. I sat cross-legged atop my rock, a favourite spot at that hour of the morning, for the light of the suns is warm upon my back, and I can look out over the lake. Siggy — Sigwide, my orting companion — sat upon my left knee, begging scraps from my bowl as usual.

Food? He said, with such pitiful hope that I could not resist him. His sleek grey fur shone in the morning sun, and his tail twitched with delight as he inspected the contents of my bowl.

I was engaged in feeding him a particularly luscious chunk of nara-fruit when a voice shattered the delicious peace of the morning.

Difficult as it was to believe, someone was hailing me.

'Hi!' said the voice, from some distance away. 'Hey! Hello?'

I looked around. Standing on the edge of the valley and gazing down upon me was a human woman. A human. In Iskyr! And as far as I could tell, she was unaccompanied. Her dark brown hair was firmly tied back, and she looked dressed for travelling. On her back she carried the most enormous kitbag I have ever seen, and I wondered how she could possibly bear it.

'Hello?' I called back, wary.

She waved cheerfully. 'Are you Llandry Sanfaer?'

I blinked. Stupidly. I probably made a fine vision of foolishness, gawping at her like she had just asked me if I was the Queen of Orstwych. Eventually I found my words and managed to return an affirmative reply, at which she set off through the valley towards me. The thick grasses came up to her thighs, but she ploughed through them with blithe unconcern. She looked like she could plough through anything with similarly unimpaired determination.

She stopped at the base of my rock and grinned up at me. 'Meriall Delaney,' she said, and dropped her kitbag onto the floor with a weary oof. 'Nice little place you have here.'

I said nothing.

Believe me, I wanted to speak. The fact is… well, I said I was shy. In truth, that is an understatement.

It's odd. I feel different as a draykon, for it is difficult to be afraid of one's fellow beings in that shape. But as a human, I have always been uncertain of myself. Strangers worry me. Many strangers all together terrify me.

And here stood a stranger, here, in my refuge, invading my lovely peaceful spot without warning.

I tried not to scowl, though I am afraid I may have failed. 'Hello,' I said at last, when I had managed to untie my tongue. I sought for something friendly to say, or at least not outright unfriendly. 'What are you doing here?'

Ah well. I suppose it could have been worse.

Meriall gave me an odd look, and shrugged. 'Where else would I go?' She surveyed my little valley speculatively and added, 'It has definite potential. I can see why you picked this place.'

I was shocked by her appearance, nervous of her presence and now I was getting confused, all of which made me a little grumpy. 'What do you mean, potential?' I said. 'And I don't understand why you would come here at all.'

It was her turn to appear surprised. 'What, is this not the site of the new draykon village? I was sure I had it right.'

Aaand I went right back to gaping. I was still busy with this when Pensould arrived. 'Minchu,' he greeted me — that is his word for mate, and he has always addressed me thus. 'I see it has begun.'

I turned my astonished stare upon him. Pense likes to change his human shape sometimes — and why not, considering it is a pure fabrication anyway? He used to get it wrong a lot in the early days, but he is doing better at it now. I noticed absently that he was wearing his favourite glossy brown hair, and he had matched his skin to my mid-brown colour. He was looking quite handsome, actually, which might have been why Meriall seemed so delighted to see him.

'You must be Pensould!' she said, beaming. She shook the hand he held out, and I was suddenly ashamed. I should have thought to offer so basic a greeting, and it was embarrassing that Pense had done so instead of me. He was barely aware of human social conventions, but he still handled the basics better than I did.

'What do you mean, Pense?' I asked him, hoping to cover my ineptitude with a question. 'What has begun?'

'I shall call it the "influx", I think, for it is a pretty word and not much used.' He smiled at me, and I noticed with bemusement that he had coloured his teeth a strange, pearly-silver hue. 'Here we have mingled our energies and made our mark upon the amasku. It is inevitable that it would attract the attention of others of our kind.'

Oh. Flushing, I thought to open my other senses — the draykon ones, for which I have no words — and examined Meriall anew. I am terrible for that. It comes of growing up human, and I was twenty before I discovered my other heritage. If I am in my human shape, I still use my sight and my hearing by default, and forget everything else.

But once I thought to look, I saw immediately what Pensould meant. Meriall shone in my mystic senses, her human frame clad in the same kind of rippling, chaotic aura that Pense exuded, albeit weaker than his. She was a hereditary draykon, like me.

She smiled at me, but not with her mouth. It's hard to explain. She did something to her aura that radiated unthreatening friendliness, something like a smile and a wave mixed together, but with no physical gesture to accompany them. I found that interesting.

'Welcome?' I said tentatively. I had not yet decided how I felt about this development. I have no idea where she received the impression that we were in the process of setting up a whole draykon village. Perhaps it was merely as Pense said: our actions were perceptible to others of our kind, and were liable to attract them. My visions of peaceful comfort in Iskyr began to dissolve, and I suffered a stab of resentment towards this lively, unthreatening woman who had not even had the courtesy to give me an obvious reason to dislike her.

She fell to talking with Pense, and they chatted comfortably about life in Iskyr, what kind of journey she had enjoyed, and the dwelling she might like to establish here. I listened, and watched. Meriall spoke Glinnish well enough, but she was not winged. I thought I detected a faint accent in her fluid speech, but I could not immediately place it. Her skin was a slightly darker brown than mine, but her eyes were an unusual deep green colour. She was unfazed by the strong sunlight, so she was clearly no Darklander.

It came to me, as I listened to her flowing conversation. Her accent reminded me of Devary's speech — Devary Kant, a friend of my mother's and of mine.

'You are from Nimdre?' I said, when her conversation with Pense finally slowed.

She smiled at me, and nodded. 'Draetre University.'

'Devary sent you,' I said in comprehension, and received an affirmative nod in response.

'He's a former professor of mine. I went through my first Change two weeks ago, and he sent me your way.'

I wasn't sure how I felt about that. What was he doing volunteering me to begin some kind of draykon collective? He knew how I disliked strangers.

On the other hand, Meriall was a newly-shifted draykon, and I was probably the only person Devary knew who could help her.

So, packing my ungracious feelings away, I set about helping Meriall to make herself comfortable. She talked, I couldn't. It was awkward.

As usual.

But Pense was right about the influx. No sooner had I grown comfortable with Meriall than another hereditary arrived: a youngish, comfortably rotund Irbellian man called Larion. He could not say how he had come to find us; he had merely wandered in Iskyr, alone from the moment of his first Change, and found himself drawn to us. Larion was quiet, laconic, and clever. He soon learned everything I had to teach, and when others began to arrive, he adopted the role of instructor.

Our little colony grew quickly after that. As I write this account a moon or so later, our tiny valley is crowded with dwellings and beginning to spill over. Our residents comprise people from all over the Daylands and Nimdre; we are of all ages and, thankfully, we wield between us a useful range of professions. It is not easy to keep everybody fed and equipped, but we are steadily learning where to reliably find food up here. Ivi comes from farmer stock. She has collected up a few volunteers and begun the process of creating some fields on the northern edge of our village, there to cultivate the strange but delicious sweetgrains that grow wild in parts of Iskyr. Loret is a tailor, and he has taught Damosel to sew. Together they are producing such garments as are necessary. In time, I feel that many of us will choose to wear our draykon forms much more often — all of the time, perhaps. But what we have at present is a collective of confused hereditaries, trying to make for ourselves a little piece of the familiar in a deeply strange world.

At the heart of all of this there is Pensould, and there is me. The settlers look to us for leadership, which I hardly know how to understand. Is it because I am Lady Draykon? Do they know, or care, about this title? Few have used it. Is it because I was the first to Change, or because we were the first to dwell here? I cannot account for it. Nonetheless, I feel the burden of this unlooked-for obligation keenly. Try as I might, I cannot deflect their expectations onto another, and to my surprise (and occasional displeasure), Pensould has consistently failed to permit me to hide behind him. I think him far more fitted to this role than I, but he only says, Minchu, I do not know the humankind like you do, and that is that. He is always at my side, but his is a silent support.

I sometimes use Meriall as a spokeswoman. She sometimes allows me to.

Our village is beginning to be known as Nuwelin, which means something like "new place" in some obscure language of Pensould's. I did ask him to think up something a little more imaginative, but by the time he had applied himself to that task, Nuwelin had stuck.

So here we are. Eclectic in our make-up, confused to a man, and unsure what the future holds for any of us. And for some reason, all of these people are looking to me to figure that last part out.

Help.

10TH DAY OF THE SEVENTH MOON (10 VII)
And So, The Ancients.

Hitherto, the residents of Nuwelin have been composed almost entirely of hereditaries but recently come into our powers. Pensould is the sole exception.

… or he was until this morning, when we received a new arrival. That by itself is par for the course by now, and we have grown efficient at welcoming newcomers. He or she is handed off straight to Meriall, who usually serves as our welcome party. She in turn tours them around all the useful people to know — Loret and Damosel, for clothing and repairs; Liat, who keeps us fed; Sophronia, who acts as our healer; and, of course, me. I have been introduced to so many new people of late, I could almost say I am becoming used to it. Or desensitised, which is not the same thing.

At any rate, incoming residents are soon walked through how to set up their own dwelling here, and we usually have them settled within a few hours.

This time was different. When Nyden arrived, *everyone* knew about it right away. This is because he showed up in draykon form.

I was sitting with Damosel at the time. We were mending shirts and chatting without too much awkwardness, which is an achievement for me. Damosel's more than thirty years older and treats me in a mildly motherly way which I don't mind at all. We were setting stitches at a leisurely pace and talking about Ivi's new crop projects, which was all peaceful and lovely, until a shattering roar threatened to blow away the shirt I was stitching up. Something properly vast shot overhead — so fast, it was gone in an instant and we couldn't even tell what it had been.

It came back a couple of minutes later. A shadow passed across the suns as an enormous, sable-black draykon sailed over our village, banked and came at us again.

It roared a second time, a sound which shook me to my bones. If you were in Waeverleyne during the draykon war, you would understand full well what I mean when I say that. It is a war cry. It sounds terrifying enough to human ears, but to a draykon it resonates on several other levels too, filling all of our senses with the promise of ruin.

Nuwelin erupted. Most of us shifted by instinct, and within moments the sky was full of draykoni ready to defend our home. Pensould was foremost among us as we rounded up the newcomer and forced him to land, arranging ourselves thereafter in a containing ring around him.

It was only as I came to land myself, threat resolved, that it occurred to me to wonder why it had been so easy. The sable draykon sat quietly, surrounded, his tail swishing lazily back and forth over the grass.

I felt an odd shiver in my mind, emanating from the menacing newcomer. I tensed, wondering what new form of attack this was. Then I realised.

… the newcomer was laughing.

Not out loud. He was snickering in my mind, helpless with mirth. He waved the tip of his tail at us in a cheery greeting.

Then he said something in a language that sounded very much like Pense's: I would translate it loosely as: 'Howdy!'

Pense — handsome and majestic in his draykon-form, with those gorgeous blue-green scales — reared up and beat his wings back and forth. He *roared*, rattling my bones again.

The black draykon did that mental-smile type thing that Meriall had done, only with almost painful enthusiasm. He positively *radiated* open-hearted friendliness, which would have been lovely if he hadn't started out with scaring us silly. *Nyden!* he said. *Ny for short. Sorry, I could not help myself.*

Pense settled down, his tail swishing with irritation. The other draykoni in the circle shifted and muttered and I sighed, fighting back a desire to smack him. A prankster… goodie.

Nobody spoke. It took me a while to realise that they, like me, were waiting for somebody else to take the lead in deciding how to greet Nyden. It took me an embarrassingly long time to realise that they were all waiting for *me*.

'Hello, Nyden,' I said with another sigh. 'I suppose it was necessary to scare the living daylights out of us?'

Nyden grinned at me, a physical gesture this time, and I can tell you, it looks alarming when a draykon does it. There's an awful lot of teeth involved. *Come on! It was funny. You all jumped like rabbits.*

'Well.' I considered how to answer that. 'This is a small village, and there was a war not long ago. We haven't yet seen anything of the draykoni who attacked Waeverleyne, but we expect to someday.'

Nyden flexed his wings, still grinning. His black scales rippled in the sunlight, and I began to understand something about him.

He is bigger than me. More than that: he is bigger than Pensould, and Pense is one of the largest drayks I have seen. Those scales are blacker than black, nightier than night. His eyes are dark, too, and narrow. If this was a storybook and I was in a fairy tale, Nyden would be the villain. He was the very image of typical wickedness, in his every feature.

Apparently he found that terribly amusing.

Whoops. I didn't think of that, said Nyden, and belatedly added, *Sorry.*

'What brings you to us?' said Pensould.

Nyden beamed again. *I just woke up. Actually, a little bit ago. It's been a loooong time.* He put a drawling emphasis on the last two words, and twitched his wings. *So, the ones who woke me were the old kind. And they were so. Dull. They have some kind of purebreed-only colony down south a ways, and there's a lot being said about humans and half-breeds and how wretchedly unfair it is that they are confined to Iskyr when they should rule the world. Or something.* Nyden snorted softly through his teeth. *'I got bored with that. I mean, who wouldn't? So I came to find you lot.* He snorted again, and added, *'The upstarts. The half-breeds.* He snickered, shaking his head. *You're a lot more fun than they are already. Can I stay?*

Here was troubling news. We had heard nothing of this colony yet, but I could have little doubt that this was what had become of Eterna, the leader of the war on my home city, and her warlike supporters.

'You can stay,' I decided, when (again) nobody else spoke. 'But, Nyden? Don't scare us like that again, please.'

His head bobbed and he grinned at me. *Absolutely not, yes. I mean, no.* He made me a funny little bow, the tip of one fang protruding. *Thank you, good Lady.*

I mustered a smile for him in return, hoping my desire to flee wasn't as obvious as I feared. 'In that case, welcome to Nuwelin.'

13TH DAY OF THE SEVENTH MOON (13 VII)
The Trouble With Me.

So, me being me, I have been giving Nyden a wide berth. In fact, after his arrival I retreated a little from everyone.

I feel bad about it, as I always do. But this sudden influx of people into my life and my personal space has been hard to adjust to. With the addition of Nyden, it was all suddenly too much. I ache for the peace and quiet of our little valley, when it was just Pense and Sigwide and me.

I have isolated myself nicely; even my beloved Pensould is not here with me. I found a distant tree, in the branches of which I created a sturdy hammock. Now I lie here, writing and feeling more at peace than I have in days. My only companion is Sigwide, from whom I am rarely willingly parted. He is curled up in the crook of my left arm, sleeping peacefully. He has a habit lately of radiating love, even while he sleeps. If only people knew how to do such things, I might be more comfortable around them. But humans are so closed. It is desperately hard to read them, and to my disappointment, draykoni senses have not helped me there.

The thing about people is… well, I do not know what it is about them that rattles me so badly. But perhaps such things are beyond explanation. What is your greatest fear? Perhaps it is heights, or crawling insects. Such phobias are common enough that they are broadly accepted as reasonable, even if they are not.

Yes, falling from a great height will kill a wingless person, but in the vast majority of cases, people do *not* fall. The danger exists, but it is remote. It is no use telling that to a person standing on the edge of a cliff, however. He or she can see nothing but the drop below, and is too paralysed with fright to assess the reality of the danger.

This is how I react to the presence of strangers, and the more of them there are around me, the worse it gets. Why do I fear people? Most of them would not dream of harming me, even if they *could*. I know this. But fear is not rational.

I used to panic if I knew I was soon to be brought face-to-face with a lot of people. Sometimes I still do, though it is rarer now. I am growing more resilient, as I gain a little in years and strength and (it is to be hoped) wisdom. But to find myself at the centre of this growing community of newcomers is disconcerting, and I never thought that such folk would look to someone like *me* to lead them. I feel the pressure exceedingly, for the price of failing in *this* scenario is higher than it has ever been before.

Anyway, enough about that. I merely wished to explain this early, because I have no doubt that it will continue to have an impact on my behaviour in the future, and if I expect my readers to understand anything about the coming moons and the way I (and we, as a colony) handle them, then the painful process of confession must be gone through.

I can only apologise for this most absurd aspect of my nature, and move on.

Words cannot fully express my gratitude for Pensould, however. He alone understands me entirely, and loves me anyway. If I need company, he is there. If I need quiet, as I do today, then he will leave me be with good grace, and await my return. I only wish that everybody could have such a person at their side.

Which is odd, considering how——

14TH DAY OF THE SEVENTH MOON (14 VII)
The First of Our Disasters.

I was obliged to leave off in a hurry yesterday, and I cannot now remember what I was going to write there. It doesn't matter. I was in the midst of composing that aborted sentence when I sensed Pensould's approach. Draykoni senses are much more… everything than human senses; we can feel each other through the aether, within a certain range. And since Pense is my spouse, our bond is stronger than most. I knew him to be on the approach when he was still a full mile away.

I also felt his urgency. He was not merely coming to check up on me, as he sometimes does. He was moving at speed, flashing through the skies so fast that he would be upon me any minute. I could feel his distress.

I dropped my journal and pen into the hammock without a second thought. Honestly, I cared nothing for what happened to them at that moment. I leapt out of the hammock and let myself fall from the tree — an exhilarating experience when done for pleasure or practice, but undertaken on this occasion for speed. I Changed halfway down, as soon as I was clear of the lower branches. Then I lifted my vast draykon wings and soared skywards, just in time to see Pense appear on the horizon.

Minchu, he called to me — speaking without words, his mind to mine. *I need you to come with me.*

What is it? I tried not to let too much of my distress show, but I think I failed. Pense can lose his temper sometimes, and it can be a little bit terrifying when he does. But it is not like him to fear, and fear is what I sensed from him as he reached me.

He soared in a circle around me and flew back in the direction he had come from. I followed. *Something is badly wrong,* he informed me.

Nuwelin?

Nay, all is well with our colony. But I have found... something. He was struggling to frame his thoughts in words, which shocked me. At last he gave up on the attempt, and instead a brief image flashed into my mind.

I saw a copse of trees: spindly, frail growths, with ice-white bark and pallid, wan-looking leaves. Their lack of colour surprised me, as such pallor is more usual in the Darklands and the Lowers. It is out of place in bright, sunlit Iskyr. The mosses and grass sparsely covering the damp earth below were also bone-white.

Beneath the pale grass, dimly sensed in the earth below: the bones of a long-slumberous draykon, its flesh long since decayed. Ordinarily this would be cause for cheer, and we might now be launching an expedition to wake a prospective new fellow.

But Pense was right: something was amiss.

A little perspective, first. As strange (and wrong) as it sounds, I first encountered my Pensould in a similar state: he was a collection of bones, and naught else. With most creatures, such a state is simply *death*, ended, done. But draykoni do not precisely die, or not eternally so. When I found Pense like that, I could feel the life-force radiating from him. It was sluggish and distant, for he had been long, long asleep, but some essential part of him still lived. Thus was he roused, and regenerated, and given life again.

These bones were dead.

Dead, utterly. There was not the faintest shimmer of potential about them, not even a whisper of energy waiting to be roused. There was nothing at all.

I did not need to ask whether Pense had ever known the like. His fear and confusion answered that question for me. We flew in silence until we arrived at a small wood, and I followed Pensould as he tucked his wings and dived for the ground.

I noticed in passing that most of the trees in the wood were not pallid at all, nor were they delicate. They grew tall, their branches thin but strong. Their trunks were covered in mottled purple and green bark, and their leaves were glorious viridian. The pale trees were confined to a spot perhaps a hundred feet wide in the centre.

Once on the ground, Pensould pawed restlessly at the earth with his great talons, ripping up chunks of mud and grass. I joined him, and we soon uncovered the skeleton.

We have highly unusual bones, as you might expect; what else is normal about a draykon, after all? Instead of bleached white, the bones of a draykon (at least a pure, ancient one like Pense — I do not know about mine) are deep indigo in colour, and they shine a bit silvery in the right light. When I saw the array of bones sticking sadly out of the earth my heart stopped dead in horror. These bones were unquestionably draykoni, but they were as pallid and stark as the grass and trees around them.

I could not detect any life about them, either, though I strained every sense I had in the attempt.

Pense stopped digging and sat back on his haunches, as speechless with horror as I. We leaned against one another and I drew a little strength from his nearness and his warmth. I was so shocked I could not think, but that would not do. *Pull yourself together,* I ordered myself, with the addition of a choice name or two which I will not repeat.

I looked again at the trees and moss and frondy plants around me, all wilting and drained of colour. Prowling about with my tail twitching with unease, I began to notice other things: a daefly lying dead upon a thin, brittle branch, the bright hues of its fragile wings bleached to sickly white. A small colony of tiny insects lying scattered across the earth several feet away from the draykon grave, every single one dead. I do not know what colour these ought to have been in life, but their dull shells were as waxy-pale as everything else around me.

Pense.

He did not reply, but I felt his attention shift to me.

Is there… do you know of a way to drain the life force out of things?

Life force? he repeated, after a pause.

Amasku, I suppose it is. Look at all of these things. I waited, nudging him until he shook off his stupor and joined me. He regarded the daefly and the insects in thoughtful, weary silence, and finally conveyed to me a mental shake of the head.

I have never seen anything like this.

It was the response I had been afraid of receiving, but had hoped not to hear. *Something has forcibly drained the life out of every single living thing in this patch of wood. Not just the draykon.*

Truthfully, Pense's reaction was alarming me quite a bit. I had never seen him so flummoxed, or so horrified. I wanted to draw him out of it, by any means I could think of, so I kept asking questions. Once the analytical side of his mind focused upon the problem, hopefully he would revive a little.

Hmm. Pense began, at last, to think, and some of my tension eased. *I do not know what could accomplish this,* he repeated. *But I can tell you that the power required to drain the life out of a draykon is… to call it considerable would be to badly understate the case.* Pense was over-enunciating his complicated sentences, as though concentrating hard on the words was of some kind of help to him. *In which case, it is perhaps unsurprising that the effects upon surrounding, lesser life forms would be profound. They surrender their lives so much more easily, after all.*

There was that touch of draykon arrogance, that comfortable certainty of superiority over every other living thing. I may have rolled my eyes, I confess, but I kept it discreet. At least he sounded more like my Pense.

And in this instance, he was not wrong. I know of no other creature that "dies" the way a pure-blooded draykon does. It is as though they simply refuse to participate in a natural life cycle, out of pure force of will. Truly, it must take a lot to rend away an old draykon soul.

I felt sick and so, so cold.

Pense had taken to prowling around behind me, but he was not investigating as I was. His attention was focused upon the grave, and he strode in purposeful circles around it, his senses alert and probing. *A female,* he informed me. *Old. Older than me, I would say, and by far. But I do not recognise… I cannot discern anything else about her.*

A flicker of anger reached me with the words, which made me feel obscurely reassured. Pense's spirit was returning. Whatever caused this atrocity, I cannot imagine, but I know that we need to find out. For that, we are going to need Pense at his best. Even if that means he is going to be in a poor temper.

I need Nyden, Pense suddenly announced, and took to the air. He was gone before I could reply.

It was silly of me, but I felt a little forlorn in the wake of this sudden departure. Nyden! What did he need Nyden for, that I could not provide? It occurred to me that it must relate to Nyden's status as a fellow ancient soul, not a part-blood like the rest of us, and that was sensible enough. But still, I could not help feeling a little dismayed. I reassured myself with the reflection that *I* had been the first person Pense had looked for, and that he had instinctively come straight to me.

That made me feel better.

I occupied myself with another sweep of the strange, pale trees while I waited, but I discerned nothing else that struck me as significant... save for a flicker of something odd on the northern edge of the circle, a faint disturbance in the *amasku* that flowed still outside the confines of that odd space. It was a little disordered, more so than usual, but the difference was subtle enough that I could discern little about it. It was flirting with the idea of creeping back in to the dead space, though it had yet to make a significant attempt to reclaim it. I welcomed the thought that the area would recover in time, and flourish again someday.

I wanted to convince myself that whatever had happened here might have been natural, that it had not been deliberately imposed. But I could not. How could any natural phenomena produce such a strange, and isolated, effect as this?

By the time I completed a second exploratory circuit, I sensed Pense on the return, with Nyden swift behind him.

The two landed, slipping lithely in between the brittle branches of the trees. I instantly felt a wave of shock and revulsion from Nyden, so powerful that I had to close myself up. It is hard to explain what I mean by that, but it is the equivalent of shutting your eyes and putting your fingers in your ears, a desperate attempt to stop anything else from reaching you. I maintained this state while Nyden walked around the grave, inspecting every part of it.

At length, he sat back on his haunches. I thought him growing more composed, so I tentatively let my guards fall.

A mistake. Nyden's head lifted, his black scales glittering darkly in the pale sunlight, and he shrieked. If I thought his battle-cry upon arrival had been alarming, I was mistaken, for this shook the earth.

Worse, he set Pense off, too. The pair of them screamed their fury at such volume, I could only assume the ruckus would be audible at the other end of Iskyr. I sat and endured, hunched up and as tightly closed to everything as I could manage to make myself, thankful that I had not brought poor Siggy along.

Eventually, they composed themselves.

I am sorry, Minchu, Pense said, and came over to nuzzle at me. I permitted him to coax me out of my huddle, though I could not immediately recover my own composure enough to reply. Nyden, meanwhile, sat by the graveside and sobbed, his misery all-consuming.

After a while, I mustered my resolve and crept a little nearer. I did not want to interrupt his grief, and I was feeling more than a little wary of him after his fit of fury. But his misery touched me, and I felt it incumbent upon me to do something. *Did you know her?*

I do not know, Nyden wept.

Oh. I wasn't sure what else to say. Considering the degree of his despair, I had expected a favourable answer.

It is the pity of it, Nyden sobbed. *And the* insult!

With that, some of his grief transformed back into anger, and he did a bit more roaring. I was thankful that Pense restrained himself, this time.

Have you ever seen something like this before? I persisted, when he had calmed himself once again.

Nyden went back to sobbing. *Never,* he replied. *Never, never. It is unthinkable.*

I felt Pense's disappointment echo my own. He had doubtless fetched Nyden in hope that the other ancient would be able to shed some kind of light on the problem. If Ny knew nothing, there was nobody else that we could ask.

Or… nobody else that we would *like* to ask.

I directed my next thought at Pensould alone, leaving Nyden to his weeping. *Eterna?* I said, hesitantly.

She would not do this, Pense swiftly replied. *Not even she. No draykon would do this to another.*

Eh, I have to doubt that. Humans kill each other all the time. Even people who seem perfectly normal and charming and kind, like Devary, can still kill at need. Are the draykoni so different, in that respect? Is there a species alive who will not, or cannot, kill its own kind, under the right (or wrong) circumstances?

That isn't what I meant, I told Pense. *Perhaps she, or one of her people, might know something about this.*

Perhaps. His reluctance matched my own. Eterna had led the war on my home; she had shown herself to be impossible to reason with, so consumed with anger and hatred that she had (in my opinion) virtually lost her mind. None of us was eager to have anything more to do with her.

But this was the kind of problem we could not ignore. We might, at last, have to put aside our distaste for Eterna, swallow our pride, and entreat her assistance.

16 VII
My first diplomatic mission
Oh, and an Arrival!

The mood in Nuwelin was sombre, once we had shared this news.

We gathered late that day in the centre of our little settlement. There is a patch of grass there which we have left as open space, for use when we need to meet or like to socialise, as the others sometimes do. There are wooden benches set in a circle, and space for a comforting fire in the middle. We lit the fire. Meriall sat with Nyden, who crouched, brooding, behind the benches. Pense and I eschewed the benches entirely and lay down beside the fire, tucked up in a large blanket Loret had made. The closeness was comforting and he calmed, though his unease did not dissipate. I could feel it rippling beneath his surface composure, spiking sometimes as some dark thought or other occurred to torment him.

For my part, I was by no means tranquil. I appreciated the warmth of Pense's embrace, and the blanket that largely hid me from the scrutiny of the people around me.

We ate, and we talked.

'We must go to Eterna's folk,' said Loret firmly. 'They must be informed, whether they know anything about it or not. This could happen again, and they have to know.'

Larion added his typically laconic support to this. The two

men have become friends in recent days, despite their very different backgrounds — Loret is a prosperous, winged Glinnish man of almost sixty years, and compared to Larion's relative youth and much more straitened upbringing in Irbel, there seems little to particularly recommend the two to one another. But they have grown close, and their opinions often coincide.

'Then send a letter,' said Sophronia, and added darkly, 'Nowt good can come of havin' aught else to do with that lot.' Like me, Sophronia was from Waeverleyne, the capital city of Glinnery. I knew she had been present during the conflict. Her resentment towards those who had tried to lay waste to our home was understandable, but I wished — I *wish* — that it was not so easy to hold on to such feelings. Eterna acted as she did precisely because she could not get over *hers*.

The debate circled and circled, and went nowhere. Our little group was hopelessly divided and incapable of reaching a majority decision, which disappointed me. I confess, I had been hoping that the first major problem faced by the fledgling community of Nuwelin might be resolved by general agreement, rather than anybody's having to make difficult decisions which would be unpopular with half of our number.

Or rather, if I must be specific: I was hoping that *I* wouldn't have to do that.

No such luck.

You will have to intervene, Minchu, Pense told me silently.

I sighed, fighting an almost overwhelming urge to simply go to sleep. I felt weary beyond belief. *Why must it be me?* I demanded. It was petulant, I knew, but I couldn't help it. The product of tiredness and anxiety and fear. I am never at my best under those conditions.

I did not expect a response from Pense, or rather I expected (and hoped for) comfort alone. He has long since come to understand my need for it, and its efficacy upon me; sometimes, all I need is a moment's warmth and understanding from him, and I can muster myself to almost any action.

This time, he took the less common step of attempting to argue me into it.

I do not think you realise how you appear to our friends, he said. *Or to me. In your own mind — and I know this, Minchu, because I have spent a lot of time there, so do not try to contradict me — in your own mind, you are a scrap of a thing, smaller by far than everybody around you. They loom and tower over your estimation of your own worth, and as such, you are cowed.*

But to others, you are quite different.

You are quiet, but they do not see this as shyness. They see you as a person who considers her words carefully, and speaks only when she has something useful to share.

You are slow to impose your authority, but they do not see this as reluctance or lack of interest. They see you as a careful, considerate leader who exercises her authority with respect for them all, and will never abuse it.

They do not see or sense your fear, for you are adept at concealing it from all but me. They defer to you because you were the first to Change in modern times, yes, and because you are Lady Draykon. But also because you are the brave defender of Waeverleyne. Your exploits in that conflict are legendary, did you know that? They respect you for that, and for your welcome of them since their arrival in Iskyr. You are a woman of wit, wisdom and bravery, and in their *minds, you tower over* them.

Fortunately, Pense seemed to be aware that I couldn't possibly be expected to find an immediate response to all of that. He nuzzled my hair and gave me time to think it over.

Which I did. In fact, I am still thinking it over. My instinct is to treat it with disbelief, and pass it off as Pense's own bias operating in my favour. But I cannot. To do so would be to insult his judgement, which he does not deserve, and besides… I cannot help hoping, secretly, that it is true.

It has never before occurred to me to imagine how other people see me, or even to imagine that their view of me might be different from my own. It is an intriguing exercise. I do not know how far Pense is correct, but… I was touched beyond words by his faith in me. I feel a glow of happiness even now, just thinking about it.

That's what I mean about Pensould. He never blames me for my failings, and he has a way of reminding me that I am not *all* absurdity.

Which is not to say that this speech performed miracles. I wish I could say that I gathered my resolve, strode forth and proceeded to be decisive, forthright and generally amazing. I wish I could say that I resolved the argument on the spot, with all the wit and wisdom that Pense is ready to attribute to me, and that this heralded an era of perfect peace and harmony at Nuwelin.

None of that happened, of course. But I did concede to

think that I must, indeed, intervene, and I probably would not be resented for doing so.

My own opinion coincided, generally, with Loret and Larion's, though I was no more eager to find myself in Eterna's company again than Sophronia. My heart still breaks when I remember the way those draykoni tore into my home, and the relish with which they destroyed the lives of too many of my people. It is hard to forgive, and I have yet to fully do so.

But I know that to nurse those resentments will only lead to more such wars in the future, and it is imperative that we avoid any further such clashes. It is my duty to do everything I can to ensure peace: between the draykoni and the humans of these worlds, yes, and also between the disparate groups of draykoni that are taking up residence across Iskyr and Ayrien.

A tall order.

And now we face a shared threat. Someone has killed a draykon, and could do so again. The others *must* be informed. Furthermore, I still hoped that Eterna, or one of her people, may have some light to shed on the force behind the unknown draykon's strange demise.

Reluctantly, I disengaged myself from the blanket and Pense's embrace and got to my feet. Everybody quieted as I did so, which unnerved me further, for I keenly felt the weight of their expectant gaze.

I took a deep breath. 'They must be told,' I said, quietly but firmly. 'It is our responsibility to share news of this event. If they had discovered the grave, we would expect them to warn us.'

Ivi was having none of that. 'All very true, but we were at war with these folk not long ago. They could attack our messenger on sight.'

Which was a possibility, but unlikely. 'They are obviously aware of us. Nyden's presence proves that. But they have made no effort to attack any of us thus far, and I think it unlikely that they will do so now.'

I waited, but to my relief, nobody wanted to argue with me on this point.

Before I could speak again, or decide on what else to say, Meriall finally weighed in. She was in her human form, like the rest of us (except for Nyden, who is too supremely comfortable in his own skin to bother with changing his shape). She waved a hand in the air. 'I will go,' she offered.

'Are you sure?'

She grinned at me, swift and mischievous. 'I am not afraid of the scary lady.'

'You should be,' Sophronia muttered.

Meriall ignored this with enviable grace. 'Anybody coming with me?'

Larion raised his hand, as did Loret. Then, to my amazement, more hands went up. It ended with everybody except Sophronia and Nyden volunteering to go.

Meriall smiled sunnily upon them all, and bowed with a flourish. 'You are too kind! But I think we shouldn't *all* go.' She looked at me for confirmation, and I could only agree. 'Nyden, if you would be a dear and bear me company, that will do nicely.'

Nyden fluffed his wings. *All the willing volunteers you have and you pick on me? What did I do to deserve that?!*

'I can't help that you are the most fearsome of us,' said Meriall coaxingly, with a sweet smile. 'Also the largest, with the shiniest claws—'

'And the only person who knows where Eterna's hiding,' I put in.

Nyden shot me a filthy look. *I left for a reason. I don't want to see them again!*

'Pleeeaase?' said Meriall, and fluttered her eyelashes.

Nyden sucked upon one fang, grumbling. *You forgot handsomest.*

'Fine,' said Meriall with a roll of her eyes. 'There is no one half so *handsome* as you, Ny, and since I cannot bear to go an entire day without your glorious visage to feast mine eyes upon, I beg you will accompany me.'

The smile she received in response was smug, and regrettably toothy. *So, so easy.*

Meriall smacked him for that, which of course he deserved.

I sighed inwardly, for I knew that I could not shrink from this. 'I will also go.'

'And I,' agreed Pensould.

Meriall nodded. 'Four is a good, stout number.'

'A respectable delegation, but not enough to appear as a threat,' I agreed. 'We will leave first thing in the morning.'

With which pronouncement, I gracefully withdrew. Or rather, I fled, and hoped that nobody realised that's what I was doing. Considering the ironic twist to Meriall's smile as I departed, though, I don't think I fooled her.

We were all four suitably draykon-shaped and on the wing very early on the day of our quest to find Eterna. We followed Nyden, whose idea of explaining our travel plan consisted of: "We bear south, and keep going." So we turned south, and we flew.

Draykoni are strong, powerful creatures, but on the whole we are better suited to short, fast bursts of flight than long journeys. We aren't able to glide very easily, the way some birds do, and it costs us a great deal of energy to maintain the motion of our wings that keeps us aloft. Iskyr, though, is enormous, and Eterna has stationed her colony a long way from ours. (Actually, it is more likely that we instinctively placed ourselves far from everybody else. I doubt Eterna cares very much where we are). We stopped every hour or so for a rest, which made for a slow journey indeed.

But I didn't mind. I may struggle in groups of people, but I can manage better with only one or two strangers around me. Meriall and Nyden are both easy-going, and Meri is talkative enough to cover any awkward silences I (inevitably) leave. When we stopped, we talked and dozed together. The first such interludes were a little uneasy, but we swiftly grew more comfortable with each other and I actually began to enjoy the interaction.

I can tell you, nobody was more surprised by this than me.

The periods of flight were also interesting. It has been some time since I have taken a long journey through Iskyr. Watching the realm's Changes happen from a position aloft is fascinating, and mesmerisingly beautiful. We flew over rolling hills looking like a rumpled, bejewelled blanket, and watched as they shimmered with roiling colour and melted into a lake of sparkling golden waters. Tiny islands of blueish rock were dotted about across the surface, sparse flecks of colour in an otherwise featureless golden sea. Later, we passed over a forest of trees grown so closely together, I could see nothing of the ground beneath. These were trees I have never seen before: they bore nothing I could describe as leaves, but their branches were thickly clad in a pale, fluffy type of something all threaded through with spidery tendrils of red. Viewed from above, it looked like a particularly plush woollen quilt covered in haphazard embroidery. I could smell the trees, too, even from up there! They emitted a thick, cloyingly sweet aroma, pleasant enough for a few breaths, but I swiftly began to feel that I would prefer not to spend much time beneath those branches.

The forest vanished in favour of an arid expanse of near desert, its sands as red as the vines of the fluffy trees. It was featureless, until we soared over a single oasis of sparkling clear water and silvery trees struggling bravely to survive in the midst.

I began to wonder where these landscapes come from. Are they generated by Iskyr itself, somehow? By which I mean, do they grow here, or were they made? See, it is possible that all of these landscapes are as natural to Iskyr as the glissenwol woods are to Glinnery, but that somehow several of them grow in the same place. The Changes happen because they fight for dominance over that space, and it varies as to which landscape wins. So to speak.

That is one theory. I also wonder how many are left behind from ages past, when these worlds were populated by multiple thriving colonies of draykoni. If I wanted to, I could land in the middle of that blood-red desert and adjust it to something else. I could change the colour of the sand, or do away with the desert entirely in favour of a rippling sea. The greater the change the harder it is, of course. I do not know if I *could* banish an entire desert in favour of water, or at least not by myself. But that is only because I am not strong enough alone. Together, we could certainly do it. The landscape bends to our will, up here, because we are part of it.

But if we did that, what would happen to the desert? I think it likely that nothing would happen to the desert at all, in that it would not be erased by our meddling. Rather, we would construct a new landscape and impose it over the top of the desert, and every other that manifests in that locale. As long as we remained and wished for it to dominate, then our sea, or whatever we chose, would remain prominent. But if we left and never came back, the desert would, sooner or later, reassert itself. So would our sea. In short, all these peculiar landscapes *might* be the leftover projects of long-gone draykoni. Somebody dreamed up those strange, fluffy trees, and the dream retains some of its power, even after the dreamer is gone.

Interesting, no? At present, there is no way to determine

which of these theories is the truth, if either. Maybe they both are. There is much yet to be done, to learn about ourselves and the effects we have on our home.

We speculated about all of this extensively, as we wended our way south. I learned that Meriall has a particularly keen mind for such theorising, and her grasp of both theories is better than mine. I also learned that Nyden doesn't much care.

Pense doesn't care either. He listens to our speculations with the mild amusement of an old man listening to the tentative discoveries of children, and contributes little.

That's okay. I love him anyway.

We passed through nine Changes before we began to sense other draykoni nearby. Nyden warned us that there would be a lot of them at Eterna's colony. I hadn't needed the warning, precisely, but the reminder wasn't out of place. When Eterna led the attack on Waeverleyne, she brought more than thirty ancient, recently-revived draykoni with her. It was reasonable to expect that most or all of these made up the beginnings of her new colony on Iskyr, and she has certainly woken others since, Nyden being one. I was prepared to encounter fairly large numbers of them, but I was still taken aback by the truth.

The colony had taken residence upon a vast mountain, which hove into view so suddenly I felt that it must have been hidden in some way before.

You could have warned us, Ny, said Meriall grouchily.

You knew where we were going. Why should you be surprised when we get there?

I didn't realise—

Thoroughly unreasonable, said Ny in disgust, cutting her off. Meriall snapped her teeth at him and he returned the gesture, grinning.

We were flying over a nondescript meadow when we crossed some kind of barely-perceptible boundary, like passing through a veil of gauze. And there was the mountain, all whitish rock with patches of alpine brush and sturdy trees. Structures like enormous, woven nests covered over with roofs and built on several levels were dotted up and down the mountain, which I viewed with some interest. Were these the kinds of dwellings that draykoni naturally preferred? Pense had always let me decide how we were to dispose of ourselves by way of a home, and Nyden had yet to fully install himself at Nuwelin.

Stop here, Pense suggested, and we obeyed, hovering at a respectful distance from the settlement. We wanted nobody to imagine that our intentions were hostile.

We had been sensed the moment we came within range of the colony, just as we had begun to sense *them* a half-mile or so back. Almost as soon as we came to a halt, a trio of draykoni soared into place before us, neatly blocking us from proceeding any farther. They were violet, yellow and white respectively, and I did not remember seeing any of them before. Whether they were part of Eterna's original group or more recently awoken, I could not tell.

Who are you? demanded the leader, the violet-scaled one. Her voice in my mind was unmistakeably female and just as unmistakeably authoritative, but unusually, she was not the largest draykon of the group. That interested me. I had previously assumed that the biggest draykon tended to lead by virtue of superior might, but perhaps that was simple-minded of me.

Particularly since I was the smallest of *my* group of four, and yet I was also the generally acknowledged leader.

Not this time, though. I refused. Not because I was afraid, although I did feel a little cowed by the numbers of draykoni before me. But because, in this instance, I was absolutely underqualified. This was a group of ancient draykoni, not part-human hereditaries like me. I had not the smallest idea how to deal with them sensibly or respectfully. Furthermore, I had the feeling that they would take Pensould much more seriously than the rest of us, for he existed on a level with them. I could have volunteered Nyden, but his… odd attitude doesn't lend itself well to negotiation. Besides, who knows on what terms he departed this place?

Pense, I said privately. *This is your world.*

He did not make me argue with him about it, fortunately, but put himself forward without complaint. I was relieved, and a little… guilty? The problem is, even when I am certain I have good reasons to hang back, I still doubt myself. Had I really delegated the role of speaker to Pense because it was the sensible thing to do, or was I just kidding myself and it was purely because I was afraid?

Sometimes I get so bored with being me.

We hail from the colony of Nuwelin, Pensould announced. *We are here with tidings for your leader.*

The three draykoni said nothing right away, and I imagined they were discussing this amongst themselves. Their manner was carefully neutral, neither trusting nor overtly wary, but I sensed a hint of unease from them.

Which was curious, under the circumstances, for I could easily see that they far, far outnumbered our little colony. But perhaps they were as poorly informed about Nuwelin as I had previously been about their settlement, if not more so. For all they knew, we part-draykoni could number in the hundreds by now.

Please wait here, said the violet draykoni at last. *You may land.*

We obeyed this politely-phrased order with some relief, for we had been on the wing for too long and were growing tired. The white-scaled draykon detached himself from the group and flew away, presumably to fetch, or at least consult, Eterna. The other two kept their position in the air above us, watchful and clearly ready to rend us to pieces should we attempt any form of aggression. This we ignored. We sat comfortably in the grasses at the foot of that sprawling mountain and dozed, at least ostensibly. In truth, I was alert for the smallest change in the situation that might herald a problem, and I am sure the others were likewise.

Eterna certainly took her time, but at length she arrived. She was the draykon who inspired my limited theory about size and power, for she was a huge creature, much bigger than any of the three sentries who had accosted us upon arrival. Her scales were mottled green and cream, though I was now able to see that they were veined with faint gold as well. I had rarely been so close to her before, and on the last occasion I had been too busy driving her into gunfire to pay much attention to her appearance.

I believe the memory of that was at the forefront of her mind, too, for she treated me with wariness. *Llandry Sanfaer,* she said, as she landed in front of me. *I cannot claim to be pleased to see you.*

I gave a draykon-shrug, which is like a little lift of the wings. *That feeling is mutual, but we come bearing important news. We could not, in fairness, fail to inform you.*

You could have sent a messenger, Eterna pointed out.

I could. But I felt I owed the respect of greater attention to your colony.

Eterna digested that in silence for some time, and I felt her attention wander over Pensould, Meriall and Nyden, lingering upon the latter some time. Nyden bore her scrutiny with all the grace of a rock, and did his level best to appear both inconspicuous and innocent. He failed the way a rock fails to fly, but she did not comment upon his return.

We made an impressive-enough group, I thought, banded together as we were. Pense and Nyden have the advantage of size, and Meriall is by no means small herself. But I felt a hint of disdain from Eterna as she looked us over. She would know at once that two of us were only partly draykon, and I know that the ancients, as a group, tend to view us as lesser.

Their loss, really. My people are in *no* way lesser.

What, then, is your news? Eterna said at last.

I let Pensould take over again, and listened quietly as he related his find of the draykon grave. He has a better idea of how to present it than I would, and there are implications to it that an ancient draykon will grasp better than a part-blood like me. He was economical with his information, expressing the situation in brief sentences. He ended by saying, *Our purpose was two-fold: To warn your folk that some danger to our kind is abroad in this land, and to ask whether you are in possession of any information about how such a thing might be done.*

Eterna considered. *You did not, then, come to accuse me or mine of the crime?*

There is no accusation, Pense replied.

Eterna radiated displeasure. *I am glad, for it is clear that there is no crime. What you describe is not possible. Your real purpose in coming can only be to get a glimpse of our colony, and take a measure of our numbers. I trust this is now concluded, and you may consider yourselves invited to depart.*

We protested, of course, but her mind was fully made up and she would not listen. She spread her enormous wings and rose up into the skies, deaf to our words. Then she was gone, leaving us to all the pleasure of three sentries with a newly hostile attitude.

We left.

So that went well, Nyden observed as we flew away.

Shut up, said Meriall.

He obeyed this order for fifteen seconds or so. *Scenic trip, though. Nice outing. Do it again tomorrow?*

Shut up, Ny, Meri and I said in unison.

Nyden sighed and fell into a sulk, which he did in silence, so I think we can say that he obeyed the command. It counts, right?

I was disappointed by the failure of our errand, but not much surprised. We may have an unspoken truce with Eterna and her people, but that is not the same thing as an agreement for mutual co-operation, and it seems most unlikely that we will ever achieve that. The memories of past conflicts are too near, and I do not hold out much hope that they will fade with time.

Eterna's immediate assumption that we were lying did hurt a little, though. Not only because it cast aspersions upon our moral characters that I felt were completely unmerited, but also because her interpretation of our motives was condescending in the extreme. Honestly. If we had wanted to scout her colony and inform ourselves as to their strength and numbers, I can think of half a dozen better ways to do so. Are we stupid enough to trail over there and present them with a wildly implausible tale, naively expecting to be believed without question no matter how absurd the story may seem? I like to think not. What a pompous… well, I had better not finish that sentence. This is supposed to be a respectable account.

We debated the finer points of Eterna's intellect, character and parentage fiercely on our way home, though our indignation soon faded. If Eterna knew nothing about the strange draykon grave, then we were back to where we had started: we had no information, and we needed to change that.

'She could be lying,' said Meriall at one point.

'She could,' I agreed. 'It is difficult to tell.'

'Maybe she did it.' We were draykon-shaped and on the wing, so we spoke mind-to-mind, but Meriall's silent voice radiated with the sardonic grin she would probably be wearing were she human. 'She has a temper. Somebody irritated her too much, and *bam*. Dead. Then she dismisses us with the pretence of finding it impossible.'

I thought about that. 'Little would please me more than being able to find her the villain of the piece.' I had to be honest: Eterna was an obvious candidate for such nefarious behaviour, and it is such a strain to me to treat her with moderation, or anything like respect. I have not forgiven.

I know that the others feel the same.

'But,' I continued reluctantly. 'We must not permit ourselves to be carried away by the most obvious, and desirable, explanation. If she is not the culprit, then there is somebody else out there that we *must* find, and soon.'

'I was just joking, Llan,' said Meriall.

'Oh.' I felt foolish. Actually, I still feel foolish about it. I am trying so hard to live up to the role I've been given that I have forgotten how to relax and laugh. I'd better work on that.

I still think it was probably Eterna.

There, I've said it. I solemnly promise not to allow myself to be blinded to evidence against her involvement, or in favour of somebody else's. I do.

But it was probably her.

Anyway, with that out of the way, I will move on.

When we arrived back in Nuwelin, we discovered that our numbers had grown again in our absence. As we drew near, I sensed an additional presence that had not been there when we left. My first thought was dismay; I was tired after the journey, and I had not the energy for the demands of meeting yet another stranger.

But then I realised this was a familiar presence, and my heart leapt with delight. The moment we reached Nuwelin, I headed directly for the newcomer, landed and Changed back to human. He was sitting in the centre, where we'd had our meeting a few days before. Everybody was there, gathered around him and the fire they had lit in his honour. They were chatting animatedly, as though they had all known each other for years.

'*Ori!*' I squeaked, and ran at him. He barely managed to turn about and stand up before I hurled myself upon him, and I almost knocked him over in my enthusiasm.

Happily, he didn't mind. He laughed, and squeezed me so hard that I almost couldn't breathe. 'Llan! Finally! Imagine my surprise when I got here to find you gone. And gone on a diplomatic mission, no less! How things have changed!'

He set me down at last, and I grinned up at him. Orillin Vance was one of the first draykon hereditaries, like me and Avane, so I've known him for longer than the rest. Unlike Avane, he is almost my own age, and he is Glinnish, like me, with wings in his human shape as well. He's tall and skinny and super cheerful. It takes a lot to drag Ori down, and he's not fazed by very much, either. He's the brother I never had, and my favourite person in the world next to my parents and Pense. Honestly, he's that important. Everything is better when Ori's around.

'A *failed* diplomatic mission,' I said ruefully. 'They wouldn't believe us! The cheek!'

'Fools! But I can't say I am surprised. You weren't really expecting rational behaviour from Eterna, were you?'

'Well… maybe I was.' I had some hopes, anyway. She has occasionally shown signs of a more reasonable attitude in the past. 'Anyway, look at you! Up here! Are you joining us?' If only Ori would stay, I felt like I could face all the demands of Nuwelin with much greater cheerfulness.

'That's the plan,' said Ori, and my spirits rose. 'I passed everything. The Summoner Guild tried to recruit me, but I told them I had a higher calling.' He grinned at me, and I grinned back.

'Of course you passed everything, and of course they did. I am glad they didn't prevail. We need you.' I hugged him by way of congratulations. He has spent months working diligently to pass all his Summoner exams, and he deserves his success.

Though I don't know why he did that, just as an aside. The Summoner Guild and the Sorcerer Guild in Waeverleyne are… well, it is a bit hard to explain. Summoning and Sorcery are the only magics we've got as humans, and they used to be all-important. I suppose they still are, but since we learned that they are merely diluted forms of ancient draykoni arts messily spread around in the human bloodlines, everything has seemed a little different. Ori was a Summoner prodigy, of course, before his draykon heritage was discovered; a Summoner of average talent might have only a tenuous link to a draykon ancestor, but Ori's as close to full-blood draykon as it gets for a human hybrid. But he's a draykon, so he has access to all of it — everything. All the things we call Summoning and Sorcery, only much more powerful, and a hundred other things besides. Why did he need a qualification in Summoning?

I asked him that, later, and he said it was because he wanted the training, not the qualification. 'It's all very well having the power, but you have to know how to use it.' That makes sense as far as it goes, but I have to express my doubts that human Summoners know better how to use these arts than draykoni.

Ori's been learning primitive, diluted human methods. If he wants to learn — if *we* want to learn — we need to go the ancient draykoni for instruction.

Which is how I persuaded him to join us up here. Hah.

I introduced him to Meriall and Nyden, both of whom took to him at once. Who doesn't? I also noted that he and Pense greeted each other with marked friendliness, which relieved me. Pense can be a bit possessive sometimes — oh, not to the extent of trying to control me, or anything like that. But he seems to be under the mystifying impression that people are practically queueing up to steal me away, and a display of mutual affection like the one I had just exchanged with Ori might be supposed likely to set him off. I am glad he appears to be comfortable with Ori, because there is no way I am going to distance myself from him!

Ori wanted to see the grave. Typically, he appeared to feel no particular dismay or alarm at the prospect of an unexplained and permanent draykon death. He is a very, very clever man — much more clever than me, if we are going to be honest here, and I did promise that I would. He isn't prone to worrying about things, either, so he saw it as an interesting problem and was instantly alive with curiosity.

We were too tired to take him out there right away, though. There was some question of his going out to the grave with Ivi or Damosel, but he declared himself unwilling to go without me (to my secret but intense gratification), so we deferred the expedition until first thing on the following day.

Which is tomorrow! It is late, now. Pensould is sleeping beside me, draykon-shaped and delightfully warm. I am curled up against his side with my journal in my lap, competing for space there with an equally slumbersome Siggy. I knew I would have to write everything down before I slept, as I have no idea if I will have time tomorrow. Are you happy, journal? What tyranny you wield over me! But I have done my duty; Lady Eva can have no cause to scold me. Now it's time to sleep.

Goodnight.

18 VII

In which we are vindicated.

I am beginning to think Ori takes a ghoulish delight in dead bodies.

'Are you sure you wouldn't rather be a detective?' I asked him. He had taken charge of the scene the moment we arrived at the grave, and kept us all back while he conducted some kind of meticulous examination of the body.

We flew as draykoni — Ori, Pense and I, that is — and I am sure he probed the site the way Pense and I had done before. But then he turned human, and busied himself with puttering about, looking closely at everything and touching the bones and saying "Hm" a lot. I stood several feet away with Pense. We folded our arms and watched in silence, because the one time I tried to say something, Ori raised his hand without turning around and I was duly hushed.

I exchanged a glance with Pense, whose expression was so bemused that I had to laugh.

What is he doing? Pense asked me silently.

Investigating, I replied.

Pense absorbed this in silence and went back to watching Ori. But he cast me another quizzical look soon afterwards, and shook his head.

But what is he doing?

I imagine he is searching for signs of foul play. Looking for clues. That kind of thing.

Pense merely blinked at me.

It is what's done at a crime scene, I explained. *The detective examines the site thoroughly for any signs as to who was responsible for rendering the victim dead.*

What kind of signs?

I had to think about that for a minute. *Well… I don't know. In the stories, it's things like fingerprints and scraps of clothing conveniently caught upon a nearby branch, and footprints, and things like that.*

What fingers? said Pense. *What clothing? What shoes?*

He had a point. A draykon crime could have little in common with human investigations; there might be no such clues, or they may be of a different character altogether. What traces might a draykon leave at a murder scene? I had no idea, and neither, apparently did Pense. Murder isn't exactly a recognised offence among the draykoni — probably because it is supposed to be impossible to permanently kill one of them. There is no precedent for any of this.

I did note in passing that, in pointing this out, Pense was climbing down a little from his earlier certainty that the perpetrator couldn't possibly have been a draykon. To my mind, it could hardly be anything else. Who but a draykon could manipulate *amasku* like this?

Ori was clearly enjoying himself, so I was reluctant to interrupt him. Pense and I waited patiently until he had finished, and then we considered ourselves free to approach.

'What conclusions have you reached?' I asked him.

Ori surveyed Pense and me gravely, and lifted a finger. 'I can conclude…' he began.

We waited.

'…absolutely nothing,' he finished, and grinned.

Pense playfully cuffed him, which drew a decidedly over-acted whine of pain from Ori.

'Enough hilarity,' said Pense. 'A dead friend lies here.'

Ori sobered at once, and nodded. 'Sorry. You're right. I was hoping I might be able to find something useful hereabouts, but I sense nothing of use with my draykon side, and I see nothing of interest with my human eyes either.' He frowned, and added, 'Except for a distinct lack of life. It is… chilling.'

We discussed that for a time, without arriving at any useful conclusions. It took me far too long to realise, with dawning horror, that the three of us were no longer alone.

On the other side of the strange, bone-white clearing there stood another human: a woman, older than me, with hard green eyes and tawny hair worn loose. She stood motionless, partially hidden behind the low, eerie-white branches of a tree. Her arms were folded, her gaze fixed upon the three of us. Her face was blank, expressionless.

I touched Pense's arm, and hushed Ori, who was in the middle of a lengthy speech on something complicated that I'd lost track of. I pointed out the woman, and we three stood looking back at her in shared amazement — and confusion.

What is a human doing up here? Ori said to us.

Neither Pense nor I replied. I could feel Pense subjecting the woman to the close scrutiny of his draykon senses, but I didn't extend mine. I had the stomach-dropping feeling that I had seen this woman before and that I did not wish to see her again…

An image popped into my mind. The Waeverleyne war, a leader held for interrogation… draykon, tucked uneasily into a new human form.

'I see you have mastered your human shape,' I said to her.

The woman responded only with a faint, mirthless smile. She neither moved nor spoke, her attention returning to the inert bones that lay, forlorn and half-buried, in between us.

Minchu? Pense queried.

It is Eterna, I told them both.

'I see that you did not lie,' said Eterna into the silence.

'Of course not,' I said, with a touch of irritation. Of course we hadn't lied. What would have been the point?

Eterna's green gaze flicked to me. 'How do I know that you did not do this yourselves?'

Ori snorted. 'Would they be foolish enough to come and tell you about it, if they had? And would we be stupid enough to stand around here chatting about it afterwards?'

Eterna inclined her head. 'It is the most obvious explanation, from my perspective. But there is sense in what you say.'

That made me a little bit angry. With hindsight, I have to remember that I, too, had instantly felt that Eterna (or one of her people) was the most likely culprit, and I wanted it to be her, because it would justify my hatred. I suppose it makes sense that she would feel the same way about us. But at the time I just felt injured and furious.

'We dealt fairly with your people during the war,' I hissed at her. 'We returned every one of your slain comrades to you for revival, when we could have kept them from you. We could have destroyed their bones — few would argue that we were justified. How dare you now accuse us of such a crime, and call us the obvious culprits?'

That sharp, green gaze settled upon me. I knew her to possess a temper in excess of my own, but I detected not a trace of anger in her eyes or her demeanour. She was coolness itself. 'You would have destroyed the bones, would you?' she said, instead of answering my question. 'How would you have done it?'

I was brought up short by that, and had to take a moment to think. 'I do not know,' I had to admit. 'But did you not...? When we talked, before, at Waeverleyne. You appeared to think it possible, then, that we might have destroyed the remains of your missing colleague.'

'It can be done,' said Eterna calmly. 'I assumed you to be aware of the means, but perhaps you were not.' That faint, faint smile appeared again and she said, 'I think I will not tell you.'

I swallowed my irritation. 'You said this was impossible,' I reminded her, gesturing at the inert heap of bones before us. 'Was that a lie?'

'Let us be clear.' Eterna moved at last from her semi-concealed position across the clearing, and took a few steps nearer to the grave. 'It is possible to interfere with the revival of a fallen comrade, if for some reason one wishes to do so. The rejuvenation of the body requires a complete and largely undamaged skeleton, of course. If the bones are scattered or too badly damaged, the rejuvenation cannot be completed. In such a case as that, the spirit is sundered and a return to life is no longer an option. That is the nearest way I have yet heard of to permanently kill a draykon, and it is absolutely forbidden among most draykon clans. Even today.'

'But that is not what has occurred here,' said Pensould.

Eterna shook her head in agreement. 'It is not. After your departure, I thought about your story. I felt there were two possibilities: either that you were lying, or that something of the kind I have just described had occurred. The latter would not be nearly so grave as you claimed, but it would be, as I have said, an offence. I came to investigate.' She stopped speaking, and stared at the grave in silence, no longer expressionless. I detected a hint of anger in her hard eyes, and a deep sadness. 'Imagine my dismay to find that you spoke nothing but the truth.'

I felt a sense of foreboding. 'Is this… someone that you knew?' I asked.

She said nothing, but at length she inclined her head once.

'I am sorry,' I said, truthfully enough. I didn't want to care about her, but the depth of her sadness could not help but affect me.

Eterna sighed deeply. 'I cannot be certain, for there is barely any trace of her left. It is all ripped away — drained, suppressed, devoured? I cannot tell.' Her jaw tightened, and she looked colder than ever. 'I do not know how it can have been done, or why anybody would have done such a thing to her.'

'Who was it?' That was Ori, because I lacked resolution to enquire further. I had a bad feeling about the probable answer.

Indeed, for a little while I thought Eterna would give no answer at all. But eventually she roused herself from her dark reverie enough to say: 'My mother.'

With that, she turned from us and disappeared into the trees. A moment later I felt a sudden rush of energy as she abandoned whatever arts cloaked her nature even from our senses, and regained her draykon form. I caught a glimpse of green-and-white scales through the tree canopy as she flew away.

None of us spoke for a while. I think we were individually struggling with how to feel about this development. Nobody wanted to sympathise with Eterna, but how to help it? For us, that forlorn and lifeless shape was chilling enough. For Eterna, it was the worst kind of loss.

At length, Pensould sighed and turned away. 'There is nothing else to be achieved by lingering here,' he said.

I had to disagree, for a strange thought struck me at that moment. 'Wait.'

Pense stopped, but he frowned at me with faint impatience. That was unlike him. I realised that he was still deeply disturbed by the place, more lastingly so than I'd known.

So I went to him and put my arms around him. He is more responsive to physical closeness than anybody I have ever known. It can be remarkably effective in altering his frame of mind, and I believe he suffers if he goes too long without it. He readily returned my embrace, and I felt him relax a little bit right away. 'What is it, Minchu?' he said, more patiently.

'This place isn't Changing.'

Ori snapped his fingers. 'That's what was bothering me. I knew there was something weird going on.'

The trees beyond the ghostly clearing were not trees anymore, strictly speaking. The forest had shifted, and everything outside of the circle had become a patch of damp, marshy woodland. I could see glimpses of dripping, spindly, putrid-green branches beyond the vicinity of the grave, and the air felt cooler and unpleasantly moist. But the grave site was unchanged; still deathly white, crowded with brittle, unearthly trees, and quite dead.

Pensould extricated himself from my embrace, leaving a kiss on my forehead as he went, and paced the outline of the clearing. Then he began stepping from the drained, white space into the marsh, and back again.

After watching this for a little while, I realised what he was looking for. I made my way to the border and stood there for a moment, eyes closed, trying to use only my *other* senses. I find it hard to do that. Focusing exclusively on the draykon part of me still doesn't come easily. I covered my ears as well, which helped a little, but not enough.

I gave up, and Changed.

Sometimes it feels like I am wrapped in swaddling, as a human, and everything is muffled through it. Shifting draykon feels like ripping it off. It can be disconcerting, as though everything around me has suddenly been amplified — colours, sounds, sensations. Overwhelming. I stood for a minute, struggling to bring it under control. When I felt more accustomed, I turned my attention to the ground beneath my feet.

This part is difficult to explain. I can only say: Imagine if you walked into a room and found it oddly, eerily silent, and for no discernible reason. Not just silent, but deeply, resonantly so, as though it has never known sound before and never will. As though something about that room takes all sound and swallows it without trace.

That is what I felt in that clearing. Or perhaps it is fairer to say that I absolutely failed to feel, or sense, anything at all in there.

But when I drew nearer to the edge of that strange, drained

patch of land, I sensed a change. Energy was beginning to flow back *in,* but sluggishly. And there was something off about it, too. It did not feel whole, as though a budding sickness lingered somewhere just beyond my perception. It troubled us all, but we could find no explanation for any of it.

When we arrived back in Nuwelin, we found only Meriall and Larion at the meeting glade.

'The others are off being productive citizens of Iskyr,' Meriall informed us as we turned human and sat down on the benches. I was weary, though I don't know why. I hadn't done anything unusually challenging. 'We thought it would be more fun to lounge,' she added with a beaming smile.

And they were lounging with enviable commitment. Meriall had laid a thick blanket over one of the benches and had subsequently stretched out full-length upon it with a pillow under her head. She hadn't risen when we approached, merely waved at us. Larion was similarly prone, wrapped in a blanket on the floor. I couldn't imagine what they had found to talk about before we appeared, but it looked as though they were having a cosy heart-to-heart. Which I think is a little bit interesting.

'What did you think?' Meriall said then, turning a curious look upon Ori.

Ori sighed and ran his hands over his hair, making it stick up. 'I don't know what to think, except that it's horrible.'

'Eterna came back,' put in Pense.

That roused Larion from his half-slumber, and he and Meriall stared intently at Pensould. 'Tell us,' said Larion.

So we did. It took a little time to cover everything.

'What about the other draykoni?' said Meriall. 'Have they noticed anything similar going on downstairs?'

I stared blankly at her. 'The other ones? Downstairs?'

'Mm.' She nodded slowly. 'The other ones. In the dark, creepy place.' She grinned.

And I felt a little sheepish. In my defence, I haven't set foot in the Lowers for some time. I may have forgotten about it. How many other draykoni are down there, and what have they been doing with the place? We have no idea.

It is high time we got in touch with Avane, which means venturing among another group of strangers.

I might have spent the last few hours in a state of mild panic about this, but the less said about that the better. Let's pretend I am a normal person with normal social capabilities and not the type to worry myself into a fever over merely having to face a group of strange people, and without making a fool of myself.

Looking on the bright side… Avane borrowed my favourite book, and I can finally get it back.

Onward.

23 VII

To the Dark, Creepy Place We Go.

The Lower Realm, or Ayrien, has always been disconcerting for me. I am a Daylander, born and raised in Glinnery, and from there I went straight up to Iskyr. I have visited Nimdre, where the natural day and night cycle remains, but I only stayed for a few days. Those night-time hours fascinated me, but they also terrified me. I am so unused to being unable to see where I am going.

At least in Nimdre, the nights ended and gave way to daylight once again. Not so in Ayrien. It is as permanently dark as Iskyr is endlessly lit. As soon as I set foot in that place, the darkness swallows me whole and I feel blinded until I get out again.

This may be why I was happy enough to "forget" about the Lowers.

On the brighter side, there is something else I had forgotten about. As a draykon, it is not necessary to open a fixed Gate to travel Off-World. Which makes it easy as pie.

When we were ready to leave, Pensould took the lead and merely glided seamlessly through the divide. One moment we were in Iskyr, and the next we were deep in Ayrien.

And so, I felt a bit better. I would not be stuck in that choking darkness. If the blindness became overpowering, I could leave in an instant.

Pense, Ori and I set off together for Ayrien, but without Siggy. He hates to be left behind, but I find myself obliged to do so more and more often. It's harder to carry him about in my draykon shape, and also more dangerous. He is so tiny, compared to shapeshifted me. And I rarely know exactly where I am going or what might await me when I get there. The dangers are too great for my tiny orting. Fortunately, he seems to have taken a shine to Larion.

We slipped through the veil and the blackness descended all at once, as though someone had thrown a bag over my head. I felt a strong impulse to panic, but I refused. Pense was serenely unconcerned, of course, and even Ori was calm. He is a lifelong Daylander like myself, so if *he* can cope with it sensibly, then so must I.

That makes it sound easier than it was. Have you ever tried to suppress an attack of terror by mere force of will? I clenched my jaw so hard that my teeth creaked, and I was so tense I almost lost my ability to fly. It was like soaring through soup, because I was fool enough to keep straining to see where I was going with my eyes.

Stop that, Minchu, said Pense mildly. *Every sense you possess is of more use to you than your eyes at this moment.*

Good point. I decided to shut my eyes altogether, which kept them out of the way while I concentrated on listening and scenting and employing some of those other draykon senses which are so hard to describe. We were flying over water. I could hear the soft shush of waves some way below me, and the air was heavy with the scent of saltwater. I could hear birds, or some other winged creatures, soaring through the skies not far away. A flock of them. I sensed their heat, each creature separate and distinct even in their tightly clustered formation. There were seventy-three. I could sense no other living beings nearby, besides Ori and Pense.

Once I had mastered this enough to feel more comfortable, I opened my eyes again — and discovered, to my surprise, that the world was not so impenetrably dark as I had thought. A moon hung in the sky, half-full and casting a soft light over the landscape. Once I adjusted my expectations, I found it sufficient to see a little by. The water shone silver below me, and I could dimly see that it stretched away over the horizon.

Boring, commented Ori with a sniff.

I think I prefer boring, I replied. *Under these circumstances, exciting would probably mean danger.*

That's when it gets fun, Ori insisted.

Until somebody gets hurt!

Psh. Ori turned a playful somersault in the air, his draykon wings beating powerfully. *We are equal to anything.*

I sometimes think Ori and I are opposite sides of the same thing. I shrink from the unknown, but Ori can be reckless in the pursuit of it. That makes a good team of us, I suppose. We balance each other out.

Pense, I said. *Do you know where we are going?*

Vaguely, he replied. *Avane is this way.*

Hm. I have no idea how he could tell, except that his perceptions must be of a higher order than mine. No surprise there. He is an ancient, and Ori and I are merely part-breeds. I made a mental note to try to recruit, or wake, a few more ancient draykoni for our colony. They are useful people to have around.

We flew for a while over more and more water, and I began to despair of ever encountering anything else. But then the horizon rippled and shimmered, and I realised a Change was about to happen. That shimmer spread until it engulfed the silvery sea, and a wave of *amasku* rolled over the landscape. In its wake, the water vanished.

The scent hit me first, a wall of floral fragrance so pungent that it drowned every sense I possess. It was like being smothered under the weight of a mountain of flowers. The landscape continued hilly as far as I could see, and I was aghast, because every inch of it must be covered in flowers to produce such an aroma.

Ori made a disgusted noise and dipped towards the ground. Then he pulsed somehow with energy, and a furrow of altered ground stretched out before him, the flowers fading away and leaving bare earth behind.

You could be at it all day without making a difference, I told him. The sea of blossoms was as broad as the ocean it had replaced, and the little patches of flowerless ground Ori was making were pitiful in the vastness of it.

Then help me!

I made no reply, because I had noticed something else. Somewhere ahead of us, a familiar presence tugged at my senses. Avane! I felt a glow of gladness at the prospect of seeing her again. She was not as close to me as Ori, probably because we have less in common. Avane is more than ten years my senior, a Darklander, and mother to a small boy. But she is a good woman, and a friend and ally. I also felt for her. She and I were sharing the same duties, but I had the advantage of having Ori and Pense at my side. Avane had ventured to the Lowers alone, which frankly makes her far braver than me.

I did a happy tumble in the air and sped up a little. I love tumbling! Ori taught me how to do it and it's honestly the best fun. I cannot do it in my human shape, or not the same way. The draykon form is well suited to the kind of barrel-roll I mean, though. You flip right over and spin. I can do five turns before I get dizzy and have to come out of it, and Ori can do seven. It's the best feeling.

But as I went into my fourth turn, I was brought up short by the sound of Ori screaming.

I have never heard him scream before. My first thought was that he must be in some kind of danger, but I quickly realised that it had not been a scream of fear. It was horror. I came out of my tumble so abruptly I wobbled and almost fell.

Ori! I yelled.

He didn't reply. In tandem, Pense and I wheeled and hurtled Ori's way. He had wandered farther than I had realised, or probably than he intended, so intent upon his destruction of the stinking flowers had he been. It took us a minute or two to catch up with him.

I saw at once what had horrified him. Ori sat hunched upon the ground, his normally white-and-gold scales looking pallid and wan in the dim moonlight. Bare earth flanked him for a few feet on either side, after which point the ocean of flowers continued. As I drew closer, I noted that the earth, too, looked paler than it had elsewhere. My other senses detected an abrupt cessation of life, as though I had crossed a firm line between the living world and barrelled into a bleak, dead one.

It felt exactly the same as that forlorn circle of destruction in Iskyr, only this area was larger. Much, much larger.

It goes on and on, Ori said, and his voice shook, even though he wasn't speaking aloud.

Ignoring the sick feeling building in my stomach, I turned a slow circle in the air, following the outlines of this new fallow field. It was easily half a mile wide. Most of it was invisible underneath those wretched blossoms, but I could feel it well enough.

Steeling myself, I landed in the middle of the flowers. There should have been the sensation of petals against my feet, stems crushing beneath me as I rested my full weight on top of them. But I felt nothing, just dry earth.

They aren't real flowers, I reported. *Not in this part.*

Illusion, Ori agreed.

Pense was still airborne, but he wasn't flying, precisely. Hovering is not easy for us. Our wings aren't really made for it. It is a laborious process, but Pense was managing it by dint of determination. I felt his mind sweep over mine, and move on. He was probing, exploring, seeking.

Bones, he said. *Far below.*

I had been too quick to count our blessings. Finding no sign of a draykon corpse on the surface of the earth, as had been the case in Iskyr, I had felt a swift surge of relief. The ground here may be dead but at least it contained no eerily lifeless draykoni.

I was wrong. I closed my eyes and ignored the floral stench as best I could, focusing on the earth beneath my feet. Down, down and down again... and there they were. Bones.

Many, many bones.

That's more than one, I said around a growing feeling of terror. More than one? That was an understatement. More than one, or two, or even five.

Eleven, Pense said after a moment. Then he added, *twelve.*

Twelve more dead draykoni. Or not dead, but... *erased.* Thirteen in total.

Whoever was responsible for this site had taken more care than they had in Iskyr. The area was ably concealed beneath the featureless seas of water or flowers, and the stench of floral perfume was so strong here that I struggled not to retch. It was a powerful deterrent to anybody inclined to investigate, failing only because of Ori's odd whims.

Pense spoke calmly, but I sensed his emotional turmoil. For once, he was closer to losing his grip on himself than I was. He has a way of sending a palpable sense of reassurance at me when I am upset, a surge of affection which wraps around me like a warm, comforting blanket. It can always soothe me, no matter what has occurred to distress me. I did the same for him, letting him feel all of the affection I had for him, and love, and my supreme confidence in everything that he is.

Slowly, he calmed. When he was stable, I gradually withdrew.

Thank you, Minchu, he said privately to me, and I felt something like a mental kiss upon my brow.

I turned next to Ori, but he had got over his immediate reaction and was now prowling around, sending swathes of illusory flowers dissipating into nothing with great, powerful pulses of energy. He meant to clear the site, I saw, and I quickly fell to helping him. Pense joined us, and within half an hour or so we had laid bare every inch of the drained earth. It was bleached white, and as lifeless as baked salt.

Pense disappeared. For a moment, I couldn't understand where he had gone. But then I saw him: small and white-furred, camouflaged against the pale bleakness. The creature he had become was of a type I have never seen before. It had a long, sensitive nose and wide front paws, shaped almost like spades. I saw the reason for that a moment later as Pense began to dig. He sent the earth flying up behind him, and soon burrowed underground and vanished.

Ori and I quickly followed suit. He had the right of it: it was certainly the quickest and easiest way to reach those far-buried corpses down below. Whether we would learn anything new by examining them more closely was doubtful, but the attempt must be made. I adopted the unfamiliar proportions of the little burrowing beast with more than a little clumsiness, but soon I had an alabaster pelt of my own and paws that felt like little shovels attached to my front legs.

We dug.

I won't waste space here with describing the process of that long descent underground. Suffice it to say that it was far worse than the crossover into the deep darkness of Ayrien, for it was velvet-black, completely untouched by any form of light, and enclosed to boot. I've never felt claustrophobic before, but it came upon me then, so powerfully that I spent a full minute frozen with the desire to escape.

I resisted, and dug, and at length we came upon the first of the bones. I had wondered if we would find them all jumbled up together, so closely had they seemed to be packed from our vantage point above. But closer up, I could sense each one, distinct and separate from the next.

I don't know how long we spent down there among those

pitiful remains. Time passed strangely under the earth, with no change of light or atmosphere to indicate its passage. But I know that, with time and focus, and the absence of anything to distract my senses, I began to discern more about these draykoni. They left traces of themselves behind. Not life, for that was irrevocably gone, but something more like a footprint. I discerned whether they were male or female, and some faint whisper of a glimpse into the creatures they had been in life: scarlet-scaled or amber, emerald green or bark-brown.

They're all ancients, Ori observed. His voice startled me, for none of us had spoken in some time, and the silence had become all-consuming.

He was right, though. I had not yet made the connection myself, but I could see the truth of it. None of the draykoni lying in this miserable mass grave had so much as a trace of human heritage about them. They felt like Pense and Nyden and Eterna: draykon to the core, drenched in *amasku*, more energy than physical creature. And ancient beyond words.

And that was an interesting point. The one in Iskyr was also an ancient, which made an unbroken chain of ancients lying in these strange white graves. That could be a coincidence. After all, there are not many human-draykoni yet, and we are still far outnumbered by the ancients.

But it might not be. Whoever had done this might be specifically targeting ancients.

Something was troubling Pense. Utilising my shovel-paws as vigorously as I could manage, I made my way over to him through the chalky earth.

Ludino, he said incomprehensibly. *Myir.*

It took me a moment to realise that these were names. *You know these two?*

They were acquaintances, once. Pense paused, and I think he was gathering his thoughts about this development. *They are far older than me. Of Eterna's era, I would guess.*

True ancients, then, in every sense of the word. That does not bode well, though I cannot say exactly why I feel that way.

I never knew they had awakened, Pense added.

Hm. Perhaps they had, or perhaps not. Had they been killed while they lived, or had their bones been stripped of their residual life while they lay deep in slumber? I could not tell.

What do you know about them? That was Ori, who had reached us by a circuitous route.

But Pense made the mental equivalent of shaking his head. *I cannot think. I must…* he paused, and I felt him suddenly fighting for air. *I must get out of the earth.*

He immediately began to burrow upwards with furious, panicked energy. Ori and I went with him, flanking him on either side. It seemed to take forever, despite our speed, as we inched our way slowly upwards and upwards and upwards… would we ever reach the surface? Were we even *going* up? There was no clear sense of direction down here. Perhaps we were tunnelling sideways, and would never reach fresh air. Perhaps we were even burrowing deeper. That damaged my composure, shaken as it already was by the twelve lifeless skeletons.

Thankfully, before I could embarrass myself by losing my calm entirely, we erupted into air and light. Gentle though it was, the moonlight seemed deliciously bright by contrast with the absolutely blank darkness below, and the three of us lay panting with relief.

That was a little bit vile, said Ori at last, with staggering understatement.

It occurred to me that these lifeless draykoni were too close to Avane for comfort. I reached for her, but I could no longer sense her. She had moved beyond my range, most likely, but I still felt a flicker of alarm.

Pense, can you find Avane?

He stirred, and sat up. Having shed his furred shape the moment we reached the surface, he was draykon once more, and I hastily followed his example. Heavens, but it was starting to feel like home to take on my scaled and four-legged shape. I am not sure if I am glad of this, or appalled.

There was a pause, so long that I began to feel troubled. We have no idea how long those bodies have been lying there. What if it had been but recently done, and whoever was responsible had run into Avane?

Yes, Pense said at last, and I breathed a sigh of relief. *She's too close to this place,* he added, echoing my thoughts. Without another word, he leapt skywards and took off in the direction I had last sensed Avane.

Ori and I heaved ourselves to our feet, groaning a little. When we undertake significant physical efforts in some alternate form, the effects of it don't wear off once we shapeshift. More's the pity. After all that digging, my arms — or rather my front legs, as they were at the time — were screaming with pain, and I wanted to rest them for a bit.

But there was no time to lose, and at least I don't have to use them for flying. I followed Pense into the air right away, Ori right behind me. We flew as fast as we could, and came upon Avane some half an hour later.

Avane was slow to master the Change, and slower still to fully adopt a draykon form. This is not because she is slow in general. She is a bright woman, by no means lacking in intelligence or persistence. But I think she felt more disconcerted by the prospect of the draykoni than the rest of us, because she is a gentle soul. The wicked teeth and sharp claws, the size and bulk, and the undeniable ferocity of the draykoni do not mesh well with her personality.

The war gave her little time to accustom herself, of course, and by the end of it she had been forced into a nearer acquaintance with the draykoni's more violent capabilities than I imagine she ever wanted. I admire her for her resolve, and her willingness to help, even though the war was focused upon Waeverleyne, a Daylander city with which she has never had anything to do.

I wasn't surprised, though, to find that she was human when we reached her. She makes a proud, beautiful draykoness, with glittering purple scales and faintly golden claws. But she still adopts the shape unwillingly, and I suspect with lingering doubts as to her ability to maintain it, or to use it appropriately.

She is somewhere in her mid-thirties, I believe. I haven't ever asked her age. She has dark, gently curling hair and dark eyes, with the pale skin of the Darklanders who've never seen the sun. She also has a mild, sweet smile, which she turned on us the moment we drew close enough to greet her.

She came first to me, which pleased me perhaps more than it should have. I Changed human and hugged her gladly. She's a good woman. Her two-year-old son, Lyerd, was with her, and he of course ran straight to Ori, smiling and holding up his arms. Ori scooped him up at once and swung him around, and instantly began some kind of game which involved a lot of giggling. He is adorable with children.

Pense hung back, silent and watchful, though he shifted human out of respect to Avane. I don't know whether he was unsure of his welcome, or merely taking the time to thoroughly check the environs for potential threats. Perhaps a bit of both, because Avane has been harbouring a secret (or not so secret) fear of Pense ever since they first met. He is draykon to the core, and even in human shape, his *otherness* is clear.

I waited while Avane greeted Ori, and took a moment to make my own observations. We had found Avane walking through a little village, so small as to scarcely deserve the name. I could see little of it, merely the looming, shadowy shapes of tallish structures in the darkness. Only one other person appeared to be in residence at the time, an elderly woman with skin as pale as Avane's and a fall of grey hair. She came to greet us, her lined face alight with curiosity, and was introduced as Wrima. I sensed a draykon soul in her, even if she was fully human at that moment.

'Oh,' murmured Avane, and conjured a light-globe to assist us. It shone faintly, so as not to hurt Avane's or Wrima's Darklander eyes, but it was bright enough to illuminate the houses closest to us. I counted six houses in a cluster, each one eccentric in design, and made from a haphazard array of materials. They were clearly human dwellings, sized for creatures of our height and proportions and fitted with staircases, doors and suchlike.

Always sensitive to unspoken things, Avane noticed our tension. 'What is it?' she said softly, and glanced around with a touch of trepidation. 'This is not a social visit, is it? Has something happened?'

'Tell us at once, if you please,' said Wrima. Her tone was calmer than Avane's, but I sensed a protectiveness about her. She had taken Avane under her wing, then. I am glad of it, for she strikes me as a steady soul.

Pense looked at me, and said nothing. Well, he was right. If Avane must hear such news, it had better come from me or Ori rather than Pense. Since Ori was still occupied with entertaining Lyerd, I indulged myself in a soft sigh and a pang of regret that such an unpleasant duty must fall to me. 'May we sit somewhere?'

Avane led us to one of the shadowy houses, her little white light-globe bobbing along over our heads. The house was warm inside, and she had fitted up a sitting-room with comfortable furnishings. I curled up beside Pense upon a low sofa, and launched into the tale.

It took a little while to explain everything, for I had to start at the beginning, with the discovery of Eterna's mother's body in Iskyr. When I came to the twelve subsequent corpses, poor Avane turned stark white, her dark eyes enormous.

'They are less than ten miles away,' I concluded. 'We came straight here. We were on our way to consult you anyway, and we were concerned for your safety.'

Avane exchanged a look with Wrima. 'Last eve...' said Avane, and faltered. She seemed unable to go on, so Wrima took up the tale.

'Last eve,' the old lady repeated. 'Something strange happened with the Changes. They have been regular around here ever since we settled, and we have had no trouble maintaining the village through the shifts. But about... oh, twelve or thirteen hours ago, the landscape flipped through eight changes in about half an hour, and everything was so badly unsettled we felt alarmed. Then that stopped, and...' She frowned, and glanced again at Avane. 'Near as we can tell, there have been no Changes since. Certainly not here, and not for quite a radius. That's where the rest of the village has gone. They're out looking for the source.'

Ori spoke up. 'That coincides with what we observed in Iskyr, more or less, though it sounds wider spread. Up there, the circular patch of ground that's been drained no longer Changes, but everything around it seems unaffected.'

Wrima nodded slowly. 'Perhaps a matter of scale,' she offered. 'Whatever was done to those poor souls must have been powerful, to say the least, if it could drain twelve of them like that. More than powerful enough to have a knock-on effect on the wider area.'

'Up to a point,' Pense said quietly. 'We saw a Change as we flew in. The site was underwater to begin with, and then the flowers came in.'

Avane gathered her son into her arms and held onto him. She was worried, of course, but she gradually calmed and her face turned thoughtful instead. 'That is likely the first Change since it happened, then,' she said. 'And that is interesting. You said northwest?'

Pense nodded. 'Northwest, westish. About ten of your miles, as Llan has said.'

'Mm.' Avane thought a little.

Pense, too, was lost in thought. Silence fell among the rest of us as we each turned over the problem in our own minds. 'You did not see or hear of anybody unusual in these parts?' I said at last, to Avane and Wrima.

Both women shook their heads. 'When the chaos began, we did wonder,' said Avane. 'But it was too extreme to conduct a search at the time. We couldn't even fly. Whatever occurred disrupted our sense of space so badly, we couldn't even tell which way was up anymore. We went straight out when it settled, but we found nothing and no one. I suppose they had already gone.'

Something about those words tugged at my memory, but I could not immediately think of what she had reminded me of. I hate that.

'I believe I note a possible connection,' said Pense slowly. All eyes turned upon him, and he smiled faintly. 'You human hereditaries have been calling us *ancients*, but we are not all equally aged. Eterna is far older than I am. Her mother must have been older still, and Ludino and Myir likewise. I cannot speak for the ages of the other victims, but three, at least, were among the most aged of our kind.'

An interesting point to note, but not one that can shed any light immediately. 'Is it true that the elder draykoni are more powerful?' I asked Pense.

He shook his head, but then hesitated. 'It is not as simple as that, though there is something in what you say. The eldest of us are certainly the most practiced, the most skilled, the most adept. And they... after so many ages of existence, they wield depths of the *amasku* that younger souls cannot reach. So in that respect, yes.'

Which did not answer the question, either, but it did alarm me a little more. What manner of draykon was so powerful as to be able to destroy Elders — and twelve of them at once, no less?

'The twelve,' I said, frowning. 'They must have been slain while still in the Long Sleep, surely.'

'Perhaps,' said Pense. 'Perhaps not.'

I sighed and leaned upon Pensould, who was kind enough to put his arm around me.

'Who could it possibly be?' said Ori. He sat opposite me, leaning forward with his elbows upon his knees, directing a deep frown at the floor. 'I cannot believe it of any of the draykoni we know.'

'Maybe Eterna's people,' said Avane grimly. The dark tone was unusual from her, and I remembered that Ori and I were not the only ones left with a lasting distrust of Eterna following the war.

'But her mother,' said Ori. 'Her mother was the first victim.'

'So it was probably not Eterna herself,' Avane agreed. 'But there are, what, thirty or forty ancients up there with her?'

'But there are more possibilities,' said Wrima. 'It is tempting to think of ourselves, our own colonies, and Eterna's people as encompassing the whole of active draykon-kind, but that is probably not true.'

'Right,' agreed Ori. 'Limbane thought only three of us would have enough draykon-blood to Change, but they were wrong. Already there are several more, and we no longer have any idea how many there will be in total. And we have long since lost track of all the ancients who have revived. It could be some other group entirely, of whom we know nothing. Maybe it's a territorial thing, or some kind of power contest.'

Pense stiffened beside me. 'No,' he said, softly but firmly. 'No such contest would result in such a massacre.'

'Then who could have?' I said, trying to be gentle. 'You must acknowledge, this kind of manipulation of the *amasku* is specific to the draykoni. Who else could drain it in such a fashion, and so lastingly?'

Pense shrugged, but I felt his stubbornness. He does not want to believe his own kind capable of such an atrocity, and I cannot blame him for that. But the possibility of monstrosities does not obligingly go away, just because we are unwilling to face it.

Moreover, just because there appears to be a pattern emerging in favour of ancients as the preferred targets, it doesn't follow that the rest of us are in no danger.

'How many people do you have with you down here?' I said.

'Eight in total,' Avane replied. 'Including Wrima and I.'

'Any ancients?'

'One.'

I frowned, troubled, for that does not seem like enough to

keep Avane and Lyerd safe.

But Avane guessed at my thoughts, and shook her head. 'This is no time to worry,' she said firmly. 'Twelve ancients slain together, at least some of which were Elders? Even had we twenty ancients with us, it would not necessarily stand against the force that is capable of such a massacre. Numbers are not the answer. Remember that the perpetrators were within ten miles of us last eve, and did not even approach us. For the present, at least, it does not appear that we are in any danger.'

That is a reassuring reflection. For that matter, the body of Eterna's mother lies not so far from Nuwelin, but we have not been targeted either. I must trust that this conflict, whatever the source may be, is not aimed at us. Not yet.

But I remain concerned for Pense, and for Nyden. They are ancients. Who can tell whether they are likely to be in danger? Until we know the reasons behind these attacks and can understand the rationale behind the choices of targets, I cannot be easy in my mind about the two of them.

But neither would thank me for interfering. I made a private resolve to speak to my fellow part-bloods upon our return to Nuwelin. We need not make a show of our concern, but I dare say we can arrange to keep a closer eye upon Pense and Nyden between us. Just to be on the safe side.

24 VII

We Seek Help From a Higher Power.

So here we have a mystery, and no clues. That is not how it is supposed to go. In the books, there is always some handy hint that the detective picks up early on, even if its meaning is not immediately clear. Every fresh mystery that arises comes with its own convenient clue attached, so I call it mighty unfair that this one is still so impenetrable.

But a useful person does not simply wait for clues to materialise. If information is lacking, the wise person goes to wherever information is likely to be found.

I have a friend in Glour. Her name is Evastany, Lady Glostrum, and she is a part-blood Lokant.

They are a race of beings far more ancient than we are. In fact they claim to have created both draykoni and humans alike, which sounds far-fetched to me, but perhaps it is true. They are capable of many remarkable things, like instantaneous travel over shockingly large distances, and limited control over the minds of others. They are addicted to knowledge, and tend to congregate in vast structures they call "Libraries" — not an unfitting term, considering they are stuffed to the gills with books and the like. But there is a lot more to those places than just shelves of tomes. Time passes strangely within, in that it barely passes at all. Perhaps it doesn't. Perhaps it is entirely static.

There is something else, too. I spent some time in one of those Libraries, not so long ago. It is where I was trained to Change, and where we taught Ori and Avane, too. In the Library of the Lokant known as Limbane, there is an enormous room whose walls are covered in a vast timeline of descent. It is like an unfathomably huge family tree, or more like five thousand of them linked together.

Since we know the identity of three of the slain draykoni, it might be useful to research their family trees. Particularly since the pattern emerging seems to be in favour of ancients, and even Elders, being targeted the most. I would be intrigued to know whether the three we know of are contemporaries of one another, and which era they hail from.

I came to wondering whether Eva has retained any contacts among those Libraries.

I shared these thoughts with Pense, Ori and Avane, and we were soon agreed that a visit to Eva might prove fruitful.

'I wonder if there are more,' Avane mused when I had done.

'More what?' My mind was focused on Eva and Lokants. 'More Libraries?'

Avane blinked at me. 'More... victims.'

Oh. More *corpses*. Of course.

The thought sickened me. Thirteen was terrible enough, but she was right. There could be many more.

'There will have to be a search,' I said. 'After we get back from Glour.'

But Pense shook his head. 'It had better be done soon. Go with Ori into Glour. I will return to Nuwelin and organise a search.'

He looked at Avane, who nodded her agreement. 'My people are few, but we will do what we can here, too.'

I did not love the idea of Pense making his way back to Nuwelin alone, under the circumstances. Nor did I love the idea of being separated from him, even if I would have Ori with me. I wanted to shriek *don't leave me,* but I swallowed the impulse. The fact that I felt it at all tells me that I have been growing dependent upon him to prop me up, and that is unacceptable.

And he was right, too. 'Very well. Ori with me!'

Ori, of course, had no objection to make. He was peppily enthusiastic at the prospect of seeing Eva and Tren again, and full of an inexhaustible energy which would make nothing of the journey. I love Ori and his cheerful nature so much. He is a delight.

I remembered something else, too, that I could get done while I was in Glour. Ivi approached me recently with a request which, at the time, I did not know how to comply with. 'Llandry, I need to talk to you. We are run through our stock of larras-grass seed, if you can contrive to get us some more. And I want to arrange to start trading litorns. They've taken well in the north-west glades and we'll have enough to begin selling or bartering within, I should think, two or three moons.'

This last was good news, since the litorn mushrooms are always in demand in the Seven. They have useful pain-killing properties, but they have always been difficult to grow down there, even in the sunlit Daylander realms. We should be able to get something useful back for those. I didn't really want to think about it just then, not with my mind full of a bigger, more dramatic problem. But Ivi was right to raise the topic. The more ordinary requirements of our daily life in Iskyr would not obligingly disappear just because we had other things to deal with.

I took out the notebook I always carry about with me these days, and wrote the two requests down. I cannot manage without that book anymore. I would forget everything.

I can probably get larras-seed at the Glour market, which ought to be running soon. You can buy practically anything there. And Lady Glostrum has links with the government in Glour. As a Darklander realm, it is completely incapable of growing litorns at all. They quickly wither and die without full, strong sunlight around the clock. As such, they may well be interested in our fledgling supply.

Ori was itching to go, and we had no time to waste. I had time only to bestow a quick, albeit fervent, embrace upon Pense by way of farewell, and to bestow Sigwide upon him for conveyance to Larion. I felt guilty as I did so. Siggy grows unhappy if he is separated from me for too long, and to be truthful, the same is true in reverse. He has been my loyal companion since I was a child, and as such, he is a vital part of my life. But I have come to a sad realisation recently.

Siggy is finally beginning to grow old.

I don't see why that should surprise me. I found him as a baby when I was but nine, so he is nearly twelve years old. His age is not yet so advanced as to cause him much inconvenience, and he can be lively enough. But he tires more easily than he used to, and I am beginning to worry about him.

Hence, if I expect to be absent from home for days at a time and I am unsure if I can care for him properly, I will leave him in Nuwelin.

Ori watched me undertake the bestowal of Sigwide with an amused smile, in response to which I could only stick out my tongue. He likes to tease me about my devotion to Siggy, but he can be just as bad, and we both know it. He has an orboe friend called Graaf. If you have never seen an orboe, let me tell you: they are nothing like Siggy. They are fast, vicious, and not usually friendly.

None of this matters to Ori. He treats Graaf like an oversized orting, and to be fair, Graaf tends to behave like one when Ori is around. They are not inseparable. I have seen nothing of the orboe since Ori returned, so I presume he is off on one of his hunting-and-marauding adventures. But he always comes back, and Ori is always delighted to see him when he does.

Anyway, the bestowal of Sigwide and other necessities being complete, Ori and I shifted draykon and set off. I could not help but focus on the receding sense of Pensould as we left, and had to swallow my dismay. I tell myself that it is not wholly about dependency, which may sound like an excuse but it is perfectly true. I love Pense. He is my other half, and I hate being separated from him.

Ori gave me a mental hug and did a spiralling tumble in the air for my amusement. I recognised it as a challenge, one which I took great delight in accepting, until it occurred to me how childish we were being.

We have work to do! I reminded him severely.

Ori waggled his wings at me with cheeky insouciance and soared ahead. In an instant he had flashed through the veil into the Seven, and I followed.

I did not relish the prospect of extending my sojourn in the eternal darks, but that could not be helped. I am a little bit proud of myself for having coped with it so competently through our visit to Avane, in spite of the horrors we found in Ayrien. If I could do that, I knew I could survive another day or two in Glour. And the moon is approaching full, which means two things: firstly that the light is growing stronger, so the darkness is not so all-encompassing. Secondly, the Glour market runs every full moon, and that should be in about three days' time.

26 VII
Old Friends, New… Stalkers?

I am becoming a big supporter of killing multiple birds with one stone, or in less gruesome terms, efficiency. My mother has been a member of Glinnery's ruling council for some years, and at last I am gaining some insight into what kind of a life it must have been for her. Hassle! Stress! Trying to do eighteen things at once! I can only add… *how does she cope?* And Lady Glostrum! Even worse, for she is an aristocrat and a social leader, the kind whose every move is followed by reporters eager to plaster her picture all over the bulletin boards. She was also the High Summoner for a long time, which must be a hectic job, and these days she has taken a leading role in establishing a training system for the partial Lokants of the Seven. She manages it all with a kind of easy serenity which I find enviable, and I can only hope I will be capable of the same in time.

Ori and I travelled to the outskirts of Glour City on the wing and then Changed human for the journey into the centre, preferring not to alarm the good citizens of Glour by flying over their heads. Happily for us, they have invested much more heavily in transport than we have in Glinnery, probably because they lack wings. We were able to hire a smart cabriolet to take us to Lady Glostrum's handsome townhouse. We regretted this when we discovered how difficult it is to *fit* our wings into a smart cabriolet. They are really not designed for it.

I have been to Lady Glostrum's mansion but once before, and have yet to grow accustomed to its size and grandeur. Ori and I stood for a moment on the doorstep, staring up at the building in awe. Its multiple storeys disappeared into the darkness some way above our heads, so I could not even tell how many there were.

'Huh,' I said, intelligently.

Ori nodded. 'What can a single person want with all of this?'

I could only shrug. These grand stone buildings are so different from the glissenwol-tree dwellings I am used to. I cannot begin to imagine what Eva does with all these rooms.

Ori rapped upon the door. Nothing happened, so he repeated the gesture with more force. I winced as three deep, tearing *booms* split the night, fearing that the stout door might buckle beneath his enthusiasm.

'Easy,' I murmured, as he drew back his fist to strike again.

He stopped at my words, which was fortunate because at that moment the door opened and a gentleman in a dark suit appeared.

'Hello,' said Ori brightly. 'We're here to see her ladyship.'

The man stared at us with palpable disapproval. 'You will find the doorbell more than sufficient for your needs,' he informed us.

Ori and I exchanged a mystified look.

'Doorbell?' I repeated.

The man extended one long finger to point at a button set into the wall beside the door. Ori, of course, could not resist pressing it immediately, his face brightening with delight as a melodic chime promptly echoed from within the house.

'Marvellous contraption!' he enthused.

He received in response a stiff bow. I began to dislike the supercilious fellow, until I noticed the faintest hint of an amused smile hovering about his mouth.

'Her ladyship is not at home to callers at this hour,' he informed us.

I interpreted that to mean that Eva was busy, and disinclined to grant admittance to all and sundry who might chance to show up at her door, many of whom would be reporters hoping for a snippet of news. I also gathered that this servant of hers was unaware of our identities. Apparently, getting past *him* was going to be our first hurdle.

Heaving an inward sigh, I steeled myself and stood a little taller. 'Please inform her ladyship that the Lord and Lady Draykon of Glinnery are here upon urgent business,' I said, trying to sound authoritative and *not* as though I felt like a child playing dress-up in someone else's clothes. Which I did. I mean... *goodness,* what a silly and overblown title!

But I had judged my strategy correctly, for the names impressed the keeper of Eva's door. He bowed to us lower than he had before and stepped back, inviting us inside. 'If your lord and ladyship would be pleased to wait in the first parlour?' he inquired. 'I will see if her ladyship is available.'

We followed the old gentleman into a sumptuously decorated sitting room, and were promptly left there as he withdrew, hopefully to summon Eva. Helpfully, he lit a light-globe before he departed, and the soft, dimly shining orb followed us around as we wandered through the room.

'The first parlour?' Ori said, looking around in amazement. 'How many more do you suppose there are?'

'Oh, doubtless dozens and dozens,' I said. 'But only think! The honour of being brought to the *first* parlour in rank, instead of something so ignoble as the eighteenth! We are very important people, you know.'

Ori grinned and dropped into the plush embrace of a handsome chaise longue. He lay there whistling something jaunty, annoyingly at his ease. I, meanwhile, stood awkwardly near the door. For all my joking words I felt badly out of place, and half expected to be tossed out again at any moment. The luxuries of Eva's lifestyle can be awfully intimidating.

When the door opened, however, it was not Eva who appeared, or even the imposing answerer of the front door. Tren came in, or Mr. Pitren Warvel, to use his full name — supposing he would allow it. He gave us such a delighted smile of welcome that I immediately felt more at ease, and he came to greet us in the friendliest fashion. I received a swift hug, and Ori a very cordial handshake.

'What a wonderful surprise!' he said. 'We had no thoughts of seeing you for some time. I hope you aren't too tired from the journey? Did Hayes offer you refreshments?'

Tren is Eva's betrothed, and one of my favourite people. He has the ability to make anybody feel at ease with only a smile and a few words. He is about five or six years older than me, though he acts with a degree of easy self-assurance it will take me another couple of decades to develop. He disappeared for a moment, but swiftly returned with the news that luncheon had been ordered. 'Eva's on her way,' he promised. 'She's got the co-ordinator with her. Goodness only knows what they've been talking about all this time. It's been three hours.' He flashed his mischievous grin.

'Co-ordinator?' I echoed. 'Of what?'

'Oh! Sorry, I forget. It's about the wedding.' His smile turned sheepish. 'It's to be a grand affair, of course. So much so that Eva needs an entire separate person just to manage the planning.'

The lady herself arrived just as he said this, and responded by sticking her tongue out at him. Her ladyship, Evastany Glostrum, is as stately and imposing as her house when she wants to be, and I have never before seen her behave with such joyous childishness. It must be Tren's influence. I think she and Tren are a perfect couple.

'You would not wish for me to deal with it,' she informed him. 'You wouldn't see me for weeks.'

Tren could only nod with rueful agreement as Eva turned to us, and engulfed me in a scented embrace. Today she was wearing a heavy emerald velvet gown with jewelled trim, her white hair swept up in combs. She looked like a queen.

I seem to have been hugged a lot lately. I do not mind, though it is not my usual habit to be so physically affectionate. In Eva's case I particularly appreciated it, for it swept away in one instant all the awkwardness inspired by the extreme luxury of her lifestyle, and all the reminders it brought of her impossibly high status. I felt that we were friends and allies again, as we had been before.

She bestowed the same salutation upon Ori, then swept the lot of us away to the dining room. Her cook had worked with remarkable speed to produce a luncheon for four... hundred, I suppose? The huge table was groaning with dishes, a situation Eva waved away with a laugh.

'I said we had hungry people to feed,' Tren said, eyeing the feast dubiously. 'I did not mean to imply that we had an army in here.'

We ate, and we talked. It was a shame to ruin the buoyant mood with the kind of news we had to impart, but it was necessary to do so without much delay. I could see that Eva was allotting as much time to us as she could, but her life would soon carry her away once more.

'I have never heard of such a thing before,' Eva confirmed once Ori and I had finished our tale. It was only what I had expected her to say, but still, I was disappointed. I suppose I had secretly hoped I had been wrong about the likelihood of her knowing something about it.

'I never heard it mentioned at the Libraries,' she continued, her meal forgotten as she bent her intellectual powers to the problem. 'Which is not to say that they don't know anything about it. Hmm.'

'I was wondering if there is a way back to Limbane's Library,' I ventured. 'If we could consult the draykon bloodlines he has there, it could be of use to us. I would like to find out if there is any obvious link between the three victims we have identified.'

'He might have books, too,' Ori put in.

'A sound idea, but not one I can assist you with at present,' Eva said, to my disappointment. 'I have no way to return to that Library, nor any way to contact Limbane or Andraly.' She sighed, looking chagrined. 'Perhaps I should not have broken off all contact the way I did. I fear I may have lost my temper a little.'

'Of course, there is the Secret Library.' Tren said this almost absently, his attention fixed upon his food. I got the impression that he was carefully refraining from looking at Eva.

Eva's chagrin grew, and she cast a swift look of censure at Tren, who serenely ignored it.

'Dare I ask?' I said.

Eva's eyes narrowed, and for a moment I thought she would refuse to respond. But at last she shrugged and said, 'Oh, very well. The Secret Library, as Tren likes to call it, is my... stash.'

'Of books,' elaborated Tren. '*Thieved* books.' He said this with an impish smile at his betrothed.

Eva drew herself up. 'They are not stolen,' she said loftily. 'They belong to me.'

'Which books?' said Ori, pushing away his plate. He had eaten enough food for about five men and looked beamingly replete. 'Tell us, tell us.'

Tren directed his most charming smile at Eva, who withstood it for all of two seconds before she visibly gave up.

'There was a time when I had unlimited access to Limbane's Library, and a fair amount of freedom to wander it at will. And to come and go, which proved a useful combination. I... may have had a few titles copied.'

'A few,' agreed Tren, nodding wisely. 'One or two. A scant handful. Nothing much to signify.'

'Thirty-seven,' said Eva.

This was more promising! 'On which topics?' I said quickly.

'Draykon and Lokant history. The Library of Orlind, with some original accounts. A couple of theoretical texts on the nature and workings of the Libraries. One or two language primers and dictionaries.' She smiled at me, and before I could speak she said: 'Yes, you may certainly borrow any that might prove relevant.'

It's hard not to love Eva.

She was lost in thought for some time after that, a process I was careful not to disturb, for perhaps she was thinking over the problem I had set before her and might yet come up with something useful. I chatted with Tren and Ori — or to be fair I listened while they chatted. Which they did, at some length, mostly about the differences and similarities between Sorcerer and Summoner training and how the two programmes might be combined. It was interesting enough, but I suppose I was only half listening.

'Llan,' said Eva suddenly, about quarter of an hour later. 'Do you remember when we were at Limbane's Library, and he was telling us about the history of the draykoni?'

I did, of course. We learned a great deal that day. But I did not remember in all that much detail, for I have never had that kind of absorbent memory. So I nodded cautiously, and awaited elucidation.

'Do you remember what Limbane said, when he talked of how they die, and can be revived?'

'Specifically?' I said. 'No.'

Eva pondered. 'I may be wrong, but I believe he said it is *almost* impossible to kill a draykon.'

'He said: Their consciousness is almost impossible to entirely extinguish,' supplied Tren, who apparently does have that enviable memory which retains things once heard, and regurgitates them at need.

'Thank you, darling,' said Eva. 'Exactly. Do you not think

that *almost* might be a little bit significant?'

Of course I did! Almost? That detail had not been relevant at the time, or perhaps I might have recalled it myself. 'Do you think he knew of a way?'

Eva pursed her lips. 'It is hard to be sure, but why else would he say such a thing?'

'I need to talk to him,' I said at once.

But Eva shook her head. 'I wish I could help you there, but who knows where he is now? I have no way to contact him, anymore.'

Curses to that. Limbane is no doubt far Off-World and beyond our reach.

Unless, of course, he has been *here*, killing off draykoni. The idea seems ludicrously far-fetched. He, or his colleagues, created my people in the first place. Why would he now be running about killing them off? Why would any Lokant? And how much reliance could we place on that *almost*, anyway? Perhaps it was just a figure of speech, a scholar's unwillingness to declare anything altogether impossible.

But it was a hint, and a thought, and that was more than we'd had before.

We were given rooms at Eva's house for as long as we could require them, but as predicted we did not see a great deal more of Eva herself. It wasn't just wedding business that kept her occupied. As near as I could tell, she seemed to be in the middle of half a dozen projects, both personal and professional, and there were several other claims upon her time. I wanted to hear more about the new Lokant heritage training programme she was setting up with Tren, but there was little time to discuss it, and our own business naturally had to take precedence. Perhaps next time.

Anyway, Ori and I contrived to pin her down about the prospect of a trade deal for our litorn mushrooms, and she promised to look into it. Then the Darklands Market rolled over Glour City, and we were free to explore it at our leisure.

I did so with mixed feelings. Oh, the market is undeniably marvellous, no doubt about that. Its name derives from the fact that it is the biggest of its kind in the three Darklands realms, and possibly in the whole of the Seven. Daylanders regularly cross the borders to browse its wares, undeterred by the darkness and the bustle. Ma and I used to visit almost every moon when I was a child, and as such it is a source of nostalgia for me. You can buy practically anything there, if you can bear the tumultuous crowds for long enough to visit all of the stalls. Which I, usually, cannot.

That is one of its drawbacks. In the past year, it has also become the site of some uncomfortable remembrances. I held my first stall here a few moons ago, selling the jewellery that used to be my trade before my life was turned upside down. Those jewels and the stones I was using at the time… well, they were the source of all the trouble since. You could say the Darklands Market is where it all started. And since a number of my customers from that fateful day ended up dead because they bought my jewellery, I cannot help feeling more than a little… guilty.

I therefore roamed the market with some feelings of distress, at least at first. But it is difficult to feel negative about anything for long when you have Ori by your side. Bright, cheerful and mindful of my state of mind without being obvious about it, he soon buoyed my flagging spirits, and we began to enjoy ourselves. The market's a beautiful site, irrespective of its wares. They set the softest, most dulcet light-globes floating over the stalls, and they look like stars brought almost close enough to touch. Everywhere is colour and vibrancy, and there is an atmosphere of merriment and excitement which cannot help but lift the spirits.

Ori and I devoted ourselves to finding the seed stock for Ivi, which took us over an hour to accomplish. That done, we roamed at will, and contrived to find gifts for our friends. I bought new, sturdy gloves for Ivi; a bag full of colourful fabric scraps for Loret and Damosel; a notebook for Larion; and for Meriall I found a tiny brooch in the shape of a winged irilapter, its colours marked out in bright enamels.

Ori rounded out our purchases with pots of spices for Liat, a soft velvet hat for Sophronia, and a box of sweets for Nyden. We were probably more delighted with our purchases than their recipients would be. Shopping for others is so much more delicious than shopping for oneself, after all. I remember that evening with fondness, for all that it was but two days ago. Looking back on it now, it feels like a last interlude of cheery normality, soon to be swept away by chaos.

And swiftly it began. We were packing Nyden's sweets into Ori's backpack when my draykon senses prickled. I had been ignoring them all evening, for if I had paid them much attention, I would soon have been swamped by a relentless onslaught of information. There were simply far too many people around for them to be useful. Indeed, those crowds could still rattle me more than I like to admit, with or without my extra insights, and the only way I could enjoy myself under those conditions was to block out everything that was not directly relevant.

As such, being so abruptly recalled to an awareness of my surroundings was jarring. Suddenly conscious of every one of the masses of strangers crowding around me, I succumbed for a moment to heart-pounding panic. It took me a few moments and several deep breaths to smother the feeling, and focus. What had distracted me?

I searched the people around us, and saw nothing out of the ordinary. Shoppers and browsers, all ordinary folk, and nobody seemed to be paying the slightest attention to Ori or me.

But I felt something amiss. There: behind me. A whisper of something… not human.

I whirled, my eyes straining to see far enough into the darkness.

Somebody was just turning away, on the verge of disappearing into the crowds, but I got the distinct impression that this person had been staring directly at me only moments before. I could tell little about the figure, not even its gender, for the person wore a cloak which concealed every defining feature beneath the folds of its heavy fabric. All I could tell was the colour of the cloak, for it shone briefly red in the soft glow of a light-globe as its owner walked away.

I tried to follow, but the press of people around me was too intense and I soon lost sight of the cloaked figure. So I stopped, closed my eyes, and attempted to follow the person with my other senses instead.

'Llan?' said Ori. I realised he had been trying to get my attention for a little while, and I had not heard him.

'Shh,' I said quickly. 'Just a moment.' Ori fell silent, and I focused.

Not human. Definitely not that. And not draykoni, either. I experienced the departing figure like a tiny mote of light in the midst of an ocean of similar motes, although it is not really light at all. That is the best way I can find to describe it. The vast majority of the lights were human: earthy or shadowy in hue and atmosphere, shot through with vivid colour and radiating warmth. The figure I followed was paler, cooler and… older. And I will say one other thing. I cannot be certain, for my eyes often betray me in the low light of the Darklands and it is easy to become confused. But I saw a wisp of hair from beneath the drawn-up scarlet hood, and I could swear that it was pure white.

A Lokant?

I stopped still, puzzled, disoriented and uneasy, for I have experienced a similar scene before. At that time I was in Nimdre with Devary, browsing a market not wholly unlike this one, when I ran into a white-haired partial Lokant who took a worrying degree of interest in the necklace I was wearing at the time. It did not end especially well. And now again: a market, and a Lokant with too much interest in me.

'We were being watched, I think,' I said to Ori. 'By a Lokant, who departed as soon as I turned around.'

Ori frowned, and said nothing. I knew he would be sweeping his own senses through the crowds, searching for the person I described. 'Are you sure?'

'No,' I admitted. 'Not entirely. But I felt that we were being observed, and I saw somebody with a Lokant aura leave the moment I turned.'

'Full or partial?' he said quickly.

'It's not always easy to tell.' And that is the truth, for a strong partial Lokant like Eva can feel very much like a full-blood, as far as my perceptions are concerned. 'But I would say full-blood, with some confidence.'

Ori nodded, his frown deepening. Partial Lokants are uncommon in the Seven, but full Lokants are virtually unheard of. I do not think any actually live in our world, nor have they for ages past. They live way Off-World, in their own Libraries. If they visit, it is always for a purpose.

'Perhaps Eva is working with someone,' I said, doubtfully. I think she would probably have mentioned that, especially if whoever she was working or training with was likely to take an interest in us. And why would they, at that? We are involved in nothing that can have any bearing on Lokant interests.

Ori considered me. 'I hate to say it, but… do you think you're maybe being a little paranoid?'

'Oh, no,' I groaned. 'Do you think I could be?' It certainly isn't impossible. My life has been a bit of a mess this past year, to say the least, and I have been followed, tracked, sought out and outright hunted by all manner of people in that time. And for all manner of reasons, many of them unpleasant or even dangerous. Was my reason beginning to slip?

'Could be,' said Ori cheerfully. 'Small wonder if you are, Llan, and don't feel bad about it.'

'It could have been a strong partial Lokant,' I conceded.

'Could have been. And it could be a total coincidence that this person was turning away at that moment. It might have had nothing to do with us.'

'True.' But if that was the case, what had made my senses prickle in the first place?

Ah… maybe nothing. After all, I was in the middle of the Darklands Market with about ten million other people around me. Small wonder if my perceptions were misleading me under those conditions.

But I made up my mind to ask Eva about it anyway, just in case.

27 VII

I Lose Ori to a Pile of Books. Again.

'Are you sure you aren't wearing Lokant-attractant perfume?' So said Tren, who naturally couldn't resist teasing me about it.

I carried a curl of my black hair to my nose and inhaled. "Hm. It's hard to tell. What do Lokants find attractive?'

We both looked at Eva, who blinked at us as though we were both mad. 'Secrets,' she said. 'And lies.'

She *really* hasn't forgiven Limbane.

'I know of one or two partial Lokants hereabouts,' she continued. 'Though I know of no reason why they should be taking an interest in you.'

'So you think it's nothing?'

Eva shrugged. 'I cannot say, just at present. But if you see anything more of this mystery white-hair, send word to me and I will investigate further.'

With that, I must be content. They are right, of course. With so little upon which to base my alarms, it is impossible to argue that there is a clear threat, or to come up with a sensible course of action. And even I think I am being irrational. Just because I've been covertly tailed by Lokants before, it doesn't mean there is anything untoward going on now.

Our business completed, we took our leave soon afterwards. I did not want to go. I like Eva and Tren, for one thing, and I rarely get to see them anymore. And for another… I admit, I am feeling increasingly out of my depth. I need to be older, wiser, calmer, more efficient, more sensible, more sociable, more… *everything,* to handle all of this. In other words, much more like Lady Evastany Glostrum. If I could contrive to spirit her away with me, I would.

Since I cannot, I will just have to work on making myself as much like her as I can. Starting with hauling myself back up to Nuwelin to address the problems I now have solutions for.

We flew home, Ori carting a packful of seed stock and me bearing a hastily-outlined trade proposal which Eva had acquired for me. I hoped they would satisfy Ivi for the time being, and leave me free to focus on the other issues.

I was a bit surprised to be greeted with real enthusiasm by Damosel. Not just Ori, who tends to elicit that response wherever he goes, but me as well. As we landed and Changed human, she came running up to us and ushered us straight into her house. There she plied us with Liat's latest cake fresh from baking and gave us a whole pot of tea between the two of us. My favourite kind, too, which proves she has been paying attention.

'How goes the search?' I enquired as we devoured our cake. I was pleased to sit down as I did so, for we had done a great deal of flying over a couple of days, and some of my muscles were aching powerfully.

Damosel felt the same, judging from the way she winced as she stretched out upon the low, padded bench she had painstakingly built for herself. 'Nothing to report,' she said, much to my relief. 'No new finds, nothing out of the ordinary. Some of the boys are still out, including Pense.'

I knew that, of course. The first thing I had done when we flew in was look for Pense, and I had been disappointed to find no trace of him. But it would be unprofessional to let that show, so I merely nodded and went on to tell Damosel all of our news.

Except for the bit about the Lokant at the market, for I was feeling a little foolish about it and really, there was nothing to tell. Ori cast me a sideways glance when I reached the end of my account without mentioning that part, but he didn't say anything.

I felt brightened by the news that there was no more news, because that meant nothing else bad had happened while we were gone. After that, we lost no time in distributing our purchases, which made everybody happy for a little while. And so I learned: never underestimate the efficacy of a well-timed gift. Ivi, thankfully, was content with our offerings and went away to study the proposed trade agreement with Glour.

It began to rain soon after that, driving us back into our shelters.

'It's time,' whispered Ori to me as we ran for my house. He had taken over one of my few small rooms, having, as yet, no abode of his own. We were working on it.

'For what?'

'The books!' Ori made let's-go motions with his hands. I could well understand his urgency, for it had taken Eva almost until our departure to find the books we wanted and hand them over to us. We hadn't yet had chance to look at them.

But my mind was whirling too much for that. I can't focus on reading with my brain buzzing like a jar full of flies. So I gave the stack of books to Ori. There are four, which doesn't sound like much but they are enormously thick tomes. They are enough to strike trepidation into my heart, but Ori just grinned and accepted them with alacrity. Well, he is a star scholar after all, whereas my schooling was more basic.

So I said to myself, in an attempt to feel better.

'You aren't staying?' he said as I turned to go.

I shook my head and tapped my forehead. 'Thoughts aswirl. I need to fix that, or I will just stare vacantly at the pages and absorb nothing.'

Ori just nodded and wandered off with his books. I tried not to feel hurt as I left him to it.

I wanted to find myself a quiet nook somewhere and do nothing for the rest of the day, but I could not justify that to myself. I had been absent for days already, and though my mission had been a productive one, I had not been pulling my weight with the more mundane activities required of our life up here. There was no reason, though, why the two needs couldn't coincide.

I found Larion at work in the kitchens, and retrieved Sigwide from him. I was instantly enfolded in orting-love, which is not a complex emotion, but there is a simplicity and depth to Siggy's affection which I always find touching.

Missed you, said Siggy as I gently scooped him up out of Larion's lap. He said it with a wave of forlorn neediness which roused every guilty feeling I had in me, and I sighed.

Sorry. I am here now.

Don't go away again.

I couldn't promise, so I didn't try. I merely pacified him with the dried berries I'd brought for the purpose, gave Larion a distracted smile, and turned to leave.

'I've never come across any creature with such a deep affection for anybody not of their own species,' said Larion.

I turned back. 'Oh?'

He smiled at me, and I realised he was trying to be reassuring. Had I come across as defensive? Probably. I tend to do that by habit, with anybody I don't know all that well. I tried to relax, and smiled back. 'I think that Siggy sees me as another orting,' I said. 'Just a bigger one. He can never understand what I have done with my tail.'

Larion nodded. He said nothing else. He's almost as quiet as I am, so for him to volunteer such a long sentence unprompted was unusual anyway.

'Thank you for taking care of him,' I said, feeling awkward again.

'He's no trouble.' Larion returned his attention to his work. He was splitting pods of some kind, and extracting the contents. I muttered a farewell and left him to it.

Never put two shy, unchatty people in a room together for more than thirty seconds. Honestly, it's just painful.

The books Eva gave us are as follows. The thickest one is also the oldest, according to what she told us. It is entitled "The Draykoni: Myth and Reality," with no credited author. The second is called simply "Orlind", which is vague but promising. There is a relatively slim one called "An Account of the 19th Cluster Construct Wars: 12th Age." That's the one Ori is reading. According to Eva, 19th Cluster means *our* worlds — the Seven, the Uppers and the Lowers. That is what the Lokants call it.

Then there is "Arts Draykus," which is an intriguingly mysterious title. It proves to be about some of the draykoni's known powers from the Lokant perspective, which is of more than passing interest to me as you may imagine.

After dinner, I went back to my house to find Ori still engrossed by these delights. I'd taken a tray of Liat's roasted vegetables in for him, since I knew full well he wouldn't stir all night, or even all week. Not until he had read all four of the books.

I found him sprawled in the middle of my ground-floor living chamber in a pile of blankets and pillows — everything that used to be on my bed, in fact. He had one of the tomes open before him, and he lay on his stomach with his nose over it, absolutely intent. I went in and said hello, and Ori went on reading as if I wasn't there at all. I had to sit down beside him and put the tray virtually under his nose before he noticed I was there, and finally he looked up and blinked at me.

'Llan! Is it dinner time? Thank you.' He ate, and went on reading.

I waited, but nothing else was forthcoming. 'Have you found anything interesting?' I tried.

Ori nodded enthusiastically, his gaze still glued to the page. 'Tons!'

I waited again, with the same result. 'Want to tell me some of it?' I prompted.

'Oh!' Ori looked up, blinking. 'Right.' He groped around for one of the books and hauled it open, leafing rapidly through it. 'This book. Draykoni, myth and reality. It's interesting because it's a Lokant-authored book of legends, accompanied by discussions of the truths behind the stories. And the stories are crazy. Their society *really* reveres the draykoni. They're seen as the pinnacle of Lokant achievement, bar nothing, and practically every conceivable power has been attributed to them at one time or another. The book calmly debunks most of it, while still emphasising how truly remarkable an achievement they were. And, check this, Galy's name is all over it.' Ori found the page he was looking for and indicated three different places upon it, proving his point. 'I don't think I am getting the full impact on this, Eva's translations are a little shaky in places. But it's compelling. Don't you think that's interesting?'

'Galywis is well known?' I said. We have met Galywis once before, in the Library of Orlind — or what is left of it. He is nice, but completely mad.

'*Famous,*' Ori replied, with emphasis. 'Very famous.'

'We knew that, didn't we? After all, he was the Master Lokantor for who-knows-how-long.'

Ori nodded enthusiastically. 'Yes, but that isn't what he is famous for. These books mention his status in passing, like it's one of the less interesting things about him. The focus is all on his accomplishments, particularly the draykoni. I think that is why they made him the Master in the first place, and how he kept the post for so long.'

That *was* interesting. Galy was a legend among his people? It was hard to picture him thus, considering I had only ever known him as aged, broken and insane. What a sad ruin to such a life.

Ori had stopped talking and looked absorbed in the pages once more. 'Anything else?' I prompted.

'Hm? Oh! Nothing significant, yet. I'll let you know.'

28 VII

Er. Where Are We...?

I lay awake for some time last night, worrying about Pense. Most of the searchers have been and gone and come back again over the past several days, but Pense's group has yet to return at all.

I should not be concerned, for he still has Nyden and Meriall with him. They have just wandered far in search of trouble, and it is taking them some time to make their way back. Or so I tell myself.

I hope they haven't found any.

I hoped that Pense's return would be the next event of note that I would record here. In fact, it is nothing so straightforward.

Today was spent in unbroken study. Ori remained inflexibly absorbed, and I was helping him, but I cannot focus on reading for so many hours together without needing a break. Everyone else was busily employed and Pense still hadn't returned, so I went out for a walk by myself. I could have flown, but my arms and back still ached from our journey into Glour and I wanted to stretch my legs instead. I stuck my journal in my bag, hoping to find a quiet nook somewhere to settle and write a bit.

I appreciated the silence as I walked. It was a balmy evening. The rain had cleared off an hour or two earlier, leaving the grasses around our valley sparkling with droplets. I wandered beyond those into a copse of frilly little trees which had appeared overnight. It can be disconcerting, the way the landscape reinvents itself. I may have been living up here for a few moons now, but I was born and brought up in Glinnery, where the countryside behaves with much more consistency and circumspection. If it was glissenwol trees yesterday, it will be glissenwol trees tomorrow. Perhaps that's dull, or perhaps it's comfortingly familiar.

I am slowly getting used to the Changes, but it takes time.

I wandered through the trees for a while, and amused myself with coaxing a few starry-shaped flowers out of the earth. I was getting a little carried away with this, covering the ground in more and more of them and adding rainbow colours, when I realised that we were no longer alone.

My senses prickled in a familiar way, and I was immediately alert. The woodland had seemed friendly and tranquil moments before, but now it began to appear dark and enclosed and bristling with threat. I stood still, sweating with sudden fear as I cast every sense I possessed around me, searching for the source of the sensation of being *watched*.

And I found the presence, perhaps thirty-five feet away. I could not see the person, for too many trees and bushes stood between the two of us. But I could feel him. That chill, pale aura reached me much more strongly than it had at the Darklands Market, either because he was closer, or because there were only the two of us present.

It occurred to me, too late, that if I had been more self-possessed I could have feigned enough nonchalance to wander back the way I had come, thereby putting some distance between me and the hidden Lokant. But I had been standing stock-still and obviously wary for a couple of minutes. If he was watching me, he now knew that I'd spotted him. If I wanted to flee, I would have to run. Or fly, which my back muscles were very much against my doing.

I didn't want to fly. Nor did I want to run, entirely. I was afraid, my heart pounding madly as I stood there. But I was also curious, or… something like it. I wanted to know who this person was, and why he was lurking around me. And I am not the person I was last year. I am not helpless.

I was not fool enough to simply walk up to him and ask him his business, however. I steeled myself and took to the air, ignoring the way my muscles protested. I flew until I was directly over the thicket in which he had hidden himself, and hovered there, looking down.

'I see you,' I called. Siggy, jolted from his sleep by my movement and receptive to my alarm, stirred in his pack and looked down, too.

Nothing happened for a moment. Then the leaves rustled and a tall, white-haired figure in a dark red cloak stepped out and stood staring up at me.

I was making a bit of a gamble with this. I've run into full Lokants before, and some of them have terrifying abilities — like, for example, the power to bend other people's minds to their will, and make you see things that are not there, or do things you do not want to do. Even Eva can do it quite well, though she is only a part-blood. I do not precisely understand how it works, but I know what it feels like, because it has been done to me before. A compulsion settles upon you all the way down to the bones, and you suddenly *need* to do whatever it is they have asked. It is extremely hard to resist. If they make you see things, that is even scarier, for you do not notice it happening. Draykoni are less susceptible to it than humans, but it can still work on us. I know, because it has worked on me before.

If this Lokant proved to be strong in that particular art, and chose to turn it against me, I was in trouble. But he had lingered around me more than once, and on this occasion, he could have overpowered my reason before I even knew he was there. He hadn't, and that led me to think that he wasn't interested in doing so.

Now I would find out whether I had been shrewd, or stupid.

We stared at each other in silence for several agonising moments, and I began to worry that I had badly misjudged him. What could he be doing save gathering himself for some kind of assault on my will?

But none came. 'If you would come down?' he called.

'Would you, if you were me?'

I thought he smiled, though I was far enough above him that it was difficult to tell. Come to think of it, was I even sure it was a he? Something about the height, and the breadth of the shoulders beneath the cloak, suggested so.

'I imagine not,' he said, and held up his hands to show how empty they were.

'You are unarmed! Excellent. Of course, one with your

abilities need not carry sharp sticks in order to be dangerous.'

'I promise, I have come with no intention of harming you.'

I was getting tired, hanging up there. Hovering isn't an easy thing to do, even when I am not already weary. But I didn't want to let that show. 'What is your business?' I demanded. 'Seeing as you have trailed me all the way from Glour City, I assume it must be something important.'

My muscles really are in poor shape. They complained, loudly. In the process, I lost control of my flight a little, and sank a few feet.

'A bit more, and we can have a proper conversation.' The Lokant reached up to me encouragingly, as though I might drop into his grasp.

What *nonsense*.

I did the only reasonable thing, under the circumstances. I kicked the living daylights out of his hands, and landed as far away from him as I could.

'Well, I deserved that,' said the Lokant, hiding his hands in his pockets.

'Emphatically.' I clutched Siggy and glared at the intruder, feeling more than a little cross. What did he mean by following me around?

To my relief, he did not try to approach me. He stood several feet away and looked me over, with an air of curiosity.

It was a scrutiny I returned, though I quickly began to wish that I had not. Most of the full Lokants I have met before have been elderly, or even ancient, but this one was different. He was tall and broad-shouldered, as I had discerned before. I now saw that his skin was slightly tanned in that golden way; his hair, just long enough to brush his shoulders, was glossy and the pure white of new snow; his eyes were very dark indeed, which was a startling effect against the white hair; and his face had the kind of perfect symmetry of feature rarely seen outside of a painting.

He smiled at me, and my heart sank about five miles down.

And I felt a surge of irritation. It is one thing to be followed about by an enigmatic Lokant who *might* have the power to crush me if he so chose. It is going *altogether too far* to give him a perfect face as well. There is no better combination for making me feel utterly, infuriatingly inadequate.

So I stood there, even more tongue-tied than usual and quietly fuming. When he made no effort to explain his purpose,

I walked past him and away.

'Wait!' he shouted, and ran after me. 'I realise this is all a bit strange, but I really do need to talk to you.'

'It's more than a *bit strange*,' I retorted, anger beginning to get the better of my reticence. 'Following me almost to my front door goes far past strange! It goes a long way past *creepy*, too, and ends up somewhere around *incredibly scary*.' If Eva was right and Limbane's lot knew of some way to permanently kill a draykon, how could I welcome the fact that a hitherto unknown one was now wandering around in Iskyr, and specifically following *me*?

'I know,' he said, and I had to admit that he had a beautiful voice on top of all his other gifts, which only irritated me more. 'I am sorry. But I realise you have had some difficult experiences with my kind before, and… I did not know how to approach you.'

That stopped me. I stared at him and then wished I hadn't, for I received another dose of his aggravatingly extreme beauty and felt very much like punching him.

'How could you possibly know that?' I said.

He looked sheepish. 'I… well, I heard about you from my grandfather.'

Oh, no.

'And who is your grandfather?' I said in a dangerous tone. I could think of two possibilities. One was Limbane, the leader of the Library where I had been trained. He and Eva had been colleagues for a while — even friends, or something like it. But that had all ended, by the time the war was over.

Then there was Krays, another Library chief, and one of Limbane's main rivals. He was behind a slew of detestable schemes and caused us a great deal of trouble, until Pense digested him. Disgusting, but Krays fully deserved it.

'Limbane Erritas.'

Well. I cannot exactly welcome a grandson of either gentleman, particularly when he insists on following me around and spying on me. But if he had said Krays, I really wouldn't have spoken so much as another syllable to him.

I looked him over, and didn't spot anything that appeared as though he might be planning to attack me with it. 'You have two minutes to explain.'

He nodded, and visibly took a deep breath. 'I need your help.'

'What.'

He stepped a little closer, which I did not like. I backed up. I definitely wanted to keep some distance between the two of us.

He stopped, and held up his hands. 'My grandfather has spoken of you, and your friends. I know you were the first draykoni of modern times, and as such you must be among the most adept.'

'That last point is debatable, but all right. Why should that interest you?'

'Well, I…' he hesitated, staring at me in a fashion I found uncomfortably intense. 'I need a teacher,' he finally stated.

That… wasn't exactly what I was expecting. I could only blink stupidly at him. 'You need a… a teacher? For what?'

He seemed uncomfortable, and unsure of how to proceed. Oddly, I found this reassuring. I suppose I like it when other people are as awkward as I can be. It makes me feel a little bit less strange. 'Let me start from the beginning,' he said.

'If you can do it quickly.' The two minutes I had allotted were already up, and he was dithering. I wanted to be safely back in Nuwelin, and I *really* wanted to find Pense returned once I got there. This creepy idiot was holding me up.

As though he could read my thoughts, he gave me a nice, reassuring smile. I found it anything but. 'My name is Gio. I am the son of Nathe, son of Erritas Limbane. And my mother…'

'Your mother?' I prompted, when he hesitated.

'My mother was a draykon.'

'That's not possible.' I said it instantly, and instinctively, before I even paused to think about it. But on reflection, I wouldn't take it back. My people had been extinct for centuries. How could he possibly have been born of a draykon mother?

He smiled faintly. 'I assure you, it is.'

I stated my objections to the plausibility of his assertion, all of which he listened to with polite attention. He then merely said: 'Just because they were extinct *here*, does not mean there cannot have been some stray one or two still living somewhere *else*.'

Such as, inside one of the several Lokant Libraries. That is possible, I suppose, but I have to wonder: Why had Limbane never mentioned it?

That's not such an obvious question as it sounds. In my experience, the Lokants have always been almost pathologically secretive, and not at all given to handing out information unless they have a clear motive for doing so. Nonetheless, considering how very *relevant* that information would have been a few moons ago, I do find the whole thing difficult to believe.

But Gio had no insight to offer on this point. When I put the question to him, he merely shrugged. 'My grandfather is not very forthcoming.'

That's an understatement.

I folded my arms. 'Supposing that to be true, it still doesn't explain what you want with me.'

'I need a teacher,' he said again. 'Who better to ask than you?'

'How about your mother?'

'I cannot. She is… um, gone. She left when I was a baby.'

Uh huh. I eyed him with undisguised suspicion. 'You need a teacher for *what*? There are whole colleges devoted to the studies of Sorcery and Summoning. Try Glinnery, or better yet Nimdre. Practically any one of the Seven, in fact.'

Gio shook his head impatiently. 'Those colleges are built around a misunderstanding of the source of those arts. Are they not? And as such, they barely scratch the surface of what is possible with the kinds of powers we are talking about. I want to learn from somebody who knows just how limited it is to split it all up into two distinct groups of abilities with their own little labels — two mutually exclusive groups, supposedly, as though one can have only one set of powers or the other! The whole thing is a lesson in how badly wrong it is possible to go if only one is *ignorant* enough. Those schools are of no use to me.'

And so, he casually trashed the entire group worth of the system I was born into and brought up under. The system that had trained my mother, my friends… his attitude did not endear him to me.

At the same time, he was perfectly right. We *had* got it all wrong, and I could not quite blame him for rejecting such a misguided course of study. I have no doubt that the colleges will rectify their errors, and learn, and come to offer much more effective teaching. But that will take time.

'There are still people far better qualified to teach you than I,' I told him firmly. 'For a start, what I know about my arts is as nothing compared to the level of understanding the ancients possess. Ask one of those.'

'I am approaching you as an individual, and also your group. Your numbers do include one or two genuine ancients, do they not?'

I eyed him with grave misgivings. He had been following me, and he knew more about my doings and those of Nuwelin than I was comfortable with. 'So you've been watching us for a while. Why? And why sneak about like this? Could you not have sent me a letter or something?'

His handsome mouth twisted into a faintly ironic smile. 'How is the mail delivery up here? Reliable?'

For a moment, I *had* forgotten that I no longer have access to such civilised things. I didn't want to admit that to this peculiar stranger, though, so I merely glared at him.

He shrugged. 'I did write to your old address, in Waeverleyne. I have to assume that you did not receive it?'

'I have not been home in a while.' To my dismay. I made a mental note to make time to visit my parents as soon as possible.

Gio nodded. 'So, I came looking for you.'

'You could have approached me at the Darklands Market.'

'Ah! You did see me. I wondered.' He smiled ruefully at me, and did an awkward little shuffle combined with an apologetic cough. 'I meant to, but I… lost my nerve.'

'You lost your *nerve*? How is that possible?'

'Well… the two of you were busy and happy and there were a lot of people around.' He blinked, and shrugged. 'It seemed like a poor time.'

I sensed uncertainty, more than he was telling me. Which frankly flabbergasted me. I am so used to being the one wallowing in uncertainty, I do not know what to do when faced with someone who can manage to feel that uncertain around *me*.

And he really, really does not look like somebody who has any business being socially awkward. I stared at his irritatingly perfect face in amazed silence for a while, until I realised what I was doing and went back to admiring the floor.

Until something else occurred to me, and I looked up with a frown. 'You don't feel like a draykon,' I told him. Probably a bit more accusingly than I had meant to.

That got me nothing more than a confused stare in response, though, and no wonder. I hadn't exactly expressed myself clearly. 'In what way?'

'Your… just, the way you appear to me in my, uh, other

senses.' I looked at him with my mind's eye, so to speak, and he was as before: a cool and pale presence, with none of the colour or the energy I would expect from somebody with such significant draykon blood.

'I don't know what to tell you,' he said, helplessly. 'I am what I am.'

Unhelpful. I thought about that for a while, without reaching any useful conclusions. How could he be half draykoni without my being able to sense any part of it? Did it mean his story was false, or was it simply that this was new territory for me? I had never before met anybody with so much Lokant blood, *and* draykon heritage. Perhaps the Lokant heritage merely runs so strong as to largely drown out the rest.

'Well, so,' said Gio, more gently. 'Can you help me?'

I was still going to say no. I didn't understand where it made sense to him to follow me around, if he hadn't wanted to approach me directly, and the fact that he had managed to follow me all the way up here was bizarre and not at all comforting.

Then I got an idea.

I know that sounds ominous. It was, a bit. I thought back to our errand to Eva's in hopes of accessing Limbane's Library. She could not help us, but here was nothing short of Limbane's own grandson, clearly a powerful Lokant in his own right (albeit only of part-blood, if he was to be believed), and begging for my help.

'I have a problem on my hands,' I told him.

He just looked at me, waiting.

I debated how much to tell him. 'I need access to your grandfather's Library. There is some information I believe he has which I have need of, and I can find nowhere else.'

Gio nodded.

I squinted at him, suspicious. Just a nod? No questions, no conditions? 'That's it?'

He smiled, horribly earnest. 'I can help you with that.'

'Aren't you going to ask me why?'

He shook his head. 'I imagine you would tell me, if you wanted to.'

Hmm. 'It's the timeline chamber that I need,' I hazarded. 'The chart room?' I wasn't sure if he would know what I meant. How familiar was he with Limbane's domain? But he nodded again, apparently unfazed by the demand.

'When would you like to go?' he said, all affability.

I wanted to go at once, but I was not so foolhardy. After all, Gio was still a total stranger, and one whose behaviour so far could hardly be called ordinary.

Feeling encouraged by his helpfulness, I added, 'I also need to talk to your grandfather.' I mean, what luck was this? A close relative of Limbane's dropping into my hands, begging to be useful in exchange for some assistance of mine. It was *too* lucky really, and my celebratory impulse was quickly dampened by yet more suspicion. But if it was typical Lokant manipulative trickery... no reason why I couldn't at least try to turn it to our advantage.

This second request provoked a more cautious response. 'Ah... I can probably arrange that, yes,' he said, but he sounded doubtful.

I felt undecided. Part of me still wanted to dismiss him altogether, but I got the sense that he wouldn't just meekly disappear. I did not want to think of him wandering about on the edges of our home, unaccounted for, doing who-knew-what and maybe spying on us. I didn't really want to take him back to Nuwelin with me, either. It was useful to know that he *could* win us access to Limbane's Library, but was that prospect sufficient to agree to his request? How could any of us know if he could be trusted?

I felt paralysed. I wanted to reject him altogether, irrespective of the use I could make of him. But I realised, dimly, that too many of those feelings were based on the fact that he was a particularly unsettling stranger. I needed to be cool and objective about it, but I couldn't be.

To his credit, Gio did not try to push me. He merely stood, looking nonchalantly around at the trees while I deliberated. I don't know if he avoided watching me because it made him uncomfortable or because he realised it made me so, but I was glad of it.

In the end, though, I did not have to make a decision.

I sensed Pense first, though he must have been a mile or two away. He was coming in fast, a distant warmth growing brighter in my mind by the second.

I forgot about Gio on the spot. My knees were so weak with relief I almost fell over, and I realised I was shaking with it. I didn't know how frightened I had been over Pense's absence until I knew that he was okay.

I Changed and flew. When he appeared on the horizon, I wanted to see him. I wanted to make certain, with my own eyes, that he was hale and whole, and without an instant's delay.

There. A deep blue speck in the distance, gaining in size as his wings ate up the space between us. Other shapes around him, naught but dark flecks against the bright sky: Meriall and Nyden.

He blazed back into life in my heart, and I waited, basking in the glow of it until he was close enough.

Then I hurled myself at him.

I didn't quite knock him out of the sky, though not for lack of trying. We made it safely to the ground somehow, and I gave him to understand how happy I was that he was still breathing.

You must understand, I am not normally so jumpy when Pense is away. But with dead ancients showing up in both the Off-Worlds and, as yet, no explanation for it, I was unusually petrified this time.

Pense took it well. He gave me a few minutes to recover my composure, during which he devoted himself to smothering me with affection. That done, I was able to pay attention to his explanation.

I'm sorry, Minchu, he said silently. *We travelled west, and the farther we flew, the more disordered everything was.*

Everything?

Instead of answering that in words, Pense sent me a mental image. By *disordered* he meant the *amasku,* and the vision I received was of a world in convulsions. It was as Avane had described: the landscapes of Iskyr flashing through Changes at frightening speed, and a sense of roiling confusion which brought with it an unsettling wave of nausea.

Pense had been flying through it. I received a clear impression of what it had cost him to do so: the confusion seeping into his own mind, sending him reeling, blurring his senses…

Something else Avane had said came back into my mind. *Whatever occurred disrupted our sense of space so badly, we couldn't even tell which way was up anymore.*

And I remembered, at last, what her words had reminded me of. There was one time in my past where I have felt something similar, about three moons ago… and Pense had been heading west.

Orlind? I asked, trying not to feel sick.

It is worse.

Orlind is the once-mythical Seventh Realm. I call it that because it was thought to be lost, and long left behind by time. It was *us* who ventured that way, after the fighting stopped over Waeverleyne. We found that it is not lost at all, not quite. Most of it is gone, but a tiny island remains. It used to be the site of the greatest Lokant Library of all, a place of such power that various Lokant groups fought over it until they destroyed it. Indeed, some of them are still fighting over it. I know that more than one has had dreams of somehow resurrecting the place.

The conflict that destroyed the Library also destroyed the land. Most of it sank into the sea, and the little bit that's left is a mass of pure chaos. The Library was so remarkable because it was bound up with the *amasku* in some fundamental way, which boosted its capabilities beyond all reason. I don't entirely understand it, I have to tell you, but Lokants get very worked up about it. And those energies have been corrupted to the point that they are wrecking what is left of Orlind.

We said, Pense and I, that we would try to heal them. We envisioned this as a project for the far future, after there had been time to do other things first. Rest and heal ourselves, after the war. Grow accustomed to our new lives, and in my case, to my new powers. Find out what place the draykoni would take in the modern world. Take time for our relationship, even, once we had decided we were having one.

I began to see that this had been absurdly optimistic.

It is leaking, said Pense.

Leaking.

Last time I was in Orlind, it was under the custodianship of Galywis, who is an unimaginably ancient and utterly mad Lokant. Famous, too, as I have lately learned. Through his efforts, the corruption there was confined to the island and was not, at that time, spreading.

Apparently that has changed.

What's become of Galywis? I asked Pense.

I do not know.

This is the worst news. If the corrupted *amasku* of Orlind is spreading, that's more than reason enough for the mess we've been seeing across the Uppers and Lowers — the mad, constant

Changes and the portals opening up everywhere. And it is only the beginning.

I remembered Avane's words once again. *We couldn't even tell which way was up anymore.* That's Orlind. That's what the corrupted energy *does*. How can it have spread into the Lowers and Uppers already? I felt a thrill of fear, almost paralysing.

What can we possibly do about this?

There was no time to discuss it further, because something had followed Pense and the others back from Orlind. I became aware of a presence, distant and unrecognisable. It came upon us fast — too fast. I had no time to react before...

... well, I hardly know how to describe it. It was like being swallowed. I was engulfed by something as irresistible as the tide, all light was abruptly extinguished around me, and I felt as though I fell a long, long way.

There was no landing. I merely realised, slowly but inexorably, that I was both stationary and alert. I lay prone on a floor that felt constructed, for all of the grass and other plants that had surrounded me moments before were gone. It was wood, or something similar, stripped bare and polished. It was warm against my cheek as I lay there.

I sat up. Too quickly, for my head spun, blood roared in my ears and my vision blacked out. When it cleared, I received my first glimpse of a new environment.

The wooden floor belonged to a kind of parlour, a medium-sized room with a large, fluffy green rug in the centre and drapes to match. There was a velvet sofa, sized to seat three, and two arm-chairs. A fire roared in the hearth, kicking out a fierce heat into the room.

Something was odd about the light. I discovered why when I went to the curtains and found no windows behind them.

I was a bit more disconcerted when I realised there was no door either.

No matter. This kind of thing has happened before. When the environment changes around me like this, it is always *amasku*, and it requires little effort to manipulate. I concentrated on the bare wall where a door ought to be, and carelessly made one.

It did not appear.

I stared in disbelief at the wall, all prettily papered in florals and... still just a wall. Shall you blame me if I confess that I felt a surge of panic? For once, I feel it was justified! Transported by means unknown, to who-knows-where, and with no apparent means of escape! I defy anybody not to panic!

Before I had time to work myself into a mess, though, I heard a creak behind me and Meriall's voice said, 'Llandry! Thank goodness! I thought I was lost forever.'

I turned in time to see her emerge from some kind of panel in the fireplace. It was not a door, just a long slab of stone which had helpfully swung outwards. Behind it I could see another room.

Under these strangest of conditions, Meriall appeared in the light of a saviour and I practically clung to her. She clutched me too, and we hung onto each other for comfort for a little while.

'How did you do that?' I asked her. My *first* question, naturally, was going to be, 'Where are we?', but it was patently obvious that Meriall had no more idea than I did.

'I think I didn't,' she said, eyeing the panel distrustfully. 'It just opened.'

I peered into the room beyond and found it shockingly different from mine. The walls were sheer glass from top to bottom, though nothing could be seen through them. Even the floor was glass, and the ceiling. As I watched, a dizzying wave of colour rippled through the room, but it was no pleasing array. The hues were nauseating and somehow… putrid.

I shuddered, and turned my back on it.

'If you are here and so am I,' I said to Meriall, 'Perhaps the others are here, too. Have you seen anything of them?' I was thinking of Pense and Nyden, both of whom had been with us in Iskyr when the transportation had happened. I felt torn between hoping they were here, for together we might better expect to find a way out, and hoping they were not, for perhaps they could find a way to help us.

'I've not seen them,' said Meriall. She was prowling around the room, touching and examining everything. 'I can't alter anything,' she added.

'Nor I.' I joined her in investigating, but to no avail. The place was as unremarkable, albeit sumptuous, as one of Eva's parlours. In fact, it struck me as strikingly like.

The sound of shattering glass distracted us from this endeavour and we turned, as one, to face the gaping panel in the hearth.

An enormous black draykon filled the adjacent room to

capacity, and then some. Finding himself ill-provided with doors, Nyden had apparently decided to bash his way through the walls instead. He crouched there, peeping through the panel at us with one huge emerald eye as splinters of glass slid slowly off his head and hit the floor with a clatter.

Hi, he said.

'Where is Pense?' I asked him. If Meri and Ny were both here then surely, so must Pensould.

I was answered by the sounds of more splintering glass, and then an equally devastating roar.

Ah. Pense was looking for me, too.

'Minchu!' he bellowed. 'How dare you be separated from me like this!' I couldn't see him, but I could feel him coming closer, and we could all hear the sounds of destruction which attended his approach.

'It wasn't my idea!' I reminded him. Really, it was too unreasonable to blame me. 'I am still breathing,' I added.

That soothed him, for the smashing noises lessened. A bit.

Then, abruptly, they stopped.

'Pense…?' I called. The sudden silence was far more alarming than the smashing and splintering had been. I strained to reach him, to understand what had happened.

The parlour walls shuddered, shimmered, and stretched. The ceiling soared upwards, up and up, and Nyden became suddenly visible in all his dark-scaled glory as the rooms we had been standing in became one, and expanded. The broken glass disappeared.

When everything settled, our surroundings had transformed themselves into a large, echoing room with a high, domed ceiling, a polished floor that looked like crystal of some kind, and long drapes which probably weren't hiding windows. A long buffet table stood to one side, with a punch bowl and everything, and there was a balcony for an orchestra. In short, it was a ballroom, and an unusually large one at that. The four of us were dwarfed in the middle of it, despite two of us being, at that time, draykoni.

Nyden stretched out his wings with alacrity, and shuffled a step or two. *Who wants to dance?*

I was unable to respond, for I was engulfed by Pense. He came at me at the gallop, and devoted himself to the pleasant task of ensuring that all of my parts were as they should be.

Somewhere in the midst of this I thought I heard a distant, small voice say, distinctly but bafflingly, 'Sorry.' It did not sound like Pense, but it must have been.

It took me a little longer to realise that we were not, in fact, four in this bizarre ballroom, but five. Concealed in a far corner, silent and watchful, was Gio. I thought he was looking far too calm, considering the mystery of our present predicament.

I marched over to him, trailing Pense and Meri behind me. 'Gio!' I greeted him, without troubling to be friendly. 'Is this something to do with you?'

'By "this", do you mean *this*?' He gestured gracefully at the ballroom.

'Actually, I do. Yes.'

'Nothing whatsoever. I am as mystified as you.' He smiled at me, as though such a response ought to be reassuring.

'It is not draykon work,' I informed him.

He merely looked quizzical. 'And therefore it must be my doing?'

'You are the only anomaly here.'

'Minchu, who is this?' said Pense, with a note of anxiety.

'I think I am not the *only* anomaly,' said Gio. 'There is me, and there is the structure we are in. The two are not necessarily related, just because we happen to have appeared at a similar time.'

'I take it he's a friend of yours, Llan,' said Meriall. I felt Nyden prowl up behind me, his curious gaze settling upon Gio with palpable menace.

Gio developed a hunted look, and I could well imagine his thoughts. If he spoke the truth, then he had not anticipated having to explain himself to so large and menacing a group of my friends — or to have to rely on my introduction. How would I describe his conduct?

Indeed, what would I say? I distrusted him and I was displeased with his behaviour, but I could not help feeling a little pity for him, pinned into a corner as he was and with no less than four suspicious and unfriendly draykoni before him.

'He is… a recent acquaintance,' I finally said. 'He has come to us seeking help with his… draykoni abilities.'

There followed a silence in which, I imagine, my three friends took note of Gio's white hair and strong Lokant aura.

'I know it seems far-fetched,' said Gio quickly. 'There is a blood link. My mother's side.'

He also claims to be Limbane's grandson, I told Pense privately.

Do you believe him?

I hardly know.

'Well, Gio,' said a dark, whispery voice I'd never heard before. I realised, to my surprise, that it was Nyden, who had always spoken mind-to-mind before. He stalked up and put his muzzle close to Gio's face. 'If you prove to be traitorous, know that it will be both my job and my pleasure to digest you.' He smiled horribly, all razor teeth, and added, 'I am particularly partial to liver.'

I waited for him to turn back into the Nyden I knew and laugh, but he did not.

Gio looked impressed. 'I am not here to hurt anybody, I swear.'

'You had better stick with us,' said Meriall.

Gio smiled gratefully at her.

'That way we can keep an eye on you.'

The smile faded. Gio sighed and bowed his head. 'I am yours to command, of course.'

This declaration appealed to Meri, for her smile turned impish and she said, 'Excellent,' in a tone of voice that bordered upon sinister.

I decided not to enquire as to the source of her satisfaction.

I don't know what Gio said next, if anything, for I was distracted by the sound of whispering. I thought that Ny and Pense must be holding some kind of private consultation, but it soon occurred to me that this made little sense. If they wished to speak privately, they would speak mind-to-mind and no one would know of it at all. Meri and Gio were not whispering, either. So who could it be?

I looked around, but the room had not changed. There was no one else to be seen, and nowhere for anybody to hide. I concentrated, but I could discern only an unintelligible babble — no words.

A flicker of movement caught my eye, and I turned, but I saw no discernible source. Nyden and Pense sat, wings comfortably tucked, in the centre of the ballroom. They probably *were* talking, for they were facing each other, and motionless. But they certainly were not the source of the movement I thought I had seen.

Was I imagining things?

Was I going *mad* in this bizarre place?

'We need to find a way out,' said Meriall decisively. She strode past me, her lack of an obvious destination no impediment to her sense of purpose, considering her no-nonsense expression. Gio trailed after her.

'There is no exit,' said Pensould.

Meriall narrowed her eyes at him. 'You seem remarkably calm about it.'

Pense twitched his tail. 'There is nothing menacing about this place.'

'You mean aside from the fact that we can't get out of it?'

'Aside from that. Can't you feel it?'

I knew what Pense meant. Strange as this place was, as unaccountable as our presence there may be, it did not feel threatening. On the contrary, there was an air of friendliness about it, and a sense of calm.

…except for those flickers of movement. Another caught my eye. Meri saw it, too, for we both turned. Nothing. We exchanged glances, her expression as puzzled as my own must have been.

Then the first figure appeared.

She was dressed for the ball, though I had never seen such a gown before. It was as white as her hair, and so light as to almost float as she twirled through the steps of a stately waltz. She did not appear to see Pense and Nyden, but nor did she collide with them.

She danced alone for a minute or two, watched in stupefied awe by the five of us.

And then, she was no longer alone. A partner materialised between one step and the next, a man with similarly snow-white hair and a suit as marvellous as his lady's gown. They waltzed together in eerie silence.

'What in the name of…' said Meri faintly.

I heard music, distant and mournful, and suddenly the ballroom was full of dancers. Every one of them was white-haired, and as oblivious to our presence as the first two. They waltzed and twirled to the faint strains of music for some minutes, and I could swear that some of them passed *straight through me.*

There was also an odd, chilling moment where I thought one

of them looked straight at me. He appeared to be about my father's age, as far as I could judge from the brief glimpse that I caught, and he had a pleasant, friendly face. His eyes met mine for a single, startling instant, and then he was gone, borne away upon a wave of music.

The dance came to an end. The waltzers stopped and applauded the musicians, and then they began to fade.

Soon we stood as before, in an empty, silent ballroom.

'Do you still want to call this place benevolent?' said Meriall shakily. 'Because that was nothing short of extremely creepy.'

I agree with the human-shaped girl, said Nyden with a strong shudder, earning himself an irritated look from Meri. *Incorporeal people give me the shivers.*

I couldn't agree. The vision, whatever it had been, had seemed a happy one to me.

But then the room changed again, and the nature of the ballroom's passing shook my pleasant feelings more than a little. The wallpaper turned to chaotically coloured slime and bled down the walls, the dome of the ceiling crashed inwards in a rain of shattered pieces which mercifully vanished before they hit us, and the curtains caught fire, burning to nothing within seconds. The flames were blue.

The walls sank inwards, shrinking the room around us — and then abruptly reversed and soared outwards again. They turned to sheet glass, through which I caught a glimpse of a forest of purple trees. Then vast drapes came crashing down, covering every inch of the walls in blue velvet.

Meriall came to a sudden stop the moment these disconcerting shenanigans began. The five of us stood stock-still, paralysed with fear that the ceiling would fall upon us, or the walls collapse altogether and bury us.

Mercifully, the tumult failed to affect us. After a minute or two of madness it calmed, and the blue velvet curtains slowly drew back.

Books. They ran from floor to ceiling in an array I could charitably term haphazard. But the word falls far short of expressing the extent of the chaos. Far too many volumes were crammed into the space, vast as it was. Tens of thousands of them there were, jumbled up in cascading piles in the corners and squashed every which way into shelves of asymmetrical proportions and uneven sizes.

As we watched, the books rearranged themselves. In fact they did this ceaselessly, jumping from shelf to shelf, opening and closing, vanishing and reappearing. It struck me that some invisible hand could almost be at work, furiously employed in attempting to impose some kind of order upon the mess. Such a being must be not only invisible but monstrously sized, and possessed of at least fifty arms besides.

I do not like this place, said Nyden, his scales shivering with tension.

Meriall agreed. 'We may not have been brought here to be harmed,' she said, narrowly avoiding being brained by a flying book by virtue of a luckily-timed duck, 'but it may well be the death of us anyway.'

And once again, I heard, faintly but distinctly, the single word. *Sorry.*

Meriall twitched, and I wondered if she heard it, too.

I reached for a book on a nearby shelf, and was surprised when it promptly disintegrated in my hand. I caught another as it sailed by, but when I opened it, the pages were blank. What were the books here for, if not for us to read?

The third I got hold of contained words, and my heart leapt. But it was verse, and the merest nonsense. The words shuffled and reformed themselves as I watched, and the nonsense became pure gibberish. I let go of it, disappointed, and it sailed away to add itself to a stack forming in the centre of the floor.

I believe we were all a bit disconcerted when the towering heap of books piling up in the middle of the room suddenly combusted. Like the curtains, they were gone in seconds, devoured by a furious inferno of blue flames.

Another pile began to form.

I don't mean to distract anyone from the show, said Nyden after a while, *But there is a door over there.*

He was right, and if it didn't sound crazy I would say that the door was going out of its way to look inviting. It beckoned from in between two bookshelves, a balmy light streaming through it in a manner most appealing. Its proportions were indeterminate. It was just the right height and width for me to pass through, but as Ny wandered over, it smoothly expanded to accommodate his greater bulk.

I could swear that I heard the strains of a gentle, soothing melody coming from somewhere beyond.

'That door is far too plausible,' said Meriall.

I had to agree. But… 'It's the only one we've got.'

'I will go first.' Pense strode up to the door before anybody could argue, supposing we had wanted to. He disappeared through it.

'It is safe,' he called back. 'Weird, but safe.'

Ny stood back with a gentlemanly inclination of his draykonic head, and waited while Meri and I stepped through. I wasn't sorry to have his comforting bulk at our backs.

Through we went.

The first thing I became aware of was a powerful and utterly *delicious* aroma, like a hundred types of fruit jumbled together.

We had entered some kind of conservatory — or it might be more apt to call it an orchard which happened to be glass-enclosed. Everywhere I looked, there were trees of myriad different species, each one bearing a heavy load of fruit. I was intrigued to note that I didn't recognise any of them.

Meriall's eyes sparkled with interest as she looked around, and when she spoke it was with approval. 'This is more like it.'

Pense merely grunted, and Ny said nothing at all, being far too busy attempting to disentangle himself from a cluster of miniature trees into which he had somehow fallen.

I went to help him. 'The turmoil grows a little trying,' I could not help remarking as I picked feathery leaves out from between his toes.

Sorrysorry, said the voice, frantic.

I looked sharply about, but saw no one.

Considering the cramped conditions of the place, crowded as it was with trees, Pense consented to turn human as we left our corner to explore. Ny, though, steadfastly refused, despite his encounter with the trees. He remained serenely oblivious to the wreckage of toppled foliage he left in his wake.

Beyond a small forest of fruit trees, we discovered that there was more to this greenhouse than propagation. An array of tables was spread out in a clearing between the trees, the glassy ceiling soaring high overhead. They were littered with tools, equipment and gadgets I neither recognised nor could guess the purpose of. Each table — though actually they were more like benches, laboratory style — bore a complement of fruits, too, a different type to each one.

Each bench also had an attendant… person.

We stopped, alarmed, but nobody looked up. They continued their work, whatever it was, with no sign that they were aware of our presence at all.

Meri tested this by drifting up to the nearest bench. A woman of my mother's age stood there, intent upon dissecting a spiny green fruit. Her white hair was caught up in a severe bun, and she wore a plain black coat.

'Hello,' said Meri.

The woman made no sign of having noticed.

'They're like the dancers,' Meri reported.

'Very like them,' I agreed, emboldened enough to explore a little myself. 'They are all Lokants.'

I stretched out my hand towards another of them, an elderly man wearing a similar black coat, and tried to grasp his shoulder. My hand passed straight through. 'And incorporeal.'

Visions of Lokants, alive or long dead I could not say. But nothing else here was insubstantial. Nyden had proved that with the trail of disaster he had left behind among the orchard.

The old man reached out for a hooked tool that lay on the bench in between us. I snatched it up before he could secure it, and waited to see what would happen.

Nothing. The man's hand curled as though he grasped the object I had just removed, and he went on working without seeming to notice that he held nothing.

Even more oddly, the flesh of the fruit he was dissecting parted in obliging obedience to his gestures, just as though he still held the tool.

I put the hook down, and noticed that my hand was coated in thick dust.

Llan, said Pense. *You must see this.*

He had wandered a little away, and it took me a moment to find him among the many benches. When I reached him, he handed me a fruit.

It was palm-sized, blush pink, and faintly heart-shaped, with a little tuck at the bottom like a dimple. I raised it to my nose to test the aroma.

'Nara fruit?' I looked at Pense. 'Where did you get this?'

He gestured behind himself. A wide bench was covered in further specimens of the fruit, each one slightly different in shape. A Lokant man was attendant over it, though he did not appear to be dissecting these. If anything, he was…

'Is he *building* that one?' I asked, aghast.

'That is what it looks like to me, also,' Pense agreed.

The man had a nara before him, about half complete. As I watched, he built up the outer shell of the fruit by slow degrees, using some kind of instrument I could not even describe for you. Then he painstakingly filled in the middle. The fruit completed, he studied it for a moment before setting it aside and beginning another.

I exchanged a wondering look with Pense.

'These are my favourites,' I said faintly. What were we seeing here? Was this a vision of past events?

Had Lokants *made* the nara fruit? Could that be possible?

Galywis claimed that Lokants made both humans and draykoni. But I don't think I ever really believed it. It seemed too implausible… and Galy is mad. But the book Ori was reading seemed to agree, and here before me was a vision of direct interference in the flora of our worlds.

For the first time, I had to seriously reconsider.

It is an overwhelming idea. Perhaps that is why I suddenly became aware of a leaden tiredness, with no particular cause. I was ravenously hungry, too; the sight of my favourite fruit was enough to remind me of that.

I sighed and rubbed at my eyes, for my vision was going a little blurry.

'Good point,' said Pense. He scooped me up and walked off with me. 'This lady needs to sleep,' he called. 'I give you fair warning, whatever you are. She requires an interval of peace and an area for repose, or I shall become angry.'

Pense has a way of getting his point across with things like that. He spoke as though he was more than capable of burning the place down if he wasn't obeyed, and he wouldn't for a second question his justification in doing so.

Fortunately, it is not an attitude he assumes very often.

His assumption that there was a sentient and responsive being in charge of our fate struck a chord with me. *Sorry, sorry…* we had both heard that voice. But would whoever it was listen to his demands? Was he, she or it genuinely interested in our well-being?

Apparently so, for the orchard reformed around us in prompt response to Pense's demands. The trees disappeared, taking their heavenly fragrance with them, and all the eerie, silent, oblivious Lokants vanished along with them.

It was replaced by a dormitory, with several neat, narrow beds lined up in a row.

Reclining in one of them with a book in his hands was Gio. He returned my quizzical look with a tiny salute. 'I wondered where you all got to.'

Never mind us. Where had *he* got to? But I was too tired to bother answering him just then. Tired, and obscurely annoyed to see him lounging there at his ease when we had narrowly avoided being burned to death in an unusually flammable library, grappled with ghostly Lokants and startling ideas and finally fetched up here, worn out and hungry.

Pense cast a disapproving eye over the furniture, but his displeasure did not focus upon Gio as I might have expected. 'I hope I am not imagined to be inclined to sleep apart from my Minchu?'

Two adjacent beds shuffled hastily together and merged into one, a picture of contrition.

'Better,' said Pense, some of his anger dissipating. He paused, and thought, and added with one of his feral smiles, 'Thank you.'

By way of response, a wave of balmy warmth washed over the room, bringing with it a comforting aroma of hot cayluch and baking bread.

Meriall coughed. 'On which note,' she said in a sweet tone I imagined deceptive, 'I am about to expire from hunger.'

A table laden with dishes appeared along one wall and danced an inviting little jig.

'I like you,' said Meri, and fell upon the food with a will.

And so we ate, and drank, and slept. Nobody asked any questions about where the food came from, or how it was (thankfully) substantial when the people were not. We were too grateful to be fed. I wanted to ask Gio what had happened to him and why he hadn't been with us, but I was too tired. Once I was fed, Pense bundled me into bed, wrapped me in a warm embrace and curtly dismissed Nyden to stand watch over us. I wondered how Ny, much older than the rest of us, would react to an undisguised command from Pense.

'Ya, I have no need of sleep anyway,' said Nyden sourly. But he didn't seem too ruffled. The table of edible delights was holding his attention nicely.

I lay awake some time in spite of my tiredness, restless in

that strange place. The things we had seen made no sense, and none of it provided any clues as to where we were or why we had been carted off like that. The presence I have several times detected may have proved benevolent, but its identity and purpose remained a mystery. What could we do, save go along with it all and see what happened? But such enforced passivity is neither natural nor comforting and I could not imagine how either Pense or Gio seemed so relaxed.

Eventually, I slept.

I woke to find Pense keeping watch, and he was glad to return to slumber while I took my turn.

Which I am now doing, and also taking the opportunity of updating my journal. Not neatly. All my fine structure is going by the wayside, because it is hard to write clearly about what is happening when I have no idea what that is. Perhaps I will be able to impose some better order upon it later.

Oh, Meriall is awake. More later, whenever I next get the chance.

29 VII (?)
I Become a Lot More Confused.
Also, Everyone Dies.

Meri approached me with a steaming mug of cayluch in one hand and a plate of some kind of fluffy bread in the other, and handed both to me. I noticed that the table had replenished itself since our last attack upon it.

When I had got halfway down the food, a tiny pot of something pink and glistening appeared on my plate.

I tasted it. Nara fruit preserves, tangy and sweet.

Meriall paused in her enjoyment of a stack of pastries and eyed the little pot. 'So,' she said. 'You know the person in charge of this little party.'

'Uhh. Not to my knowledge, no. Why do you say that?'

She nodded meaningfully at the preserves. 'Somebody seems eager to please you. And couldn't comply quickly enough with Pense's demands yesterday.' She took another bite of pastry and chewed thoughtfully. 'I can't help feeling that all of this is focused on you and Pense, somehow. The rest of us are just extras.'

'All of what, though? I can see no sense in anything that's happened, no pattern. The dancers, the library, the burning books, the orchard… if there is a mind behind it all, what is it for?'

'I don't know. But it has something to do with Lokants, that much is obvious.'

Yes. Everyone we had seen in the various visions was a Lokant. 'The naras,' I said slowly. 'If it is true that they created them… it is something that must have happened in the past. A *long* way in the past.'

'A very long way.'

'Maybe they aren't visions so much as memories.' I thought of the voice I had heard, twice now. *Sorry*. And the man who had almost seemed to look straight at me as he had waltzed past me in the ballroom…

'It doesn't make sense,' I said, growing frustrated. 'I want to conclude that we are in a Lokant Library, but I've been in such places before. They do not behave like this. This is more like the Changes in Iskyr, which is draykon magic, but we cannot influence it.'

'It is my belief that we are in the Library of Orlind.' Gio had risen from his bed without our noticing, so engrossed were we in our thoughts. He wandered past on his way to the food, giving me another little salute when I caught his eye.

'How could that be possible?' I demanded. 'We were nowhere near Orlind when we were… um, swallowed.'

Gio nodded, and took a long gulp of cayluch with obvious appreciation. 'So we weren't. But there are some things about our Libraries which you might not know about.'

He stopped to eat, which was irritating. 'And?' said Meriall, fixing him with a disapproving glare. 'Talk first, eat later.'

'Sorry.' Gio swallowed hastily. 'You know that they move around?'

I blinked. 'What?'

'Some of them,' he amended. 'Orlind among them, for a time. It was eventually anchored in your world, on the island which you still call by the same name. But before that, it drifted.'

My mind spun. 'So if it could be… unanchored?'

'Right. If it could be wrested free of its moorings, so to speak, you wouldn't have to be on the *island* of Orlind in order to end up in the *Library* of Orlind.'

'But how could it be removed? Is that even possible?'

Gio shrugged and went back to his plate. 'I have no idea if it is possible,' he said with his mouth full. 'I would certainly guess that the consequences of doing so would be… significant.'

I took a deep breath to steady myself. If Gio was right…

I have been in the Library of Orlind before, with Pense and Eva and Tren. It had crashed wildly through Change after Change, just as this place did. I would have made the connection sooner, save that it had appeared to be geographically impossible.

But what did that mean for Galywis?

I mustered my courage. 'Galy?' I said softly. 'Is that you?'

The beds all leapt three feet into the air in perfect synchronicity, startling Pense who was still in one of them. Then a jubilant little tune played from somewhere, growing swiftly into a noisy fanfare. The tumult woke up Nyden, who uncurled himself with a snort of irritation.

I felt faint.

'Galy!' I shouted over the noise. 'What are you doing? What has *happened* to you?'

See, last time I saw Galywis he was in the Library of Orlind, yes, but very definitely as a separate physical presence. What was he now? *Where* was he? He seemed part of the building in ways which frankly disturbed me.

These were his memories we were seeing, or his ideas… perhaps some of both. The man who'd caught my notice in the ballroom? Now that I thought to make the comparison, his features were Galy's. I had seen Galywis himself, as he had been in his younger days.

Galy was gone from the Library of Orlind because he had *become* it. He had merged his own mind with it for reasons I couldn't begin to guess at. And when Pense had shown up near the island, he had recognised him as a friend and followed him.

And thus, here we were.

Pense sat up and stared sleepily at me. 'What's going on?'

'Um. Galywis has become a building and is trying to tell us something.'

Pense had nothing to say that right away, nor did I expect him to. He stared at me, sleepy and confused, and finally nodded. 'Aha. Of course he has.'

No reply had come to my question to Galywis, which served to prove that ordinary communication was beyond him. I thought of the library full of books and how they had been either empty, or filled with gibberish. And the bonfires, which now struck me as a sign of… frustration.

Galy had been terribly mad when I had met him a few

moons ago, and that was *before* he became a Library and wandered off. Communicating with him was not going to be easy.

And I didn't want to think about what kind of emergency had occurred that could push him to such extremes.

I explained all this to Pense, Meri and Ny, as quickly and simply as I could. Nonetheless, Meri was looking a little wild about the eyes by the time I finished, and Nyden gave me one of his toothy smiles. *I knew you would be more interesting than Eterna's gang*, he said. *But I did not anticipate just how much.*

Pense took it in stride. He ran a hand through his dark hair, messing it up even more than it already was, and nodded once at me. 'Interesting,' was all he said.

'This Galywis is somebody that you've known for years and years, of course,' said Meriall.

'Well… no. We met him only once.'

Meri blinked. 'Ah. But he proved himself to you in some obscure but decisive way, and you would trust him with your lives.'

I frowned and thought, and finally nodded, but with less certainty than I would like. 'We fought off a Lokant invasion of Orlind together, and… er, well, he *was* on our side.'

'At the time,' added Pense helpfully.

Meriall's lips quirked into a wry smile. 'Wonderful,' she muttered.

I watched Gio. I wasn't sure I agreed with Meri, that she and Ny and Gio had ended up in here with us by accident. Was it a coincidence that a Lokant happened to be along just when we had disappeared into a Lokant Library? For that matter, was Gio's appearance in my life truly unrelated to these events at all? He claimed to be the grandson of Limbane — and Limbane was one of the people whose wars over Orlind had led to its destruction.

On the other hand, he *had* been the source of a piece of useful information. I didn't trust him, but as the only lucid and coherent Lokant we had access to, he could be tolerated.

Well, he would have to be. We couldn't get rid of him.

I hesitated, torn between wanting to talk to him and wanting to avoid him forever. He sat now on the edge of his bed, with none of Pense's rumpled appearance. His white hair was perfectly ordered, his clothes neat in spite of his having slept in them. He looked annoyingly handsome and even more aggravatingly at ease as he sat, oblivious to my scrutiny.

I sighed inwardly, cursed myself for an idiot, and went over to him. We would never find out anything more about him if we didn't ask. If *I* didn't ask.

'You seem very comfortable,' I told him. I sounded a bit more sour about it than I had intended.

Gio looked up at me, bemused. 'Should I be panicking? But I am having a wonderful time.'

'You're what?'

He smiled, his eyes lighting up with enthusiasm. 'This is the Library of Orlind! I have heard tales of it since I was a child — its history, its extraordinary nature, its remarkable powers. I never imagined that someday I might stand within it myself. More! That I might glimpse something of the *old* Library, before it was destroyed! I am grateful beyond words to Mr. Galywis for this magical tour.'

This was a way of looking at it that I had not considered. 'Huh,' I said, at my most searingly intelligent.

Gio raised an eyebrow. 'Do you see nothing to enjoy?'

I was struck by this question, because truthfully, trying to *enjoy* anything that happened in my life was never a priority. In fact, it wasn't even on my agenda. I was always too busy fearing something, or everything, and trying to manage anyway. And, more recently, trying to juggle my new responsibilities, just as soon as I figured out exactly what they were.

'I am concerned,' I told Gio, 'because I think something catastrophic must have happened, to produce this result.'

Gio looked me over thoughtfully, and nodded. 'I can understand that you might.'

I decided I'd had enough of Gio. I turned my back on him, and returned to my friends. 'Are we all ready? I think we had better not delay any longer than is necessary.'

I am, said Nyden peppily, and Pense gave me a nod.

Meri looked about as happy about everything as I was. She stood with her arms wrapped around herself, her face grim. But she met my gaze, sighed, and relaxed her forbidding posture a little.

'All right!' she yelled. 'Galywis, Mad Master of the Library and self-appointed director of our fate, let us have it!'

I barely had time to reach Pense and grab onto him before

the dormitory disintegrated in a shower of dust and darkness fell around us.

What followed was… confusion. When the light returned, it brought with it a sequence of Changes so rapid, we could not follow them. A succession of rooms and scenes and faces spun around us at dizzying speed, as though Galy was mentally flipping through the book of his memories, trying to fix upon a place to begin. The effect was staggering. After a minute or so of this, I shut my eyes and covered my ears against the blur of colour and sound and waited for Galy to settle down.

I was roused from this by Meri digging an elbow into my ribs. 'Llan!' she hissed.

I opened my eyes.

'Uh,' was all I could think of to say.

We were not in a room anymore. It was dark, wherever we had ended up, and the space was clearly not intended for habitation by humans. The walls curved oddly — if they could be called walls. They were soft-looking and reddish, and they glistened oddly. Strange structures, vast and unnameable, rose on all sides, most of them flexing or rippling or pulsing as with some indefinable function. Far overhead, a long beam curved away into the distance, oddly constructed out of matched segments melded together.

'What is that sound…' said Meri.

Rising above a plethora of noises I could put no name to was a dull *thud-thud* sound, regular and profound enough to echo.

'It sounds like a heartbeat,' I said, tentatively, for how could it be that?

'It is a heartbeat,' said Pense. He pointed at one of the structures, a pulsing, convoluted thing about six times our size. 'There is the heart.'

It did not look like a heart. Not that I would know, really, for I have never seen one. But it was undoubtedly pulsing in time with the double *thud* of the beat. I frowned at it.

'And that,' continued Pense, pointing at another of the things, 'is a stomach. And there is the spine.' He pointed upwards at the long, curving beam.

I now saw that what I had taken for an odd kind of roof structure was undoubtedly a rib cage. I swallowed a sudden flutter of mild panic as I realised what the shapes and proportions must mean. 'We… are inside a draykon.'

Pense gave me one of his more disturbing smiles. 'Life with Galywis is never dull.'

I could find no response to make to that. We were *inside* a draykon. The fact that it could hardly be a real one and must be but a semblance of one was of some comfort to me, but not that much.

'Life doesn't get any less weird,' I muttered.

'It's not boring,' agreed Meri.

Gio merely seemed fascinated, for he wandered off at once to explore. Ny just sat humming some mad little tune to himself, his tail tapping out the beat.

I cleared my throat. 'Well, Galy, we are with you so far,' I said. 'What are we meant to be seeing here?'

The organs around us vanished. Muscle, flesh and cartilage melted away until all that remained was the skeleton of the beast, shimmering in those beautiful colours I had always admired.

The bones pulsed with a flow of raw energy, shining silvery-pale. *Amasku.* We were witnessing the natural flow of the stuff. To see it like that, bound into the very bones of a draykon, brought home to me the extent of the connection between the two.

I then realised that the shine I had noticed in the flesh was derived from the same thing. It wasn't just the bones. Amasku was knit into every part of every draykon, so deeply that the two could not, by any imaginable means, be separated.

As we watched, mesmerised, the silvery light dimmed and began to fade, the beautiful silvery energy extinguished almost to nothing. The bones soon began to suffer, turning pitted and pale and fragile. Some of them crumbled.

I watched in horror as bones dissolved around us one by one, and the rib cage that formed both walls and ceiling fell inwards.

The spine began to fail.

'Galy!' I screamed as the skeleton crashed in upon us.

Whatever I had been standing upon crumbled and gave way. I dropped, screaming. My wings flared open to catch my descent, but before they could slow my fall I was grabbed, as by an invisible hand, and whisked sideways. Light blazed, searing my eyes.

When the light faded, I saw a corridor stretching away before us, apparently into infinity for all I could tell. The ceiling was... missing. Above us yawned the heavens, dark and starlit and somehow more vast than they had ever appeared to me before.

Doors lined up along the corridor on both sides, set almost edge-to-edge. Each was a different shape, size and colour and I could not even begin to imagine what might lie behind them.

When I turned around, I saw much the same thing stretching out behind us. There must have been hundreds of doors.

'Galy,' I said, foolishly looking around as though I might see him somewhere. 'We might need a little guidance here. Where do you want us to go?'

No reply came, nor any sign as to what we were expected to do. The corridor was empty save for ourselves, and eerily silent.

Ny shrugged his scaled shoulders, his wings rippling with the movement, and pointed the tip of his tail at a green door with thorns engraved around it. 'That one, Mer!' he commanded.

Meriall shrugged, too, and went to open it. Beyond it lay a tiny, one-room cottage with a stove, a neat table and chairs and wooden cupboards built into the walls. Colourful rugs covered the floor and the table was set for tea. There was nothing at all out of the way about it, except that it was upside down. The fact that the floor had taken up residence upon the ceiling did not appear to inconvenience either the rugs or the furniture very much.

I was intrigued.

But Ny merely said, *quaint*, and turned his back on it. Oddly fascinating as it was, I had to agree that its relevance was somewhat questionable, so I let it go.

By unspoken agreement we committed ourselves to opening as many doors as possible until we found something useful, and we spread out along the corridor. I went through a succession of portals rather quickly, and found behind them the following: an opulent bedchamber with a four-poster bed, its walls crusted with bright jewels; a square, featureless room flooded with steaming water, and filled with the scents of flowers; an apothecary's shop in a state of disarray, half of its contents strewn all over the floor; some kind of closet containing about seventy examples of the same ruffled dress, in seventy different colours; and a tiny conservatory crammed with nara trees, though each one bore fruits of different shapes.

'I feel like we have ended up in Galy's cupboard of ideas,' I said to Pense as I passed him.

'Likely,' he agreed. 'What would yours look like, given physical form?'

'Half empty, probably. With statues of you all over the place.' I was childish enough to stick out my tongue at him. For this sally and its accompanying gesture I received a dig in the ribs and a kiss. Not a bad prize.

We went on, calling out our finds as we discovered them. I found a garden; a dark copse of mostly dead trees; a pit full of sand the colour of blood; a bubble of golden light and a room full of silver pipes all playing themselves at once. And, marvellously, a glade with a single tree, tall beyond belief, its trunk set with little doors and windows all the way up as though somebody lived within.

Meriall and Ny found a pool of pink water; a room full of sheets of parchment, all blank; an adjacent chamber full of broken pens; what looked like the inside of an egg, empty; and, alarmingly, a sheer drop into nothing.

Pense and Gio's finds ranged from kitchens and dining chambers and other such mundanities through to an infinite expanse of stars and a cluster of spheres oddly suspended in mid-air, each one crowned with a miniature palace.

All of this interested me more than I can say, and I wanted to explore every single room (except for the sheer drop). But none of it bore anything that appeared to hold any relevance, either to the vision we had previously received or to anything Galy might reasonably be expected to tell us. It was all enchantingly, but frustratingly, random.

'Galy?' I called again as I closed a purple crystal door upon a small mountain of glittering gems. Ny passed by at that moment and wedged his tail in between the door and its frame, preventing me from closing it fully. His eyes lit up with avarice. *I like this one*, he informed me.

I nudged his tail out of the way with my foot. 'You can't have them.'

Why not?

'Because they are Galy's.' I shut the door.

He invited us here. He wants me to have them! They are a gift!

'They probably aren't real.'

You don't know that! The food was real!

I shrugged that off. 'Shoo. We have work to do.'

Llandry! Open the door!

I refused, and Ny gave up the point eventually, albeit with very poor grace.

As he turned away, though, I noticed that his scales glittered oddly.

'Ny.'

He stopped, and I went closer to examine him. 'Your scales are diamonds,' I said faintly.

They were unmistakeably so, black diamonds cut somehow into scaled shapes and laid over his hide like a coat. Then a mantle of gold and purple gems materialised over his shoulders, a crown of jewels encircled his head, and his claws turned to dark, glittering emeralds.

See, said Ny smugly. *I knew they were for me.*

This sign of Galy's presence both reassured and troubled me, for should he be able to alter *us* with the same ease with which he Changed the Library around us? Had he, or was it just an illusion? I surreptitiously checked my own hands, in case my fingernails had turned into mother-of-pearl or something.

They hadn't (slightly to my disappointment). I *did* notice, however, that arrows had appeared on the floor, pointing back down the corridor behind me.

I turned.

What *was* a long, straight corridor had now sprouted about a hundred new passages which went in a hundred different directions. (All right, I am exaggerating, but it might as well have been a thousand for all that we could expect to navigate that mess.) Worse, they shifted as I watched, swapping places, closing up only to open again in another spot, drifting up heavenwards or swooping away into the floor… it was dizzying.

The arrows led straight into the heart of the chaos.

I sighed, squared my shoulders, and set off. 'You couldn't make it any easier, could you Galy?' I asked, without much hope.

About three of the corridors obediently winked out. The rest writhed, if anything, more furiously than before.

'Good try,' I sighed.

Pense caught up with me and captured my hand, and we followed the arrow trail together, Ny and Gio and Meri falling in behind us. The arrows led into a passageway that soared skywards, and continued to do so even as we trudged up it. Its walls were translucent, and through them we could see the deep darkness of the sky outside, and the faint twinkle of its many stars. It was quiet, deeply so. The *clink* of Nyden's bejewelled scales was all I heard, for our feet made no sound upon the floor.

At the distant end of the passage, there was a single, black door. It was perfectly round, with a large handle set into the centre.

Walking wasn't getting us any closer to it. If anything, the door was growing farther away with every step we took. The corridor stretched, and the door all but disappeared from sight.

'Galy!' I said sharply, for I felt an almost palpable sense of fear. The walls pulsed and shivered with it. What was happening to him, that he was so afraid? Was that why he had been unresponsive before? He was in some kind of danger, I felt sure of it, but what could we do?

The door shrank almost to nothing — but then rushed back towards us with alarming speed. The floor buckled at the same moment, all but throwing us at it.

Pense got the door open, and we fell through it.

It slammed shut behind us with an echoing *boom.*

After such tension, I expected to find something remarkable and probably dramatic on the other side. Instead, we found a dull peace and thoroughly unprepossessing surroundings. The room we were in could even have been called bland.

It looked like somebody's office. A large desk of uninteresting design dominated one wall, its surface stacked with books and papers and objects I had no name for. The rest of the place was so dull I can scarcely remember the details.

Things got a little more interesting when Ny barrelled through into the too-small space and crashed into said desk, smashing it to pieces. The office hastily reformed to accommodate his bulk, but not before he had managed to polish off the chair and part of the wall, too. The noise he made suggested that the disaster came attended by a fair amount of pain for him, and I winced. Ny, though, lay in an inert heap upon the rapidly-expanding floor, giggling.

Oops, he cackled.

'Stop wrecking Galy's stuff, Ny,' said Meriall grouchily. She was nursing a grazed elbow, and her forehead had apparently come into contact with something solid, too.

I took a look around to make sure that Pense and Gio had made it through without incident, which they had. The sense of danger had completely receded, and in the quiet and apparent calm I was able to calm a little myself. We all took a moment to breathe.

Then it was time to explore.

It took little time to establish that the office really was as boring as it appeared. All the books were unreadable and so were the papers, which disappointed me a little. How could we expect to find out anything if all the clues were illegible or written in some language none of us speaks? Even Gio was no help there, merely returning a helpless shrug when asked to investigate.

So we abandoned the office in short order. The door we had fallen through proved to have quietly unmade itself, but another had appeared opposite. We followed it, with some caution. I have no doubt that Galy means us no harm, but it is also clear that he is not wholly in control of the situation here. Or even of himself.

We went through a number of similarly featureless corridors and rooms — I won't bore you with the details, they were thoroughly uninteresting. Eventually these gave way to some labs, which were not very interesting either.

Then we rounded a corner and ran into another person, the first we had seen since entering the maze of officy dullness. A Lokant, male, relatively young. He wore a blue coat and carried some indecipherable object, which he was referring to with such absorption that he did not appear to notice the group bearing down upon him.

Not that there was anywhere for us to go to escape him. He looked up a moment later and I braced myself for interrogation. But to my relief, he seemed as oblivious to our presence as all the others we had seen. He looked straight through us, staring into the distance in a thoughtful fashion, before returning to whatever it was he carried.

I saw his face, and almost had a heart attack.

'That's *Krays*,' I choked out. And it was, undoubtedly, even though I had known him as an elderly man and this was a much younger version of him. His features were unmistakeable.

Pense had not made the connection, for his brows contracted in surprise. As Krays walked past him, Pense wheeled about and pursued him down the corridor, circling, scrutinising everything about him. It was a menacing attitude, not least because Pense was primarily responsible for the eventual demise of the real Krays.

The Krays-ghost — or dream, or whatever he was — vanished around a corner and Pense came back.

'It is him,' he reported.

'I wonder where he is going,' said Meriall.

'Let's follow him!' said Ny enthusiastically.

'Yes, let's,' I agreed, and we did. Gio said nothing, and his silence struck me as odd. I watched him trailing down the corridor after Pense, who strode out decisively in pursuit of Krays. Gio's expression was so impassive, I couldn't help wondering what he was hiding behind it. He must have *some* feelings or thoughts about the appearance of someone like Krays, but he showed nothing.

We caught up with Krays and kept pace behind him. It felt odd, openly following him like that. He really looked solid, like a real person. There was nothing about his appearance to suggest that he was only a vision, so I couldn't shake the feeling that he would realise we were there any moment and challenge us.

He did not, of course. He walked down so many corridors, I wondered how he could possibly remember his way around. But he barely heeded his environment, so at home was he. We all passed so many doors I soon lost count, but he showed no interest in any of them until, at last, he stopped before a large set of double doors made of some kind of metal. He looked at them and they opened, without his even touching them. Through he went, and we followed.

Beyond lay a massive, domed chamber, a sudden and surprising change from the featureless offices. For a moment I could barely see, for I was struck by such a tumult of chaotic energies that my external senses were blinded by it. *Amasku*, purer and richer in character than I have ever before experienced. The place was drowning in it, but it was not as chaotic as I had initially thought. There was a structure to its pattern, infinitely complex. I was dazzled. I have only known its flows in the Off-Worlds, where they have been so long disordered I suppose we have never known how it ought to feel.

Or how it ought to *behave*.

When my other senses returned, I found I had eyes for nothing but what dominated the centre: the carcass of a huge draykon.

At least, I thought it was a carcass at first. It looked half-decayed, its gleaming indigo bones exposed in some areas and covered by muscle and flesh and glittering golden scales in others. I stared in confusion at the flurry of activity around it. Many other Lokants were at work in here, doing something completely inexplicable to the poor creature. Given its semi-skeletal state I could not help assuming that they were disassembling it, and my stomach turned over.

'They are harvesting its bones,' I said, horrified.

But Pense stared at it with a deep frown upon his face, and finally shook his head. 'They are not, I think,' he said softly.

Ny took to the air. There was enough room in that place for him to fly, even with all his bulk. The chamber was certainly made to accommodate draykoni proportions. We watched in dumb silence as he flew over to the creature and circled it.

'Are they... *adding* to it?' said Meriall at last.

'Yes, exactly,' said Gio, surprising me, for he had not spoken since we had tumbled through that strange black door into the first office. 'They are adding to it. Or in other words, building it.'

His tone was a trifle condescending, but we cared not for the implied slight upon our comprehension, for we were too thunderstruck by his words.

Of *course* they were building it. That seemed obvious, now that it had been pointed out. My heart twisted in excitement. We were in the centre of the Library of Orlind, and here was a vision of perhaps the most important moment in its history — perhaps even the history of the Seven Realms as a whole.

The first draykoni were being designed and constructed *right here*. And that was surreal. If I was uncomfortable before with the idea that my race — *both* my races — had been conceived of and created by some other species, I was appalled at seeing the proof of it before my eyes. And also fascinated, and awed. What kinds of people were Lokants, that they could do such things? I was forcibly reminded of how little we really know about them.

Krays's presence here both interested and bothered me. I hadn't previously known that he was involved in this project at all.

'Forgive me if I'm being impertinently curious,' said Meriall, drifting closer to me. 'But who is Krays, why are we following him and why does it matter that he is here?'

'Krays is the person who caused all the trouble a few moons ago,' I told her. 'He was behind the return of the draykoni, and everything that happened because of it. He wanted to restore the Library of Orlind, the Master Library, so he could control all the other Lokant Libraries.'

There came a ripple in the air as I spoke and a kind of… *buzzing*, not a sound but a palpable sensation in my bones. It felt like anger, or frustration, but it was gone before I could decide.

Meriall pursed her lips. 'Was he indeed? I might like to shake his hand.'

'You can't, he is dead. Pense ate him.'

Meriall blinked. 'Oh.'

'Anyway, a lot of people died because of his actions.' I felt a surprising flicker of anger towards Meriall, that she could behave like Krays deserved to be congratulated for his efforts. He had acted out of ambition and selfishness and with a ruthless disregard for anybody else's wellbeing. How could she applaud him?

'And for that, he can never be condemned enough,' said Meriall. 'But nonetheless, we are all here because of him. Not everything that came of his deeds was bad.'

I sighed, and rubbed at my forehead. A headache was threatening to emerge. I didn't like the line of thinking Meriall was taking. Everything started with a spate of murders over the draykon bone, and culminated in a war that destroyed half of my home city. Yes, I had also rediscovered my heritage and come to know Pense as a result of the same things, but even so. How could I do otherwise but wish it all undone? It was almost like saying it was worth all those people's deaths just so I could have better wings and a mate. I felt deeply uncomfortable.

There are more. Ny's voice broke in upon my musings, shattering my train of thought. I wasn't sorry. I felt him signalling off to the left, from the far side of the vast chamber. Krays had gone that way, too, and we had been steadily drifting in that general direction. We picked up our pace and hurried after Nyden, trying to ignore the crowds of busy Lokants we passed through. It is really the strangest feeling, walking through clusters of people like that and having them act like you aren't there at all.

Several big, double doors lined the curve of the far wall, all of them thrown open. A glance revealed that each one led to chambers identical to the one we were in, and each contained another partially-constructed draykon. I saw a crimson one, a deep forest green, a silvery one and a violet-hued, all differing in size, and wondered what the intention might have been behind the variety of colours.

What interested me still more was the variation in design of each creature. The golden draykon looked fairly familiar to me: its pointed snout, slender build, wing shape and coiling tail all resembled my own, nearly enough. But these others were vastly different. One had only two legs. Another had a stockier frame and a rounded, blunt snout. A third had no wings and looked more proficient at swimming than flying, all sleek contours and undulating curves. I stared in wonder at this array, mesmerised, because here was a creative process that I recognised. I was a jeweller, once, before all this madness upturned my life. The process of experimentation, of trying design after design until you arrive at the optimum combination, was so familiar to me.

Pense had gone after Krays. I keep a little part of my mind fixed upon him at all times, when we are together, and so I still did in spite of my distraction. So when Pense got upset, I knew about it at once.

'Trouble,' I said tightly, and grabbed Meri and Gio. I had no idea where Ny had gone, but no matter, there was no time to worry about him now. I dragged the others after me as I dashed in Pense's direction. If he was in danger, he might need all of us to help him.

It wasn't until we got closer that I realised there was no fear in the feelings I was sensing from him. Urgency, yes, but nothing to justify the extent of my alarm. I do get oversensitive about Pense, I suppose.

We found him three chambers farther along, watching as Krays argued heatedly with another Lokant, in a ripple of words I could not understand. The other person was Galywis. Whatever the cause of their dispute, they were both incensed by it. Poor Galy was shaking with fury.

This room was smaller than the others, and rather bare. Its walls were covered in an odd display that reminded me of the genealogy trees in Limbane's Library, though this was composed mostly of figures and anatomical drawings of draykon-like creatures. They changed as I glanced at them, as though the ideas behind them were being adjusted as I watched. They were oddly reminiscent of the bulletin boards back home.

The room felt different. The *amasku* here lacked the perfect order I had sensed everywhere else. Something was deeply amiss with it. It bristled and spiked in my mind, making my skin shiver, turning my stomach nauseous. I thought back a little, remembering the collapse of the draykon whose body we had briefly inhabited, and shuddered. I could well believe that the effects of this kind of energy, so broken and disordered, could be catastrophic.

We received visual proof of this in short order.

It began with a distant roar, a tortured sound which instantly captured the attention of everybody in the room. Even Krays and Galywis stopped shouting at one another. They froze in place, eyes locked in mutual horror.

If anything, their reaction frightened me more than the sound itself.

Galywis breathed something that could only be a curse, and he and Krays leapt into action. There was a heavy metal bar upon the door which I had not noticed before. Krays ran for it and slammed the bar into place, barricading himself and Galy against whatever approached. Galy meanwhile ran around the walls in a strange frenzy, staring at the shifting diagrams with intense dismay. They shifted and changed themselves more and more quickly as he passed by them, writhing through formations like wild things.

The roar sounded again, much closer this time. The walls shook with it. Fear hit me so hard I could hardly breathe. I knew that whatever might occur was unlikely to affect me, for we were clearly lost in some kind of vision. Nonetheless the growing panic was palpable and we all felt it. Pense rushed for me, stationing himself directly before me as though he would repel all threats by bodily force alone. Meri and Gio backed up until they hit a wall and stayed that way, eyes wide. Gio was shaking.

Krays's barring of the door, though a sensible enough thought in itself, proved useless in the end because the draykon came through the *wall.* That roar sounded again from mere feet away, so loud and tortured that my ears threatened to shatter and my heart twisted in my chest with fear and compassion because that was a draykon call, deranged with some kind of pain I could not understand. I only sensed that it was intolerable, that the only possible cause was madness.

Then a huge section of the wall crumbled into pieces and a draykon crashed into view, a female. Greenish coloured, not one that we had seen before. She was only partially built, for patches of her hide were missing and her inner flesh shone through, ropes of muscle and gleaming bones beneath. What there was of her hide was ripped and torn and bruised by her insane, destructive progress through the Library but she did not appear to notice or care about the damage she was doing to herself.

In fact, I fear it was worse than that. It would have been easy to assume that the maddened rampage was intentionally destructive, that she was trying to destroy either the Library or the people in it or both. But she was so crazed with pain, I felt that she was scarcely aware of her surroundings. It was *herself* she was attempting to destroy, ripping herself to pieces upon anything she encountered.

Everybody scattered. Krays and Galy got the barred door open again and vanished through it at a dead run, barely in time to avoid being crushed by the poor maddened draykon as she barrelled, unstoppable, through the room and crashed through the opposite wall. Gio and Meri ducked out of the way, an instinctive movement in the face of such a rush of oncoming fury.

The draykon disappeared from view. All that remained was the noise of continued destruction, interspersed with her cries of pain and fury. Both rapidly grew fainter as she receded.

I exchanged long, appalled looks with Pense and Meri. Nobody spoke.

Then, as one, we wheeled and ran after the tormented draykon.

By the time we caught up with her, they had brought her down. She lay thrashing in the middle of a pile of rubble, her poor body riddled with long metal spears. The machines that had fired the barbs were stationed nearby, but I had noticed them only peripherally before. It was not until later that it occurred to me how significant their presence was. These people were prepared for this kind of madness. It had happened before.

The draykon was screaming, and oh, it was far, far worse than her earlier rage. I felt her pain — probably only an echo of what she was feeling, but it was enough to crush the air out of me. My muscles turned to water and I fell, sweat pouring off me as every part of my body rebelled at once.

Then she died.

The pain stopped, leaving me breathless and trembling. I got to my feet carefully, unsure if my jellied legs would hold me. There was an awful silence, heavy upon the air, and people moved sluggishly if at all.

'*What* just happened,' said Meriall shakily. She was hanging on to Gio. They were hanging on to each other, looking as shaken as I felt.

I found Pense and clutched him. We both needed comfort after that, and for a while we simply held each other. 'I don't know,' I said at last, though I had some small idea. That complex, perfectly ordered *amasku* had warped like buckled metal around the crazed draykon as she flew, as though her very presence corrupted it more and more by the second. Or vice versa. Or both?

Was this how such corruption occurred? Was it the madness of the draykoni that bled into it, changed it, broke it? Or was it the other way around? Did they corrupt each other?

But how had such madness occurred? And why was it that the Lokants who had created such a beautiful creature were so well prepared to destroy her, too? I watched as the people of the Library picked themselves up, set about rectifying some of the mess she had made, and removed the corpse. The process was a swift one, well-ordered, as though they had done it several times before. Probably they had.

I remembered something I had heard from Galywis once before — a few moons previously, when we had stood in the ruined Library of Orlind in the presence of the real Galywis, when he was whole and sound and still a separate being from the Library. The project to create the draykoni had been his, and I could the better believe it now that I had seen him at work upon it.

He had talked of merging the Library of Orlind with the energies of our world, and steeping the first draykoni in the latter, as though they were fruit and the *amasku* wine. *Up to the eyeballs,* he said. *It changed their brains.*

It changed their brains.

The process had ultimately been a great success, for it had

spawned a race of beings whose mastery over their surroundings was virtually absolute. I should say *our*, for I am one such, strange as it can still seem at times. But what if that same process sent some of them insane? It was a circular state, if true. Their own madness polluted the energies that filled them, twisted it until its presence was pure, screaming agony, and that sent them further insane until all they could do was destroy themselves in their urgency to escape it.

The thought makes me shake so badly I can hardly hold my pen.

We were not given long to reflect upon any of this, for the vision vanished in a whirl of colour and a different scene shimmered into view. A greenhouse, remarkably large and soaring to impressive heights overhead. Flourishing greenery covered most of the clear glass walls, and I saw neat, compact trees everywhere, heavily laden with fruits both familiar and strange. The air was pleasantly warm, and smelled delicious.

I realised with a frisson of surprise that I had been there before, the last time I had visited the Library. Back when it was still on Orlind, and Galywis was still the Master there (albeit deranged). This was *his* greenhouse, his beloved fruit trees. I could picture him, standing in the little clearing in the centre, delightedly offering us an armful of fruits.

I relayed this to Meriall and Gio — noting in passing that Ny still had not reappeared. What had become of him? I tried to sense him but he was nowhere nearby.

I was on my way to Pense when he abruptly faded away. So did the others. I spun, heart pounding, looking for any sign of where they had gone, but... nothing. I could neither see nor sense them.

I was alone.

My muscles moved of their own accord. I slouched slightly, my shoulders rounding, and I began to fidget, like I couldn't bear to stand still. My head turned this way and that, eyes darting anxiously, alert for any sign of intrusion. I have never been paranoid like that, never stood or behaved like that — what was happening? I could feel my heart racing in my chest as I strained to override whatever had taken control of my limbs, but I could not.

Sorry, said Galy's voice in my head. He said more, a muddled garble of faint, barely audible, haphazardly spilled syllables which

I could not comprehend. His voice rose with a growing urgency as he desperately tried to communicate, but I could understand nothing. Time seemed to freeze around me as he struggled to make himself heard; the air grew heavy and still, and nothing moved.

'Galy,' I said at last, speaking low. 'Calm. I cannot hear you, you must show me.'

Well, he did. The strange sensation of suspension faded, colours brightened again and my mind snapped to alertness. I tried to accept the loss of my autonomy, forced myself to relax. It was petrifying to lose control of my own body, but at least it was Galy — he could mean me no harm.

I retained this comforting belief for a good two minutes. When I heard a quick footstep behind me, I tried to turn, but too late. Arms wrapped around me, strong and paralysing, crushing me so hard I could not breathe. I struggled ferociously, but I was too tightly held to escape.

I felt the cold touch of sharp metal against my throat. A line of fire blossomed there; blood flowed in a shocking, hot flood. My limbs weakened all at once, strength flowing out of me with the blood that poured down my chest, soaking my shirt.

I barely felt myself collapse as the arms released me, leaving me to fold limply to the floor. Vision faded and I knew no more.

I was not dead, of course, or how could I write this account? But so convincing was the charade that I was surprised to wake, an unknowable time later, sprawled still upon the floor of Galy's greenhouse. I flexed my limbs experimentally, and was relieved to find that they responded once more. Shaking and nauseated, I climbed to my feet, sweating with the remembered horror of apparent death.

Or rather, murder. I was *murdered* a little while ago. And yet, I was alive. Was it my own death I had experienced, a future event yet to happen? Was Galy trying to warn me? The prospect shook me so badly I could not breathe, couldn't think, couldn't stand still. I paced frantically as panic rose, gulping desperately for air the moment my throat ceased to constrict.

'Minchu.' Ah, the blessed relief of Pense's voice as he found me at last and swept me up in his arms, squeezing me almost as tightly as those terrible arms had moments before. This embrace, though, was welcome. I buried my face in his shoulder and waited for the panic to pass, confident now that it would.

Pense was shaking, too, almost as violently as I was.

'Did someone cut your throat, a minute ago?' I asked him when I could speak.

He nodded grimly. 'I died. Did you?'

I nodded in reply. We stared at each other, and I saw my own fears reflected in his eyes.

'Well,' came Meriall's voice. 'That was easily the worst thing that's ever happened to me.'

I looked round, relieved to see both she and Gio returned. Ny, too. They looked about as delighted with recent events as I felt.

'Either we are all going to die,' said Gio blandly, 'Or something else is afoot here.'

That was true. It was certainly possible that we could all be murdered in the same way, but not especially likely.

I remembered the way my posture had changed, my movements subtly altered, my behaviour so different from my own.

'I think we were Galy,' I said in a whisper. I could barely speak, because if I was right, we had experienced Galywis's death and that meant...

'Galy,' I called softly. 'Are you alive?'

Silence. And then, mournfully and so softly I could barely hear him, *Sorry*.

Tears sprang to my eyes. 'Oh, Galy,' I sighed. He was an odd, odd soul, the strangest person I have ever known. Quite mad, not a scrap of sanity remaining, and as a Master Librarian I could not doubt that he had taken decisions in his life that I would find questionable. But I had known him only as a lonely old man, doggedly devoted to his self-appointed task of guarding his precious Library, and capable of both a surprising enthusiasm for little, bright things and a disarming sweetness in trying to share them with us.

Someone had murdered him — cut his poor throat and left him to bleed out on the floor of his own Library. Why?

And did they know that his mind had survived, if his body had not? Did they realise that he and the Library were now one and the same?

We were subdued in the wake of this news, though Galy was

not. I sensed a growing urgency from him, at odds with his more buoyant behaviour of the previous day. Something had happened to him, I felt sure. Had there been a threat to the Library, while we worked our way through the corridor of doors? Whatever it was, he was anxious and eager and I was not surprised when his greenhouse dissolved around us as soon as we had deciphered his message.

I could make little sense of what followed, though. We were in a laboratory, watching as young-Krays and a Lokant woman I had never seen before worked together on a project we could discern nothing about. We saw Krays and the same woman arguing about something, presumably many years later, for they both appeared rather older. But the substance of their conversation was impossible to understand, for they spoke rapidly, and in a tongue which I could only half comprehend.

A bare, white-walled room filled my mind, featureless and empty save for a fully constructed draykon skeleton stretched upon the floor, its bones yet to flare with life.

A laboratory again, and a machine of some kind set upon a table. It looked vaguely familiar to me. A split second later it exploded, and a flurry of metal shards flew across my vision.

Then a succession of draykoni replaced the laboratory, all fully-formed and of the shape and proportions I was familiar with. Not partially completed creatures, these, or early test projects; they were finished, hale and alive. But we saw little coherence. It was more like flicking through Galywis's mental catalogue of the beasts, contextless and confusing. I scarcely had time to note anything significant about each draykon, save for their general size and colour. Steel-blue, carmine, ochre, night black, cerulean, violet, cinnabar, cream, russet, maroon... so many, and so fast. At length Galy either came to the end of his inexplicable list or he lost his concentration, and it was over.

Then, suddenly, *everything* was over. The air grew heavy with panic, and I heard Galy babbling crazily in my mind. I could understand nothing of what he said, not a single word, which frustrated me because I have no doubt that it was *important*.

He gave up with a scream of despair, a raw sound which tore my heart in two. The walls convulsed around us, pulsing in a way that was oddly like... well, it seemed like...

All right, I cannot find a graceful way to express this. The Library of Orlind retched around us and vomited us forth. We were expelled from its confines in a violent surge of energy, propelled some distance through mid-air before we finally hit the ground, hard.

I lay, dazed and aching, in what felt like soft moss. Pense was nearby, I sensed him close. A slightly pained turn of my head brought Meriall and Gio into view, lying sprawled but apparently whole a few feet away.

Nyden was a dark, inert mountain of flesh somewhat beyond. I was grateful that he had not landed upon any of us in the chaos of our involuntary departure.

We were somewhere in Iskyr, I judged. Two suns hung in the sky, and a dewy golden light bathed the glissenwol forest we had come out in. The sight of those towering trunks and broad mushroom caps soothed me a little, for they looked so reminiscent of Waeverleyne, my home.

A flicker of movement caught my eye, and I sat up, briefly repentant of doing so when bruised muscles pulled. I saw a building half-concealed among the trees, a slim tower with too many windows, an oversized and crooked roof and altogether too many colours daubing its walls. If its appearance wasn't peculiar enough, its behaviour certainly was, for it was fleeing into the distance.

On *legs*.

I watched it disappear, blinking, wondering whether I had hit my head in the fall and was now hallucinating. But no, of course I was not. That was the Library of Orlind vanishing into the trees, crashing into a sapling in its haste and almost toppling it. Galy had either completed his objective in absconding with us, then, or he had grown so spooked that he had lost his wits and fled.

The legs were a strange touch, but Galy was odd like that. He might be a building now, but he had been a Lokant for centuries, with ordinary limbs. If he wanted to move around in his new state, perhaps his befuddled mind would naturally reach for the familiar tools for doing so.

Meriall sat up. 'Is that... the Library?' she said faintly.

'Mhm,' I said.

'And is the Library legging it, in a more literal sense than one would expect a building to be capable of?'

'Looks that way.'

Meriall blinked, twice, and then lay back down in the moss.

'It's possible that I need more sleep,' she mumbled. 'I am not at all sure that my wits haven't been permanently disordered.'

Gio just sat, gazing after the Library long after it had vanished from sight. He caught my eye, and gave me that flickering, sardonic smile of his.

'What do you make of all of this?' I asked him.

He shrugged and stood up. I did so, too, encouraged by the hand Pense reached out to assist me. I hurt, there was no denying it. I hurt in lots of places.

Much as I appreciate Galy's efforts, I cannot help wishing that he had managed to eject us just a *mite* more gently once he had finished.

'It's a riddle,' Gio said after a thoughtful pause. 'As to what it means, your guess is as good as mine.'

'Great.' I was unable to suppress a sigh. It was ungracious of me, perhaps, but I had been hoping that Gio's presence would be of more use to us. He was, after all, the only Lokant member of our involuntary little company. He had offered one or two useful insights, but had ultimately contributed little. He had barely even *talked*. He was a silent presence, following us around, sharing nothing of whatever his thoughts might be. True, he had done nothing to justifiably draw suspicion to himself, but nor had he done anything to earn our trust.

Nyden still hadn't moved. Pense and I went over to check on him, but he was out cold, oblivious to our presence. I bent over his head, murmuring something both soothing and wakefulness-inducing (or so I hoped) and lightly touched his face.

Pense grabbed a stick and poked him with it.

'Ow,' whined Nyden, his scaled hide twitching mightily. 'Stop that.'

'You were unconscious,' said Pense.

'I was not.' Nyden was indignant as he rose, swaying, to his four legs and shook himself. 'I was *tired*, and this moss is deliciously soft. I think I want some at home.'

Pense jabbed him with the stick again, earning himself a reproachful look. 'Where were you these past few hours, anyway?'

'Nosing around,' said Nyden, punctuating this comment with a jaunty thrust of his undeniably pointy muzzle into the air. 'Did you know there is a hot spring in the Library? It was *almost* big enough for bathing, even for me.'

Pense sighed, and shoved his hands into his pockets. It is a gesture he picked up from Tren, I think, but he only does it when he is annoyed or dejected. 'Good to have you with us, Ny,' he muttered.

I helped Meriall up and conducted a quick, covert assessment of everybody's state of health. Ny was right, the moss was deep and soft, but Galy had hurled us forth pretty hard. We were stiff and hurting but we were sound, so I turned my attention to the next problem.

'Galy's afraid,' I said. 'And dead. Sort of. And the corruption of Orlind is spreading and a lot of draykoni are dead and maybe more are that we don't know about and maybe some more will be if we don't do something soon.'

Not my most eloquent speech, to be sure. I received nearly identical puzzled looks from the others.

'Agreed,' said Pense after a moment.

I rubbed at my forehead, feeling tired. I had no idea how long we had been stuck in the Library more specifically than *too long*, and it was an exhausting experience trying to keep up with it. I felt disoriented at suddenly being released, and completely confused by everything that had happened. 'What does it all *mean?*' I said at last in frustration. 'Everything is a mess and Galy's chosen us to solve it but we have no idea what he has been trying to say.'

'Nonsense,' said Meriall stoutly. 'With five good brains between us, I am sure we can figure it out. Let's think. What are the connections between a stack of uncharacteristically lifeless draykon corpses, a ballroom of Lokant ghosts, a library full of unreadable books, the spreading corruption of Orlind, an orchard of nara fruit, mad draykoni prototypes and that nutter they call Krays?'

'Don't forget watching a draykon die from the *inside*,' said Gio.

'And the corridor of doors to everywhere,' added Pense.

And being brutally murdered, put in Ny, and added brightly, *That was fun!*

'Yes, the death of Galywis,' I said, frowning. 'Why would anybody kill him? They must have been trying to get at the Library, surely.'

Gio nodded. 'It always did attract that kind of attention. Powerful things do.'

Powerful things.

'All right, so somebody wants the Library,' I suggested. 'Much like Krays did. He probably isn't the only Lokant alive who would like to step into Galy's old shoes as the Master.'

'It did occur to me,' said Meriall in a careful tone, 'that Krays's story is perhaps not over.'

I stared at her. 'What? It has to be. He was *eaten*.'

'Yes,' she said patiently. 'And I have no doubt that dear Pensould did an admirable job of digesting him. But he was not working alone, was he?'

I was struck with two impressions: horror at the idea that killing Krays himself might not have been enough to destroy the ambitious projects he had been pursuing, and annoyance at myself for failing to imagine the possibility sooner.

So. Here we are again, facing a complicated problem, with the shadowy presences of Limbane and Krays looming. The total absence of one and the death of the other *might* be reason enough to believe them uninvolved, but... I tend to doubt it. Lokants are tricky like that.

'Krays was the Lokantor of a Library called Sulayn Phay,' I said with a sigh. 'An entire Library. You are right, it is by no means impossible that they are intent upon carrying through his plans even without him.'

'They probably have a new Lokantor, by now,' Gio offered.

I looked at him for a moment. 'Those draykoni they were building. The genealogy charts, Gio. We need to see them.'

Pense gave me one of his watchful looks. 'Do you have an idea, Minchu?'

'Maybe. I need to see the charts.'

Gio looked more trapped than eager to help, which was disappointing. 'Ah...' he said. 'All right, I will see what I can do to arrange that.'

I opened my mouth, but had no chance to harangue him further. He pulled Eva's trick, which is to say that he looked intent for a moment and then vanished.

That Lokant thing. He just *thought* himself to somewhere else, or something. I have no idea how it works, but Eva can do it with about as much difficulty as breathing. Or so it appears.

'Bye then,' said Meriall.

'We won't wait for him,' I decided. 'Who knows how long he will be, and I am not comfortable about standing around here for too long.' We had no idea where we were, but Galy-as-Library had passed through not long since, and whatever was plaguing him might not be too far away. 'We need to go home and see Ori. He's had plenty of time to read those books by now, and he might have found something. Gio will catch up with us there.'

I was a little bit surprised — and secretly, pleased — by the way everybody agreed with the plan and willingly fell in with it. Admittedly, I wasn't sure how much Ny was even listening, Pense tends to back me up whatever I do, and Meriall would have been highly in favour of any plan which involved going home, getting a bath and her idea of "proper" food. Nonetheless, I felt decisive and resolute and maybe, just a little bit, in charge.

It felt good.

Before we left, though, I was briefly distracted by something else: a note of disturbance in the energy in that part of Iskyr. Nothing too severe or too striking, just a ripple of unpromising potential somewhere beneath the surface... it might be nothing, but I note it here just in case.

It wasn't until much later that I thought again about the vision of the mad draykon, and the way she had been brought down by her creators. They had merely shot her with spears and dragged the carcass away — killed her, in other words, by mundane means. It was a death she ought to have been able to revive from, if such a feat was already feasible in those early days.

If Lokants knew of a way to permanently destroy her, why had they not used it then? Had they had some reason to refrain, or was my theory nonsense? Perhaps that telling *almost* from Limbane meant nothing after all. Perhaps he and all his kind were as ignorant as I was, and had nothing to do with this mystery.

The idea is a depressing one, for it threatens to set me back to the beginning. But I don't feel inclined to dismiss the idea. Something about it makes sense, on a fundamental level I cannot explain. I don't yet know how or why, but I feel certain that, once again, the separate fates of draykoni and Lokantkind are still very much intertwined.

10 VIII
Ori is Enlightened, and Also Hopping Mad.
I Learn That I am the World's Worst Person.
And Gio Whisks us Away.

We were in the Library for *days*. Eleven of them, to be precise. How that was possible, I have no idea. We slept only once, and if I had to guess I would have called it two at most.

That said, time does move oddly in the Libraries. I may have assumed that wouldn't apply to Orlind anymore, considering how broken it is, but perhaps it does. In a broken way. Usually time passes slowly in those places, if at all. I have never heard of an accelerated passage of time before.

Anyway, we went home. Tired and worried and eleven days late.

Ori was unhappy with us.

'Where have you *been*?' he bellowed the moment Pense and I entered our house. 'I have been going *crazy* wondering what happened to you! Everyone was certain you'd been murdered and buried a million miles away and we would never know what became of you! How could you stay away for eleven days without TELLING me! Or taking me with you! It's bloody unfair! Sigwide agrees, don't you, Siggy? He wants you and he hates me for not being you and we both hate you right now.' Ori finally exhausted his flow of words and stood in the middle of

136

my living room, dishevelled and furious. He clutched handfuls of his hair in shaking fists and shuddered violently, taking great gulps of air. 'I thought you were *dead!*'

I had been frozen, shocked by this tirade from sunny Ori. But this sign of suffering melted me and I ran to him, throwing my arms around him in a huge, engulfing hug. 'I am so sorry,' I said into his shoulder. 'We did not mean to, I promise. We'll tell you all about it, but we are well, no one is hurt, and no one is dead. Well,' I amended, 'at least, not one of us.'

That may not have been the wisest speech I have ever made, especially that last part. Curse my thoughtless tongue. Ori had relaxed fractionally as I held him but he stiffened again and stared at me. 'Llan,' he said dangerously, 'I think you'd better tell me everything, and at once.'

So we did. Pense and Ori and I flopped tiredly all over my floor, making full use of the colony of cushions Ori had assembled in there, and we went through the story as quickly as possible. Ori being Ori, he soon forgot his fear and his anger and drank up every detail of our tale, asking many questions I could not answer and thinking much more deeply about the implications of it all than we had had time or energy to do.

Somewhere in the middle, Siggy crept in. I'd been aware of his presence from the moment I entered the house; he was a tiny bundle of warmth in the next room, tucked up peacefully asleep. Or so I had thought. I'd opted to leave him in peace while I tended to Ori, but I regretted that the moment he came into the room, for a sorrier picture of woe I have never seen. He tiptoed up to me as though unsure of his welcome, head and tail drooping, and stood waiting for me to acknowledge him.

I have never felt like a worse person in my entire life. Even Ori's fear was nothing compared to my poor Siggy's utter wretchedness.

I stopped speaking at once, unable to form another word, and scooped him up in my arms. He would not speak to me, though I apologised in seven different ways and soothed him every way that I knew how. He, too, had been so certain I would never come back that he had disappeared far into grief. His normally silky grey fur was dull and coarse and falling out in patches, and he was rail-thin — I wondered when he had last eaten.

In leaving him behind, I had thought I was doing right by

him — keeping him out of danger, letting his aging bones rest peacefully at home while I dashed madly about. I had never meant to be away so long, but my intentions made no difference to Sigwide.

I resolved on the spot, never to leave him behind again. Better he take his chances with me than I keep abandoning him, as he saw it, and leaving him in so unhappy a state.

Tears coated my cheeks and I hadn't noticed. I am unsure whether it was just poor Siggy, or Ori's fear and Galy's death and everything else that had happened all hitting me at last. I had a cry for a while, and Ori wept a bit and everybody hugged everybody until we all felt better.

Once we had calmed ourselves, Ori told us what we had missed. 'All was quiet for several days, but then about four days ago Ivi found another dead drayk, a ways west of here. It's like the others, dead beyond revival, no identity. And two days ago, Avane came up to report another couple found in Ayrien. No idea who they are, either. Nothing else has turned up since.' He paused, and said with a stern look at me, 'I decided not to tell her you were missing. She would only worry.'

I winced, feeling guilty even though we'd had no choice about our unscheduled absence. 'Three new ones. Um, anything significant or different about them?'

Ori shook his head. 'Not really. They more nearly resemble the first one than the mass grave under those horrid flowers. Tiny, localised dead area, carcasses found individually. There was just one odd thing about the one Ivi found.' He reached into a pocket and pulled out a handful of metal objects.

'What are they?'

He shrugged. 'Nobody knows. They look like parts from something, but who knows what. Maybe they have nothing to do with the corpse — could be a coincidence that they were there.' He put the bits of metal back into his pocket.

I thought of one of Galy's final visions — a machine exploding, shards of metal flying through the air. But that had taken place in the Library, not in Iskyr.

That machine, though... something about it nagged at me. Lokant-built? Most likely. Had it been used against the dead drayk, somehow? Was it some kind of weapon? It seemed another piece of evidence in favour of Lokant involvement, but my thoughts on the matter were too foggy and vague to be of use.

So I merely nodded, trying to think of something intelligent to say. But I was too distracted by the sick feeling in my stomach, and there wasn't much to add anyway. At least it seemed to exonerate Gio.

'What about the spread of taint from Orlind?' I said instead, glad enough to divert the topic of conversation.

Ori gave me a blank stare. 'The what?'

Oh… of course. Pense and Meri and Nyden had been on their way back from that discovery when they ran into Gio and me, and were subsequently swept away by the Library. That news had yet to reach Nuwelin.

I let Pense tell it. The narration left Ori visibly worried, and intrigued as well. 'Now, that is interesting. Galy was keeping that under control, of course, so it might just be his absence that is doing the mischief. What's the rate of expansion?'

Pense replied, 'Slow, but faster than we would like.'

'No sign of anything else going on there?'

'We have yet to conduct a thorough investigation.'

Ori nodded and fell silent. His sharp mind would be turning over the problem, perhaps developing all manner of ideas and theories that hadn't occurred to us. I felt suddenly, deeply grateful for Ori and his intellect, his diligence, and his flair for research. How would we manage without him?

'Speaking of which,' I said, forgetting that I had not shared my thoughts aloud, 'How fared the hunt?' I gestured at the books.

Always happy to talk upon the subject of his research, Ori instantly forgot everything else. He was revived by then, restored enough to say, all in a rush, 'I have read every single word in those bloody books, many of them multiple times over because there was nothing else to distract myself with while I was planning how to manage the rest of my life without the two of you and wondering how to extract revenge upon the parties unknown responsible for your obvious demise and *by the way*, there really is a lot of useful stuff in there. I have a lot to tell you, and I'd better start right away because we've lost about ten days and also I am *starving*, when was the last time you two ate?'

So we acquired food, and sat restoring ourselves while Ori talked. I set my poor limp Sigwide in my lap and coaxed him to eat as I listened, feeling a little better with every morsel of fruit I persuaded him to swallow. His little body relaxed bit by bit until he grew sleepy, tucked his nose under his tail and dozed off.

I love you, he said just before he fell asleep, and my heart ached more than ever.

'This book,' Ori said, showing us one of the fattest tomes. 'Arts Draykus. I don't know if that's Eva's translation or a Lokant term, but whatever. It's a more in-depth look at what the draykoni can do, and how that compares with what they were designed to do at inception. The former far, far exceeds the latter, by the way. Did you know we are infinitely more amazing than anybody thought we would be? Doesn't that make you feel shiny?' Ori beamed, paging rapidly through the book. He had filled it with bookmarks. There was little paper up here, so he had used dried leaves, blades of withered grass and an occasional pressed flower to mark his place. I wondered how he had contrived to make notes, for I could hardly imagine he would fail to do so.

'I won't bore you with all the details just now,' he muttered, still busily sorting through the pages. 'We can take a closer look later. But there is an entire chapter devoted to their — or I should say, *our* — regenerative abilities. Here.' He thumped a page marked with a faded purple leaf. There was a whole sheaf of makeshift bookmarks distributed through the pages that followed. 'Right, noteworthy points: this is one of those things that nobody thought we would be able to do. It came out of nowhere. Which is why your story of their shooting down an early drayk interests me so much. It didn't revive?'

I shook my head. 'Not that we saw, but I thought nothing of it at the time. The vision was over as soon as the drayk died, and we didn't see what happened next. They might have revived it, or… I don't know.'

Ori's lips tightened. 'No, Llan, I don't think they did. Here, listen. *The draykon power to regenerate is considered one of the species' most noteworthy and remarkable characteristics, but it is impossible for our scientists to take credit for so unique and miraculous an ability. The initial plans for the species projected for no such power, nor was it included in the developed outlines as the project progressed. The first example of this extraordinary magic was observed post termination of subject thirty-eight, when its creche-mates stormed the laboratories and effected the revival in situ.*' He looked up. 'It goes on to discuss various theories about how it was done, most of which strike me as a bit wide of the mark. But how do you like that? The drayks were getting away from their creators *very* early on. I get the sense that this project was badly out of hand almost from the moment they began it.'

'Wide of the mark?' I repeated. 'You mean they don't understand how amasku *works?*' I felt bemused by that, but also excited, because here was an explanation as to why they had not revived that mad draykon — or destroyed her permanently. If Lokants ever learned how to extinguish us, it must have been later.

'Doubtful,' said Ori. 'It has to be a hard thing to study from the outside.'

That struck me in particular, though I couldn't immediately say why. I had known for some time that Lokants had been deeply involved in the original design and creation of my wilder, more magical self, so I had assumed that they knew its functions and potential better than I yet did. The likelihood of their ignorance intrigued me. How was it possible to create something and not understand what you had made?

And what did that mean, for our current problems?

'Termination,' said Pense abruptly. 'Is there more said of that, Ori?'

Ori shook his head. 'No, and I checked thoroughly because that occurred to me, too. But you brought an answer back with you, no? They merely killed that poor mad drayk in a usual kind of way.' He frowned as he spoke, and I could well understand why. The impersonal way in which the poor creature — subject thirty-eight — had been treated, brought to life and then dispassionately killed, was chilling. I wondered whether it had been maddened, like the one we had seen in the Library.

'I wonder what happened after it was revived,' said Pense.

'Yes,' I said, frowning. 'If they killed it because it was mad, what would they do when it came back? And what did the rest of its "creche-mates" do?'

'It isn't said.' Ori turned a few more pages. 'But here, look. Umm, I'm going to paraphrase this bit, it's long.' He read for a moment, and nodded. 'That trick of coming back from the dead? It caused them some problems, it seems — probably with the mad ones.'

Here, I thought, was a possible motive for their developing some way to more permanently erase us. If they felt their creations were turning mad beyond repair, and were opposed to their revival, perhaps they had gone looking for a way to more lastingly disable the poor creatures.

'Which is another interesting question.' Ori abandoned the book and looked hard at me. 'How did she go mad, that one you saw?'

'I hardly know, we saw little of her. But… it was as though her *flow* had become twisted somehow, like… like it had turned inside out, started running backwards. I'm not explaining this very well.' I paused and thought, frustrated with the effort of trying to articulate so obscure a phenomenon.

'It felt like a very small, localised version of what has happened at Orlind,' said Pense.

'Yes!' I said. 'Not the same exactly, not at all, but *similar*. And it probably felt similar to the draykon, too. Her flight was erratic, like she had trouble working out which way was up or down, and she scarcely felt like a sentient being — like she had lost her own sense of identity.'

'You don't know how that happened?'

I could only shake my head. 'The first we saw of her was when she came crashing in, already mad.'

'But termination,' Pense interrupted. 'We were not finished with that, Ori.'

'Oh, yes.' Ori went back to his book, brow furrowed. 'This book was written some years after the project was concluded, I gather. Listen to this: *It is difficult to separate the body of a draykon from its animating essence, as the two are intrinsically bound up with its personal amasku, or life flow. Each draykon is a spark of the same fire, and to extinguish any individual flame is almost impossible. The degree of force required to accomplish this is beyond the scope of most scientists, and certainly beyond the scope of this study.* Ori looked up. 'That's all it says. There is nothing about how it's done.'

Little though there was, it was enough to excite me. 'That's what Limbane must have meant when he said *almost impossible*! There is a way, and the Lokants know it!'

Ori was in full scholarly flow, and wearing his dubious face. 'Maybe. There is nothing in here to suggest that this is anything but a theory, perhaps an untested one. We shouldn't be too quick to lay the whole thing at Limbane's door because of it. Or Sulayn Phay, or any of them. It's still far more likely that another draykon is the culprit.'

'We shouldn't rule them out, either,' I argued. 'The draykoni are still united in declaring it impossible. This is the first sign we have had that somebody out there believes it isn't.'

Ori's head turned towards the door and he frowned. 'Something is happening out there.' He rose to his feet with a fluid grace I could only envy. Sometimes it seemed as though Pense's early awkwardness with his adopted human form had been succeeded by a mastery of it that *I* would never achieve, despite having been born into it. I suppressed a fleeting sense of inadequacy and stood up, gathering my still-sleeping Siggy into my arms.

By then I could hear it, too: a babble of approaching voices, rapidly coming closer. Ori and I exchanged a startled look, with perhaps a little wariness. I, for one, was worn out with surprises.

We stepped outside. Assembled in front of my house was every citizen of Nuwelin, most in human form and looking uneasy. I noticed a new face in the crowd, a winged Glinnish woman with abundant dark hair and bronze skin. I remembered to smile at her, a gesture she hesitantly returned.

Walking in front of them was Gio, looking still more uncomfortable.

'Hello, Llandry,' he said when he saw me. 'Do you think you could let these good people know that I mean no harm?'

'What did you do to alarm them? They are usually much more welcoming.' I surveyed the gathered knot of people with confusion, for their reaction was out of character. We were used to all sorts of people finding us up here, most of them new hereditaries looking for assistance. We were accustomed to providing it, and making all manner of strangers welcome at a moment's notice. What had upset them about Gio?

He raised his hands in a clear gesture of culpability. 'I, um, appeared in the middle of the camp. It was unwise of me.'

'It isn't a *camp*, it is a village.' That was Meriall, standing arms-folded a couple of feet away from Gio and scowling mightily upon him. '*Camp* sounds haphazard, disorganised and temporary, none of which we are.'

Gio sighed. 'Apologies. I translocated into the centre of your lovely *village.*'

'Most of us have never met Lokants before, Gio,' I told him. 'You shouldn't take my familiarity as characteristic of everyone.'

'So I have learned.' He fixed his pretty eyes upon me with a beseeching expression. 'May I please be introduced to your fine friends? And if you would be so kind as to reassure them so they won't kill me, that would be wonderful.' He gave me a big, hopeful smile.

'Gio,' I said in an unfriendly voice. 'Are you trying to charm me into charming my friends for you?'

His smile disappeared. 'Well, I… yes, actually.'

I glared at him. He had kicked up a ruckus and the upshot of it was that Sigwide was awake. His first deep, proper sleep in days, and Gio had ruined it with his carelessness! I clutched Siggy closer, stroking his fur, and wrapped a section of my loose shirt around him.

I glanced at Meriall, who could have vouched for Gio as well as I could. But the closed expression of her face told me she had no such intention.

It would have to be my job, then. So be it.

'Everybody, this is Gio. We've met before. He's a Lokant and they do weird things like that all the time. He probably isn't here to kill any of us.' Probably. I was still by no means certain that he wasn't the author of all our troubles, utilising some shifty, nasty Lokant art (or machine) to wipe out our draykon fellows. But in fairness to him, he had never given me any solid reason to imagine him guilty of the crime, either.

With these words I strode past him, on my way to fetch some more food for Siggy. Which was *much* more important.

'Um,' Gio said as I passed him. 'What do you mean, probably?'

'I mean you are still an unknown quantity and a highly suspicious figure and I cannot say for certain that you're safe to be near.' I let him trail after me, unwilling to pause to talk to him. 'I am also well aware that translocation requires prior preparation, by the way. When did you mark yourself a travel-point in the middle of Nuwelin?'

He hesitated. He was probably wondering how much of a lie he could get away with, I thought sourly.

'Um, before I met you the first time,' he admitted at last. 'I just, um, wanted to be able to return easily.'

'*Before* you even spoke to me?' I stopped then, aghast, and stared at him. 'What if I had told you to get lost, the way I wanted to?'

'Er. I was hoping you wouldn't.' He gave me those damned beseeching eyes again. If anything, they'd actually grown bigger and twice as soulful in the last couple of minutes.

'Setting that aside for a moment,' I said. 'Why the middle of my village? Wouldn't you more reasonably have chosen a spot a more discreet distance away?'

He looked down, shamefaced. 'It's hard to explain.'

I took a deep breath to control myself. 'I have just vouched for you before my entire village. Grudgingly, perhaps, but I did it. That means you now have access to our tiny community and they will, in time, accept you. If I have done that only to find that you are a traitor after all…'

I didn't know how to finish that sentence. I wanted to remind him that Nuwelin looked peaceful enough as a small gaggle of humans, but we were draykoni to a man (and woman) and more than ferocious enough to defend ourselves when roused. But it immediately struck me how futile a threat that was. How could we pose any meaningful menace to somebody who could disappear with a stray thought?

'It's… comforting,' said Gio, eyes still fixed upon the floor.

'What.'

'Your village. Nuwelin. It is a comforting place and I like being here.' He looked up and met my eyes at last, and this time I saw more sincerity there than I ever had before. I think it cost him something to say those words. 'My home is… isn't… it's not like this.'

I hated the way my heart thawed on the spot, for what if he was lying? He *could* be. Easily.

But I couldn't help responding to the vulnerability he'd shown, and the admission of such a simple and essentially endearing need. Nor could I help being touched by the implied compliment to Nuwelin. We have a hard task, here, but we are doing it with as much trust for each other and compassion and hope as we can muster between us, and I love to hear that it shows.

Maybe I shouldn't be so hard on Gio.

'All right,' I said, a little reluctantly but the words came out intact. 'We'll let it go. Did you come here with news for me?'

He smiled and held up something that looked like a badge. It had a symbol on it that I did not recognise: some kind of stylised plant bearing a single orange fruit. 'I did.'

'What's that?'

'It's a pass! To Estinor Library.'

'To where…?'

'To my, uh, grandfather's Library. Limbane's.'

I squinted at the badge. It didn't look very official. 'Are you sure?'

'No, well, *this* isn't official. It's just something I put together, I… thought it might be fun.' He put the badge back in his pocket, looking abashed. 'Um, an official pass would hurt more.'

'Oh?'

'It would have to be implanted.'

'Let's… not do that.'

Gio nodded agreement. 'I can get you there. And straight back, with my handy travel-point right here.' That winsome smile emerged again, with perhaps a hint of smugness around the edges. He knew he'd got me on that one. 'When would you like to go? I would advise soon, because Limbane's absent for a bit and it's quiet out there.'

'We'd like to go at once!' I enthused. I had been afraid that Gio would fail on his promises, and felt elated that he had come through. It was a shame that Limbane wasn't around, as I still wanted to interrogate him. But then again… perhaps it wasn't.

Here is how my projected conversation with Limbane goes in my head:

Me: Hello Limbane! Do you happen to know how to kill a draykon? Permanently?

Limbane: Why yes, I do. Let me tell you all about it.

Me: Super! And, er, have any of you been using it a lot lately?

Limbane: How did you guess? Let me tell you all about that, too!

Here is how it would probably go in reality:

Me: Hello Limbane! Do you happen to know how to permanently kill a draykon?

Limbane: I have never heard of any such thing.

Me: Really? But you said—

Limbane: Really. Now get out of my Library.

Maybe a bit of exploratory investigation in his absence is a good place to start.

'We?' said Gio, blinking.

'Me and Pense and Ori. Meri might like to come, I don't know about Ny—'

'Wait, hold on.' Gio held up his hands in a *stop* gesture. 'There is only me to take us, so I'll have to drag everybody along all by myself. Mighty as I am, I cannot hope to carry more than three there and back.'

'Oh. Of course.' I should have remembered that, for I had seen Eva travel that way many times and never with more than two or three passengers. 'Me, Pense and Ori, then.'

'Great. Fetch the team, and we'll go.'

I beamed at him, and ran.

We assembled back at my house. I had not had to search far for Pense, because he had been following me — discreetly. Keeping an eye on Gio, of course. Ori, though, had given up on the dramatics outside and gone back to his books. I found him sprawled once more upon the floor, reorganising his bookmarks into some new, presumably more useful, configuration.

'Adventure time,' I told him, and hauled him up off the floor.

He bounced smartly to his feet, adjusted his rumpled shirt, attempted and mostly failed to arrange his hair, and nodded at me. 'What's it to be? Exploration and espionage? Breaking and entry? Stealth and surveillance?'

'Dire peril in the pursuit of exciting heroics,' said Pense.

Ori smiled, a trifle uncertainly. 'Ah... really?'

'No.'

I patted Ori on the back. 'Dire peril in the pursuit of academic research, actually.'

Ori brightened at once. 'Oh, that's *much* better.'

Gio appeared at the door, somehow looking both smoothly composed and diffidently unsure of himself at the same time. 'Are we ready?'

Ori surveyed Gio with interest, then raised an eyebrow at me. 'Is this our tour guide?'

'He's taking us to Limbane's Library.'

'Mmm, there are *lots* of books there. Lead on, Gio my friend!'

I was amused by Ori's enthusiastic acceptance of Gio. If he had felt any doubts in that direction before, they were all borne away by the promise of books. Ori would love anybody with access to a good library.

Gio looked startled by the word "friend", and directed a hesitant smile at Ori.

Ori beamed back. 'Books?' he prompted.

'Yes. Come with me.' Gio held out his hands.

I took one of them, and Ori gripped the other. Siggy was installed in his carry pack and lay sleeping against my chest, a willing comrade due to being blissfully oblivious.

Pense, though, was slow to join us. *Are you sure about this, Minchu?* he said privately.

Hard to be sure, isn't it?

He could be taking us anywhere at all. It could be a trap.

I know. But how else are we going to get the information we need? Nobody else can take us to any of the Lokant Libraries, not now that Eva's given up her access.

He was silent. I watched his face, feeling torn myself. I wanted to trust Gio, not just because we needed him but because... I was starting to like him, a little bit. I hadn't wanted to. His story was thin and I still hadn't figured out what he really wanted from us. And he was a Lokant, which didn't help, for they had never proved to be trustworthy. But his aloof composure seemed to hide the kind of vulnerabilities I could only sympathise with, and I found his uncertainty disarming. He never presumed, only… hoped. It was getting harder to maintain my suspicion, and most of my irritation with him had faded. I *wanted* him to be everything he said he was.

Are you coming with me? I said to Pense.

He joined me, reluctant but at least he came. He wrapped one strong arm around my waist, attaching himself to me. *Always.*

Gio nodded. His grip tightened upon my hand, the world shifted sideways, and we disappeared from Nuwelin in a nauseating rush.

We ended up in a dark, windowless box.

'What is *this*?' whispered Ori in disgust.

'It is a maintenance closet,' replied Gio.

'A bit of warning would have been nice,' Ori muttered. 'You never know. *Some* of us might suffer from claustrophobia.' His tone was sarcastic, but I suspect he spoke the truth, for I have never heard Ori sound so grouchy before.

'Sorry,' Gio replied as we strove to avoid jostling each other in the enclosed space. 'It was the only place I could think of to bring you that wouldn't attract notice.'

'Is this really necessary?' I said. Limbane might not be best pleased to find us wandering around in his Library, but was such extreme caution warranted? He wasn't even home.

'It would be better if we could complete this errand unobserved.'

I chose not to argue with him about his approach. After all, he must know Limbane better than we did. 'Where is the door?' I said. It was too dark in there to see anything.

'Um.' There came a hastily-suppressed clattering sound as Gio, presumably, embarked upon a hunt for the exit. The rest of us opted to stay where we were. The potential for disaster was far too high; knock one thing over in the crowded cupboard and everything else could topple with it, creating a terrific racket.

Then a set of hinges creaked and a thin line of light pierced the darkness. 'Here it is!' said Gio proudly.

Nobody answered him. We were too busy holding our collective breath, waiting to see if anybody was around to notice the closet door's opening itself.

'We can proceed,' he said, throwing the door wide and stepping out into the corridor beyond.

We followed. Siggy shifted in his carry-pack and I soothed him, anxious to keep him calm. I couldn't have him growing alarmed and trying to jump out. What if I lost him in this mystifying place?

I was immediately reminded of how disappointing the Libraries could sometimes be. They are some of the most remarkable structures in the known worlds; wonders untold emerge from their laboratories, and they possess caches of knowledge beyond imagination. Not to mention their curious ability to float just on the edge of time, barely touched by it, everything inside preserved far beyond any natural lifespan.

In spite of all this, parts of them resemble public and government buildings at home in the Seven: bland, featureless corridors with identical doors set into them and no features of interest whatsoever. We looked up and down the length of a particularly boring example, nonplussed.

'Lead on,' I said to Gio.

He nodded, but looked uncertain as he glanced about. I saw him visibly square his shoulders and then set off, his steps purposeful.

'It is the chart room you want, yes?' he threw back over his shoulder.

'Yes!' I had a mixture of feelings at that moment: some uncertainty on Gio's account, and some trepidation, because there were a number of exciting ways in which the venture could go wrong. But at Gio's words those doubtful emotions gave way to a surge of excitement. The chart room had fascinated me before, and I was delighted at the prospect of visiting it again.

I also had high hopes that we would, at last, discover something useful. I was beginning to feel that it would not take much to begin to make sense of the mess. We had assembled many pieces of a muddling puzzle, and perhaps we needed only a few more significant clues to resolve it into a coherent picture.

Gio led us with confidence and caution, a combination I approved of. We traversed several of those dull corridors, twisting and turning through a labyrinth I could not hope to comprehend. I wondered how Gio could find his way, familiar though he must be with the place.

We met no one at all, which began to trouble me as much as it reassured me. Was it usual for such a place to be so empty?

'Almost there,' said Gio after a while, which confused me still more, for I had seen nothing I recognised. Pense caught my eye, and I read a similar doubt in his face.

But then Gio stopped and opened a door, and there was the chart room, exactly as I remembered it. Gigantic, circular and distantly domed, its size was hard to fathom; I felt dwarfed the moment I stepped through the door. The walls were pale, and made of something I cannot name. If you think of the bulletin boards across the Seven and the way they change to display the latest news, you might be able to picture the chart room well enough. I have no idea if they are made of the same thing — in fact, I have no idea what the bulletin boards are made of in the first place, nor how they operate — but they strike me as similar. Flat, smooth and faintly shimmering, displaying information in constant flux.

That information is names. Thousands, perhaps hundreds of thousands of names, all arranged in neat genealogical timelines. I presume it dates all the way back to the first draykoni, and presumably the first humans too.

Somewhere in there is my name, coloured in gold because I am draykoni. Eva's and Tren's names are up there too, in blue and purple and silver — all coded to indicate the different kinds of heritage they possess and the powers it bestows. I imagine that all the residents of Nuwelin are represented somewhere upon the walls. Of course, it would take about three weeks to find them all.

That wasn't why we were there.

Gio shut the door behind us after we had all filed in, pausing to check the corridor once more before he did so.

'Quickly, I suggest,' he said, taking up a guard position near the door.

Quickly? I stared at those endless walls, feeling dizzy just looking at them. 'All right, our objective,' I said, forcing myself to think clearly. 'We have the identities of three of the murdered draykoni: Pense's friends Ludino and Myir, and Eterna's mother. We need to find them all, and look for links between them. They are all Elders, so presumably we will find them nearer the top of the walls.'

This was broadly accepted, and we spread out. I pressed Gio into service as well, for there was little point to his standing guard. The best he could offer us would be a few seconds' advance warning of somebody's approach, and the room was far too big for that to be of any use. We could not hope to reconvene in time to escape before anybody approaching could open the door. Better to complete our errand as quickly as possible and get out.

One of the amazing things about the chart room is how you can manipulate the display. It responds to certain gestures, which Limbane taught us in days past. If I hold out my hands towards the walls and pull them downwards, the names will begin to scroll. The more sharply I do this, the greater the effect. By this means, I was able to access the beginnings of the timeline fairly rapidly, though it still took a minute or two to run through so many generations.

The names thin out very quickly at a certain point, and gold names crop up more and more frequently. Gold means that the person possesses enough draykon blood to shift. I noticed that the shades of gold altered, too, becoming brighter and purer the farther back I went.

At last, the scrolling stopped at a very sparse display: one pure gold name, with two others descending from it. It was not a name I recognised, but I had hit the beginning and found one of the very first draykoni — made, I suppose, in the Library of Orlind.

I ran the display sideways, more slowly this time, reading each name in hopes of encountering something familiar. But it was Ori who reported the first result.

'Myir!' he crowed. 'Here she is. Golden as a sunny afternoon and splendidly alone up here.'

I wanted to run over and look, but that would waste time, so I stayed where I was. 'An original?' I prompted.

'Looks like it. No parents recorded.'

I beamed, already feeling vindicated. I'd had a secret theory growing in my mind, but lacked the certainty to share it with anybody. It was only a hunch. But here was the first point of possible confirmation: Myir was a first-generation drayk, a prototype.

Pense found Ludino soon afterwards. 'Also an original,' he called. 'Which, I never knew.'

'Pense. Those you think of as *elders*. Are they all first generation?'

He shrugged. 'I do not know. We have never phrased it in such terms amongst ourselves, for … well, if any of us know of our true origins, it has not been widely discussed. We only know that some of us are far older than the rest.'

'Is Eterna an elder?'

He paused to consider. 'No,' he said at last. 'I would say that she is *ancient* but I would not apply the term *Elder*. But before you ask, I cannot articulate why.'

I smiled, satisfied. My theory was quickly coming together. At that point, I would have bet money that Eterna was no elder because her mother was one, an original.

It was me who found her upon the charts at last, though I almost scrolled straight past her in my hurry. *Eterna*. I had adjusted my focus a little as my theory developed; I expected to find Eterna a generation or two farther down, but probably only one. So it proved. Both her parents were recorded: Astrand, a female, and Tynval, a male. Neither had progenitors listed.

'Astrand!' I shouted, forgetting caution in my exultation. 'That's it. All three are first generation. What's the betting that the rest are, too?'

Ori adopted the idea at once, which pleased me greatly, for he is so much more analytical than me and consequently more likely to see problems I overlook. But he said, 'Llan! You are a little genius!' and fell at once to theorising further upon the point. 'Of course, we have considerably more than three corpses to account for, so it is early to become *too* attached to the idea. But three out of three makes for a significant emerging pattern! What if all the dead drayks *are* first generation? We have assumed one of two things: either the violence is random or it is personal, with some kind of vendetta against each individual victim. What if it is both more specific than the former and more general than the latter? It could well be! Somebody wants all the first generation draykoni dead!'

Pense said nothing. He was frowning.

Pense? I said, tentatively. I didn't want to disturb his train of thought, whatever it was, but his expression troubled me.

'Am I on here?' he said aloud.

'You must be. We all are.'

Pense shook his head. 'When we were here before, with Limbane, he said that I was not listed — because I have no descendants, and because my parents were never recorded. He said I predate this system.'

I blinked, shocked. I had forgotten that entirely. 'Are you sure?' It was not that I doubted him, but his words made no sense considering everything we had just found.

'Perfectly.'

Now I was frowning, too. 'How can you predate this? These are the oldest draykoni there are.'

'Do we know that for certain?' said Ori. 'Or is it merely that they are the oldest according to *this* study? Perhaps the information is incomplete.'

'No,' said Pense firmly. 'I am no Elder. I cannot be older than Ludino and Myir. They were most certainly my seniors.'

'Forgive me, Pense, but I have to ask you how you are so certain of that,' said Ori apologetically. 'I hardly imagine the draykoni have birth records.'

Pense opened his mouth, but shut it again without speaking.

'Um,' said Ori, suddenly diffident. 'You do remember your parents, Pense? Right?'

Pense sighed, and ran both hands through his hair. Another gesture he had picked up from Tren. 'I have forgotten many things,' was all that he said.

'Oh.' Ori stood, blinking, and said nothing more.

I did not like the direction this was going in. If I was right and somebody wanted to eradicate the oldest draykoni, where did Pense fit in with that? If he was older even than Ludino and Myir and Astrand, would that make a target of him, too?

'I cannot be,' Pense said at last, more confidently. 'There is… an *aura* about the Elders, something about them that is indefinably different from the rest of us. It is their Mark. And I have it not.'

Hmm. As far as I know, I have never met a real Elder — not a living one, anyway. I have been thinking of the term as merely meaning *pretty old,* and apparently I've been wrong to do so. I cannot say that I knew what Pense meant by *Elder,* if not that, but I found his certainty reassuring. I take his word over Limbane's.

The discrepancy is odd, though.

'If you have what you wanted,' said Gio suddenly, 'I might suggest that we go.'

Which was a fair point. We had got so carried away with the thrill of success that we had forgotten the danger of discovery.

But now that it came to it, I felt torn about leaving. 'This is a Library,' I said.

Ori grinned at me. 'Gosh, is it? Good work, Llan.'

I stuck my tongue out at him, only belatedly remembering that I was meant to be projecting an aura of maturity and competence — for Gio's benefit, if for no other reason. I didn't want him thinking me immature.

Too late.

'What I *mean,*' I persevered, 'is that this is the ultimate source of information for all the topics we are interested in. We could find all the answers here, instead of trying to glean them from a mere handful of Eva's books.'

'In theory,' said Ori, 'but it would probably take us weeks of searching to uncover anything useful. You remember how big these places are, right?'

I sighed, feeling deflated. 'That is true…' I had to concede. But my gaze strayed to Gio. 'Unless we had help.'

Gio had no trouble catching on to where my line of thought was taking me, for he looked up at once. 'Uhh, it is not that simple. I don't know where everything is in this Library, either. You would need an … archivist, you would call it.'

'Which is?'

Gio looked at the door and then back at me, shifting restlessly. 'Oh, archivists are the ones who devote their lives to organising their Library and keeping the collections current and maintained. It takes an unthinkably long time to become useful at it and there are not many of them.' He smiled at me and added, 'And no, before you ask. I do not happen to have a conveniently open-minded and discreet archivist friend I can introduce you to.'

I paced a moment, thinking. 'Is there no way we can quickly identify what we need?'

'No.' Gio looked at the door again. 'Orillin is right, I think you are forgetting the size of the facility. There's eons worth of information in here, spanning more worlds than you can imagine. Without the help of an archivist, it could take weeks.'

I felt a new respect for Eva's tenacity — or perhaps her persuasiveness — in tracking down the several books we had already consulted, as well as managing to have them copied. She was devious.

'We need to go,' said Gio, more urgently this time.

'You can come back any time you like, can't you?' I said to him.

He looked at me with narrowed eyes. 'No, I am not searching this Library top to bottom looking for books for you.'

'Why not?'

He struggled with various unvoiced thoughts and shared none of them. Finally he rubbed at his eyes and shrugged. 'All right, if I must. But I can promise nothing. What is it that you want me to find?'

'We need to know how it is possible to permanently kill a draykon. That is the core problem.'

'Fine. Now can we please go?'

I wondered what was making him so restless — until I heard voices approaching, and the sounds of footsteps.

'Yes, that is most definitely someone coming,' said Gio with a grimace. 'More than one person, so if we could please move along?'

Gio's urgency was contagious, if hard to explain. Pense, Ori and I all ran for Gio full speed, and barely in time. I reached him first, being the closest; his hand closed over mine in a crushing grip. Gio gathered up Ori a second later, but Pense had wandered far and could not close the distance in time.

The door opened.

I *sensed* Gio's fear, a gigantic, shocking surge of it that far dwarfed my own. For a horrible moment I thought he would vanish on the spot and leave Pense right there, but he managed to hold.

Pense sensed it, too. He gave up on reaching us on foot and simply dived, hitting Gio in a tackle. Gio fell, dragging Ori and I with him — but before we hit the ground there came that nauseating surge and we were elsewhere.

We fell in a tangled heap in the middle of Nuwelin. I lay dazed for a moment, conscious of a sharp pain in my back. It took me a few seconds to gather myself, and then my first priority was to check on the others.

Gio, Ori, Pense — all present. Siggy safe in his carry-pack upon my chest, though most definitely *not* asleep anymore. He was wriggling wildly, alarmed and frightened. I think that the level of fear among the four of us had badly got to him, he has always been sensitive like that.

Whaaaaaaat. That's all I could hear in my head, Sigwide screaming that word at me.

I sighed and sat up carefully. As I soothed Siggy, I was interested to note that the spot Gio had chosen to travel to really was right in the middle of Nuwelin. We had landed not far from our meeting place, and it was occupied.

'Morning,' I said weakly.

Larion raised a hand in languid greeting, not troubling to move from his semi-recumbent posture upon the floor. 'Everything all right?' he said.

'Fine,' I croaked. I staggered to my feet with a groan and shook myself, relieved to find that my back still functioned, however much it hurt. Pense and I went through our usual ritual of checking each other over for injury — how sad is it that we have had to do this so often, in our relatively short time together?

'As a mode of travel,' said Ori, 'the thing has its pros and cons.' He stretched, wincing.

Gio merely lay prone, making no move whatsoever to get up. He folded his hands underneath his head and smiled vaguely at me. 'Normally it is conducted with more style and significantly fewer bruises.'

I watched him, thoughtful. He looked calm now, supremely

so, all his earlier fear gone. Or perhaps it was not so much fear as… blind panic, out of all proportion with the extent of the risk. It was never very likely that we would be caught, but what was likely to happen if we were? Limbane would be displeased and perhaps angry with Gio. And so what? That prospect was nowhere near terrifying enough to explain Gio's fear.

What kind of trouble did he expect to be in, and why?

'Why were you so rattled?' I asked him.

He met my gaze briefly, and looked away. 'Some of my grandfather's people are touchy about intruders. And the chart room is not exactly open access, even to me.'

He was way overdoing the show of relaxation, maybe in an attempt to compensate for his panic before. I watched as he plucked a blade of grass, saluted Larion with it and began to chew upon the end.

I dismissed him from my mind for the time being, and turned to Larion. 'Any news?'

Larion shook his head. 'Nothing. In fact, everything has been remarkably peaceful while you were gone. An occasional corpse, of course, but that's only to be expected.'

I wanted to see the new gravesites, but I had to accept there must be little point. Ori would have investigated them, and if he said they were typical of the pattern then I trusted him.

I felt an urge to kick Gio, lying so lazily upon the ground instead of hunting for the books we needed. But I could not help sympathising with his probable feelings in the aftermath of such fear, even if the source of it mystified me. I had felt such panic often enough myself.

So I let him be for the present.

Pense joined me. *Minchu, I am returning to Orlind. Do you wish to accompany me?*

I grasped his point at once. *The corruption. Yes, of course we must attend to it.*

He nodded. *I cannot help thinking that, as pressing a problem as the dead draykoni are, this may be more so. And it is being overshadowed by everything else.*

I could hardly argue there. I felt a momentary shame at permitting myself to be so distracted, but I suppressed it. Not a helpful attitude. We were but few, and we were outfaced by the variety of problems we were trying to deal with.

That stray thought, though, gave me an idea. *We need help*, I told Pense. *We need to know the extent of the problem, and we need some idea of what may be causing it, besides Galy's absence. It could take us days or weeks to cover enough ground alone.*

Pense eyed me, slightly uneasily. *What do you have in mind?*

For a start, we must send Nuwelin out to survey Iskyr, and get Avane's people to do the same Below.

Pense nodded, still wary. *That is sensible.*

And… I also want to talk to Eterna.

That won me a long sigh. *Must we go through that again?*

Do you think I enjoy her company? I would far rather never see her again. But this is her home, too, and her people. The threats we face — the corruption, the deaths — affect them all equally, and they deserve to be informed no less now than before.

Pense rolled his eyes. *You have an exaggerated sense of honour.*

It is not just honour. It is their home, and they are as responsible for defending and preserving it as we are. And we could use the help. This is all getting away from us, Pense, and you know it.

I expected another argument, but I was surprised by a hug instead. *That's my Minchu,* he said with a mental chuckle. *One half honour, the other half uncompromising practicality.*

This was no description of me that *I* recognised, but if it meant Pense was happy with me and willing to go along with my plans, then I would gladly take it.

11 VIII

Hurrah, More Problems!

It was decided that Meri and Larion would take word to Avane, Pense and Ori and I would travel to Eterna's people and the rest would begin the task of determining the extent of the corruption in Iskyr, guided by Nyden. Gio was dispatched to undertake his search at his grandfather's Library. The discussions proceeded smoothly enough, to my relief, and few argued with me this time.

I would like to think this is because my decisions have, thus far, been proved broadly sensible and they are coming to trust me.

It is probably more that they do not much care. After all, they have never been to Orlind, never experienced the corrupted *amasku* for themselves. We can tell them that it is dangerous, and they will believe us, but it lacks the impact of actually walking through it, of learning how it feels and what it does to you.

Sadly, they would soon learn.

Before we could depart, I had the problem of Sigwide to solve. It is easy enough to cart him about with me when I am human-shaped, but I intended to shift and fly with my bigger wings for this errand, and I have yet to perfect a means of carrying a tiny orting along while I do it. He is so small compared to my grander shape, it would be easy to crush him, or lose him and fail to realise it.

I ended up strapping his carry bag to my foreleg. Actually Ori did it, since I could not manage it myself once I had Changed. He was secure there, with little chance he would fall out, and I could see him even mid-flight and make sure he had not got lost.

It would have to do. Unwilling to waste any more time, we attended to this problem as quickly as possible and then took to the air. The rest of the people of Nuwelin departed around us, soaring away in groups of two or three, and for a short time the skies were vivid with the coloured scales of myriad draykoni.

And so we flew south once more, and a little westerly. My mind was fixed upon Sigwide as we took off. I was unsure how he would react to this new experience of flight, though he was accustomed to flying with me in my human shape. I fly a lot faster as a drayk, apart from anything.

I was braced for distress, but instead I received a different reaction. As soon as my four feet left the ground, a sound I had scarcely ever heard from Sigwide before filled my mind and it took me a moment to identify what it was.

My orting was giggling.

Hysterically, perhaps, for my timid Siggy could scarcely be enjoying himself? But I felt no fear from him. He was having fun.

How I can still underestimate him after so many years together, I do not know.

Hehehehheeehhheeehehehee chortled Siggy in my mind, and on I flew, my spirits lightened by the sound of his mirth.

I was mentally prepared for the same long, tiring journey we had undergone before, but we had been travelling for barely three hours (as far as I could guess) when we encountered a sight which halted us at once.

We were flying over low hills which rose to small mountains in the near distance. Those mountains were so beautiful: dramatic swells of craggy, silvery rock, their sides coated in bright green mosses and flecked with blue and violet alpine blossoms. The light of the twin suns glinted off them in shimmering waves, which only made them more achingly beautiful to behold.

It also made it really easy to see the legion of draykoni approaching on the wing, spreading over those glittering mountains in a wave of colour.

STOP! I yelled, banking hard. I had overdone it, I fear. My scream must have resounded painfully in the minds of my friends because Ori, probably half dozing, almost fell out of the sky.

Who are they?! I was still shouting, but honestly, I was shocked. And afraid. I thought I knew all the draykon colonies in Iskyr and here was another! Out of nowhere! And we had passed this way fairly recently. Where could they possibly have come from, and most importantly were they *friendly?*

Calm, Minchu. Pense enfolded me in a mental hug until I pulled myself together, and then gently let me go.

Embarrassing, I know. The heroes in adventure stories never panic, do they? It is lowering. In my defence, I was almost as dozy as Ori at the time.

Anyway, as far from the mystery flock as we were, it was impossible to discern anything about them. We held a hurried and tense consultation between the three of us, a conversation to which Sigwide added an occasional sleepy syllable by way of support, and ultimately decided that it was too late to try to go around them. We would have to approach in good faith, and hope for the best.

The mystery was resolved when I noticed that the lead figure really was unusually large, it was no trick of the distance or the light. She also had green and white scales.

I could say *she* with complete confidence at that point because it could be no other than Eterna.

All right, I said, more intrigued than alarmed. *What is Eterna's colony doing this far north?*

It took us another quarter of an hour or so to reach them, which was plenty of time for us to turn over a variety of theories between the three of us. Perhaps something had happened to their home site and they had been forced to move. Perhaps they were simply in search of a better spot. Maybe there was some threat they sought to avoid.

Maybe they're just having a family day out, suggested Ori with a mental smirk.

A pleasant constitutional around the mountains, added Pense, which interested me, for he is not so likely to joke as Ori or Tren. They're really rubbing off on him.

It all struck me as a little irreverent, considering that some catastrophe might have befallen them. But I had to admit, they did not look like they were in trouble. There was a serene quality to their flight, an insouciance to the angle of their wings, that belied any ideas of trauma.

It turns out that distance can indeed be deceiving.

Eterna flew on ahead of the rest of her folk to meet us, and as she drew closer I was obliged to relinquish any fond ideas as to her serenity. She came at us in a blaze of bright green hide, the colours dazzlingly intense in the strong sunlight, and when she reached us she flashed teeth and claws in a display of fury.

Every draykon knows, she hissed. *Every true draykon, pure in blood and sage in the ways of our kind, knows to avoid Orlind! Every one of us! But* you, *in your ignorance, your infantile overconfidence, had to meddle where it was* not *due. See what has come of it! I wish to the sun and skies that your miserable kind had never been drawn forth to plague us!* She focused on Pense and bared her teeth once more, a low snarl accompanying the gesture. *I have not forgotten* your *presence, wing-brother. What company you keep! How could you permit yourself to be drawn into such dangerous meddling!*

This tirade left all three of us speechless. *Orlind.* Surely the corruption could not have spread so far as to disturb Eterna's colony? I felt a growing dread which robbed me of words entirely.

Calm, wing-sister, said Pense at last, at his most soothing. *Tell us what is amiss.*

Now is not the time for calm, Eterna replied contemptuously. *We are forced to flee, but where can we go? Soon all the realms will be engulfed by the sickness and we shall all be mad.* Upon which encouraging words she soared in a tight circle, turned her back on us, and winged away.

Wait! I yelled after her. I beat my wings hard, determined to chase her down. *We need your help to mend this!*

Eterna ignored me, but there was no way I would let her lay the blame for this at *our* door and then refuse to assist us. I flew faster, my muscles aching with the effort — she is much larger than I, and her wingspan dwarfs mine. I cannot long keep pace with her.

Please! I threw after her. *You're right. If we do nothing, Iskyr and Ayrien will be lost and where will that leave our people?*

Eterna slowed at last, and banked to face me. She said nothing immediately, and I was left to enjoy her palpable hatred uninterrupted. It rolled off her in waves, mingled with frustration and more fear than I believe she wanted to display. The effect was stifling, and I struggled to breathe.

You should have sought my guidance sooner, she said at last, wintry-cold and unmoved. *I told you to stay away from Orlind.*

If we had done so, it would now be under the control of a Lokant whose interests have nothing to do with protecting or preserving our worlds. My kind are here because of him!

Eterna gave a mental shrug. *He is also the reason why I am once again alive, I and all of my people. What if he* had *taken back Orlind? Perhaps he would have mended it, and we would not now have this problem.*

How can you talk so? If there has been meddling afoot then it is he who bears the blame. *Lokants have torn our world apart in pursuit of their own goals, and if unchecked—*

Is this all that you wished to say to me? Eterna interrupted. *You are wasting my time. Go back to your pathetic village and enjoy it while you can.* She cast me a final look of shrivelling contempt, accompanied by a kind of mental gesture which was like… well, it was as though she had spat at me.

Wait, I said again. *Your mother's death.*

She froze. *What of it?*

Is it a coincidence, that these deaths occur at the same time that the corruption spreads out of Orlind? Perhaps, but I doubt it. They are connected — they must be.

It wasn't enough. Eterna showed me her tail and flew away, not deigning to answer me. She flew with all her speed, and I could have no hope of keeping up with her this time. I could only watch, sadly, as she disappeared into the distance.

Pense and Ori had caught up with me by then. *You tried, Llan,* said Ori. *It is no fault of ours if she is too stupid and stubborn and lazy to listen to us.*

But we need their help, I sighed. *It will be so much harder to do it alone.*

We will find a way. That was Pense. *We have achieved much already, largely unaided. And now we have Nuwelin, and Avane's folk.*

Perhaps it would be enough. *I wish she had at least told us the extent of the spread into her territory,* I replied, feeling more grouchy than dismayed. How dare she blame us *and* make our job harder in one stroke! She had always infuriated me.

We were going there anyway, pointed out Ori. *Let's continue. We can find out for ourselves.*

So we did. The relative tranquillity of our earlier flight was all lost this time. We flew in a state of heightened alertness, searching for any signs of a disruption in the flow of *amasku* around us, dreading that we would come across it at any moment.

Somewhat to our relief, we flew a long way before we encountered the first sense of it. It was hard to miss, though it is difficult for me to describe how or why in words. If you imagine… a correct flow of *amasku* is like a sunny day, with clear skies and a fresh breeze and that delightful feeling of serenity and possibility and hope. It empowers us, strengthens us, keeps us calm and at the height of our abilities.

When we drew near to the corruption, it was like seeing a dark, heavy storm-cloud appear on the horizon. The closer we got, the more disturbing this effect became, like that feeling of tension and dread that builds with an oncoming storm. That is the best I can do, and it falls far short of encompassing everything that I feel. I can only apologise.

We were forced to stop at last, for we dared not get too close. We hung there in the skies, clumsily hovering as we surveyed the damage.

There was no visible sign of trouble in the landscape below, not yet. If the dry, barren island of Orlind was anything to go by, that would come in time. For now, the marshes spread before us were thriving, all flourishing vegetation and scurrying animals. The creatures I sensed, though, were beginning to feel it: there was a feverish quality to their movements which there ought not to be, and a hint of panic reached me from more than one source. Some were struggling to maintain their sense of direction, growing steadily more confused.

Corrupted *amasku* affects my kind worst of all, for we are formed of that energy and cannot help being tied to it. We are a part of its flow. But no creature is safe from it — not beasts, not humans. Left unchecked, it will eventually kill everything it touches. I thought of one of Galy's visions, and the way the draykon's bones had turned dull and crumbled.

Ori finally broke the depressed and frightened silence. *We are a long way from Orlind.*

It is spreading faster, Pense agreed.

Much too fast, I said. *We must mend this, now.*

Ori shook his head in frustration. *Yes, but how? Even Galywis couldn't mend it. He could only contain it.*

Galywis is not a draykon.

Right, which is probably the only reason why he could dwell there and only go acceptably *mad. We were hopeless in Orlind. It affects us too deeply.*

We were not hopeless. We managed for a while, though it took some effort to counteract the effects. If we co-operate as a larger group, we can manage for long enough to look around, gather some information.

That will have to be enough, then, said Ori, not sounding convinced. *We can try it.*

We should go at once, I said. *No use in mapping the extent of the corruption any more — we know enough. There isn't time.*

And so we returned to Nuwelin, faster than we could easily bear and already tired from our long flight. It was not my favourite, of all the journeys I have ever taken. By the time we reached our home we were dropping with exhaustion, and poor Sigwide was a shivering ball of distress in his flight bag.

I Changed human again, shuddering with tiredness and the pain in my limbs. I forced my trembling legs to walk about a little, afraid that if I lay down it might take me hours to move again.

The village was largely empty, the others apparently not yet returned from their own errands. I did find Gio, though, lying in Larion's usual spot in the centre. He smiled as I approached with Pense, Sigwide lying in a boneless heap around my neck.

'Morning,' he said, then looked at the sky with a frown. 'At least, I think it is? It is so hard to tell up here.'

'It is always morning,' I told him. 'And afternoon as well. The terms mean little in Iskyr. We speak of days, but the span of time is pretty arbitrary up here.'

'Fair.' He produced something spherical from a pocket and showed it to us, a satisfied smile on his handsome face. 'I brought this for you.'

It was bluish and opaque and I couldn't even tell what it was made from, let alone guess at what it was for. My blank face must have said enough, for he hastily added, 'Oh, it is a… book.'

'It does not look like a book.'

Gio sat up. 'I know that. It is a book in another format, a way of storing information. It doesn't matter how. It contains records from some of the original draykoni projects, unaltered.' He frowned and amended, 'Hopefully unaltered. One can never be sure.'

Ori reached for it, brightening at once. 'Oh, *interesting*. How do I read it?'

'You can't from here. I would have to take you back out to the Library, to a reading room. And you would need my help deciphering it, for it is in an old tongue which is too far removed from yours to be comprehensible. I think.'

'You found that very quickly.' I frowned at him, unable to help feeling a twinge of suspicion. What had he said about the vastness of the collections?

'Not at all. It took a great deal of time — weeks, you would call it. Time passes differently in the Libraries, you must know that.'

I had known, and had briefly forgotten, my mind on other things. 'We have a bigger problem at the moment,' I said, feeling torn. 'I am not sure we can spare Ori to pursue that until we have mended Orlind.'

'Llan! We must. Remember what you said to Eterna — what if there *is* a link? Those records could hold the answers to both problems and I need to see them.'

I looked at Pense, too troubled to think clearly.

He is right, said Pense gently. *We can manage without him while he searches the records, and he is the best person to take on that task.*

There was a time when Pense was always losing his temper and flying into a rage. Somewhere in recent moons, though, he has all but lost this tendency and become a voice of reason instead. I scarcely recognise him as the person I first knew.

I sometimes wonder how much I have altered, in the eyes of my friends. I know it must be a lot, for here I am: far from home, leading a fledgling colony I could not even have imagined a year ago, and grappling with problems that would once have been unthinkable. I have not seen my parents in weeks, and have barely had time to notice, let alone regret the absence of their protection and comfort.

How things change.

'All right, go,' I said. 'As fast as you can, Ori.'

'Yes. But remember, time passes differently up there. I could probably devote weeks to the project and still be back in time for tea.' He gave me a quick kiss on the cheek and a hug, and hugged a bemused Pensould with even more vigour. 'Luck in Orlind. Be careful out there.'

Ori helped Gio to his feet and gave him a hearty slap on the back, a gesture which sent the unwary Gio into a slight stagger. 'Let's go!'

The two young men linked hands and vanished, leaving me alone with Pense. He approached me at once and gathered me close, nuzzling my neck. *I cannot remember the last time we managed to be alone,* he said silently, echoing my own thoughts.

And there is no time to take advantage of it, I replied with regret. In the distance and coming rapidly closer was Nyden, a mote of warmth and brightness in my magical senses.

Pense sighed and released me. *I do wish the worlds would stop ending,* he said, half joking and half sincere. *It is inconvenient.*

Nyden arrived in such a hurry, he almost landed on us. *Wotcha,* he said, or something like it. *Are you busy?*

Not excessively, said Pense gravely.

Great. Orlind is sinking and I thought you might want to look into that.

Sinking…? I repeated, and the word matched the sensation in my heart.

Yeah. Not that badly, just a bit around the edges. But sinking is sinking, right? Loret and I snuck a peak over the mountains. Oh, the corruption has gone way into Iskyr but you knew that by now. It grows at maybe a foot's length a day.

I looked at Nyden's clawed feet. They were much bigger than mine, and probably encompassed three or four of what I would think of as "feet".

My heart began to pound with alarm. *That's too fast!*

You bet it is. Oh and there is a castle in the middle.

A… castle? In the middle of the island?

Big place, nice turrets. Flags. Black as night, though, and looks mad as fire. If a building can look mad. It can, right?

Do you mean mad-crazy or mad-angry?

Both.

That answered any questions I might have had about where Galy was right now. *That will be the Library, but I thought he was running* away *from Orlind? What is he doing there?* It felt odd, referring to a building as *he* or indeed referring to Galy as *the Library,* but no matter. *Weird* and *my life* are practically synonymous terms by now.

No idea, said Nyden. *We took a look from a nice, safe distance and then it was time to fleeeee.*

Pense spoke up. *Where is Loret, out of interest?*

Ny's head snaked around on his long neck. *Uh. Good question.* He ran several steps and launched himself into the air, clumsier than normal. Was he merely tired, or was what Eterna called the *sickness* getting to him, even though he had kept a clear distance from Orlind? That was a troubling thought.

All right, we need to go. I set off for my house as I said it, conscious of the likelihood of Ori and Gio returning to an empty village. I scrawled a hasty note on one of Ori's dried leaf bookmarks and left it on top of his stack of books. I hoped he would find it there, but could do little to make sure of it.

Then I put Siggy back in his pack and slung him around my neck, pausing to grab a handful of berries for him before I left my house.

No, he grumbled, and writhed.

We have to go out again, Sig. You don't want to stay here alone, do you?

He thrashed harder by way of response, but he quieted when I dropped the berries into the bag. *I am sorry,* I told him softly. *Soon we will be finished with this, and can be peaceful again.*

Siggy munched berries noisily. *Whuff,* he said, which is a word I have never heard him use before. I still have no idea what it means.

Good, I said, choosing to take it as agreement. *Then we go.*

And we went.

12 VIII

To Orlind, and Victory!
… or Doom. Probably Doom.

Having already flown a long way south to Eterna's (abandoned) colony and back, it took a great deal out of us to set off for Orlind again so soon. But we had no choice. Matters were now far too urgent to admit of delay, regardless of how much I wished we could stay at home and sleep.

We had forgotten to eat for some time, too, and had little opportunity to rectify this along the way. Soaring into chaos both sleep-deprived and underfed was no wonderful plan, but what else could we do? The island was sinking and Galywis was holding the fort — *literally* — all alone. We would just have to be all right, somehow.

We found Nyden again somewhere along the way, and Loret too. *Get everybody to Orlind,* I told them in passing, having paused only to ascertain that they were well and had no further news for us. *If you find the others, or Avane's folk, please send them after us. And come yourselves, when you can. We need all possible assistance.*

They were weary, too, and I felt terrible issuing such instructions when they clearly needed rest. But urgency compelled me. This was no time for weakness.

When we crossed over into corrupted territory, I felt it almost like a physical blow. It knocked the breath from me and made my head spin, my stomach churn. I had to slow dramatically or I might have fallen out of the sky.

The effect was not as bad, yet, as it had been on the island. I wondered whether that meant that it began mildly enough but would grow worse in time, or whether Orlind was so bad because it was the centre of the disturbance. I hoped to reverse the spread well before we would have time to learn the answer.

Of course, I had no idea how. I quickly put that thought out of my mind before doubt could halt me altogether, and we flew on.

There are some obstacles in between an intrepid adventurer like ourselves and the island known as Orlind. For one, there is a considerable mountain range running along the west coast of Irbel. That barrier is the reason why nobody set foot in Orlind for so many ages, and we had trouble enough passing through on the last occasion.

After that, there is water to cross, for as soon as the mountains end, the ocean begins. Fortunately, what is left of Orlind is not so very far out — it used to be part of the mainland, of course, before much of it fell into the sea.

Then there is the peculiar enchantment that hides the island from sight under a shroud of mist, blocking out much of the light as well as prying eyes. At least we knew what to look for, this time.

I will not recount our struggles in passing these obstacles, wearied as we already were. It was a series of trials and a great strain, and I am in no more hurry to dwell on the remembrance of it than you probably are to hear every detail of that journey.

I *will* share my dismay when I realised I had given Nyden no instructions on how to pass through those mountains.

Ori knows, Pense reminded me.

Ori is not here!

He will be. Remember, time passes differently in the Library.

That could not be good enough. I landed on the gentle slopes before the peaks really began, taking a moment both to catch my breath and to think.

I needed to leave somebody here to guide the others, but who? Pense could not be spared and neither could I send him on alone without me. I thought briefly of Sigwide, but swiftly dismissed the notion. Much as I adore my orting, he is not blessed with sufficient… elasticity of thought, shall we say, to hold and relay such a complex idea.

That did give me a different thought, though.

We had already observed that there were traces of a corrupting taint even in Irbel. *Amasku* is not so strong a force in the middle realms, as we think of them — or Irtand, as they are known elsewhere. Those sensations of wrongness gave me prickles of disquiet, for I had not expected that the problem might infect anything beyond Iskyr and Ayrien.

The animals thereabouts were feeling it, too, though to a lesser extent, and they could have no understanding of the cause of their distress. They only knew that they *were* so; uneasy, alarmed, slightly confused. I closed my eyes and focused upon the creatures nearby, seeking their traces of warmth and bright notes of thought and feeling.

A few daeflies drifted from flower to flower — too small. I sensed subterranean creatures I could put no name to grubbing through the earth and rock below. Birds wheeled through the skies, confusing me with their erratic patterns of flight and gabbling streams of thought. Not useful.

At last I found what I was hoping for: a trace of a drauk, not too far away.

I turned human again, and set off after it. They are small beasts, and would only flee if I tried to approach in one of my larger shapes.

I cannot imagine you have ever tried to have a conversation with a drauk, and if not, I do not especially advise it as a hobby. They are crotchety creatures, prickly and paranoid and totally uninterested in chatting. I could only get this one's attention by appealing to the unaccountable fear I knew it was feeling.

I know why your spine itches and your head aches, I told her. *I know why you cannot rest and your prey runs from you, too frenzied to be caught. I can mend this, but I need help.*

Such promises I had taken to making. As I spoke yet another, I hoped fervently that I could keep it.

The drauk, busily scuttling away from me one moment, stopped and turned to face me. They are curious animals, simultaneously graceful and graceless, with long, thin bodies, glittering black scales, pointed snouts and spiky ears. Not to mention their wickedly sharp claws, which I had no intention of coming into contact with.

What do you want?

Drauks are not particularly gracious creatures either.

It took me a little time to explain my idea, and to persuade the drauk into going along with it. That done, the drauk scuttled away to fetch its brethren and I resumed my search.

The search paid off spectacularly when I encountered an orboe. PERFECT!

I did suffer a moment's regret that Ori was not there. When it comes to managing animals he is far more adept than I, especially the larger ones.

But in Ori's absence, I steeled myself and went after it. If you haven't seen an orboe (and probably you have not, for they are not commonly found wandering around in the Seven) then permit me to paint a picture here: a typical orboe is a four-legged beast, more than six feet long and shaggily furred. Everything fearsome you can imagine by way of teeth and claws is probably applicable. They have massive jaws, and look like they could chew through my leg with minimal trouble.

This particular one was grey-furred, paler than Sigwide — a pretty shade, like benign summer clouds. That did not make it look any less fearsome to me, and I did wish a little that I did not so badly require its help.

Then I realised how silly I was being. I am, after all, a *draykon*. It might have been more appropriate to pursue a drauk in human form, but it wouldn't hurt at all to have my own claws and teeth for this part.

The orboe could not help but notice when he developed a draykon audience of one. At first he took fright and squared up to me, teeth bared. I had to give him full credit for courage, for in that shape I was by far the stronger.

But then he stopped, and the fight slowly drained out of him. I felt scrutinised.

Then I was hit by a surge of joviality. The orboe actually ran at me and rubbed his fur all over my leg.

Hallohellohellohallohullooo! he said. He even touched noses and thoughts with Sigwide, fully as though they had met before. That part *definitely* confused me, for an orboe could eat an orting in one bite.

Graaf...? I said doubtfully.

Graaf! the orboe repeated with dazzling cheer. *Where is my Ori?*

Coming, I assured him, which only increased his delight. *Graaf, what are you doing wandering around Irbel alone?*

Graaf thought about that. *Ori left me here*, he finally decided. *Right here?* When had Ori been this way, and what for?

Not right *here*, Graaf amended. *Near. Maybe? Somewhere.*

I gathered from this that Graaf was growing as confused as the other creatures hereabouts. Ori had probably left him in Iskyr and he had wandered through a rogue gate into Irbel.

Graaf, I want you to help me, I told him. *And I need more of your kind.*

The last part took a little longer to arrange. I opened a gate through into Iskyr, a more stable one than the rogue ones that sometimes emerge, and held it while Graaf went in search of any nearby orboes. He came back fairly quickly, to my relief, with three females, and another two joined us soon afterwards.

Perfect, I told him.

When Pense and I took flight again, we left behind a trail formed of drauks and orboes. The drauks may be small, but their deep black scales stand out well upon the slopes, even from the air. And the orboes, of course, are easy to spot.

When Nyden or any of the others reach this place, they will see a line of beasts pointing the way towards the pass through the mountains. Graaf promised faithfully to keep the line together for as long as possible and to add others to it. I hoped his attention would not wander away from the task too early.

That is possibly the strangest thing I have ever seen you do, Minchu, said Pense with wry amusement as we soared up into the mountains.

I think it is *the strangest thing I've ever done*, I agreed, laughing. As I said, my life doesn't get any less weird.

I admired my obedient line of beasts for as long as they remained in sight. Soon, though, we were deep in the mountains, winging through Ori's pass as fast as we could. The air is thin up there, the wind is fierce and I cannot say that traversing it is an enjoyable experience. At least we knew what to expect this time, which made it a little easier.

When we came out of the pass, we were faced with a vision of the island of Orlind which differed rather markedly from before — insofar as, we could actually see it. We were forced to search for it last time, because it was hidden in a shrouding mist way out over the sea. Now the mist was gone, and the sky was virtually cloudless. We saw the island at once, a small plateau of land adrift not far from the coast. It looked dry and bare from this distance, a patch of desert in the middle of the sea.

Do you want to rest? asked Pense.

I thought about that. *Yes,* I said fervently. Fatigue weighed down my wings and made me feel heavier than ever, and sluggish. Worse, my thoughts were sluggish too. *But we have not time, I think.*

Pense's wings twitched, and I sensed his disapprobation. But my attention was diverted from anything else he might have said, because something odd caught my eye below.

We had not yet reached the sea. The mountains sloped gradually down to the coast — no sheer cliffs in this part, at least — and those slopes were as thickly grown over with alpine plants as they were on the other side. These, though, were vividly purple and lavender and blue and green, except for a neat, pure white patch not far from the shore. We were so far up that the white area was but a fleck in my vision, and I almost missed it.

My heart sank.

Going down, Pense, I told him. I folded my wings and dived.

I suppose I hoped that it was merely a little anomaly in the plant life here, a patch of albino vegetation or something. Of course, it was not. As I drew closer to it, I could see that it was a neat patch of stark white decay, everything in it stone dead.

We landed on the edge of the circle and gazed at the place in silence. Another collection of lifeless draykon bones, a perfect skeleton, whole and undisturbed. There was not a flicker of *amasku* discernible, not only within the corpse itself but also the whole of the lifeless circle.

So close to Orlind. It was the clearest link we have yet discovered between the dead ones of our kind and the beleaguered island… perhaps I had been hoping that they were not related, that the troubled and troublesome Library was not responsible for yet more death. No such luck.

I thought back to our first conversation about this, before everything had become so much more complicated.

What could drain the life out of something like this? I had asked that of Pense, and he had not known.

The power required to drain the life out of a draykon is… to call it considerable would be to badly understate the case.

I thought of the shattered pieces of metal Ori had shown me, a collection of unidentifiable shrapnel carelessly gathered from one site and as carelessly preserved.

Pense, I said, and my thought held so much tension that he stopped at once and looked at me. *Did we see Limbane at the Orlind laboratories, in Galy's visions?*

Not that I recall.

If Limbane knew it was not impossible to extinguish a draykon soul, I bet Galy knows it too. And probably Krays. Somewhere in those visions was a clue...

The white room, said Pense.

That skeleton! I interpreted it as partially constructed but it wasn't, was it? It was dead, like this one. And everything around it was dead, too, only it was one of those empty white featureless laboratories so it didn't show...

And then a spray of metal...

The machine we saw. I was thinking faster now, fully alert for the first time in some hours, my mind alive with realisation and horror. *It did not look like the ones Krays built, but it was not that different either. It was the same thing, Pense! An energy collector. Krays didn't invent those — or if he did, it was not recently. In Galy's mind we saw an early version, and Krays's ones were an improvement upon it.*

Yes, Pense agreed. *But they still explode if they are overburdened.*

I felt sick. *Which they would be, if somebody used them to drain the life out of a draykon,* and *everything around it.*

Or more than one at once, Pense added. *As we found in Ayrien.*

Damn Lokants and their secretiveness, their coldness, their ruthlessness. They created wonders, but at what cost!

Any of them could have used those collectors, I said with frustration. *Limbane, Krays, any of their people. But why would they? What do any of them gain by killing the results of their own projects?*

Pense just shook his head. *We cannot yet know.*

I rubbed at my eyes, hit by another wave of tiredness. And more. The taint of corrupted Orlind was stronger here, and I felt it with every heartbeat. It muddled my mind, nauseated me, made my heart pound with a nameless fright. *We have to press on,* I said to Pense. *There can be no more answers here.*

We left the poor skeleton behind, and I felt a pang of regret at leaving it there alone, its grave unmarked.

We flew, and the island expanded in my vision. I saw the black castle Nyden had described, planted in the centre of the barren land. It looked stark and forbidding, its flags flying defiantly.

Orlind is sinking, he had said.

Was it smaller than it used to be? I could not tell.

The island was still undergoing Changes last time I was here, but I saw nothing of the kind now. It seemed more lifeless than ever — no animals, nothing growing, nothing moving. Just those dark, ugly flags whipping in the wind.

Pense, I said, struck by another thought. *That's why the sickness is spreading. Those machines that Krays brought here, to siphon off the amasku... I wonder if somebody has taken them away? They're being used to kill Elders instead, and the structure Galy made to contain the problem is broken.*

Could be, Pense agreed. *We will ask Galywis.*

If we could wring any sense out of him, yes. We would have to try. He was the only person who knew where he had hidden those machines in the first place.

It grew steadily harder to forge onwards, assaulted as we were by the sickening whirl of energy that marred the island. We flew slower and lower, forced to fight to stay alert, to keep a grip on our senses. I felt that wave of befuddling confusion again, my mind insisting that I was upside down, sideways, inside out... it hits you with frightening force the moment you reach the island, and it takes the fiercest concentration to resist it, to remake the space around you as it needs to be.

I gritted my teeth, forced down the wave of panic that it always induces in me, and flew on.

A moment later, I realised we were not alone on the island. Two figures paced around the base of the castle, one a youthful male figure wearing a red cloak, his hair pure white...

Is that Gio? I said in shock.

The figure turned and saw us coming.

An instant later, he vanished. So did his companion, a woman with the same characteristic snow-white hair.

That was Gio! What is Gio doing here?! And who was that with him?

He did not wish to give us the opportunity to ask him that question, Pense observed.

My bad feelings grew. Gio, who I was beginning to trust because he had shown signs of being a real person after all and I wanted to like him. Gio, who had taken my Ori away and had not yet returned him. If he betrayed us I would *eat him piece by piece.*

I was alarmed to realise that I meant that last part.

If Gio is here, where is Ori?

I felt Pense's concern echoing mine. Ori had gone off with Gio alone — we had *let* him go alone.

Hail, fellows! came a distant voice. *If you go in the creepy castle without me I will be eating you when you come out.*

I banked and turned. Nyden was behind us, winging his way across the sea with enviable insouciance. He was but a black speck on the horizon at first, but he approached swiftly, swiftly on those enormous wings of his. Behind him came Ivi, Larion and Meriall.

For a second I could almost have wept, so relieved was I to have help. I was more certain than ever that we were going to need it.

Nyden flashed his teeth in a grin as he drew level with us, and dipped his wings in an oddly dandified greeting. *You waited! I love you.*

Be careful here, everyone, I said. *Orlind is tricky and it will dump you on your head if you don't watch out.*

We noticed, said Meriall drily, and indeed, she was weaving about with an air of confusion, visibly steadying herself. So were the others.

I looked back at Nyden, puzzled, for there was no trace of distress with him. *Ny, do you not feel the chaos?*

Yep, he said cheerily. *What a ride.*

A *ride?* I stared at him in utter disbelief. Nobody could possibly feel that and be *entertained* by it.

Nyden gave me a sudden, penetrating look, as though he had never seen me before. *Is that an orting strapped to your foreleg?*

Yes it is.

He blinked sleepily at me, and sucked thoughtfully upon one long fang. *May one be permitted to ask why you carry tiny, edible passengers bound to your fine and shapely limbs?*

Sigwide sensed that he was under discussion, though the cheery greeting he gave Nyden suggested he had missed the substance of the conversation.

Nyden grinned, wide and toothily. *Hello, snack. I am delighted to see you too.*

He is not edible!

Dear lady, he most certainly is. Tasty, too, though they make no more than a morsel.

Sigwide is not for eating, and stop changing the subject. How does it make you feel, Ny? This place.

Can we please land for a minute, said Ivi. She was struggling, and I reproached myself for not thinking of it sooner.

We winged down and perched upon the shore, keeping to the edge of the island. It grew swiftly worse the nearer you got to the centre, and we all needed a little time to gather ourselves before we ventured that far.

Not too close to the edge, though. I saw what Nyden meant: the pale, lifeless earth had turned boggy near the water. *Sinking indeed.* I stepped a little too close to the sea and my foot sank deeply into mud which felt more like quicksand. I hastily withdrew.

Ny? I prompted, as he lazily floated down and landed, light as a daefly, upon the bare earth. Pense and I landed rather more heavily, and Ivi, Larion and Meri all but collapsed onto the ground, graceless and frightened and relieved.

Alive, he replied. He was restless, dancing from foot to foot and shuffling his wings. Energised, certainly — perhaps too much so. But his reaction was markedly different from the others. He was thriving on this messed up place, though not in a healthy way. He was frenzied, everything in him going too fast. For all his habitual display of laziness, I got the sense that he was barely in control of himself.

A thought occurred to me. *Ny, are you… old?*

Way old!

Really old?

Really really. Ny's tail swayed back and forth contentedly.

Do you, uh… remember having parents?

Nobody remembers having parents.

In other words, no. I eyed him with some fascination. Pense was filling the others in on our discoveries, and Ny bent his head to listen, his tail tapping with lively interest. I focused on Nyden, surveying him first with my eyes and then with my other senses.

In my mind's eye, Larion, Meriall and Ivi were patches of flickering brightness and warmth in the writhing mess of energies that was the island. Chaos seethed around them, tugging at them, tormenting their peace, tearing their brightness into pieces. I quaked, seeing how easily they could be engulfed. I had no doubt I was the same.

Pense was a brighter, stronger presence. He radiated a fierce vibrancy the others lacked, his heart's energy an ordered pattern.

If Meriall flickered and Pense glowed, Nyden *shone.* He was a tiny sun, a self-contained bundle of strong magical energy. I watched as chaos reached for him with hungry little hands and was… absorbed, its broken patterns melting smoothly into the perfection of Nyden's. But it did not disappear without trace. He was soaking it up, I think involuntarily, and I could feel its effects upon him — the first flickers of danger in the frenzied currents of his life force. But those energies swirled through him in a rush and flowed back out, creating a little space around him where the patterns matched his own. More or less.

Pense, I said to him silently. *Ny is an Elder, isn't he?*

Yes. He answered me absently, still engaged in discussion with the others.

Look at him. I mean, really look *at him.*

Pensould turned, and subjected Nyden to the full weight of his scrutiny. Nyden had drifted off into a world of his own by then and sat crooning some mad little song to himself, oblivious to all the attention he was attracting.

I think we can conclude that you are not an Elder, I told him. *You are much older than the rest of us, and pure draykon besides. Apparently that means that your connection to this world and these energies is stronger than ours. But the Elders are in a class of their own! Look at him. He breathes it like air, and he is imposing his own order around him.*

Temporarily, perhaps, for chaos whirled around all of us, as ferocious as a storm and as far beyond control. The fact that Nyden could influence it at all was remarkable.

Pense stared at Ny, as electrified as I was. *But… if the aim of Krays's Library is to restore Orlind, why would they be killing off the very people who can positively affect it?*

Perhaps they are not killing anybody. Maybe someone else is responsible for that.

My head ached at the idea that we might have multiple Lokant factions involved, and some of them unidentified. Was Limbane lurking about somewhere, sticking his fingers into the Seven Realms pie yet again? If so, what was he up to? I hated to think that *he* might be the one killing Elders. We might have parted ways with him in the end, but I still struggle to think of him as so outright a villain.

We need to know more, said Pense, his frustration echoing my own. I thought again of Ori, and wondered if he was safe, and what he had found.

We also need to keep a closer eye on Nyden. I thought for a second, and added, *And we need to get hold of more Elders.*

Pense nodded, following my line of thinking without needing to enquire. The corrosive effect of the island was probably the single biggest obstacle to our accomplishing anything useful here at all — either helping Galy, or renewing the land. But so many Elders had been killed, and Nuwelin had only ever had Nyden.

I thought of Eterna, and cursed her again in my mind. How many Elders did she have among her much larger colony?

Ny, Meriall. Larion. Did any of you get hold of Avane?

The lady's on her way. Nyden's words radiated a thrumming appreciation, which slightly took me aback.

With her people?

All the everybody. It will be a fine family party.

Meriall rolled her eyes. *Ny flirted with her disgracefully.*

I felt Ny's mental grin, even without looking at him. *She is delicious.*

I let that pass. *How many Elders are with her?*

Nyden shrugged his wings. *I did not look.*

I can't tell, said Meriall, and Ivi agreed.

None, said Larion.

Meriall blinked at him. *How do you know that?*

Larion shrugged his wings, echoing Ny's gesture. *I have no idea. They just feel different to me.*

Another interesting point. Pense could spot Elders easily enough, but those of us with human heritage struggled — except Larion. *Larion, you are going to be useful for that. Keep an eye out for Elders, please, and let me know if we encounter any?*

Larion did not reply, but he nodded seriously at me.

No more Elders, then. Just Ny. It would not be enough. It was not just the question of Galy/the Library being under some kind of siege and the unpromising presence of unidentified Lokants on the island. There still loomed the question of how to renew this place, if we could, and seeing Nyden's effect on the environment I could not help formulating the beginnings of a hopeful plan. If we could gather enough draykoni here, as many of them Elders as possible, perhaps we could really achieve something.

But that was for later. The place was still contested. Galy was still dead, murdered by an unknown person. Somebody — possibly the same person — had sent him fleeing from Orlind and had pursued him across Iskyr. Somebody was still killing

Elders. Eterna still hated us and refused to work with us at all. Ori was missing and Gio's motives were in question, more directly so than ever before. Oh, and Orlind's sickness was spreading across Iskyr and Ayrien and even infecting the Seven a little.

We had a host of problems to deal with before we could think about mending this place.

I looked at Nyden again, and Larion and Ivi and Meriall… and another unpromising thought darted into my mind.

'How are they finding the Elders?' I said aloud.

Everybody looked at me blankly. 'What?' said Ivi. 'The Lokants?'

'Yes. Whoever is responsible for *killing* them. There are multiple draykoni colonies spread over the whole of Iskyr and Ayrien — finding any individual draykoni is no easy task to begin with. Once found, how can they tell which are Elders? Even most of *us* cannot easily tell. Nobody without our heritage should have any idea.'

'But the chart room?' said Ivi. 'They have better information about the Elders than we do.'

'They are just names,' I replied, shaking my head. 'Just names written on a wall. How do you match a name to a particular individual? They knew that *Ludino* and *Myir* were Elders but how could they know what they looked like or where to find them?'

'The closer you are to being an Elder, the easier it is to spot the others,' said Meriall grimly.

I nodded, unwilling to voice the rest of my thoughts aloud. Pense's face prevented me. He looked stricken, and sick to the soul.

'They have had help,' he said at last. His wings flexed abruptly, and he let out a roar of disgust.

'Yep,' said Meriall. 'You are right, Pensould: it probably is not draykoni killing other draykoni. But some of us, somewhere, are helping the killers.'

I felt sick, too. How could any of us so betray the others? I thought of Eterna. She was the only one I knew who could be cruel enough, who could hate enough… and she had shown a surprisingly sympathetic attitude to Krays. But would she? Her own mother had been one of the victims. Why would she do it?

'Why, though?' said Ivi, echoing my thoughts. 'They must be getting something out of it.'

I shut my eyes for a minute. Everything was getting badly on top of me. There was so much going on, so many questions to which we had no answers — only more and more questions. It never ended. My mind was awhirl with it; I felt dizzy with the pressure and the frustration.

'We need Ori,' I said at last.

Larion had said little, though he was by no means inattentive. Every time I looked his way, I saw his eyes fixed upon a different part of the island, surveying everything. At length, he spoke. 'That castle is moving.'

We all whipped around as one, and stared at the looming black monstrosity in the centre of the island. Or, it *had* been in the centre when I had last looked at it a few minutes before. It was not moving now, but it was closer.

As we watched, the flags all changed colour from black to white, and grew bigger. The sheer face of the fortress's front had no door, but now it developed one, a vast round portal which opened in clear invitation.

'I think Galy wants to talk to us,' said Meriall, frowning. 'Again.'

We could not deny such a request, though I think none of us was thrilled at the prospect of being swallowed once more by such a confusing, chaotic and sometimes dangerous building. This time, though, we were different: all in our draykon forms, we made a much more formidable group. And we needed to talk to him. We launched ourselves skyborne and flew, mostly in a straight line, though there was some weaving about on the part of Meri, Ivi and Larion.

When we were halfway across the intervening distance, the castle made a sudden lunge for us. One moment it was still far away; the next, it loomed directly above us, dark and forbidding, its portal gaping wide.

'Oh Galy, please don't do that again…' I began, but too late. The open door yawned wider; black brick and an onrush of shadow engulfed our senses and we were swallowed whole into the depths of the fortress-that-was-Galywis (and the Library of Orlind).

Light, air and freedom vanished with a booming *snap* of the door behind us.

We tumbled in a heap onto a cold, dark stone floor. I was knocked back into my human shape by the shock of it, and for a moment I lay limp, too surprised to react. Sigwide's whimpering recalled me to myself, for he had fallen out of his sling and lay curled in an unhappy ball a few feet away.

Or... no, not whimpering. He was giggling again, and by no means unhappy. He curled himself into a tighter ball, his fur sticking up in a bristly grey thatch, and began rolling madly about, bumping willy-nilly into the various prone bodies lying inert upon the floor.

Siggy, I sighed, and gathered him up. It was an amusing display, but exactly then was not the time.

He protested. *But I like it.*

You like berries, too. Here's some. I retrieved some of my dried supply from a pocket and offered them by way of a bribe, which was as effective as always.

This done, I hauled myself to my feet and looked around. What manner of place had Galy made for us this time?

We were in a vast, stone-built hall, and... that was it. The structure was enormous, and poorly lit, so I could see nothing of the ceiling or even the farthest wall. There was no furniture, no windows, no adornments, nothing. It was just empty space.

Pense had hung onto his draykon shape and lay on the other side of the hall. He got to his feet as I watched and shook himself, grunting his displeasure. Nyden was his usual self: scaled, as inky-black as the hall, and blithely untouched by the abrupt change in our circumstances. He stretched lazily and curled his tail around himself with a sleepy smile. *I like this game.*

The others had all lost their grip on their draykon selves, like me, and were staggering shakily upright. Nobody seemed to be lastingly hurt, which quieted my concerns somewhat.

'Galy,' I called. 'We are delighted to see you, of course, but what are you doing here? And what are *we* doing here?'

In answer, one wall cleared and brightened and turned transparent, like a single, vast window. Through it, we could see the cracked, bare earth of the island beyond and the glittering, sunlit sea farther still.

It was no longer empty.

The two Lokants we had seen before had returned. One of them was definitely Gio, I saw to my mingled disgust and dismay. His companion was a Lokant woman of much more advanced years. Her white hair hung loose in a tangled mess, and she appeared to be similarly uninterested in neatness of dress, for her simple black shirt, trousers and coat were rumpled and shabby. She and Gio looked at ease together, I thought, like they knew each other well. Though, it was hard to tell with Gio. He always looked impassive.

With them came others: three that I could see, two women and a man, of various ages. I could determine little else about them: they were as featureless in dress and appearance as Gio's unidentified companion, and they carried nothing that might give us a clue as to their intentions.

What worried me more was Galy's reaction to this group. If he had still been a man, he would have been quivering with rage. As it was, his stones shook and rumbled with anger and waves of fury beat upon us, almost a palpable force. I stretched out a hand and found stone, even if I couldn't see it. I laid my hand upon it in an instinctive gesture of comfort, though I doubt that it helped.

'Galy, who are these people?' I said. I was not very hopeful of a useful response and I received none, but the question hung in the air.

'What are they doing?' asked Meriall.

Galy either did not know or could not tell us, for nothing changed. We could only watch as the little group of Lokants approached the castle and stood staring up at it, conferring amongst themselves. We heard nothing of their conversation. I wondered if they could see us as we could see them, but that was unlikely; they gave no sign of having spotted us, and did not appear to realise that they were observed.

I wanted to march out there and interrogate Gio. What was he doing on Orlind, with such company? And *what had he done with Ori?*

'It's *Gio,*' said Meriall suddenly.

Had she only just noticed? 'Yes, it is.'

'No. I mean, Gio must be the one helping whoever's killing Elders. He is half draykon, isn't he?' Her eyes narrowed, and she folded her arms indignantly. 'After we were so welcoming, too.'

I mostly remembered Meri being witheringly sarcastic to Gio and blatantly distrustful of him, but I said nothing of that. 'He might be,' I said cautiously. 'But if so, he is much less draykoni than most of us here, and we have a difficult time spotting Elders ourselves.'

'But it is possible.'

I felt torn. I hated the idea that Gio was so complete a betrayer. I wanted to be vindicated in my decision to trust him — and if he was so far in league with the Lokant killers, what did that suggest about Ori's safety? My heart fluttered with trepidation at the idea.

On the other hand, he was a convenient culprit because he was not one of us. If *he* was responsible, we did not have to face the prospect that one of our own had aided so cruel and ruthless a regime. I could see why Meriall so readily seized upon the idea.

Her suggestion found willing agreement from Ivi and even Larion. Pense, too. This eagerness to turn upon him with no real evidence troubled me, and I felt more strongly than ever that I wanted to defend him.

But how could I? I had no evidence that he was trustworthy either, and here he inexplicably was: wandering Orlind where he should not be, and in company with a group of Lokants we knew nothing about. The chances that they were here to help anything *we* cared about seemed slim.

For a second I was really tempted to go out there and confront him. I was growing tired of the lack of answers, tired of having to wait for something to change, for somebody to slip up and reveal something, or for somebody else to hand us the information we needed. I felt like wringing Gio's neck until he told me everything he knew.

These uncharacteristically violent tendencies were forestalled by an arresting sight which swiftly distracted my attention: a flutter of colour on the horizon. I held my breath, unsure what I was hoping for except for... *something*. Something good, something useful, a change. I hardly dared hope for Ori.

The flickers of colour resolved into a line of draykoni, advancing on the wing at terrific speed. I saw shades of red, purple, green, blue, everything... my eyes strained, searching for the one I was most anxious to see.

There, in the midst of the approaching crowd: a large, muscular drayk with a familiar shimmering golden hide.

'That's Ori!' I yelled, relief and hope making me unusually loud in my excitement. I found I was bouncing on my toes, so delighted was I to see him coming.

I wanted to run out of the castle again to meet him, and see who he had brought with him. Only, there remained a group of Lokants in between them and us. It might be better if these people were not informed that they had such a large number of draykoni ranged against them, but it was too late for that.

'Galy...' I began, but faltered, unsure what to say.

'We need to get out,' said Pense.

'No, we need to stay here,' said Larion.

'Bring Gio here, and get rid of the rest,' Meri added in a cold voice.

'Galy is keeping us safe,' Ivi said, with a rare smile. 'Isn't that right?'

Galy rumbled his agreement... or perhaps it was disagreement. Stone blocks are not especially easy to interpret.

We were certainly safe. Nobody would get in without Galywis's permission. But we were also confined, and our situation could quickly turn into a siege if we were not careful. What would be best to do?

I thought over the possibilities, and made a decision. 'Galy, can you please get our friends in here?'

There was a clamour of disagreement from my companions, which troubled me more than I cared to show. It is a new experience, having to make difficult choices and alienating others in the process.

It is especially difficult to oppose Pense. If he is not with me, I feel lost.

'We have few options,' I persisted. 'We have no idea who those Lokants are, or what they are doing here. We don't know what Gio's up to, we don't know what Ori has found out, we don't know who killed Galywis or the Elders or why — we hardly know anything! What we *need* before we can proceed is information, and that means we need access to Ori and time and safety enough to hear him out. So, we need to get him in here, and everybody he has brought with him, because they are our friends and we do not know if those Lokants pose a threat until we have heard from Ori. Does anybody disagree with any of this?'

Silence, which heartened me a little.

'Does anyone have a better plan?'

Heads shook, and nobody spoke. Pense began to pace, but he did not raise any further complaints.

I understood. We had spent enough time cooped up in the Library, and the fact that we could not necessarily rely on Galy to release us when we wanted him to was a concern.

Nonetheless, we needed to talk to Ori.

'Well then Galy, please scoop them up.'

The draykoni were over the sea by now, and closing in upon us fast. We watched as they winged closer and closer, and swooped over the heads of the startled Lokants.

At exactly the perfect moment, the roof of the Library vanished with an artistic puff of mist and the building took what felt like a huge, gulping breath.

'Er...' I said, realising fractionally too late what was happening. In our discussions and pacings we had wandered into the centre of the hall and that suddenly looked like a very bad place to be. 'To the walls! *Run!*

We scarpered, dashing for the safety of the walls at top speed. I managed to scoop up Sigwide in the nick of time, and all but fell against the nearest wall just as a rain of draykoni fell in upon us.

The ceiling snapped into place with a satisfied sigh, and a ghostly smile drifted briefly across the dark expanse of stone.

'Nice job, Galy,' I said shakily.

The smile widened, and disappeared.

All around us, shocked and bruised draykoni staggered to their feet and shook themselves. A clamour of voices filled my head as everybody wanted to know where they were and what had happened, all at once.

I left Pense and Larion to explain and answer questions. I scanned the crowd, looking for those familiar to me.

Ori! I hurled myself at him, too delighted to see him to remember my dignity.

Oof, he said and tackled me. We rolled a bit, snorting with laughter. *This is lovely,* Ori continued, *but what did I do to deserve so much enthusiasm?*

I thought you might be dead, I explained, curling up on him.

Dead? Why?

He sounded so nonplussed that I felt foolish. *Er. Because Gio is here on Orlind with some other Lokants and he was supposed to be with you.*

He's here? Ori craned his neck, but he couldn't see past the crowd of draykoni to the window-wall.

Right out there, with a much older woman and a few more.

Ori's tail swished. *He didn't mention anything about that. What is he doing here?*

We don't know.

You haven't asked him?

No... not yet. I probably would have done that next, if you hadn't shown up. Ori, did you find anything in Limbane's Library?

Nope.

My heart sank like a rock, all my hopes dashed in one flat syllable. *Nothing whatsoever?*

No, because... Ori stretched his wings and refolded them, swaying. *Because I wasn't in Limbane's Library.*

What?

I wasn't in Limbane's Library. Neither were you.

I don't understand. Gio took us there.

Gio took us... somewhere else. Ori seemed troubled now, restless and fidgeting. *I need to see him,* he said abruptly.

Ori... it could be dangerous to go out there right now. We have no idea who he is with or what they want.

I won't go outside. Ori shouldered his way through to the window-wall and sat hunched, gazing out at the little group of Lokants. They had retreated some way from the castle walls and were deep in discussion, all of them looking rattled and perhaps irate. Well, the sudden appearance and then *dis*appearance of so many draykoni would test anybody's nerves.

Gio was prominent among them, his red cloak drawn closed against the sea wind. He appeared to be doing much of the talking, and I wished that we could hear what he was saying.

Ori, I prompted him after a while. *What did you mean, Gio took us somewhere else? What did you learn?*

Gio took us to Krays's Library, Sulayn Phay, Ori replied grimly. *He is Krays's grandson, not Limbane's.*

I was shocked into silence, my mind awhirl. *Oh, no,* I whispered at last. *We trusted him and it's my fault.*

Ori's tail lashed. *Just because he is related to Krays doesn't make him a villain, Llan.*

That... is true...

Necessarily. But here he is, and with her.

What? Who is she? I looked more closely at Gio's female companions. I decided at once that Ori must mean the elder, for Gio never strayed far from her side.

Her name is Dwinal. She is Gio's grandmother.

Krays's widow?

Ori shrugged. *I have no idea if Lokants marry or anything like that, but in effect. Yes. And she is definitely bad news, Llan.*

What about his mother? Was she really a draykon?

I don't know.

I watched Dwinal and Gio, my stomach churning. They looked... like they were used to each other. Although that said, I detected some small signs of discomfort in Gio, usually so composed. He darted an occasional look at the castle when Dwinal wasn't looking his way, his perfect brow furrowed, and every time he did so he paced an uneasy step. But it was impossible to guess what he might be thinking.

I spent a lot of time with him, up there, Ori said abruptly. *He's all right, even if he is Krays's grandson. Or so I thought.* He shook himself. *Right, let's gather everybody. I know what they're doing out there and everyone needs to hear it.*

It took a little while to gather the attention of all the draykoni now crammed into Galy's hall. There must have been thirty at least, a mixture of hereditaries like myself and purebloods like Pense. No Elders, though, if I was any judge — save only for Nyden of course. Most of the rest of Nuwelin had made it here, and Avane's people. There were even a few purebloods I recognised from neither group, and I wondered where they had come from.

We have a few defectors from Eterna's mob, Ori told me by way of explanation.

More like Nyden. Interesting. Speaking of whom, I saw him sidle up to Avane with an insinuating smile, his tail curling around her possessively.

I did not think she looked entirely delighted with this development, so I went over at once and drew her away from him, ignoring the dirty look Nyden gave me.

I am not going to eat her, Ny said resentfully. *I am just going to... devour her.*

I judged he said this to me only, for Avane made no sign of having heard. I ignored it.

How is Lyerd? I asked her as we made our way back over to Ori.

He is well. I've left him with Wrima. She says she is too old for saving the world.

It does take some energy, I agreed. The thought proved to be an unwelcome reminder of how weary I was, but I ignored that, too. At least in the Library, the constant pull of corrupted *amasku* was muted. We were insulated from it here, and the respite was most welcome.

Though that was an interesting point. How was it that this Library, so intrinsically bound to the island's energies as it was, could be so comparatively peaceful? It must be Galy's doing. He was shielding us somehow.

That made me madder than ever that somebody had killed him. If anybody could devise a way to renew the island, it would be Galy. Even if he, too, had been emphatic about its impossibility.

Right, quiet down, Ori said, his voice rising over the babble. We had arranged ourselves into a circle in Galy's airy hall and Ori stood in the middle, looking majestic and surprisingly at home there. *Everyone has been brought up to date with what we are doing here, and why? Yes?*

There was a rumble of general agreement.

Great. First, then, those people outside. That's Dwinal and Gio, widow and grandson of Krays respectively. Gio is the one who claims to be half draykoni, currently unverified. The others are Danalt, Hyarn and Tynara. They are all members of the Library known as Sulayn Phay, once led by Krays and now by Dwinal.

We have long assumed that Krays's intention here was to revive Orlind, the Master Library — that's what we are currently standing in, by the way, if you didn't know. If he succeeded, we thought he would install himself as the new Master of the Libraries, a position Galywis long held, and so wrest control of all the subsidiary Lokant Libraries that there are. It's an ambitious plan, fitting for an ambitious and ruthless man. But that is not what he was doing.

Galywis is a legend among his own people for his achievements, greatest amongst them being: every one of us. His is the mind that conceived of us, designed us, created us, and he is revered for it — rightly enough, even if the project itself left much to be desired, and ended in disaster. Galywis called an early halt to the draykon project because something went awry, though I could not find out what. The records were incomplete, I suspect partially destroyed.

That was a surprise, and an unpleasant one. I had grown used to thinking of Galywis's project as an unqualified triumph. What could possibly have gone so badly wrong that Galy had abandoned the project altogether?

Many people seek fame, Ori continued. *Krays was no different. He wanted to be a legend, like Galywis — to surpass him, even. In order to do that, he had to equal and then outdo Galy's achievements. That means creating something even greater, even more remarkable, than us.*

For that, he needed this Library, or to build such another structure himself. I do not know whether he intended the former, or whether he was here to study Galy's creation in order to learn how to replicate it. Either way, Galywis was an obstacle. One which Hyarn recently removed, or so he thought.

Hyarn. Galywis's killer, finally named. I felt a ripple of anger from Galywis, and the walls rumbled and shook with his displeasure.

Krays was siphoning amasku from Orlind and taking it back to Sulayn Phay. He rigged up a network of draykon bone in his laboratories and used it to anchor the energy, and he's fixed it up so that its patterns mimic the healthy energies that Llan and Pense and the others saw in Galy's visions. And he's using that as a creche for his new, superior race of draykoni.

How do you know all this, Ori? I asked.

I have been to his Library. I saw the laboratories he has set up there, and what he is doing with them. They look like everything you described, Llan, everything Galy showed you. His design is a little different, but in essence the project is the same. He was trying to build a new version of us. New, improved, better than Galy's. Perhaps it was only meant to be an intermediary project, a learning experience prior to his embarking upon a project entirely his own. I cannot tell.

Krays may be dead, but Dwinal and the rest of Sulayn Phay are committed to finishing his work.

Galy was growing angrier, and agitated. The Library shook around us as though an earthquake rippled through the island, and I began to fear for the stonework. For once, I could guess the direction of his thoughts.

And Hyarn? I prompted.

Ori's tail lashed again. *Gio told me.*

Gio. Loyal to Sulayn Phay and his grandmother, not Limbane at all. His presence here with Dwinal and Galy's murderer could scarcely be misconstrued. He had approached us in order to learn about us — *that* was why he wanted to be taught the ways and arts of the draykoni, not because he had any such heritage himself. What else had he lied about?

I thought back to our visit to the chart room — supposedly Limbane's, but actually a copy. I was not surprised that there was a similar chamber at Sulayn Phay, because Krays had modelled much of his Library on others. That appeared to be a common habit of his, emulation. Perhaps his records were more complete than Limbane's, however. Limbane had been more concerned with living draykoni, or those with sufficient heritage to become so. Krays was more interested in long-past history. It explained why Pense's name was absent from Limbane's chart room, at least.

Something Ori said was nagging at me, and I ignored the babble of voices as others began asking questions. What was it...

Gio told me.

Did Gio take you to those labs, too? I asked Ori.

Yea. And he got the records from the original draykoni project from the same place. He said it was his grandfather's copy.

He told you himself, about being related to Krays?

Kind of. I realised after a while that we were not at Limbane's and then he had to explain.

I frowned, thinking. There was something else yet, something that teased at the back of my mind...

Study. Krays was studying the Library of Orlind, the original records from Galywis's project... what else had he been studying? How else could he learn the details of Galy's achievement?

If it were me, I would certainly be curious about draykoni like myself and Meri and the others.

Were we designed to Change? I asked Ori.

No mention of it in the records, he said briefly, distracted by the questions of others.

Limbane had once claimed that his people were the reason why mine originally began to take human shape. It was something *they* taught us to do, towards the end of the devastating wars between draykoni and humankind. To hide us, to allow us a chance to survive. I thought that meant they were responsible for our ability to change our shape altogether.

But there was no mention of it. A number of things about us had taken even our creators by surprise. We had developed in unexpected ways, perhaps because even Galy hadn't fully understood the *amasku* and all that it meant. No wonder Gio had been sent to investigate us.

But if it were me, I would also want to study the ones Galy had constructed himself. The prototypes. The *Elders.*

I thought about the energy collectors we had seen before.

We had known since moons past that Krays had wanted to siphon off the *amasku* from Orlind, but we had never fully understood what he planned to do with it. We had assumed that he merely wanted to get rid of it, as part of an attempt to cure the Library of Orlind. But we were wrong there. He simply needed the energy, as much of it as possible, and presumably from the closest source to the original.

Where *else* could he — or his heirs — collect such energy?

The Elders weren't being killed, I said, sickened to my core. *They were being harvested.*

My words cut across the hall, and Ori stopped talking abruptly. His head snaked around to stare at me, and silence stretched.

Bastards, he said at last. *Of course they were.*

The realisation that Elders were dying for so dispassionate a reason chilled me more than I can say. It seemed *worse,* somehow, for it was so cold, so impersonal. Dwinal and her colleagues neither knew nor cared who any of those people were, what kind of lives they led, what they might have done with the rest of their days. They were captured and stripped of useful parts, like... like harvesting a crop of vegetables. I cannot imagine the callousness of the person who can do that.

But that's Lokants for you. Their distance from our worlds is so great, and their erstwhile power over us so complete, I do not think they view us as people at all. Not even Galy had shown any real empathy for the draykon prototypes he had built and driven insane in the process. They, too, had been casually destroyed to make way for the next one, and the next one.

I had clenched my feet so hard, my own claws were digging into my hide. I forced myself to breathe deeply and relax, shaking my head to loosen tense muscles.

Pense spoke up in a shattering roar. *They will destroy NO MORE OF US. I pledge my life against it.*

I went to him, though it was difficult to calm him when I was so agitated myself.

But who has been the betrayer? said Avane. *That is yet unknown, is it not?*

She was right. Until we learned who had led Dwinal to her victims, we could not guarantee that there would be no more.

I looked around at the hall full of draykoni, and shuddered inside. It could be anybody in *here,* even. How could we possibly know?

We need help, Meriall said. *Lokant help. We can't get anywhere near Dwinal and her crazy friends without it.*

There is only Gio, said Ori. His tone struck me as wistful, and I caught him gazing out through the window-wall in a manner I can only describe as forlorn. He looked away quickly as soon as he saw me watching him, and his tail twitched a restless, staccato rhythm upon the stone floor.

He cannot be trusted, I said, firmly but not without regret. It still stung, that I had vouched for him only to find that he had lied about everything.

Ori sighed.

He's coming here, Avane said.

I looked outside. She was right: Gio had separated himself from his group and was approaching the castle. He made a fine figure, striding purposefully and confidently across the barren ground with his red cloak flapping in the wind. He stopped at the wall and, to my surprise, knocked politely upon it.

Hushed silence fell in the hall.

What is he doing? Meriall said at last. She sounded as annoyed as she was confused. *He must realise he is not welcome in here.*

A few of the draykoni actually shrank back, visibly frightened. That struck me as odd, given the considerable difference in size, might and ferocity between them and the lone figure of Gio. But we had just heard that Gio was part of a group whose technology had successfully killed many Elders, in ways previously thought impossible. Their fear was natural enough.

Somewhat to my surprise, I found I was not afraid. Fear was so natural to me, I felt strange without it, as though I had forgotten an important article of clothing. Nonetheless, I was filled with sadness and regret and disgust and urgency, but not fear.

Oh, and *anger.* I was with Meriall and Pense in that.

It is all right, I said reassuringly. *He cannot get in.* The Library had been closed against us when we had first come to Orlind, there being no door even to knock upon — or stairs to reach it, which was a major obstacle considering the building had been floating some way above the ground at the time. We had made stairs and a door, something we could do because we were able to manipulate the rich energies this remarkable Library was steeped in. Galy had permitted us to do so then, but he had denied all of us the means to influence his beloved *old girl* since. *He would have to be a drayk after all even to try, which I doubt, and anyway Galy would never allow —*

I stopped. Gio had taken a step back and surveyed the sheer face of the castle with an air of purpose, and then actually cracked his knuckles in preparation to do... what?

That question was soon answered when a door appeared in the stone.

It was misshapen and shaky, and his first attempt wavered and vanished after a mere few seconds. But it *happened.*

His next attempt was much better. A plain wooden door appeared, square at the corners and hung upon simple iron hinges and, by all appearances, perfectly functional.

Gio knocked again, and the sound echoed weirdly through the hall.

He waited.

Galy won't let him in, I said again, though my confidence was wavering. How had Gio made the door? Gracious, had he been telling the truth about something? Was he half drayk after all? Why had Galy allowed it?

He never felt like a drayk to me. I'd probed him repeatedly with my magnificent magical senses and never felt a whisker of the drayk about him.

'Did you do that, Galy?' I asked the air.

I felt his *no* shiver through the floor beneath my feet.

Oh, dear.

'Don't let him in,' said Meriall. She stood, arms folded, watching Gio with a scowl.

'Let him in!' said Ori urgently. He had been watching through the wall for a while, and something he had seen was distressing him.

What's the matter, Ori? I asked him.

While we were talking, Gio had a massive fight with his grandmother. I thought they were going to hurt him. I need to talk to him!

The door creaked open. Gio dashed inside, and the door not only slammed behind him but disappeared as well.

We stared at Gio, and he stared back.

'Hello,' he said. 'Um. Any chance of shelter for a homeless ex-Librarian?'

Nobody knew what to say to that, least of all me. There had

been too many surprises, and I was too tired. My brain refused to process his words for several long seconds and then I hardly knew how to feel. What in the world was he up to *now*?

Gio's eyes shifted from drayk to drayk, probably looking for somebody he recognised. He grew steadily less comfortable under my eyes, his customary composure fraying by the second. I realised he was upset, genuinely so.

Ori shifted human in a flash and ran for Gio. To my further surprise, the two engulfed each other in a tight hug and held it, oblivious in that moment to the scrutiny of their audience. After a while, Ori drew back and gave Gio a searching look. 'Is this the truth?' he said softly.

Gio nodded. His eyes were huge, and he looked petrified. 'I swear it.'

Ori's smile could have put the suns to shame.

I exchanged a look with Pense.

What exactly is going on here? Pense said.

Um. Looks to me like the question of Gio matters a lot more to Ori than to the rest of us...

I Changed back to human as well, and collected my sleepy orting on my way through to Ori and Gio. I deposited Sigwide in Gio's arms, to his surprise, though he instinctively curled his arms around the dozy bundle of fur, his fingers gently stroking. I approved of that as a good sign.

'You look like you need a hug,' I told him.

I turned to Ori. *What's going on?* I asked him silently.

Gio's all right, he said, repeating his earlier assertion. *He's had a terrible time with them, Llan. His family are appalling and they've used him all his life. He needs us.*

Ori's mental voice shook with emotion, and I felt a sense of foreboding grow, because it was obvious that my sweet, cheery, bright and lovely Ori had fallen in love. What's more, it appeared to be mutual.

I surveyed Gio anew, making no secret of my scrutiny. He bore it patiently, though I thought he looked more tired than resigned. He fully expected to be rejected; I read it in the slump of his shoulders, the shadows under his eyes, and the way he found it so difficult to meet my gaze.

'If your grandmother wanted a spy in here, you'd be the perfect person to send,' I said flatly. 'And what better way than to stage a fight and pretend you have switched sides?'

'I realise it must look that way,' said Gio softly. 'But it's not like that. I swear.'

And once again, it came down to a simple choice: were we going to trust him, or not? Would we choose to have faith in another person and help him, whatever his background, or would we choose suspicion and cynicism in order to protect ourselves?

Thoughts? I directed the question at Pense, Ori and Avane.

I believe him, said Ori, not at all to my surprise. *Please help him,* he added, so forlornly that my heart bled a little.

It clearly affected Avane as well, for she melted at once. *I say we give him a chance. We can keep an eye on him... Ori can keep an eye on him.*

I looked at Pense. He stared back at me, his eyes dark with worry. He looked at Ori, then at Gio, then back at me. *All right. We give him one more chance.*

I felt proud of Pense just then. Even after everything he had just heard, and in the midst of his justifiable rage, he could still have mercy upon Gio.

Could I?

I stepped closer to Gio, and looked him in the eye. 'If this is a trick, you will be sorry,' I said. 'If you betray us, I will take it upon myself to make you regret it. And if you hurt my Ori, you'll follow your grandfather down Pensould's gullet. Is that clear?'

Gio blinked at me in total disbelief. 'You're... not kicking me out.'

'Nope. Though, I do want the truth, and all of it. How did you make that door?'

Gio sighed, and looked wearier than ever. 'I am not half draykon,' he said in a subdued tone. 'My mother was a Lokant, like all my relatives. I have no other heritage.'

That did not surprise me. The story had rung hollow from the beginning. 'But then how did you manipulate the Library?'

Gio bit his lip, hesitated. 'I was not born with draykon heritage, but I was... given it.'

I felt cold, as the weight of Gio's meaning settled upon me. *Given it.* My thoughts flew back to Krays... and to Griel, Krays's partial-Lokant thrall. One of Krays's more chilling ideas had been to take the bones of shapeshifted draykoni and transplant them into Lokants, thus conferring upon them limited access to draykoni powers. I had thought he had managed to accomplish this only on himself and one or two of his more unfortunate allies...

'Your bones?' I whispered.

Gio grimaced, and nodded. He handed Siggy back to me with endearing tenderness, and pulled up his sleeves. There were the scars, scars of the same kind of incisions I had seen on Griel's arms. 'I have draykon parts enough to attempt some limited arts, but... I don't. I try not to. It is repellent to me, employing arts stolen from the literal flesh of another...' He trailed off, looking nauseated and so downhearted I couldn't blame Ori at all for catching him in another hug.

Gio returned the embrace, and steadied himself. 'I was sent to Nuwelin,' he admitted. 'Grandmother insisted. She said she'd do worse to me if I refused, and I believed her. She is ruthless enough for anything. But... I wanted to be there, too. I was curious about all of you. I watched you for a while before I dared to approach you, and I saw... the kind of bond I have never experienced before. You... care about each other, even the newest among you. I was astounded. I... wanted to be part of it.'

Even Meri looked softened by this narrative, for her scowl disappeared and she stopped looking like she wanted to punch Gio.

Pense, though, focused on a different aspect of the tale. 'What were you supposed to do in Nuwelin?'

'Two things. I was to find out as much as I could about your arts in general, for Grandmother knew by then that our supposedly extensive knowledge of Galywis's creations was by no means exhaustive. You've advanced a great deal since the days of the original project, and much of it is a surprise. Especially the humans amongst you who can shift draykon, rather than the other way around. That electrified everybody, particularly since there prove to be so many more of you than we thought there would be. There were supposed to be only three with enough draykon blood...'

True, that. Limbane and his Librarians had been involved in manipulating that heritage, trying to keep the draykon bloodlines alive, but even he had got it wrong. Me, Ori and Avane: only we three had been identified as capable of the Change. This hall was full of evidence to the contrary.

'And the other thing?' Pense said, grim and apparently unmoved by Gio's suffering. But I knew better. I could feel his pain, pain that he was adding to his store of rage.

'I was to find out if there were any *alyndim* among you. Um, originals. Elders, you are calling them? Grandmother overreached herself with that, for I cannot identify who is *alyndim* and who is not. But I told her nothing of that. I told her you had no Elders, and she looked elsewhere.'

So, Dwinal was the one looking for Elders. I had been right to think that Lokants were behind the trouble, though the thought gave me no satisfaction. If not for Gio's deception, Nyden might have been targeted — perhaps killed.

Gio sighed deeply. 'I wish I had told you everything at the time, but... I thought you would never believe me. I thought you would lynch me, actually. Especially you.' He looked at me.

Me. Me! I had spent most of our acquaintance feeling uncomfortable and inadequate around him, as I did with so many people. I could only gape at him.

He smiled faintly in response. 'I do not speak out of ingratitude,' he assured me. 'I know that I would never have been tolerated as long as I was, without your support. But you... are more fearsome than you know, when it comes to the ones you care about. I realised how severe would be the consequences if my duplicity was discovered. I was quite frightened of you, and Pensould.' His eyes flicked to Pense and back to me, and he reconsidered. 'I *am* quite frightened of you and Pensould.'

'They won't hurt you,' said Ori quickly. 'Llan looks grim and forbidding sometimes but she's lovely. She only does it when she's afraid, and she's probably been more afraid of you than you were of her.' He smiled encouragingly at Gio, and I tried to stifle my desire to smack him.

Gio's brows rose. 'Afraid of *me?*' he said, incredulous.

'People worry me,' I said shortly. 'Strangers especially. Odd, unaccountable strangers most of all. It's a trait of mine. Can't help it.'

'I'm not sure that it's true anymore,' said Ori with an apologetic smile for me. 'When did you last feel that way, Llan? When did you last have *time?*'

Ehhh, so. Nothing like a series of world-shaking disasters to improve your social skills, right?

Gio was still staring at me as though he couldn't believe anybody would be afraid of him. That feeling was mutual. How could a man like him fear me?

It made no sense, but I will be honest with you: I enjoyed the feeling, just a little. I have gone through my whole life feeling so helplessly, unaccountably afraid of everyone else, it is… nice, to feel on the other side of that power relationship for once. A *tiny* bit nice. I don't actually want to scare people, I swear.

'I might, though,' said Pense. He had taken up his human shape at some point during the discussion and now stood watching Gio with folded arms, his face impassive. Not forbidding, but not welcoming either.

'Might… um, hurt me?' said Gio, eyeing Pensould uneasily.

Pense nodded once. I thought he would not speak, but he added as if by afterthought: 'Your grandfather tasted terrible. I would not like to have to repeat that experience.'

Gio swallowed, but he rallied himself enough to reply: 'I hated him, you know. You did all of us a service in removing him.'

A muscle twitched in Pense's cheek. I had no trouble guessing at his feelings: he had not expected to be *thanked* for killing Krays, particularly by the man's own grandson. *Especially* when he had just been threatening that same grandson with a similar fate.

'Nobody will be eaten,' I said firmly. A stray thought wandered through my mind, and I frowned. 'Gio. If you were sent to us by your grandmother, why were you so afraid of discovery when you took us to Sulayn Phay?'

He looked slightly abashed. 'I, um, did not have her permission to do that. I wasn't supposed to help you, just watch you.'

Knowing that he had broken Dwinal's rules and risked punishment in order to help us made me feel a bit better about trusting him now. 'Thank you for that,' I said, and he rewarded me with a surprised, delighted smile which broke my heart a little bit. 'We are going to need your help again, if you are with us.'

'I am with you,' he assured me earnestly. Ori leaned closer to him and took his hand, a gesture of support which Gio seemed to appreciate. 'Anything I can do,' he added, and smiled at me.

I smiled back. 'Thank you. We need to get those energy collectors back off your grandmother, to start with. They removed some of them from this island, did they not?'

Gio nodded, and grimaced. 'We spent a few happy days searching, and it was dirty work unearthing the things. I don't think Grandmother got them all in the end, but enough.'

That was probably one of the things that had so agitated poor Galywis. 'Did they know what they were doing to the island by removing them?'

'They knew they were important in some way but not how, exactly. I don't think they cared.' His head tilted at me in a question. 'Come to think of it, I have no idea either. What were they doing?'

I eyed him speculatively. 'Do those bones you carry give you much by way of draykoni senses?'

He hesitated, and shut his eyes. 'Not… not much, I think. What am I looking for?'

I closed my eyes too, the better to try to describe the experience. I felt for the undercurrents of energy that swirled around me. 'The energy of these worlds, what we call *amasku*. Galywis used it to make us, and bound us into its currents. It is like… a sense of pressure, and a flow, like water but, um, not.' Glib as ever, that. I frowned, and tried again. 'You can't see it or touch it but it's there. A pattern…' Actually not much of a pattern there, it was too disordered. The currents wavered and rippled oddly, never quite able to settle into the coherent state they naturally assumed. Outside the Library it was far worse: the flows tossed and frothed like a stormy sea, dizzying and nauseating.

I had described nothing useful, but perhaps it was enough, for Gio gasped and said, 'I… there is something. It's not… right, is it?'

'It is a terrible mess,' Meriall said bluntly.

'Thanks to Krays and Limbane and their people,' Ori put in. He squeezed Gio's hand as he spoke, reassuring him that he meant no reflection upon Gio.

'It is a huge problem,' I said. 'When our world is in such a state, all is chaos. The disorder affects everything: animals, people, plants. It is why this island is so dead. It has been broken by it. Those machines were keeping the flow in check, thanks to Galy, and the corruption didn't spread beyond the borders of Orlind. But with the machines removed, that's disrupted, and it's moving into the Off-worlds. If we don't fix it, those realms will ultimately end up like this place. It could even happen to the Seven.'

Gio stared at me, shocked. 'Um, I don't think Grandmother

realised that.'

'Whether she did or not, we have to solve this problem. And we want to do more: we want this place healed, flourishing again. To start with, we must get those collectors back. Maybe you can help us there. Where are they keeping the machines, and how can we get at them?'

Gio chewed his lip thoughtfully. 'They are kept at Sulayn Phay, when they are not in use. I have broken with the lot of them, and it won't be long before they revoke my access to the Library, so we had better move fast if you want to get them back.'

I nodded. 'Right. Ori, Pense and I are with you.' I could say this with confidence even without asking Ori or Pense — no prizes for guessing where they would prefer to be. 'And… Meri? Larion? There are probably several of them and they are big, heavy. I doubt we can carry more than one each.' I thought about that for a second. 'Or not. Gio, can you carry five of us?'

Gio eyed us doubtfully. 'I can try. If I cannot take all at once, I will take us in two groups.'

Meriall and Larion exchanged glances, and finally nodded to me. 'What's another mad adventure, after all?' said Meri, and grinned at me. 'Let's try not to die though, right?'

I grinned back. 'That's always a priority. While we are at it…' I looked around at the assembled draykoni. Most of them had lost interest in the discussion some time back and had wandered off to other parts of the hall. They crouched in small groups, conferring amongst themselves.

'We need to find out who's been feeding information to Sulayn Phay about the Elders,' I said, lowering my voice. This part was trickier, because we honestly didn't know where to look. I had a strong hunch that it must be another Elder, but I could be wrong. Even if I was right, that only helped us so far. I was going to have to gamble a little.

I doubted that it was a rogue Elder wandering around alone. Whoever it was needed to stay close to groups of draykoni in order to learn who to target. There was only one place to go looking for a group of Elders, and that was Eterna's colony.

'Nyden,' I said.

He was leaning close to Avane, unnoticed by her. It sounds predatory of him, especially given Ny's undeniable advantages of size and bulk compared to Avane. But his manner was surprisingly tender, and he just seemed… happy to be near her.

Albeit a bit guilty, for he snapped to attention when I called his name and took a hasty step away from Avane. 'Yes, boss!'

'How do you feel about an espionage mission?'

His eyes gleamed, and he sat straighter still. 'I was *born* for espionage,' he purred.

I refrained from pointing out that he hadn't been born, exactly, as he had no parents. 'You're a treasure,' I informed him. 'How do you feel about turning turncoat on your turncoat?'

'I have always been afflicted with grave fickleness,' Ny said, swaying mournfully from side to side. 'I never could make up my mind. Now I come to think of it, Miss Llandry, I do not think Nuwelin is for me after all. I feel a powerful desire to return to the sheltering womb of Eterna, so to speak, and embrace my pure-blooded heritage once more.'

'You will have to eat some humble pie,' I warned him. 'Can you manage to look suitably shame-faced and repentant?'

Nyden's head drooped and his eyes appeared to double in size. He looked piteously at me, a soulful show of remorse somewhat belied by the mischievous glint of one protruding tooth.

'Your fang's showing,' I said.

It disappeared. 'I'll practice.'

I beamed at him. 'Good. Who are you taking with you?'

His eyes widened and he sat up very straight, chest puffed out with pride. 'Oh my, I get to *pick a team?*'

'If you please. It would help if we could get an idea of who's willing to go along, of course.' I addressed the latter to the group in general, afraid that nobody would volunteer.

Nyden eyed Avane hopefully, but she hesitated, and said nothing. His shoulders drooped a little.

'Right, I need recruits!' he bellowed. 'Smartish, we do *not* have all day.'

In the end, he managed to round up five: two of the people unfamiliar to me, together with Liat from Nuwelin and two from Avane's village, Anshalin.

Avane herself approached me soon afterwards, still clad in her wings and scales. *I am worried about the corruption,* she told me. *If we don't stop it spreading, it will reach my village. I have to take a group and deal with that, somehow.*

Take as many ancients as you can get. Elders, if you can find any. I caught her up on our findings there, and Nyden's curious effect upon the putrescent energy of Orlind. *Careful, though,* I finished. *It won't easily touch them, but... we saw what happens when an Elder goes mad. If it does get on top of them, it won't be pretty.*

Avane twitched her tail three times, a gesture characteristic of her. It seemed to mean general approval. *I will take everybody who's not already assigned elsewhere. There ought to be enough of us to make a difference.*

And with that, all was agreed and arranged. Nothing remained but to throw ourselves upon Gio's mercy once more and venture back to Sulayn Phay. I couldn't quiet the voice in my mind that questioned my sanity in doing so. We still had no way to be certain that Gio could be trusted, only a gut feeling that he was sincere. But we had no other choices by then. We had to act quickly. There was no time to delay while we searched for some other Lokant with access to Krays and Dwinal's Library, and of whose trustworthiness we could be more certain. It would have to be Gio, and we would have to make it work.

I had to take a few deep breaths before I was ready to leave. We were heading back into danger, and so much was riding on our success... or failure. I felt the pressure keenly.

But I would have Pense and Ori, the two people I trust most in the world besides my parents. And we made a group of five drayks and one Lokant, which made us by no means powerless. We would be all right. We had to be.

I toyed briefly with the idea of leaving Sigwide behind once again, but he was so unhappy at the prospect that I swiftly dismissed the thought. Besides, I had no one to leave him with. Larion would be coming along with me, and everybody else was assigned to some other task.

You will have to behave very well, Sig, I told him with a vague attempt at sternness. *This is important, what we're doing. And dangerous.*

Sigwide said nothing, but he touched his tiny nose to mine and quivered with love and I had to be satisfied with that.

Galy opened up the roof, and Ny's team began to depart on the wing. I stole a glance out at the remaining Lokants; all they could do was watch as a half-dozen draykoni emerged without warning from the black fortress and vanished into the distance. I took heart from their perplexed and faintly worried expressions. It must be clear that much was afoot, and they could guess at none of it.

'Hold the fort, Galy,' I said aloud. 'We'll be back.'

The stones rumbled in reply.

'Will he be all right?' Meriall said doubtfully. 'He's already been murdered by these people.'

'Yes, that was when he was a squishy human. I mean, Lokant. Now he's a building and he could squash Dwinal with a single block of stone. None of them will get in here without his say-so.'

'Ready?' Gio said. He looked nervous. So did Larion... actually, so did everyone. Even Pense was unusually tense.

'Not at all,' I said, with a tiny smile. 'But let's go anyway.'

15 VIII

We Band of Fools Go After the Lokants.

I am losing track of the date, again. There is no real calendar in Iskyr, no time-keeping. There isn't even a cycle of days as there is in Glinnery. That problem is much worse in the Lokant Libraries. Venture out there and who knows where you end up in the timestream.

So, all this probably happened on the fifteenth. Who knows. Who cares.

Gio translocated us into Sulayn Phay in two groups: me and Pense and Ori first, then Meri and Larion. He took us to the same closet as before, which was even more fun with extra people. We had to wait in the enclosed space until Gio had all of us assembled, and then we waited again while he ventured out to check if it was safe to emerge. He was noticeably more cautious this time than he had been before. Word of his defection would spread fast, and he could not rely on going unchallenged if he was spotted.

'Be careful,' Ori whispered before Gio left.

Gio nodded. 'It will be all right. If anybody asks, I am here to collect my personal effects.'

With that, he was gone, leaving us to huddle in doubtful suspense until he returned.

He was not long. 'Come out,' he whispered, opening the

door a crack.

We emerged and stood blinking in the white light of that same, stark hallway. Gio set off at once, leading us in the other direction this time. 'The route from here to Dwinal's quarters is clear for the moment, but we will have to move fast.'

We obeyed, traversing corridors as quickly and silently as we could. Gio kept up his station some way ahead, checking each turn in the hallway before he permitted us through.

All went smoothly. 'Three more minutes,' Gio said tersely.

But at the next turn, he stopped abruptly and held up a hand. *Wait.*

We waited, hardly breathing. Footsteps sounded close by, and Gio nodded to somebody just out of our sight. He spoke, in a dialect I could not decipher. It was *almost* familiar enough for comprehension, but not quite.

Somebody replied, a male voice.

Gio took a step back, and another. He held up his hands in a gesture both placatory and, I thought, an attempt to prevent the further progress of whoever he had encountered.

But in vain, for another Lokant swept past him and stopped in shock upon seeing us. The man was about Gio's own age, but thinner and sickly-looking. His eyes narrowed when he saw us, and he rounded upon Gio, a torrent of angry words pouring from his lips.

Gio merely stared at him, and the flow of vituperation came to a swift end. Then the sickly man's head bowed in submission. He turned and walked away again, back the way he had come.

What just happened? asked Meriall.

Lokant thing, Ori replied. *Gio just laid a compulsion on him.*

Which means what?

Dominated his will, made him see and do whatever he wanted. It's his strength. He is amazing at it. Ori's mental voice rang with pride at this display of Gio's skill, and I gathered he had seen Gio do it before.

That is creepy beyond all reason, Meriall said flatly.

I had to agree. Eva is pretty good at it, too, but it has always chilled me to watch her do it. It has its limits — Eva could only so manipulate one person at a time, and it did not last indefinitely. Soon, the sickly Lokant would shake off Gio's commands and remember the truth. But in the hands of somebody skilled and trained, it is frighteningly powerful.

Gio did not look happy about it, however. I wondered whether the man he had just manipulated had been a friend, once.

Gio stepped out again and we followed. There were no further interruptions, and we arrived at a door Gio found relevant within a couple of minutes.

The door looked featureless to me, not even a doorknob or a handle in sight. But it was not so to Gio, apparently, for he laid a hand against it with a practiced gesture and waited for three seconds. Then he pushed at the door, confident that it would open.

It didn't.

He stopped, blinking in surprise, and tried again. The result was the same.

Gio sighed, and rubbed at his eyes. 'That was fast,' he muttered.

Ori touched his arm. 'What's amiss?'

'Grandmother has already had me locked out of her quarters. I need to find someone with access. Wait here.' He set off up the corridor.

'We can't just stand here,' Meri called after him, but to no avail. Gio disappeared from view.

Larion shrugged, and took up a relaxed stance against a wall. 'Nothing we can do but wait.'

Pense walked away a few steps and took up a guard posture. He was ready to Change at a moment's notice, if necessary, and I had no doubt he would eat anybody who tried to harm us. I hoped, for the Lokants' sake, that nobody would come this way before Gio returned.

Ori and I followed his example, and waited. My heart was pounding uncomfortably hard, though I tried not to show fear. I felt horribly exposed, standing helplessly in the middle of a corridor somewhere in Krays's Library with no Gio, nowhere to hide at need, and no way of getting out either. A traitorous thought snaked through my mind: what if Gio never came back? What if he had left us here?

It took him far too long, twenty minutes at least, and each minute seemed twice as long as the last. We waited, nerves growing by the second. But he did return.

'Sorry,' Gio mumbled as he reappeared. He hurried to the door and laid his hand against it again. His hands were bloodied, and he had something small, complex-looking and metallic strapped to his wrist. That, too, was covered in blood.

The door opened, and he hustled us inside, and shut the door behind us.

We were in a sitting room, reassuringly empty and ordinary enough, with arm chairs and a rather chic table. I scarcely looked at it. Gio's bloodied hands had all of my attention.

'Gio…' I said. 'Er. How did you get us in?'

He looked down at his hands with a frown, and rubbed them on his dark red cloak. It didn't really help. 'Access is biological,' he said in a hurried way, his eyes scanning the sitting room. 'Grandmother lets all her relatives in here, until she doesn't. If that stops working then I have to do it the hard way, which means taking somebody else's access. If you aren't a blood relative it's done by way of an implant.'

He stopped there. It was not necessary for him to elaborate. Had he really tracked down some hapless Lokant with access to Dwinal's quarters and hacked some kind of an implant out of them? I was shocked to silence, and so was everybody else, for nobody spoke.

'He won't die,' Gio added, his frown deepening. 'It was the only way I could help you. You *did* say it was important?' He looked at Ori, uncertain.

Ori looked taken aback, but he recovered quickly and smiled at Gio. 'We couldn't get this far without you.'

True, but I could not help feeling shocked. What manner of upbringing had Gio had, that he could coolly cut open one of his former colleagues and seem so unaffected? But considering what his family were like, he probably deserved credit for not being much *more* of a psycho.

'We have to walk a bit,' Gio said, setting off towards a door at the back of the sitting room. 'All her personal chambers are irrelevant, she keeps nothing useful in those. What we want is at the back. There's a lab and a storage room and a cell.'

A *cell*? Seriously, this family is messed up. Who keeps a cell at the back of their personal quarters?

'We need to be quick,' said Gio tersely. 'Someone will find Gharo before long and there will be trouble.'

We ran into the second problem at the door to Dwinal's lab. Her rooms had been empty up until that point, but a low growl and an echoing snarl spelled the end of our period of peace.

Pacing up and down before the door was a whurthag... or something like it.

You might have seen those before, in the news if not in the flesh. A few moons ago, when the realms were in chaos and gates were opening everywhere between the worlds, we had a lot of whurthags roaming through the Seven. It wasn't a good time. They are brutal and vicious and hard to subdue. I had hoped I had seen my last whurthag some time ago, for they are native to Ayrien and not Iskyr and the Summoners' guilds are keeping them out of the Seven.

It took me a moment to realise that this one was not quite a whurthag, or not as I knew them. It was black-furred and big and four-legged as I would expect, its massive jaws bristling with teeth, its eyes ghost-pale and eerie. But its movements were odd, its shape peculiar. It was half mechanical at least, its hide stretched over parts made of something else — metal or whatever.

How very Krays. He had terrorised my poor Waeverleyne with mechanical draykoni, fire-breathing and everything. How like him to co-opt the design of another fearsome creature and make a weird mechanical hybrid of *that*, too.

We stayed well back from the creature, alarmed by its snarling but mildly reassured that it had not yet attacked us. It was intent upon guarding the door, and as long as we did not approach it seemed it would not leave its post.

'Typical,' Gio sighed. I expected something more from him — some idea of how to deal with the creature, perhaps, some attempt at formulating a plan.

Instead, he tensed and hurled himself at the thing.

The whurthag-thing greeted Gio with a flurry of snarls, and man and creature rolled in a mass of black hide and red cloak as Gio fought with it. I could not even tell what he was trying to do.

Ori leapt forward with a cry of alarm, his body a blur as he began to Change — only to realise that the room was far too small to accommodate his draykon shape. Pense and I were a step behind him, though there was precious little we could do. Could I Change into a whurthag? I had never done so before, and there was no time to think about it.

'*Stay back,*' Gio shouted.

Then it was over. The whurthag slumped to the ground and

lay inert, eerily so. It looked like a model, like a thing that had never had life enough to move.

Gio stood up shakily, his arms striped with bloody wounds inflicted by raking teeth. 'They can be disabled, if you know where the switch is.'

'And if you don't mind it tearing you to ribbons in the process.' Ori growled the words, rigid with anger, but he was gentle enough as he tore a strip off Gio's cloak and bound up his bleeding arm. 'Idiot,' he said roughly, but he softened the accusation with a kiss, and Gio did not appear to mind too much.

I watched with some alarm. Twice in quick succession, Gio had gone to extraordinary lengths to help us. Either he was determined to allay our suspicions in the furtherance of some nefarious scheme, or he really was as desperate to please us as he seemed. The one possibility filled me with foreboding, but the other tore at my heart.

In another moment, Gio had the door to the lab open.

And there were the energy collectors, or some of them. We found only three, though we searched thoroughly. The lab struck me as too neat and too unassuming by half. Considering we had wandered into the lair of evil here, I was expecting something more sinister than clear benches, a neatly-swept floor and cupboards full of nothing especially recognisable or interesting. A half-completed project would have been nice — something that clearly demonstrated both the intent and level of progress our opponents had achieved. Failing that, some kind of manifesto of villainy would have been acceptable too. A sheaf of notes, perhaps, clearly detailing what they expected to get out of haunting Orlind, murdering Galy and a slew of my people and setting Gio on us.

They were singularly uncooperative villains, alas, for there was nothing of use. Just three of the cumbersome energy collectors waiting quietly at the back of the room.

'Only three?' said Meriall in disgust. 'That's a let-down. I can hardly imagine that will be enough for us to do anything useful with.'

'But it is three fewer machines with which they can kill Elders,' Pense said, and hefted one of them. He grimaced, his arms shaking. 'They are heavy. I advise two to each machine.'

I hurried to help him. Meri and Larion secured a second

between them, and Gio and Ori took the third. 'Moment,' said Gio. He went silent, his eyes closed, and I wondered what he was doing. 'Right,' he said then, and vanished with Ori, leaving the rest of us to await his return.

He was soon back, reappearing in precisely the spot from which he had departed moments earlier. He had set himself a translocation point, then, in Dwinal's lab. I never did understand how that works, because I do not think Eva can do it — she can only use those points set by full Lokants. Gio is a handy ally to have, in that respect.

Away Gio went again, this time taking Meri and Larion and the second energy collector with him. Ori had returned with him after his first trip, but the others did not; when Gio reappeared he was alone.

'Last one,' he said to me with a smile. He looked tired, whether because translocating frequently and with such burdens was so exhausting, or because of the strain of transgression and the fear of discovery I could not guess. The lost blood cannot have helped, either. I felt a little concern for him.

'Thank you,' I said to him as he took hold of us, and smiled back at him.

His smile turned warmer, but he looked startled. I felt that tug of sympathy at my heart once again. How could a person be so surprised and so delighted by a mere smile? It was like no one had ever treated him kindly in his life before.

I braced myself for the nauseating whirl of translocation, but before we could depart, I felt a wild writhing and scrabbling against my chest. Sigwide was going mad, clawing at his carry-pack and chattering at the top of his voice.

LetmeoutletmeoutletmeoutletmeDOWNIneedtogodownletmeout!

'Wait!' I cried, frightened that Siggy would fall out just as we vanished and be left behind. *Siggy, this is not the moment —*

LETMEOUT.

I had to put the collector down in order to get hold of him, but I was too late. He surged out of his sling in a flurry of twisting limbs and fell to the floor.

Then he ran away.

Sigwide ran away from *me*.

Pense and Ori stared, as shocked as I was. 'Did that just happen?' Ori said in awe.

'Maybe he was more affected by Orlind's mess than I

thought,' I said, stricken with guilt at having brought him along. But leaving him behind would have been no better.

I ran across the lab after him, but in his wild flight he was too quick for me. He did two crazed circuits around the room at top speed, then careened madly across the floor, neatly dodging the attempts of Pense, Ori and Gio to catch him. He had stopped talking to me, and flatly ignored all my demands for his return.

'Something is weird about this…' I said. 'I don't think he is frightened, exactly. More… overexcited…'

I left the sentence unfinished because Siggy chose that moment to disappear.

We also heard Dwinal's voice from the adjacent room, shockingly sudden, for we had not heard her approach. A look of terror crossed Gio's face and he made a frantic we-need-to-go motion.

I felt a similar panic almost overwhelming my sense altogether. For a second I was too panicked to think, and I couldn't breathe.

Hold fast, Minchu, said Pense, and his reassuring voice in my mind brought me out of it. I forced myself to think clearly.

Sigwide does not vanish. He is not capable of disappearing into thin air. So: either something disappeared *him*, or there was a more mundane explanation for his vanishment.

He was also not at all given to such fits of disobedience, and he had never run from me in his life. Therefore: he was not running *from me* so much as running *to* something else, something that had attracted his attention in an unusually powerful way. And which he considered important enough to pursue that he was prepared to disobey me.

We have to find him, I told Pense and Ori silently.

We have to go! Ori replied, shooting Gio a look of concern.

You go. The voices from the next room had not come any nearer, and I hoped I would have a few minutes to retrieve Sigwide and find somewhere to hide before they did — if they did. Perhaps Dwinal would leave again without coming in here.

Ori gave me a look of anguished indecision, then grabbed the energy collector and nodded at Gio. The two disappeared with the machine, leaving me and Pense in Dwinal's laboratory.

I would not leave you here alone, Pense told me. I could only spare a moment to send him a wave of love and gratitude, most of my attention fixed upon the problem of Sigwide.

He had been near the back of the room when he had disappeared, in the far left corner. I could see nothing there that would explain it, but when I approached something shifted subtly in my perception, as though that corner was deeper than it ought to be.

Another step and my foot sank, the floor being apparently a few inches lower than it appeared. I almost fell, barely stifling a yelp of surprise. *Pense, here.*

He joined me and took my hand. We stepped forward together, and when the floor vanished from beneath our feet and the walls disappeared, we fell together.

We fell a long way, down and down. There was nothing around us but bright, white light, featureless and blinding. I shut my eyes and held tight to Pense's hand, my heart pounding as we plummeted farther and farther, gaining speed… I knew with conviction that I had erred, we had strayed too far, we must die when we hit the ground.

I'm sorry, I told Pense, wretched with futile remorse.

He merely gripped my hand tighter.

There came a moment where I stopped bracing for impact, stopped reproaching myself, stopped regretting, and… let go. I cannot describe to you how I felt in that moment. There is such freedom in simply falling, such peace in taking what comes without fear or worry or doubt. It is perhaps the only time in my life when I have managed to feel that way.

It's a shame that I have to be put in a position of inevitable, imminent and unavoidable death before I can manage to relax and accept what comes of my life. I may need to work on that.

Anyway, we did not die. Our rapid descent slowed and we began to float, drifting gently downwards in a cocoon of warm air. The light around us dimmed gradually until I could safely open my eyes and look around.

We were high in the air over a beautiful island surrounded by a glittering green sea. The land was thickly forested and those trees were a mix of kinds: fronded with leaves of cerulean, azure and indigo, and laced with flurries of gold; vibrantly, shockingly green and as plush as forest moss; pale and ethereal and feathery, like clusters of cloud swaying in the breeze; even the broad, painted caps of my own beloved glissenwol. A grand, curving lagoon spread its sparkling waters over one side of the island,

and in the centre, directly beneath us, was a building of such size and splendour that I could only stare in awe. It was a cluster of spires and turrets and towers, each architecturally unique and distinct from the rest. The walls were a pure white which shone in the sunlight, and the towers were a flurry of glorious colour.

We drifted down and finally came to rest atop that building. A little raised platform sat in the centre of the roof and upon this we landed, as gently as though deposited by a careful hand. A door was open nearby, though the interior was too dark for us to see beyond the portal.

Pense had not released my hand. We looked at each other, mystified.

'Well,' I said after a moment, 'we are alive.'

'That is always nice,' Pense agreed.

'What do you suppose will happen if we go through the door?'

'We might die.' Pense said it with a straight face, though I detected a trace of amusement.

'Something good might happen, too,' I said, albeit dubiously.

Pense grinned at me and scooped me into a swift hug. 'That is the first time I have heard you not only accept but volunteer the possibility of a positive outcome. I am proud.'

I laughed, a bit ruefully. He wasn't wrong. 'Let's find out.'

'Onward to death.' Pense released me. He made to move ahead of me in his usual protective way, but hesitated, and finally bowed. 'Would you like to go first?' he said instead.

I took hold of his hand again, and kissed it. 'I think we can manage to go together.'

'Together it is.'

And so, hands joined and braced for disaster, we approached the door.

On the other side stood a Lokant man, his hair closely cropped. His face was a little lined with age, but he was no ancient. He looked spry and fit and energetic, and he smiled at us with an attractive twinkle in his grey eyes. He was carrying a familiar bundle of grey fur.

'Yours, I think?' he said, and held Sigwide out to me. His smile widened and he added, 'Little creature loves this place. They all do.'

I took back my orting, gratified and relieved by the way Siggy snuggled back into my arms. Apparently his rebellion was over.

'Thank you,' I said cautiously. This was one of the Lokants we had seen with Dwinal not long before, standing outside Galy's fortress… 'Are you Hyarn?'

'Good guess.' Hyarn bowed his assent. 'Will you come in?'

'You killed Galywis.' I backed up a step, and now Pense did step in front of me, growing visibly taller in the process.

Hyarn held up his hands. 'There are some things you do not understand. If you come this way, I will explain them to you.'

I took another step back, as did Pense. It was futile, for we well knew we had nowhere to go. We were on the roof of a staggeringly tall building and we could hardly fall back *up* to the lab again — and Gio and Ori, if they were there.

'You killed Galywis,' I said again. 'You crept up on him from behind and cut his throat. Why would you do that?'

Hyarn frowned. 'That is only part of the truth.'

'You do not deny it.'

Hyarn sighed and lowered his hands. 'It was necessary. You will understand why, if you will permit me to explain.'

'Then do so, but stay where you are. We are not coming in.'

'Very well.' Hyarn folded his hands behind his back and met my eyes squarely. 'You will be aware that Galywis has long been mad, but perhaps you do not know of the extent of it. He lost his grip upon reality long ago, and his behaviour has become more and more out of control. You are aware that he has bonded his consciousness with the remnants of the Library once known as Orlind?'

I nodded.

'Did you know that he has long been able to do this?'

That took me aback. I stood there, mouth agape, and finally shook my head. 'I thought it happened after he died.'

'We first became aware of this ability some little time ago, when he interfered in Lokantor Krays's attempts to divert the *amasku* of Orlind. Galywis and the Library were melded for a time, and he walked the place around the island, remaking it according to his preferences. There is a sea in between the island and the mainland, of course, so we had thought that these wanderings were confined to Orlind. As such, his activities did not much concern us, and we were content to leave him in peace. But we were recently proved wrong.'

'Wait,' I said. 'How could you be unconcerned when he was directly interfering in your Library's doings there?'

'I said he had disrupted Lokantor Krays's project,' said Hyarn gently. 'Our leader he may have been, but it does not follow that the whole of Sulayn Phay slavishly followed his whims or even agreed with his ideas.'

I felt all my recent certainty slipping away, leaving me disoriented. 'Oh…'

'There was a flaw of some kind with the draykoni,' Hyarn continued. 'Galywis knew it, of course, as did our Lokantor. I do not believe Master Galywis ever managed to isolate the cause of the madness that sometimes took hold of his creations, though it was not for lack of trying. It broke Master Galywis's heart to see it, and when he could not mend it, he concluded the project early.' Hyarn shook his head sadly. 'There was talk of seeking a way to terminate all of the draykoni, for their own sake. But Master Galywis stayed his hand, and thankfully the trait seemed to breed out over time. Within a few generations it largely ceased to manifest at all.'

I remembered what Ori had said about the project's cancellation. Here was why. Too many of those first draykoni were utterly, horrifically, painfully mad, and even Galywis had not known why, or how to help them. I could not help thinking again of the female we had seen in those long-lost laboratories and her desperate, self-destructive flight.

I swallowed, remembering Nyden's odd way of interacting with the energies of Orlind; the way he absorbed it, melded with it in ways even I could not match. As long as his own core energy remained pure, he was largely untouched by the sickness around him. But time and excessive exposure must erode his resistance, and eventually he would take that sickness into himself and break…

Gio had said Dwinal had no real idea what she had done to the island when she removed those energy collectors. I wondered if Galywis had been ignorant, once, that *amasku* could be corrupted, could sicken…

Had the Library of Orlind really broken during the Lokant wars, or had the essential damage happened much earlier, and the Librarians had not even realised? Had some of those original draykoni gone mad because they were wrought from pure *amasku*, and born of energies already twisted and sickened beyond repair?

My mind reeled and I felt sick. *There was talk of terminating all of the draykoni, for their own sake.*

'Did... did you kill them?' I asked, horrified. 'Our Elders. Have they been going mad again? Did you decide to end everything after all?'

Hyarn shook his head. 'Galywis did,' he said, gently enough, but the words still hit me like a punch to the stomach.

I wanted to reject them. I wanted to cry, *Not Galy!* Not sweet, confused Galywis, who had welcomed us to his beloved *old girl* and tried so trustingly to share its beauties. Galy, who had come searching for *us* when he was frightened and in danger, and looked after us so carefully – even Nyden, an Elder, but our friend. Poor, mad Galy, who had sacrificed his sanity and finally his life for the sake of his beloved Library.

But I could not, because it made too much sense. We had seen the sweet side of Galywis, but we had learned more about him since. Galy had presided over the casual destruction of any draykon prototype who went mad. There was *talk* of terminating every one of them, *for their own sake*. Galy might not have followed through with it at the time, but… burdened by his own madness, had he reconsidered?

I thought back to everything Galy had shown us himself: the vision of that mad drayk and her appalling pain; the way he and his colleagues were helpless to stop her or cure her and could only destroy her; the way the *amasku* had eaten through the carcass of a draykon, leaving it barren and dead in its wake. Had that been Galy's way of showing us what he had done, and why? Had he used the Library itself to take back the energy it had granted in the first place? Nothing to do with the energy collectors, nothing to do with Krays or Dwinal or even Sulayn Phay…

Another thought struck me: the parade of draykoni he had shown us at the end, flashing by colour by colour. It *now* occurred to me that the hue of one of those glorious creatures matched that of the maddened and destroyed drayk. Had that been Galy's mental library of Elders, or *alyndim* as they were called? Or had it been his catalogue of those who had gone mad, and subsequently been destroyed?

'I believe he acted out of compassion,' said Hyarn, breaking the appalled silence. 'I have read his original accounts of the project. It always tormented him, that failure in the design and the pain it caused. It troubled him that there was no reliable way either to cure the afflicted creatures, or to — to put them out of their misery, as it were. Having at last discovered a way, perhaps it was a relief to him to use it.'

'But — but —' I stalled, scarcely able to put my objections into words. I took a breath and tried again. 'Do you mean to say he has been destroying all of the *alyndim* merely in case they happen to go mad someday? Pre-emptive destruction is not compassion!'

'That is a question which has much occupied this Library, of late,' admitted Hyarn. 'Either he has taken it upon himself to ensure that no other *alyndim* suffers such pain again, by extracting them from your world before it can happen — and remember that, in his own madness, that may seem to him a perfectly acceptable solution. Or, the very madness he feared and regretted has come upon some several of your number all at once, and he has merely reacted to it.' He spread his hands in a helpless gesture. 'If the latter, I do not know what could have caused such a widespread problem.'

'Galy could not kill indiscriminately,' I said, though my words sounded hollow to me as I spoke. Was this merely useless, misplaced trust on my part? 'He is no monster.'

Hyarn merely said, 'Perhaps.'

'He need not have involved us,' Pense pointed out, and I sensed that it cost him something to speak so. He was angry in a dangerous, simmering way, and it would take very little to draw out his rage. 'He tried to tell us what was happening, and what he was doing about it. We merely failed to understand.'

I sighed, and put a hand to my head. A dull headache was pounding there, and I had only just noticed. 'His visions were so mixed up, so incomprehensible. Even now, I don't know... why did he show us any of it?'

'Good... um, morning?' said Gio from behind us. I jumped violently and spun. He had just alighted upon the little landing platform, Ori close behind, and my heart gladdened to see them both. But Gio did not look as though he knew where he was, for he and Ori wore matching expressions of confusion. Ori also looked delighted, though, but Gio looked wary and oddly... hunted. His face darkened when he saw Hyarn.

'What is this place?' he said coldly. 'What is going on here?'

Hyarn smiled at him. 'Welcome, Gio.'

Gio blinked stupidly. 'Welcome? What...?'

Someone else was descending: a woman in shabby black. Dwinal. She had swept back her wild white hair into a hasty ponytail, which made her look less forbidding, but only slightly. Hers was a hard face, devoid of congeniality. She landed directly behind her grandson and patted him on the shoulder.

'Let me begin by apologising for Gio,' she said to us. 'He has always been sadly easy to manipulate, but at least he is useful.' She was unsurprised to find us there, and instead of violently expelling us the way we might have expected, she gazed upon us with satisfaction. Even smugness. She *wanted* us there.

Gio stared at his grandmother in utter horror. 'You mean you...' He looked around wildly, and up into the distant skies. 'This was all a set up? You used me?'

Dwinal gave him a quick hug around the shoulders. Under the circumstances, that affectionate gesture was out of place. 'I had to,' she told him, unapologetic. 'This is more important than you.'

The look of betrayal on Gio's face should have melted the coldest heart, but Dwinal was unmoved. 'I had no idea,' Gio said helplessly, and his eyes strayed to Ori's face. 'I am so sorry...'

It could have been an act, but I doubted it. His dismay was so raw, I could feel it.

Ori drew Gio closer, scowling. 'Why are we here?' he demanded of Dwinal. 'What is it that you want of us?'

'I needed to talk to you,' she said. 'I take it Hyarn has informed you as to the nature of the problem?'

'I have,' said Hyarn, still smiling.

'Why use Gio?' I demanded. 'If you wanted to talk to us, you could have just told us the truth, and asked.'

'Would you have believed a word I said?' Dwinal asked, her pale eyes piercing and cold. 'Would you even have given us the chance to try?' Her mouth twisted in disgust as she added, 'Krays's wife, forever tainted by his glorious legacy. Could I approach those who opposed him and expect to be trusted? No, indeed. I needed to get you *here,* but I could only achieve that by manipulation. So be it, and here you are.'

Considering that we had seen her standing right outside Galy's fortress and had not tried to communicate with her, I cannot honestly say that she was wrong. I wondered, fleetingly, whether the energy collectors were relevant at all, or if they had simply been used as bait to draw us to Sulayn Phay. 'But where *is* "here"?' I said. 'Is this still part of your Library?'

'It is a... model, of sorts.' Dwinal looked out over the gorgeous forest, the hard lines of her face softening a little. 'It is Orlind, as it once was.'

'A model.' Ori repeated the word flatly, and folded his arms. 'It is an extraordinarily realistic "model", not to mention unusually life sized.'

Dwinal shrugged. 'A plan, then. A layout, a blueprint, whatever you wish to call it. It is a vision, a projection. Not real, but adept at pretending to be so. Before a permanent site was chosen for the Library which came to be called Orlind, several locations were considered and projections built. This is the one that was selected.'

'And lovely it is,' said Pense. 'But why are we here?'

'We need your help.'

Ori laughed. 'Oh, do you? And why would we help Krays's wife?'

Dwinal gave a mirthless smile. 'You assume that my former husband's goals must be mine, and I can have no separate aims. It is a common mistake. A wife must support her husband in everything, of course.'

Ori folded his arms. 'Even if you had nothing to do with anything *he* did, we still have no reason to trust or help you.'

'No reason?' Dwinal looked pointedly at Gio.

'You've only used and betrayed your grandson,' Ori said in disgust. 'He is another good reason not to trust you.'

I cleared my throat. 'Ah... why don't you tell us what you want?'

I received a look of reproach from Ori for that, but it had to be said. It was of no use locking verbal swords with Dwinal all day. She had a good reason for luring us to her Library, and I wanted to know what it was.

Dwinal nodded to me, and exchanged a glance with Hyarn. 'The Library of Orlind has long been a bone of contention among my people,' she began. 'It has been the focus of severe conflicts in the past, as you will know. In more recent years it has largely faded from notice, broken as it is. But now the draykoni are returned. Master Galywis's achievements have been much talked about and there are those — my former husband among them — who look once more to Orlind as a beacon of hope. Some would see it restored to its place as Master Library, and used once more for the kind of visionary projects Galywis dealt in. Others would take up my husband's work and try to surpass even Galywis's supreme creation — for which they would also require the use of that Library. It will not be long before you will begin to see other Libraries making exploratory incursions there, in pursuit of some one or other of these ideas.'

I exchanged a worried look with Pense. This was unsettling news indeed. When Lokants interfered in our Worlds, they invariably caused a great deal of trouble.

'Others disagree,' continued Dwinal. 'I disagree. I believe the Library of Orlind has long been a liability, not just for your worlds but for ours as well. My people are disintegrating into factions and the strife could destroy us, as it almost did once before. There could be another war, and it will tear up your Worlds as it will fracture mine.' She grimaced. 'I am Lokantor for Sulayn Phay, but my will does not entirely hold sway here. Some of my people are of my own opinion, others opposed. The strife has already begun, and I cannot guarantee that I can hold Sulayn Phay out of the conflict.'

An inscrutable look passed between Dwinal and Hyarn, and Hyarn took up the tale. 'Galywis was beyond help,' he said softly. 'Believe me, we tried to assist him. We tried to remove him from the Library, which was of paramount importance, for it is the Library and his long residence there which destroyed his mind. But he would not be moved, he would not be helped. He was too far gone. When he began destroying his own creations, we knew it was too late for him. He had to be stopped, and in the end there was only one way to achieve that.'

The softness of his voice did not blind me to the coldness of his logic, and I could not help feeling a shiver of revulsion and horror at his words. 'So you just killed him?'

Hyarn's gaze flicked to me. 'I didn't "just" kill him. It is the worst thing I have ever had to do, and a deed for which I will never be able to atone.' His mouth hardened into a grim line. 'But it had to be done. It was the only way to separate him and the Library from one another, and protect our people's single greatest achievement. Left unchecked, he might have destroyed all of you.'

I felt a little faint at that prospect. It seemed a ridiculously far-fetched statement, but as soon as I thought of the field of dead draykoni in Ayrien, hidden under that vast meadow of putrid flowers, I had to revise my ideas. What other power could have achieved destruction on so large a scale, and covered its tracks so effectively to boot? My stomach twisted and my heart bled at this vision of Galywis, but I could not reject the possibility of its truth. I did not want to accept Dwinal's visions of future war, either, but there is no doubt that the Library of Orlind has spawned violent conflicts in the past. Could I reject her fears?

'We need to talk to Galy,' I said faintly.

'We hope you will,' Dwinal replied. 'See, we were not prepared for what happened after the death of Galywis. That he could bond with the Library even after his body was gone seemed inconceivable to us. But so it came to be, and our solution only made the problem graver. Now Galywis and the Library of Orlind are forever entwined, and I fear they are both made stronger by it. And more dangerous, for the madness of Galywis's mind infects the Library, and the Library's brokenness exacerbates Galywis's condition. It is the worst of all possible outcomes.'

I began to feel an uneasy premonition, one I saw reflected in Pense's face. 'What do you want us to do?'

'You want your island restored, do you not?' Dwinal looked at Gio. 'So my grandson tells me. It is corrupted, and its corruption is spreading into your realms. Is that the truth?'

'It is,' I said, 'and the effects will be grave indeed if we do not mend it.'

Dwinal nodded. 'It is the Library's presence there which causes the disruption. It is the rotten fruit in the barrel, and its decay is too advanced to be reversed. If you would prevent the farther spread of that decay, then it must be removed. And its removal will also divert the possibility of a war which neither of our peoples want.'

'Removed,' said Ori bleakly. 'You mean destroyed.'

'Yes.' Dwinal stared him down, unmoved. 'That Library's continued existence causes nothing but trouble for all of us. It must be destroyed, and forever. But Galywis will listen to nobody. Nobody but you, that is.'

I felt sick. 'You want us to turn on Galy.'

'By any means necessary.' Dwinal turned her cold stare upon me, and I am sorry to admit that I quailed a little. Her ruthless commitment to her purpose was intimidating, to say the least.

'Talk to him. Perhaps you can get him to see reason, somehow. Perhaps there is lucidity enough left in him to hear the sense of your argument. Believe me, all of us hold Galywis in the highest possible respect, and his loss is a great blow to our people.' Her voice softened a touch at last. 'But he was lost long ago. He is no longer the Master Lokantor that we knew, and all his genius is turned to destruction. If he will not see reason… then you must do whatever is necessary. Trick him, trap him — anything.'

'Betray him,' Ori said coldly. 'Say that to our faces, if it is what you mean.'

'If you see it as a betrayal, then yes: betray him. For he has betrayed *you*. You sought the killer of your people: we have given him to you. Do what you must, to protect both your Elders and your island. And we will do as we must, to protect *our* people. An alliance between us is vital, if our separate ways of life are to be preserved.'

I mentally revised my assessment of all the decisions we have had to make in the past few moons. Few of them struck me as either so grave, or so impossibly difficult, as this one. 'How can we know that you speak the truth?' I said desperately. 'We have heard so many tales, so many points of view… they cannot all be true. How can we know?'

Dwinal looked at me, and I thought I detected a faint note of sympathy in her cool gaze. Perhaps it was wishful thinking. 'Talk to Galywis,' she advised. 'He trusts none of his own people any more, but he trusts you. If you ask him for the truth, I believe he will give it.' She indicated the lush island before us with a sweep of her arm. 'In the meantime, I encourage you to explore this projection. It is an accurate vision of your beautiful island as we found it. Perhaps it could be a vision of the future, as well as the past.' She glanced briefly at Gio and added, to my surprise, 'Whatever you decide, do look after my grandson.'

Dwinal and Hyarn left us then, with few words and no ceremony whatsoever.

For a while, silence reigned. Pense and Ori and Gio and I could only look at each other in speechless dismay, and nobody knew what to say.

Gio finally spoke up. 'Listen… for what it is worth, my grandmother is known for her brutal honesty. I do believe that she speaks the truth.'

'Why would she lie?' Ori asked. 'Maybe she has some other

reason to want Orlind destroyed, and maybe we would not approve of it. But however that may be, we do not want to risk more Lokant wars spilling into our Worlds. They did enough damage last time.' I could see that he hated to speak those words, for he looked weary and disgusted and appalled. But he could see the sense of her words, just as much as I could.

'And she may be right about the Library,' I added. 'It may well be the source of the corruption...' I shared the thoughts that had struck me earlier, about the Library's sickness and the madness of those early draykoni. By the time I had finished, Pense looked grimmer than ever.

Ori groaned, and briefly put his face in his hands. 'Such a mess,' he lamented. 'The last thing I want is for Dwinal and Hyarn to be right about any of this.'

Gio leaned against Ori's shoulder, a silent comforting presence. It seemed to help, for Ori calmed a little at once, and awarded Gio a grateful smile. 'I'll be all right. But we had better be certain that the Library really is causing the problem, before we even think of...' he trailed off, unable to finish. *Before we think of colluding with Sulayn Phay to destroy Galy.*

'I have a theory on that,' I said, reluctantly. 'The pattern of corruption has spread so much faster than we thought it would, but not evenly. It has spread farther and faster in some places than in others. Is that not the truth? We have not finished mapping its reach, but the pattern there is clear enough, or rather the lack thereof.'

Ori nodded slowly. I could almost see him putting the pieces together in his head, his quick mind having no trouble following my lead. I was more surprised that I had arrived at this conclusion before *him*. 'Oh,' he said at last, and sighed.

Pense and Gio wore twin looks of befuddlement. 'What is your theory, Minchu?' said Pense. 'Enlighten the challenged amongst us.'

'I think the corruption follows the path of the Library. If the Library's mere presence causes the disruption, what would come of Galy running off with the place? Wherever Galy and the Library have gone, they have left a trail of broken *amasku* behind them. Only subtly so, barely perceptible, but it is there. I have felt it.' And I had, though I was not able to identify what I was feeling at the time. At each of those sad, pale graves I had felt traces of that kind of disturbance, like a strange footprint in the *amasku.*

'All this can be confirmed,' put in Pense, 'once we return to the Seven. Avane should have more information for us.'

I nodded. 'We know some of the places the Library has passed through, because we saw it ourselves. And if the trail extends to all the places we have found slain draykoni, too...' I could not finish the sentence, for it looked so black for poor Galy.

Ori sighed. 'Fine. If all of that is confirmed, then we will have to try to talk to Galy.'

'No easy task,' I agreed.

'We will try.' Ori leaned sadly upon Gio. 'You are not hiding any more secrets, are you Gi?'

Gio shook his head, emphatic. 'No, and never shall again. I am worn to shreds with the strain of it all.'

I could easily believe that, for he looked it. He was paler than ever, which brought the shadows beneath his eyes into stark contrast. He was a little rumpled and a little disordered, no longer the scrupulously neat and perfectly groomed man I had first known. He had dropped his air of untouchable composure, too, or simply lost it somewhere along the way. The strain was visible on him.

'Let's explore,' I suggested. 'This is a Library, we have time. Then we will go home and... figure things out.'

'I am *game* for that first part,' Ori said, his smile returning as he looked out at the trees. 'This place is so beautiful I could almost cry.'

Pense's curiosity equalled Ori's, though he was less effusive about it. He and Ori and I Changed our shape, and Gio helped secure Siggy into his flight-sling upon my foreleg. Then he climbed up onto Ori's back.

Here we go, Ori said as he rose into the air. I saw a look of pure delight cross Gio's face as he experienced flight for the first time.

After you, Minchu, said Pense.

It was bittersweet, soaring over those glorious trees. Orlind-as-was lay spread before us like a banquet of life and colour, and the contrast with the bare, dead island of my memory could not be more stark. We flew over a twinkling stream which flowed into a serene lake; the beds of both were littered with chunks of purplish, crystalline rock, tinting the clear waters with bursts of lavender colour. We saw exquisite glades, carpeted with cloudy moss and fronded with sprays of misty foliage. Some of the trees soared to unimaginable heights, and here the glissenwol were the tallest of them all, their caps sheltering delicate leaf-bedecked trees under their care. This vision of the island had been captured in late summer, perhaps, for some of the trees and bushes were vibrant with flowers, while others had already begun to bear a delicious array of bejewelled fruits. I wished it could be possible to sample some of them, for I recognised few of the species that I saw.

And the animals! We saw them everywhere, soaring aloft or scurrying through the grasses, the mosses and the ferns of the woods. There were plump, soft-furred meerels searching for their favourite fat fruits to eat; kreeays on the wing, white-feathered and swift; curly-tailed irilapters with their iridescent wings; drauks and ortings, worvillos and woles, even a whistworm caught out in the daylight hours, quick to withdraw into its ground dwelling as we flew over.

It was a heartbreaking picture of all we had lost with the fall of Orlind, and it brought the importance of our task into clear focus. What had become of our beautiful Seventh Realm was a tragedy. If it could be reversed, it was our duty to do all in our power to try. And it was our utterly inescapable duty to prevent a similar destruction from happening to any other part of our cluster of worlds.

We concluded our tour at last and reconvened on the roof of the fabulous bejewelled building — a structure standing in for Orlind itself, in what had once been a hypothetical future. Pense and Ori were as resolute as I, and even Gio had changed. His confusion and wretchedness had faded, and he and Ori stood close together, clearly a united team.

'Ready for this?' Ori said.

Pense said, 'Yes,' without a trace of hesitation.

'I think so,' I said, unable to equal Pense's certainty but more than willing to try.

Gio merely nodded. I thought he looked a little nervous, which put me in sympathy with him. Small wonder either, for he now had strong ties to both sides of this chaotic adventure, and that could only be an uncomfortable position to occupy.

'Here we go, then,' said Gio.

I braced myself for the whirl of translocation, and took one last, longing look at the beauty and peace around me. I wanted to fix it in my heart and mind, so I could always summon it at need. The road to the renewal of Orlind would be a long and difficult one, and I wanted to have this vision always, to guide and sustain me through it.

So we went, leaving the gorgeous vision of old Orlind for its broken and bare reality.

And all that delicate peace I had so carefully stored up was shattered in an instant, for we arrived to find the island in chaos.

16 VIII

Everybody Goes Mad.
And Some Things Explode.

Gio transported us to a spot on the edge of the island, which was lucky because the rest of it was engulfed in what looked like a miniature war.

Galy-as-fortress had taken possession of the centre of the island, and when I say that I mean the foreboding black castle was far larger than it had been before, and looked grimmer than ever. The battlements had sprouted long, wickedly sharp spikes which pointed outwards and upwards, aimed to discourage airborne assailants. The walls were as sheer as a cliff face and completely smooth, unclimbable. There were no doors or windows, and a moat had appeared around the base of the building, wide and deep and filled with something too green to be water. It stank, too; we could smell it even from our relatively safe distance.

The air was full of draykoni on the wing. As we watched, a unit of ten launched themselves at the castle, teeth and claws bared, screeching curses. They were aiming for the roof; perhaps they thought they could find a way in up there, considering that's how my group had gone in and out not long before. But they never made it. Slits opened up in the walls of the castle and missiles shot out. I could not see what they were — rocks, arrows, bullets, something else entirely? But they served Galy's

229

purpose. Three draykoni dropped, their wings shredded. Two others howled in pain and swerved away, abandoning the attack. The rest were forced to retreat, too, and Galy stood victorious.

I recognised none of them.

'What the...' whispered Ori.

I swallowed. 'Anybody know what this is about?' I said.

No one did. We watched, stupefied, as a second team launched a similar attack upon Galywis, with identical results.

'We need to do something,' said Pense.

I agreed of course, but what? Why were our people attacking the Library? I searched the land and the skies for anyone I recognised, and at last I spotted Loret on the other side of the island. I thought I saw Avane, too, and a couple of her folk.

'There,' I said, and pointed them out.

Ori surveyed the mess of injured, furious and brawling draykoni in between us and them and squared his shoulders. 'Right. Should be interesting.' He looked at the skies and then back at the ground. 'For once, I'm going to say that now is not the best time to be gigantic and airborne.'

I watched dismally as another rain of missiles shot down two more draykoni, and could only agree. 'Let's be tiny and hard to spot,' I suggested.

Like me! Sigwide put in merrily.

'Good idea. Ori, do you want to wait here with Gio? We will return once we know what's going on...' I stopped because I had seen a familiar shape in the air, not attacking the castle but overseeing the assault. Enormous, with green and white scales... 'That's Eterna! What is she doing here?'

'No prizes for guessing that she is mixed up in this,' Ori muttered. 'Where there's violence, there's Eterna.'

I stared at her, eyes narrowed, trying futilely to divine her purpose merely from watching her. Last time we had seen her she had been a long way from here, seeking a new home for her people in Iskyr. Now she had brought them to war — again.

'You would think her failure at Waeverleyne would put her off war games,' I muttered, irritated. That woman was far too much trouble.

Pense and I hurriedly Changed, and soon afterwards three ortings scampered away in search of Avane: the two of us, and Sigwide.

One of the interesting things about shapeshifting is how

much of an effect the physical shape you choose can have on the way your mind works. There we were in the midst of a raging battle, injured drayks all around us and more falling all the time, and the most forbidding castle imaginable coming ever closer as we ran. And I felt fear, yes; my little orting heart pounded furiously as we dodged and swerved and ran as fast as we could to reach the other side of the island. I also had to maintain my efforts to resist the muddling, nauseating effects of the *amasku* thereabouts, or I would have somersaulted my way to Avane, and probably ended up in a broken little heap about halfway there.

But alongside that, I was also oddly enchanted by the feel of the wind in my fur as I ran, the bounding motion of my lithe little body and the enthralling mixture of scents that reached my nose. It was *thrilling*. I wanted to skip with glee, and had to restrain myself from dancing my way past the fortress.

If that is how Siggy feels all the time, no wonder he is such a merry soul.

I was so distracted by the conflicting mixture of impressions and sensations that I failed to spot the bronze-coloured drayk falling out of the sky directly above us. Pense and Siggy dodged. I did not. I knew nothing of it until Sigwide barrelled into me, sending both of us rolling for about twenty feet. I stood up, dazed, all my fur standing on end with fright.

The ground shook as the draykon came down, one leg landing barely three feet away from my nose.

Watch out! Sigwide bristled with fury, his teeth bared in a snarl as he berated me. Considering that he was, for once, slightly larger than me, the effect was surprisingly intimidating.

I tucked my tail between my legs, trembling, and bowed my head. *Sorry.*

Siggy touched his nose to mine and leapt into a gallop once more. I followed. We skirted the moat, and found Pense and Ori waiting for us on the other side of the castle.

Minchu, you —

I know, I am an idiot.

— make a beautiful orting, he finished.

Oh. I touched my nose to his, as Siggy had just done with me, my tail wagging.

On we went, this time without mishap. Avane loomed as we approached, impossibly huge and stupendously purple. I squeaked as, with a casual sidestep, she almost squashed Pensould.

He hurriedly Changed, opting for his drayk shape rather than his human form. *Avane.*

She jumped. *Oh goodness, I almost killed you.*

I still breathe. What is going on here?

I Changed, too, though I took human shape so I could scoop up Sigwide. For all his irritation with me, he was not paying nearly enough attention to the forest of draykon legs hereabouts and almost got himself stepped upon, too.

Avane moved restlessly about, trying to watch the battle and talk to us at the same time. *Llan, Pense, it's Galy. He has gone mad.*

He was always mad, Pense pointed out.

Yes, but now he is dangerously so. Look there. She pointed her nose a ways over our shoulders. We turned.

Near the water's edge, a patch of stark, dead white land had blossomed. We must have run past it, but so intent had we been upon not getting crushed that we had failed to notice it.

Galy did it, Avane said, and she sounded both frantic and upset. *We saw the patterns, Llan, in Ayrien and Iskyr. Everywhere there are corpses, there are traces of corruption — a trail. We followed it back to Orlind, and when we arrived… Eterna was already here, doing all* this. *She said she saw the fortress swallow one of her people and spit him back out like — like that over there. I didn't want to believe her. But then he sucked in one of the Elders before our eyes, and the poor creature ended up over there, like* that.

Avane grew more upset with every word. Pense and I soothed her as we could, but it was hard, for we were gutted by the news.

I hadn't wanted it to be Galy. Seeing Eterna there had given me hope, for a little while. Maybe it was her after all, maybe the blame lay with somebody I already hated, someone I had little reason to like or sympathise with…

Instead, I had to accept that someone I liked and trusted was capable of terrible, unthinkable things. Perhaps Hyarn was right, and Galywis thought he was acting out of compassion. But that changed little.

Avane, was the Elder… mad?

Avane's tail swished as she thought about that. *I hardly know. She was enraged, yes, roaring fit to burst and intent upon destroying the castle with her claws alone if she could. But most of them are like that at the* moment.

Did that mean most of Eterna's people had gone mad, or that none of them were? Watching the airborne draykoni intent upon their assault, I had to agree with Avane: it was hard to tell. They were unstoppable, no matter how many of their people fell, and that did not speak well for their sanity just then. But battle fury could produce the same effects.

I saw something then that sent a chill through my heart: Nyden on the horizon, approaching on the wing with the half-dozen others he had taken with him. Ny, the only Elder in Nuwelin — the only Elder among my friends. And here he was, in the one place that posed a significant threat to him. I'd taken brief comfort in the notion that he was elsewhere, perhaps still searching for Eterna's folk in Iskyr. And here he was after all.

Ny! I screamed, almost delirious with fright. *Ny, you have to get away from here. GO!*

He could not hear me, or perhaps he simply ignored me. As he drew closer, I felt waves of fury radiating from him. He was *angry*, but I did not think he was mad — not yet.

Pense hissed suddenly, and spat. *Llan. Look.*

I turned back to the fortress in time to see Galy's roof open wide, revealing a yawning black pit of an interior. A shrieking draykon with cinnabar-coloured scales disappeared inside, its wings beating frantically in a futile effort to escape.

The roof reappeared with a cheery twinkle, sealing the creature inside.

Cinnabar. *Pense, all those drayks Galy showed us during the visions. That was one of them! I think they are the ones he is targeting!*

That thought turned my stomach, for among the dizzying parade of colours there had been one as night-black as Nyden...

Galy had had a few opportunities to kill Nyden already, and had refrained — perhaps because Nyden had only ever appeared in our company, and I would like to think that Galy would hesitate to destroy a friend of ours, even in his madness.

But that would continue only as long as Galywis remained rational enough to consider the matter. And from what I was then hearing and seeing, he had left all lucidity behind.

I was running before I knew it, straight for the dark fortress. 'Galy!' I screamed. 'Galy, you have to stop this! Let the draykon go! DO IT!'

Like Nyden, he either failed to hear me or ignored me. I ran on, Pense two steps behind me, but bringing myself closer to those walls did not make me either more audible or more persuasive. The castle loomed, impenetrable and untouched, and the draykon did not reappear.

Change, Minchu, Pense ordered me, and I obeyed. We soared aloft, spiralling out of range of Galy's missiles, and I tried again. Pense joined his voice to mine, and we roared together: *'Galywis! We adjure you to stop! In the name of your friends and your people, remember yourself!'*

He heard us. I cannot say how I knew, only that something shifted in the atmosphere, and I felt a brief flicker, a flutter of attention from the castle.

I held my breath. The strain of hovering there, far above the ground of Orlind, weary beyond words, my senses topsy-turvy and my head spinning, quickly took its toll and I almost fell.

I gritted my teeth, and held.

I saw a blur of gold out of the corner of my eye: Ori, Changed and on his way to us.

Llan, you crazy woman! he yelled. *What are you* doing?!

Something! I screamed back. *Whatever I can!*

But nothing happened. The fortress stood, Galywis unmoved.

Enraged beyond sense, Eterna shrieked her fury. As one, every one of her people who could still fly hurled themselves at the castle. Some of Avane's people joined them, and even some of mine — I saw Liat in the middle of the fray, and even, to my shock, Sophronia.

Their numbers were considerable, and they were *draykoni* — physically formidable, and born of a magic they wielded as easily as breathing, even in the midst of the chaos of Orlind. United in fury, their assault should have been impossible to withstand.

But Galy *held.* Slits opened up all over his walls and a hail of missiles poured forth, drowning his attackers in a deadly flurry. Draykoni screamed and dropped, bleeding and despairing, and still their stolen comrade did not re-emerge.

Even my people, powerful beyond words and maddened with fury, could not prevail against the man and the place that had birthed them.

War, then, could not solve this.

We need to go, said Ori, and I knew instantly what he meant.

Yes, said Pense.

Let's go, I said.

We spread our wings wide and flew high, and higher still. We winged our way over the heads of the attackers, keeping as much distance as possible in between us and them. I *hoped* it would be enough to protect us from Galy's missiles, but I could not be sure. Would he be able to distinguish us from the others? Even if he could, would that prevent him from targeting us? I could no longer say. The Galywis we saw that day was a terrifying stranger; our friend had gone.

We flew on, aiming for the centre of Galy's roof. Ori bellowed and cursed, hit by a stray *something*, but he did not stop. *I'm fine*, he insisted, his voice strained. *Keep going*.

We were directly over the roof and closing fast upon it when it abruptly opened. A draykon skeleton floated forth, stripped bare of its flesh and its energies, reduced to a bundle of pale, lifeless bones. The corpse drifted gently to the ground where it was laid tenderly down, as though deposited there for a peaceful slumber. The ground immediately around it turned shockingly white.

Eterna's scream of rage and grief made the world shake. I felt it in my bones, and when every other draykon nearby joined in, my ears almost broke under the pressure.

It took me a moment to realise that I, too, was screaming.

'GALY!' I roared, too angry to feel any longer afraid. I folded my wings and plummeted downwards, aiming straight for the open roof. Galy had not yet sealed it again, but he could do so at any moment… I felt Pense join me and then Ori, and the three of us closed upon the castle at frightening speed. If the roof reappeared before we made it through, the impact would probably kill us.

We didn't hesitate.

I braced myself, teeth gritted, and closed my eyes…

Heads up, came a dark voice out of nowhere, and my eyes flew open again.

Ny fell gracelessly past us in a blur of black shadow, and disappeared inside the castle.

NYDEN! The word emerged as a despairing shriek, for I had thought him distant still, distant *enough*, safe…

Then I was through into the depths of the fortress, Pense and Ori arrowing in behind me.

The roof snapped shut, and we were left in darkness.

So, said Nyden, *There is no traitor among our lot.*

I lay in a heap, too stunned and pained to move or speak for the moment. I had hit the ground way too fast, and no doubt acquired a number of new bruises for my collection in the process. I could see nothing, but I sensed Pense and Nyden and Ori not far away.

I gathered that, I replied with a sigh. *It made sense at the time.*

At least Pense would be pleased about that. He had said from the beginning that no draykon would so harm or betray another, and apparently he was right.

'Galy,' I said as I staggered to my feet. 'Can we have some light, please?' I felt some trepidation in addressing him, for I was all too aware that I knew nothing of this Galywis. Did he remember who we were? Did he still see us as trustworthy?

For an agonising moment the answer seemed to be no, for the darkness did not lessen one whit.

'Please,' I said again, and at last he complied. Light flooded the castle, and I saw that we were back in the same bland, stone hall where we had held our draykon-moot. That meeting had taken place only hours before, but it felt like a lifetime ago.

'Thank you,' I called, eager to keep Galy happy if I could. I had dropped out of draykon shape when I fell, and the chill of the hall raised goosebumps on my skin. At least, I chose to interpret it as an effect of the cold, rather than a physical manifestation of the nerves and uncertainty that set my stomach churning. I felt woefully ill-equipped to deal with this.

Ori, too, had resumed his human form, though whether voluntarily or not I could not say. He looked as shaken as I felt, and I noticed a little blood in his hair.

I am fine, he told me, noticing the direction of my gaze. *Just hit my head a bit.*

Pense was both unaffected and seemingly unperturbed by the fall and our predicament. He stood, arms folded, waiting in silence.

I went to Nyden. *Ny, I told you to get out of here…*

He had not troubled himself to stand up but continued to lie in a heap, splayed lazily across the cold stone floor. *You may not have noticed,* he replied, *but the fighting does not appear to be achieving much. Eterna has lost her wits. She is merely getting everyone killed.*

It is not wholly out of character for her, I reminded him.

So I hear. He stretched out comfortably, resting his snout upon one extended leg. *I thought I would come and have a chat.*

With Galy?!

Why not? Throwing draykoni at him is a waste of time.

You made bait of yourself?!

Nyden winked at me. One enormous wing flexed, and I felt the light touch of it brushing over my hair. He'd patted me on the head. *It will be all right,* he crooned. *You worry too much, noble leader. He did not eat me before, did he?*

All of which was so patronising I felt like smacking him. The twinkle in his eyes and the ironic twist to his lips told me he knew that, had wielded it like a tool with which to distract me from my fear. *Better irritated with me than afraid of him,* he murmured in my mind.

He was right. I summoned up all my memories of Galywis as I had known him before: the mad but harmless guardian of the Library of Orlind, who had welcomed us, talked to us, fed us his favourite things and never threatened us with any kind of harm. Even the Galy who had swept us up into the Library not long ago and carried us off. He had not harmed us then, either; all he had tried to do was talk to us.

Which sparked off a new train of thought in my mind. I had assumed he was trying to tell us of the danger to himself, to our people and to the island, in order to lead us to the culprits. But in light of everything we now knew, that no longer made sense. What *had* he been trying to say?

And what was he planning to do to Ny?

I went and stood by him, as though that would help at all. Whatever Galy's plans for Nyden might be, it seemed unlikely that Pense or Ori or I could do a great deal about it. But I wanted to try to express to Galy that Ny was more than someone we travelled with from time to time. He was a friend.

'We need to talk, Galy,' I said, making sure that my voice held steady and betrayed none of my inner tremors. 'What is going on here? Why are you doing all this?' And silently I thought, over and over, *don't hurt Nyden. Please not Nyden, don't hurt Ny…*

I do not know what manner of answer I expected. Perhaps another whirl of confusing visions, or a door opening into some hitherto unseen chamber of the Library wherein some new clue might be found.

Instead, Ny twitched and shuddered and then groaned, a guttural, inhuman sound which shook me anew. He began to thrash wildly, his claws scrabbling helplessly at the stone floor.

Then he screamed, and convulsed.

'*GALY!*' I yelled. 'Not Nyden! *Don't hurt him!*'

'*I thought you wanted to talk,*' said Nyden, but it was not his voice. It was lighter in tone, milder, but also strained, as though every word cost an effort to utter. '*Welcome back! Me and the old girl are always happy to see you.*'

'Galy?' I whispered, horrified. Nyden lay still again now, but he was far from relaxed. His whole body was contorted, and only the whites of his eyes showed.

'*Thought we would never speak again, hey?*'

'But what… how… how are you doing this?'

'*With difficulty. Hurts a lot, me and him both. Cannot do it for long. What do you want to talk about?*'

I took a deep breath, and swallowed my horror. 'You've been killing our Elders! Why!'

'*Helping them,*' corrected Galy-as-Nyden. '*Helping me. You suck the energy out of them, see? Like this.*'

I have no idea what he did then, but Nyden roared and convulsed again, and his hide burned under my hands. Then he collapsed, shivering.

'Stop it!' Ori shouted. 'Demonstrations are *not* required.'

'*Sorry,*' said Galy, in that small voice I had heard so many times.

'What are you using it for?' Ori said, more calmly.

'*I showed you all this.*' Galy sounded irritated.

'Sorry, but your cocktail of visions was hard to interpret.'

'*I thought you would help me.*'

'Help you kill our Elders?' Ori gaped, too flabbergasted to say any more.

'*Help me to — to—*' Nyden's jaws opened wide in a kind of soundless scream, and nothing more emerged. He shuddered and writhed, and his evident agony cut me to the core.

'Quickly, Galy,' I gasped. 'Help you to what?'

No more words emerged. Instead, the castle rocked around us, the stones rumbled and shook, and a whirlpool of *amasku* rose up to engulf us. My senses drowned in a flood of chaos and it *hurt*, the pressure of it beating upon me in wave after wave and I couldn't breathe or see or hear anything save the roar of stonework splitting apart and I felt nothing but the tremors of the ground beneath my feet and then everything *exploded* and I exploded with it, bursting apart into a rain of blessed nothingness. And I felt… *relief.* Peace. Calm.

I opened my streaming eyes and blinked, surprised to find the castle still intact around me. Just a vision.

I tried to speak but my words emerged as a thin croak. My throat was parched, my lips felt wooden.

'Galy,' I managed in a hoarse whisper. 'Are you trying to destroy the old girl?'

'*YES!*' Poor Nyden shouted the word and choked, coughing and retching.

Pense ran to us and fell to his knees beside Nyden, bracing him. 'Why the Elders?' he demanded.

They are replete with the energy I need, and they are broken anyway. MAD like me, mad like we are. Only one way to make it go away, hey?'

'What do you even *mean!?*' Frustration overwhelmed me. Galy's riddles and half-spoken truths, his omissions and his garbled revelations… at this rate he would drive me insane, too.

Galy ignored me, and went on with his rambling. '*Design flaw. Sends 'em round the twist, like a flick of a switch. See? Show you.*'

'*NO!*' roared Pense and Ori and I as one. We grabbed for Nyden, as though physically holding onto him would somehow protect him from Galy.

'*No. Look.*' The stone hall melted away and we were back in the labs of old, watching again as that maddened female drayk rampaged through the Library. '*Never could find the problem,*' Galy-as-Nyden said. '*Hoped it would breed out. Seems to. But the first batch are a mess. Found one of them loose on my island, mad as you like. Poor fool. Did the only thing I could think of.*'

'You turned the entire Library into an energy collector,' I guessed.

'*Not a bad idea of Maeval's,*' Galy mused. '*Oddly circular, of course. Takes a drayk to catch a drayk.*' Draykon bone glittered all around us, pulsing with *amasku,* and then faded away. '*Works though.*'

Another of Galy's visions flashed through my mind: one of Krays's energy collectors, exploding to bits. 'So if you overload the old girl with enough *amasku,* you think she will burst. And you with her.'

Ori shook his head. 'Galywis, this is the wrong way to go. You cannot destroy our Elders *just in case* they go mad! And you propose to destroy your Library and yourself, the same! No! It has to stop. There must be something else we can do.'

The lab vanished around us, but nothing replaced it. There was only light and heat and a wave of frustrated rage from Galywis that smothered the breath out of me. *Do you think it is fun to be mad?'* he roared. *Do I make an amusing figure to you? Does she?'* Colour flickered briefly across my vision, outlining the maddened draykon once again, her body contorted in agony. *Like to try it yourself, hey? You'd soon see.'*

Ori held up his hands, visibly frightened. 'No, Galywis,' he said firmly enough, though his voice shook a little as he spoke. 'But perhaps they will not go mad. Perhaps they can be cured, mended. Perhaps the Library can be mended. Perhaps you—'

Nyden shook his head furiously. *Too late, too late. For her, for me. I am* dead, *but there is no release, no end—'* He broke off, and a terrible silence fell. No comfortable silence, this; it felt like a brief lull in a raging tempest, and a heavy tension hung in the air. Then Nyden's labouring lungs swelled with a mighty indrawn breath and Galy-as-Nyden roared: *I would wish this on NO ONE!'*

Blood leaked from Nyden's nose and his eyes met mine. I saw the real Nyden in there, somewhere beneath Galywis's all-consuming possession, and he was terrified.

I'd never seen Nyden anything but laid back before.

'Galy, you have to let Nyden go!' I ran my hands over Ny's dark scales, trying to soothe him the only way I could. 'You're killing him. Stop.'

Another wordless burst of anger seared my senses, and then Nyden collapsed, boneless and exhausted, onto a floor turned to cold stone once again.

'Ny?' I bent over him, trying to see into his face, but his eyes were tight shut and he did not respond. I shook him. 'Ny!'

One eye cracked open and focused blearily upon me. A drop of blood leaked from the corner. *I award the experience a two out of ten,* Ny said faintly. *Would not recommend.*

I was so relieved I could have cried. *Two? As many as that?*

I am not dead. It could be worse.

He got hugged a bit then. I will not say how much, that would be embarrassing.

But Galy's anger and frustration had by no means abated. The walls rattled and the ground heaved beneath our feet, sending us staggering. Ori laid his hands against the nearest wall, striving to calm Galywis, and I saw him talking in a stream of words I could not hear over the rumbling of the stones. He shook his head, frustrated, and I thought I saw the glitter of tears on his cheeks.

Tears streamed from my own eyes, unheeded. I think Ori and I both knew we had lost Galy; despair had carried him far from us, and we could no longer reach him.

It was Pense who realised the danger. When the first stone fell from the roof overhead, he looked up sharply and stood in one swift movement. 'We need to go,' he barked. '*Now.*'

'Go where?' I looked around wildly, but the castle was as enclosed as ever.

'We make a door. Like we did before.' He strode over to Ori and forcibly dragged him away from the wall, just as a cluster of rocks rained down and struck the spot he had been standing in with a loud *crash*. Galy was shaking himself to pieces and he would crush us if we didn't find a way out.

'*Ori!*' shouted Pense, and pointed at a clear spot upon on an as-yet-intact wall. 'Door. There. All of us.'

It was hard, almost too hard. We had wrought a door in the Library of Orlind before, upon our first visit; we knew we could do it, if Galy permitted it. And it was not that he opposed us, directly. But he was so deep in rage and madness that he could only impede our efforts, whether he meant to or not. Even with all three of us focused upon the task — and that was no simple matter, what with the building collapsing around us — we struggled. It was like trying to fight through endless layers of gauze; all we could do was tear away layer after layer, hoping to find clarity somewhere on the other side.

The faint outlines of a door appeared, a tracery of cracks in the stone.

Pense wasted no time. 'Go!' he barked at Ori. 'Get everybody away from the castle. He's going to draw on anybody within range, do you understand?'

Ori turned white as snow, and the objections I saw in his face went unvoiced. He ran for the shaky door and shoved his way through. I saw him Change on the other side, and he disappeared in a blur of golden scales.

'Minchu. Nyden.'

I had already run to Ny, but my efforts to lever him up were futile. He was too big, too heavy, and too much hurt. He tried to stand, but his shaking legs gave out beneath him and he toppled to the ground with a ringing *thud.*

Go without me, he said, and for once there was no trace of fun in his words.

'Not a chance,' I snapped. 'Ny, I know you object to shapeshifting but now's the time to lighten up a little. Change, now. Something small.'

He gave me the eye, and snapped his teeth together in irritation. *The things I do for you,* he muttered.

'Just do it.'

It hurt him, I could see that. His whole body shuddered with the effort, and he whimpered with pain, despite a clenched jaw and tightly gritted teeth. He shrank, slowly — too slowly.

'*Now,* Nyden!' I yelled. Our makeshift door was rapidly vanishing and I could hardly keep my feet upon the rippling floor.

Nyden groaned, and Changed all in a rush. I barely noticed what form he had taken — something small and fat and furred and above all, *portable.* I scooped him up as I ran for the door, Pense two steps behind me.

The door resisted. We pushed harder, to no avail. The stones sealed up, leaving no trace of our erstwhile exit route.

Pense pounded uselessly upon the stone, and bellowed something incomprehensible. A massive block of stone fell directly behind him, missing him by inches; the floor shook anew with the impact.

I took a deep breath.

'*GALY!* If you were ever truly our friend, prove it now and let us *go!*'

Pense gathered me close and shoved me beneath him, putting his own body in between me and the falling masonry. I did the same for Ny, holding him protectively against my chest and trying to ignore the seeping blood that stickied my hands.

Minchu, said Pense. *You are a queen among draykoni and I love you.*

Those words brought fresh tears to my eyes. Pense is never effusive.

A sudden rush of fresh, cold air cut off any response I might have made. A door didn't so much open as the entire wall fell away, and collapsed in a heap upon the earth.

Go. Pense pushed me before him and we tore out of the Library, gulping in clear air as we ran. It rained beyond the walls and we were soaked within minutes. The water hung heavy upon my wings as I flexed them and took to the air, striving to put as much distance between me and Ny and the Library as quickly as possible.

Ori was ahead of us, a frantic presence in the skies as he desperately tried to herd draykoni back from the castle. He was succeeding poorly. They were not listening to him, and if anything they saw his attempts to repel them as an attack. He strove doggedly on, defending himself as best he could from the teeth and claws of those he sought to protect.

And there were many, still. Some of those who had fallen earlier were approaching the castle on foot, trying to swarm inside from the ground. Many others were still airborne, closing fast upon the fortress now that Galy had ceased to fire his missiles. Eterna was among them.

Pense took one look at this and Changed, turning draykon in a single breath. His scales glittered, piercingly blue in the rain, as he took one swooping circuit of the castle.

Nuwelin! he roared. *Anshalin! FALL BACK!*

Some of our people were trying to help Ori. I saw Meri and Larion heading for him, with Sophronia and Damosel not far behind. But Pense's shout cut through everything. I have never known him to muster such raw power as he did then, nor to wield it with such devastating effect. Our friends wheeled about and were winging away before they even had time to process what he had said, and to my relief I saw Avane and Loret also in retreat. Even some of Eterna's colony bowed to the pressure and withdrew.

I went for Ori. I could not shift without dropping Nyden, who still crouched, shivering, in my arms, and in my human shape I was too frustratingly *slow.*

'Ori!' I yelled, as soon as I was close enough for him to hear me. 'Move. We have to go.'

I can't yet. They will not listen!

'It's too late! GO!'

He cast one last, desperate look at those too furious, too vengeful, too deranged or too stubborn to hear him, and I felt his anguish at leaving them. It echoed my own. If only we had been able to reach them in time. If only we had been able to reach *Galy,* found the right words to say to ease his despair, dissuade him from this terrible course of action.

It was too late for *if only*. Ori and I dived beneath the doomed draykoni, tucking our wings and rolling to evade raking claws and teeth. A flash of white caught my eye: Gio, staring up at us in dismay and far too close to the castle. Did his stolen draykoni magics put him in danger?

Ori swerved, grabbed Gio in his claws and shot skywards once more, his wings pumping desperately.

We managed to put perhaps another hundred feet in between us and the fortress before the end began.

It was as though the Library inhaled, and with each mighty indrawn breath it devoured wave after wave of energy. Distant as I was by then, I felt it still: life and vibrancy and will left me in a rush, leaving me wearied almost to the point of exhaustion. My pace faltered, slowed, and I almost fell, my legs suddenly too weak to hold me. Pense and I collapsed against one another and dragged each other onwards. I tried not to look at him, for the ashen hue of his face frightened me, and I knew that my own visage was as drawn and deathly as his.

I could only hope, desperately, that Nyden was sheltered still, for in his weakened state he could scarcely bear to lose more…

But the silence that fell then frightened me more than anything else. All the clamour of rage and war died out almost at once, and I dared not look behind me for fear of what I might see. Galy had not stopped. He drew in more energy, and more still, not just from those living draykoni around him but from the land as well. I could feel it streaming away from us, the sudden flux turning its nauseating chaos into a maelstrom of disorder. Sick, weak and dizzy, I fell at last and lay inert, unable to tell the sky from the ground or the air from the earth.

Nyden twitched beneath me and lay still.

The terrible hush stretched. Then the ground began to shake, the threatening rumble of an approaching earthquake. Intense pressure built, lying heavy upon me like a physical weight and choking the air from my lungs. I curled around Nyden and Pense curled around me and we lay, hunched and shaking, waiting.

When the explosion came, it rocked the island in a terrific blast of energy. The ground bucked and shuddered and rolled, and debris rained down upon us in a deadly hail of stone and glass and metal. The noise was unbearable. I thought the tumult would go on forever but at last the noise lessened, the ground stopped shaking and the sickening, pulsing waves of expelled energy slowed and finally ceased altogether.

Pense and I sat up slowly. We were both shaking uncontrollably. My teeth chattered with the convulsions of my poor tormented body, and my ears rang in the wake of the explosion. I steeled my nerves and looked around.

Part of the island had dipped and sunk into the sea. It looked lopsided now, and the glittering waters were fast rushing in to claim more of the tortured land. No trace of the castle remained, save for the litter of debris which lay scattered over every surviving inch of ground.

Not a single draykoni was on the wing. All had fallen. They lay, toppled like freshly scythed grass, some sluggishly moving but more lifelessly inert. Those who had been nearest to the fortress would never move again; naught remained of them but bare bones. I counted at least eleven stark carcasses spread over the earth, their pale bones glinting mournfully in the wan sunlight.

Ori lay some way ahead of us, twined protectively around Gio. They moved as I watched, pained and aching, drained as we were, but alive. Relief washed over me, and if anything I trembled more in the wake of it.

Nyden stirred in my arms and groaned. *How do we get mixed up in these things?* he whimpered. *I vote we start a book club instead.*

Seconded. I wanted to move, but I could not. I felt like I might never move again. It seemed impossibly difficult even to keep myself in a seated posture, let alone to get to my feet. Every part of my body ached and shook with pain and weariness, and I could barely think.

One distant impression finally seeped through to my awareness, however. The island felt… different. The muddlesome whirl of broken *amasku* had not dissipated altogether, but it was much lessened, ebbing like an outgoing tide.

A fear I had scarcely been aware of eased, and I took a deep, shaky breath.

Some few of the hardier, or perhaps just luckier, draykoni had stumbled to their feet and were moving around, testing their weakened bodies and checking on their fellows. I saw Avane heading for us, which prompted another rush of relief, for I had long since lost track of her in the chaos.

And my poor Sigwide, too, who hung limply in Avane's shaking hands like a broken little doll. My heart raced again with swift panic laced with crippling remorse. Where had he been, when the Library exploded? Was he *dead?* I forgot my weakness and staggered to my feet. I could not quite muster a run, but I hastened towards Avane as fast as I could.

She, at least, seemed hale enough, her pallor and bruise-mottled skin notwithstanding. She was squinting against the sun, her Darklands eyes streaming with tears, and I realised she had maintained her weaker human form purely in order to deliver Siggy to me.

'He is all right,' she said quickly, and held out the sad little shape. 'He fainted, I think, but he breathes.'

'I will trade you,' I said, thrusting Nyden's furred little form into her hands as I took Siggy. He didn't move, but I could sense his heartbeat pulsing faintly on, and he was uninjured.

Avane accepted the bundle of fur that was Nyden with a doubtful frown, though being Avane she instantly sensed his fragility and handled him with the utmost care. It was only then that I realised what a mess Ny had made of his shapeshifting. He had the tail and ears of an orting with the body of a wole, albeit larger than was typical. I could not guess where he had drawn the contours of his compact muzzle and delicate paws from, or the purplish colour of his fur, but he had made a fine patchwork of himself.

'That's Nyden,' I told her.

Avane frowned. 'Nyden-who-never-shapeshifts? That Nyden?'

'It was an emergency.'

'I think he has fainted, too,' said Avane, holding him gingerly now that she knew who he was.

Nyden's tail twitched at that, an irritated little *swish*, but he made no move to extricate himself. *I do not faint,* he informed us severely. *I may occasionally* lose consciousness *in an impeccably masculine fashion, but swooning I absolutely decline to do.* He glanced up at Avane's face, and paused. *Unless, of course, I am cradled in the arms of the most beautiful woman alive.* With which comment, smoothly uttered, he made a creditable impression of a graceful swoon and hung limp in her hands.

You aren't too badly hurt, then, I said, feeling just a little peevish.

He made no reply, nor did he move when Avane gently

shook him. I cautiously probed him with my other senses, and discerned slowed heartbeat, sluggish energy and only the barest flicker of residual life about him.

'I... I think he really has fainted,' said Avane.

'Just put him down,' I recommended. 'You need to change your shape before your eyes burn out.'

'But... won't he be in danger? He is hurt, he needs tending to.'

'He'll be fine.'

Nyden's tail lashed like a little whip, and he growled. *Spoilsport,* he muttered resentfully.

You make a wonderful damsel in distress, I retorted, and sat down. I hadn't entirely meant to sit down, but my knees refused to hold me up anymore, and the rest of my body generally agreed that being recumbent might be nice. I smiled up at Avane, cuddled Sigwide close, and barely noticed when my eyes drifted shut.

She's going to swoon, too, warned Nyden, and I wanted to object that I do not do *swooning* either, and had no intention of breaking my general policy just then. But I had lost the energy to speak, or move, or think. So I just sat and held Sigwide, and allowed the floods of conflicting feelings to wash over me as they would. I didn't notice I was crying until Siggy's nose touched my cheek, and his little tongue poked out to lap at a falling tear.

It will be all right, he told me.

I looked at the devastation of Orlind and the gaping space where the Library had once stood, and at that moment I only felt doubt. Would it? Will it? Only time can tell.

25 VIII

Our Adventure Draws to a Close.
And I Fob Off a Problem Upon Eva.

I am running out of space in this journal; only a handful of pages
remain to be filled. But I am nearing the end of this particular
tale, and soon it will be time to put this book into Eva's hands
and begin another.

I have not had chance to write much for some days. The last,
oh, many pages were written as I recovered, and that is a process
which lasted a while. I cannot describe the extent of my
weariness following the explosion, nor the physical toll those
days took upon my body, but I was useless for some time
afterwards. Pense and Ori were little better.

Ny made a great drama out of it, of course. *I may never walk
again,* he declared, when he was recovered enough to regain his
usual shape. *I shall be a cripple for all of my days.*

Whether or not you will forever be a cripple, you will always be a baby.
That was Meriall of course, with her customary lack of sympathy
for Nyden. I did not altogether agree. Ny has to exaggerate;
that's the way he is. But the pain he suffered is no laughing
matter, and small wonder if he was overcome by it for a time.

Avane will never love me, he wailed tragically.

Meriall was unmoved. *Avane will never love you anyway.*

Nyden sniffled and whimpered and sighed for days, but since
he used the situation to shamelessly cadge sympathy and hugs

off all of us, I do not think he suffered too terribly in the end.

We returned to Nuwelin, leaving Orlind to the temporary custodianship of Avane and of Eterna, and what was left of her people. We slept for days together, and when that period was over, I woke and ate and wrote and slept until I had recorded everything for Eva.

And then we cleaned up Orlind.

By the time we returned to the island, Eterna had already seen to the removal of those of her folk who were slain in the conflict. None of the dead were ours, to my relief, nor Avane's either, but there had been injuries aplenty among our colonies and those took their time and tending to mend, too. We went to the island at last as a united force, half expecting to have to wrest control of it from Eterna.

But we found her in an unusually subdued mood. She even nodded her head to us as we landed, and made no move either to oppose our arrival, or to stake any claim over the territory.

It will take much, to restore this place. She looked out over the island, still littered with the broken remnants of the Library, one side half-submerged under the onrushing sea. *Is it your wish to make the attempt?*

It is, I told her.

Then it is for you to try, for it is not mine. Not ours. She stretched her wings to the sky and beat them once, slowly, her nostrils twitching as she tested the scents of the air. *I should have listened to you,* she said at last.

Such a concession from Eterna surprised me extremely. And it humbled me, considering how convinced I had been of her guilt; how much I had hoped that she was behind everything, because it was easier.

I should have been quicker to forgive, I told her in reply.

She looked at me, and I thought I saw the barest hint of a nod from her. It might have been my imagination.

That was all. She turned her back on us, and soon afterwards her colony took to the skies. We watched as they rose and rose, spiralling into the clouds above Orlind. Then they vanished, flashing through into Iskyr in the blink of an eye.

'That was unexpected,' said Meriall.

I had no answer to make. Eterna had paid dearly for her realisation, for it was the second such costly mistake she had made. I could only hope that she would remember this in years to come, and be slower to turn to violence.

And I hope I will remember this in years to come, too, and be less inexorable.

We arrived in Orlind with one pressing question to be answered: was the Library truly the source of the island's disturbance, and would its removal take the disruption away with it? A few days ought to have been enough to allow the tumultuous swirl of energies to settle, or so we hoped.

We knew the answer as soon as we set foot there, for the difference was striking. Maybe too striking, for instead of the mess and the madness we encountered an environment eerily... dead.

Well, not wholly dead. *Amasku* flowed still, but weakly, faded almost beyond perception. What there was, though, flowed pure and sweet and true, and my heart lifted. We remained a while, steeping ourselves in that delicious flow, letting it strengthen our bodies and our resolve alike.

We can do this, I said at last, *but it will take much. Who is with me?*

Pense I knew I could count on, a confidence he swiftly confirmed. *Always, Minchu,* he told me, and my heart glowed.

'We can give it a spin,' said Meriall, ostensibly with indifference, but I knew her by now. That was a sparkle of interest in her eyes, and she looked around with as much satisfaction as dismay, intrigued by the prospect of a challenge. I smiled at her, and she gave me a tiny salute in reply.

'Yes,' said Larion, laconic as ever, but it was all I needed.

My people are in agreement, said Avane, her draykon eyes shaded and dark. I knew it would be hard for her and the rest of Anshalin, here in the Daylands, but I was touched and grateful that they were willing to bear the discomfort. Avane had developed some way of adjusting her eyes when shapeshifted, which filtered out just enough light to make it bearable for her. I hoped it would be enough.

Sophronia had yet to get over her indignation at Eterna's behaviour and subsequent departure; not even her reluctant concession could evoke the smallest forgiveness in her heart. But she set that aside enough to offer her support, and I was satisfied.

Everyone of Nuwelin joined our venture, to my delight and relief. Only Ivi hesitated, clearly disconcerted by the barrenness of the place.

We will make it thrive, I told her, hoping my confidence would not prove to be misplaced.

Then you will need me, said Ivi sourly.

I smiled inwardly, for it was enough.

Ny had to be difficult about it, of course. He had got over his ordeal enough to cross the seas on the wing, but he was not yet ready to relinquish his claim to sympathy, and walked with an ostentatious limp when he thought himself observed.

Now he sprawled all over the bare earth of Orlind, disgustedly twitching his tail out of a pile of splintered rocks. *It is not much, is it?* he drawled with palpable disdain. *With new accommodation one expects somewhere good to bathe, at least. And there is* nothing *to eat.*

I took the tip of his tail in my claws and pinched. Hard.

Ow, he whined.

We all know you will help us, I said. *We are relying upon it, since you are the only Elder we have.*

Nyden sighed and flopped down, lying fully prone in a posture of utter defeat. *Fine,* he said grumpily. *I would rather be frolicking among the daeflies in Iskyr, but if it pleases all of you...*

I released his tail and patted it gently. *Avane will be here a while,* I reminded him privately. That worked a treat, for he looked up at her with a glint of interest in his dark eyes, the tip of one long fang mischievously protruding.

Ori was with us that day, along with Gio, because the two of them were inseparable. Poor Gio had suffered badly for a few days, expecting a rebuke or outright rejection from everybody he met in Nuwelin. It had finally sunk in that he was neither resented nor unwelcome, and then... he had completely transformed. All his careful composure, his distance, his reticence disappeared and he could hardly do enough for any of us. He was quick to offer his aid to the project, quicker even than Ori.

I Changed human to speak to him, and surprised myself as much as him by giving him a hug. 'Actually,' I said, 'I have another task for you, and for Ori. If you're willing. There is something else needing to be done, and only you can help with that.'

Gio's smile faded a little, and I imagined he knew exactly what I meant. 'If I can,' he said. 'You know you may rely on me.'

I felt bad for asking it of him. All he wanted was to settle with Ori, as far away from his old life as possible, and be happy. But I couldn't allow it; not yet. Because we are not done here.

Dwinal showed up but once, after poor Galy's death and the explosion of the Library. She and Hyarn looked around the shattered island with approval, and they actually had the gall to congratulate us.

'Quick and efficient work, Miss Sanfaer,' Dwinal commended me.

Fevered with weariness and pain and grief as I still was, I felt in no mood to accept her praise graciously. Absent was any sense in her that anything had been lost, either by Galywis's ultimate passing or by the total destruction of the former Master Library. She was almost merry with delight, and that made me instantly suspicious.

'It was none of our doing,' I told her. 'Galywis made his own choice.'

That sobered her a little, but not much. She nodded briskly and looked but once more at the wreck her people had made of our beautiful Seventh Realm. 'Either way, we appreciate your assistance. You will not regret it, I trust.' She made a kind of half salute to me and Pense and Ori, bestowing only an ironic smile upon her grandson. 'I do not think we will meet again,' she said, though this was not necessarily directed at Gio, for she gave him a questioning look. He returned it with only a cool stare, at his most aloof.

She shrugged, and smiled at me. 'Good luck with this place,' she said. 'You will need it.'

Then she and Hyarn vanished, leaving us with the task of cleaning up their mess unaided.

Well, I could not say I was surprised.

Some days later, I travelled to Glour with Pense, Ori and Gio, leaving the clean-up of Orlind under Meriall and Avane's direction for a time. We found Eva and Tren unusually unsettled, and were surprised to learn that they had been trying to contact us for some days. The explosion of the Library had been felt some distance away, it seems; there were some aftershocks in western Irbel and it had set off an avalanche in the mountains there. Eva being Eva had guessed at the probable source accurately enough. They calmed much upon seeing us, and later we sat tucked up in one of her cosier parlours, drinking cayluch and eating cakes and relaying all the news.

'She was far too happy about the whole thing,' I said of Dwinal, at the conclusion of our tale. 'She was thrilled that the Library was gone, and that reaction seemed out of place. Like it meant more to her personally than averting a possible risk of conflict. It seems unpromising.'

'Agreed,' said Eva, adding with a faint smile, 'A happy Lokant usually means bad news for us.'

'I cannot help fearing there was much more to it than she told us,' I said, in between cakes. I do not know how Eva contrives to acquire such exquisite delicacies but I can never get enough of them. 'She *said* it was all about concern for her people — eternal conflict over the Library, factions and divisions, that kind of thing. But she did not seem grieved by Galy's passing, nor relieved, or anything I might have expected. She was *gleeful.*'

'Positively bounding with it,' Ori agreed. 'It was pretty disgusting.' He cast a quick, apologetic look at Gio as he spoke, perhaps remembering belatedly that he was speaking of Gio's grandmother. But Gio merely gave a tiny, rueful smile.

'She is not the monster my grandfather was,' he offered. 'But she is certainly no good, either. I do not recommend trusting her very much, if it can be helped.'

'You do not have any idea what else she might have been up to?' Tren asked, in his mild way.

Gio sighed, and shook his head. 'What can I say? Everyone at Phay is a compulsive secret-keeper. I had access to her private rooms for years, but I avoided going there as much as possible. I never knew about the construct of old Orlind, and was never given more than a general idea of what my grandfather was working on. They made me a most unwilling party to it, but not an informed one.'

'There is also the question of Krays's energy collectors,' Pense pointed out. 'We thought they were being used to drain energy from the dead draykoni, but if that was the work of Galywis, that interpretation no longer holds. What was their intended purpose in Dwinal's hands?'

I'd had an idea about that. 'It is possible she knew more about the corrupted *amasku* than she admitted to. We know now that she wanted our help to destroy the Library of Orlind, and Galywis with it. She might have removed the energy collectors in order to allow the corruption to spread, thereby forcing our involvement.' I frowned as I spoke, because who knows? It is just another theory.

'She claimed to be separate from your grandfather's work,' Eva said to Gio. 'Do you think she spoke the truth?'

'She might have, but it may not mean very much if she did, because she was also telling the truth about factions. Sulayn Phay was always somewhat divided, but it has been more so since my grandfather's passing. She is Lokantor, but she leads a fractured Library. If *she* is not continuing Krays's work, it does not necessarily follow that nobody else is. And she was interested in draykon Elders, but I never found out why.'

'I wonder what they might be doing that would benefit from the destruction of Orlind,' Eva mused. 'Whether it is related to Krays's projects or not, it is an unusual approach. Every other Lokant I have ever met was dying to revive that Library somehow, provided of course that it could be kept under their own control. I cannot help but be curious as to why Dwinal and Hyarn deviate so far from the usual attitude.'

'I had hoped to leave that problem in your hands,' I ventured. I had to force the words past a flutter of nerves, for I knew that Eva could not welcome being burdened with such a task. She was extremely busy already, and she had bid farewell to Lokants and their messes with relief.

Indeed, she lifted an eyebrow at me, and the sardonic twist to her lips made me quail just a little. But she merely sighed, and nodded. 'Somehow I guessed that was the intention.'

'We have not the wherewithal to investigate it fully,' I apologised. 'We have only Gio, who is more than willing to assist you.'

Eva gave Gio a speculative look, but it was Tren who said: 'I imagine you are as thrilled with the prospect as Eva, no?'

Gio smiled faintly. 'I am in no hurry to tangle with my family again, but Llandry is right. There is more afoot than my grandmother acknowledged.'

'It could be construed as someone else's problem,' Eva said, with faint hope.

'Perhaps,' said Pensould. 'Perhaps not. The destruction of the Library *may* mean that the focus of their attention has now passed from our realms, and we will be troubled no longer. But on the other hand, it may not mean that at all.'

I felt warmed, both by Pense's unquestioning support and by his use of the word *our*. I sometimes wondered how invested he felt with this modern world, so different from everything he had known in his youth. It reassured me to know that he saw our Seven Realms as his own.

Eva muttered something incomprehensible, and slouched down in her chair. It was an uncharacteristic posture for her, decidedly inelegant, but from the look on her face I could see that she didn't care. 'Lokants cause too much trouble,' she decided. 'Interfering wretches. At this rate, I will have to establish a network of defence just to keep an eye on them.'

'A Lokant Investigation and Deterrence Bureau,' Tren suggested, eyes twinkling.

'Perfect. We will pull in all the Partials we can find, train them up, and set them loose. Any full Lokant who dares set foot in the Seven again will be sent packing post-haste.' She laughed at the idea, but sobered soon enough and set down her empty cup of cayluch with a snap. 'I will be honest, Llan, I have no immediate idea what we can do with this problem. But with Gio's help, perhaps we are not without options.'

'Ori's, too,' I said.

Eva cast a sharp look at Ori and Gio. Perhaps it was only just occurring to her to notice how closely together they were sitting, or how absorbed in each other they became the moment the conversation progressed to any topic which did not immediately concern them. She smiled faintly, and said, 'Perfect,' with such alacrity I wondered what she was referring to. 'We will benefit from draykon company, certainly.'

'Thank you,' I said with relief. 'It rests my mind to know that you will take care of it.'

Eva raised a brow at me, and I expected one of her sardonic responses. But she said mildly enough: 'We will make enquiries, and see what we may discover.'

'That is more than enough,' I hastened to assure her.

She nodded, and looked from me to Pense. 'You two will be out at Orlind?'

'Yes. We have a real chance of renewing the island at last. We are hoping that the combined efforts of Nuwelin and Anshalin will be enough.'

'We may seek aid from Eterna's colony, also,' Pense added. 'They are still richer in Elders than we.'

I had my doubts about the likelihood of help proving forthcoming from that quarter, but Pense was right enough: we should at least try.

'I will also be travelling into the Seven fairly often,' I added, belatedly. It had been easy, and indeed necessary, to forget my duties as Lady Draykon for a while, but I could not lastingly do so. And since our Lord Draykon would be away with Eva and Tren and Gio, those duties would fall entirely on my shoulders.

'I have a new contact for you,' Eva said. 'Board of Agriculture. Very interested in anything you are exporting from Iskyr.'

'Or indeed Orlind,' Tren put in. 'Given time.'

That was fine news to take back with me, and would certainly please Ivi.

The conversation passed then to other things. We talked until very late, and I sat up later still, recording these final thoughts in my journal. In the morning I will put it into Eva's hands, and Pense and I will depart for Orlind. I leave Glour with some regret, for I miss my friends here, and I will miss Ori too. Even Gio, whose true personality I have scarcely had time to discover, but which I very much like.

In spite of this, I am eager to return to Orlind. The time has finally come to reverse the fortunes of that beleaguered place and mend all its ills, and I am keen to begin.

I am also eager for some peace, a time of quiet with Pense and our friends, old and new. I am proud of the community that has built around us, and around Avane. I do not know what will become of us all in time, nor how our efforts in Orlind and Iskyr and Ayrien will turn out. But I feel confident, now, that we will endure, and that brighter times lie ahead.

And for the first time in my life, I can say with certainty that I am exactly where I should be.

MORE STORIES BY CHARLOTTE E. ENGLISH:

THE DRAYKON SERIES:

Draykon
Lokant
Orlind
Llandry
Evastany

Seven Dreams

THE MALYKANT MYSTERIES:

Death's Detective
Death's Avenger
Death's Executioner

www.charlotteenglish.com